Praise for

BRENDA JOYCE

"A hot contender for the
historical romance crown."
Toronto Star

oyce delivers a powerful story,
ife with compelling characters
and steamy sensuality."
Los Angeles Daily News

"She keeps the reader
on an emotional seesaw . . .
Her characters are fresh
and wickedly sympathetic."
Publishers Weekly

and

SCANDALOUS LOVE

"A page-turner . . . Bewitching and poignant,
Scandalous Love is the
essence of romance."
Affaire de Coeur

"Brenda Joyce brings a woman's
romantic fantasies to life.
Emotional, poignant, and highly sensual,
Scandalous Love is potent passion at its
ultimate . . . [It] will certainly make a romance
reader's heart sing with happiness."
Romantic Times

Avon Books by
Brenda Joyce

VIOLET FIRE
CAPTIVE
BEYOND SCANDAL
THE GAME
AFTER INNOCENCE
PROMISE OF THE ROSE
SECRETS
SCANDALOUS LOVE
THE FIRES OF PARADISE
FIRESTORM
INNOCENT FIRE

BRENDA JOYCE

Scandalous Love

This is a work of fiction. Names, characters, places, and incidents are products of the author's imagination or are used fictitiously and are not to be construed as real. Any resemblance to actual events, locales, organizations, or persons, living or dead, is entirely coincidental.

AVON BOOKS
An Imprint of Harper Collins*Publishers*
10 East 53rd Street
New York, New York 10022-5299

ISBN-13: 978-0-06-123525-2
ISBN-10: 0-06-123525-3
www.avonbooks.com

First Avon Books special printing: August 2006
First Avon Books paperback printing: November 1992

Printed in the U.S.A.

10 9 8 7 6 5 4 3 2 1

This one's for Adam Matan Senior, born at 2:30 A.M. on September 14, 1991.

Welcome to the world, darling!

And always, it goes without saying, for my best friend, my greatest love, my husband— Elie

Prologue

Clayborough, 1874

The Hall was filled with guests. Animated voices, happy laughter and the jubilant strains of a string quartet rang through its corridors. The small boy lay in his oversized bed two floors above the ballroom, listening to the sounds echoing through his home. His small fists were clenched in his bedcovers as he stared sleeplessly into the darkness.

He did not like the darkness, but he was six years old, no longer a baby; he would not turn on the light by his bed. Instead, he stared at the shadows on his wall, shadows made by the old-fashioned sconce lights in the hallway that shone through his door, left carefully ajar by his nanny.

He imagined the flickering shadows were people, not monsters; women in glittering jewels and men in midnight black tailcoats. He imagined that he was one of them, and not a boy, but a man, a real man, as strong and powerful as any of the lords below. As strong and powerful as the Duke, his father. *No—stronger. More powerful.*

The fantasy made him smile. For an instant, he felt adult. And then he heard them, and his smile vanished and he sat bolt upright, trembling.

They were outside his door, in the corridor. He strained to hear them—when he did not want to hear them. His mother, her voice soft, almost a whisper. "I didn't expect you back. Here, let me help you."

And his father. "So eager to rush me to bed?" There was nothing soft about the Duke of Clayborough's voice.

The small boy gripped the quilt more tightly. The shadows no longer frightened him. For the monster was now outside his door, in the hall.

"What's the matter, Isobel?" Francis Braxton-Lowell demanded. "Have I distressed you? It's obvious you're not pleased that I'm here. Afraid I might attend to the guests in my own home?"

"Of course not," his mother replied calmly.

The boy did not want to get out of bed but he slipped to his feet, crept to the open door and peeped around it.

The Duke was tall, blond and handsome, his mother was blonder, stunningly beautiful and elegant. His fine evening clothes were rumpled and he was unshaven, she was the picture of perfection in her ice blue sateen gown and glittering diamonds. Distaste etched itself clearly onto the Duke's face and he turned abruptly, stumbled, and lurched up the corridor. His mother's facade dropped. Anxiously she followed him.

He peered after them.

The Duke paused outside of the door to his suite. "I don't need your help."

"Are you going to come downstairs?"

"Afraid I'll disgrace you?"

"Of course not."

"You lie so well. Why don't you invite me downstairs, Isobel?"

His mother's back was to him so he could not see her expression, and her voice was not quite so calm. "If you wish to join us, why don't you change your clothes first?"

"Perhaps I will!" he snarled. His gaze suddenly settled on the strand of diamonds at her throat. "I've never seen that patch of paste before."

"I had it made recently."

"Damn me—that doesn't look like glass and paste at all!"

Isobel did not reply.

Silence fell heavily between them. The small boy had crept forward and he crouched behind a lacquer prayer table. Dread filled him. The Duke's eyes were widening, and suddenly, violently, he ripped the jewels from his mother's throat. Isobel choked off a scream. The boy leapt forward.

"This is the real thing!" the Duke shouted. "By God, these are real diamonds! You traitorous bitch! You've been hiding money from me, haven't you?"

The Duchess stood frozen.

The boy froze too, panting, just behind her.

"Haven't you?" Francis shouted. "Where did you get the money for this? Where? Damn you!"

"From royalties," Isobel said, the slightest quaver in her tone. "We have received our first royalties from the Dupres Mining Company."

"First you rent my land without my permission," Francis yelled furiously. "Now you hide my money from me? You never stop, do you?"

"How else am I to save your patrimony?"

Francis moved with surprising speed for one so drunk and he struck his wife hard across the face. She cried out and reeled back against the wall.

"You've always been a fraud, Isobel, from the day I met you. A fraud and a liar!" He lurched toward her again, arm raised.

"Stop!" the boy shouted, tackling his father around the knees. "Don't hurt her! Don't hurt her!"

"Damn you and damn him," Francis shouted, hitting his wife again.

The blow took her across one cheek and this time knocked her to the floor. The boy reacted. He pummeled his father's thighs viciously, as hard as he could, filled with a blinding rage. He hated his father so much it hurt.

As if his son were no more than a stray kitten, Francis plucked him up by the scruff of his neck and tossed him aside. He landed on his back, his head hit the floor, and for one moment he saw stars.

"You puny brat! You think you're a man, do you? Well tomorrow you'll get a man's punishment for interfering where you shouldn't!" His father towered over him. "A puny brat and a fraud—just like your mother!"

The boy blinked to clear his vision. His father was gone. But not the words, not the cruel, hateful words, for they lingered in his mind. For a moment he lay trembling in pain. It felt like a fist in his chest, in his heart. It hurt terribly. But it hadn't been caused by his father's physical blow. He closed his eyes, and sweat staining his brow, he fought himself until everything subsided, the pain, the need for tears, the hatred, everything. Until there was nothing left at all.

And when he opened his eyes he saw his mother, still prone. He scrambled toward her just as she sat up, tears falling down her cheeks. "Mother? Are you all right?" He did not sound like a child; he sounded like an adult.

"Oh, darling!" Isobel cried, wrapping her son in her arms. "Your father did not mean it, he did not!"

Patiently, the boy let her hug him then he moved away. He nodded expressionlessly, although he knew it was not true, while his mother sobbed silently. He knew that his father had meant every word, every action. Just as he knew that his father hated them—hated him. But it did not matter.

Not anymore. For one good thing had come of this night. Finally, the pain was gone. He had learned how to control it, how to chase it into the night. He had learned how to embrace emptiness. And it was vast.

Dragmore, 1898

"You have callers, my Lady."

"But I never have callers," Nicole protested.

Aldric looked at her, his lined face unfathomable, although his brown eyes were twinkling. "The ladies Margaret Adderly and Stacy Worthington, my Lady."

Nicole was surprised. Of course, it was an exaggeration to say that she never had callers, for her best friend, the Viscountess Serle, as well as the local gentry and her family, did come calling rather frequently. But they didn't really count. What counted was the fact that she herself did not have the usual bevy of callers like other young ladies of her class. Not in the past several years. Not since the scandal. What could these ladies, whom she had never met, possibly want?

"Tell them I'll be right down. Have refreshments served, Aldric," she told the butler. A bubble of excitement rose up in her.

Aldric nodded, but before leaving he raised one bushy white eyebrow. "Perhaps I should mention that you will be a few minutes, my Lady?"

She understood and chuckled, looking down ruefully at her men's breeches and muddy riding boots. Although it was almost the dawning of a new era—the twentieth century—women did not wear men's clothing even when they had just cause. Some things never changed. "Good of you to remind me, Aldric. I shouldn't chase away my illustrious visitors before I even find out why they've come."

Still chuckling, she waited for Aldric to leave, imagining the shock the two proper ladies downstairs would receive if they saw her attired like a man. It just wasn't done.

Nicole sighed, honest enough with herself to know that her carefree attitude and rather improper sense of humour did not help her situation—not that she was really in a situation, she reminded herself. After all, she chose to remain in the country. As she riffled carelessly through her armoire for the appropriate undergarments, she admitted to herself that it was nice to have young women come calling. It had been a long time. Not that she wasn't happy at Dragmore, for she was. Her life was Dragmore, horses and books. It was just that, well, it *had* been a long time.

Nicole donned a combination, stockings and a petticoat, as quickly as she could. She hated corsets and refused to wear them, even though she was twenty-three and five feet ten inches in her bare feet. She was bigger than most women and then there was her age. She refused unequivocally to try and cinch in her waistline as if she were five feet tall, eighteen years old and a scant hundred pounds. If people knew, they would talk. People loved to talk, Nicole had found out firsthand. But in this instance, no one could possibly know, and even if they did, Nicole was adamant.

It wasn't just a matter of comfort. Nicole was a voracious reader. She agreed with some of her favorite women authors who favored knickers and bloomers instead of the current fashions, which were, they held, unhealthily constrictive. *Like corsets.* Just as modern society had invented rules of decorum expressly to keep women in their place, so too it had invented fashions for the exact same purpose.

After all, a corseted, fainting woman could not be expected to do more than smile and breathe. A fainting woman could not run, ride, shoot or think. A fainting woman was demure.

Nicole was wise enough to know that she should keep her wisdom to herself.

When she had finished dressing she paused one instant to look nervously in the mirror, aware of the tightening knot of anticipation in her belly. She scowled at herself. It wasn't that she disliked her quiet navy blue jacket and skirt, for she couldn't have cared less about clothes as long as she was not constricted by them. It was other aspects of her appearance which displeased her.

She sighed. "Well, what did you expect?" she asked her reflection seriously. "To be shorter? To be blonde? What are you, a nitwit? If people judge you by how you look, why, they're not worth one pence!"

Her door opened. "Are you calling me, mum?"

Nicole blushed. If the servants ever caught her talking to herself she'd never live it down! "Uh, yes, Annie, would you take my breeches to Sue Anne? The left knee needs patching." She smiled brightly, waiting until Annie had taken up the pants and left. Then she looked at herself with a frown. She was still ridiculously tall and much too dark. She had inherited all of her father's swarthy looks, and nothing from her petite, blonde mother. She wasn't morose by nature, but couldn't her hair have been brown instead of jet black?

She should have asked Annie to help her with her hair instead of making up a story about her britches, she thought, trying to run a comb through it, because the thick, wavy black mass fell to her waist and was untamable without a second pair of hands. It was too late for that now, and Nicole tied it back quickly with a ribbon. The ladies Adderly and Worthington were waiting. Her belly clenched again. If she delayed another minute it would be downright rude. Abruptly Nicole left her room and flew down the stairs, forgetting she was in skirts until she tripped and was forced into a more sedate, ladylike pace.

In the hall below she paused to catch her breath and calm her quivering nerves. She told herself that she was being silly—she was only receiving callers, something other young ladies did every day of their lives. Hurrying down a long, marble-floored corridor, she wished that her mother, the Countess of Dragmore, was home to give her a dose of good advice. But Jane was in London with Nicole's younger sister, Regina, who refused to remain in the secluded countryside when the season was in full swing. Nicole wished her parents would let Regina get married and forget about the fact that she, the elder sister, was unwed and likely to stay that way forever.

She paused in the doorway of the large, bright yellow salon. Instantly, the two young ladies on the chintz sofa froze, their conversation ceased. One was blonde and perfect, the other a stunning brunette. Both young ladies stared at Nicole out of wide blue eyes. For a silly instant, Nicole felt like an exotic *something* under a magnifying glass, and then the feeling passed.

Smiling, she entered. "Hello. How kind of you to come."

Both girls stood, their gazes openly curious as they drifted over Nicole's tall body while they exchanged introductions. Nicole felt massive standing next to them, for she towered over their diminutive five foot frames. "Lady Shelton," said the blonde, "I am Lady Margaret Adderly, and this is my friend, Lady Stacy Worthington."

The formalities dispensed with, Nicole urged them to sit, seeing that they had been served tea and cakes. She sat facing them in a brocade wing chair. Stacy Worthington regarded her too intently.

"You do know about the Duke?" Margaret asked excitedly.

She could only be referring to one man. "The Duke of Clayborough?" Nicole said, wondering what he could possibly have to do with anything, much less these two young ladies.

"Yes!" Margaret beamed. "He has come into possession of Chapman Hall. You do realize that he is your neighbor!"

"Of course," Nicole said, somewhat perplexed. She knew nothing about the Duke except that he had indeed just arrived at Chapman Hall, a mere mile from Dragmore's front gates. She had never heard of him before that week.

"He is my cousin," Stacy Worthington announced. She smiled smugly, as if being the cousin of a duke was a matter of great importance.

"How fortunate you are," Nicole managed.

Stacy did not catch Nicole's implied sarcasm. "We have known each other since childhood," she said grandly.

Nicole smiled.

"He is in residence," Margaret said, "and this Friday we are holding a masque in his honor at Tarent Hall. After all, he must be welcomed properly to the country."

"Yes, I suppose so."

"I am sure that if the Earl and Countess were in residence, they would have the honor of hosting the event, but as they are not, my mother has decided to do so."

Nicole nodded.

Stacy smiled. "We knew that you were here, *not in London*, and of course it would be most improper if we did not invite you. So, here we are."

Nicole blinked, stiffening. She was astonished at what Stacy had said and the way she had said it. She had just been given the rudest invitation, the implication clear that she had to be invited whether she was wanted or not. At the same time, the young woman had referred to Nicole's not being in London with her parents and sister and all the other unwed young ladies of means and position who were husband-hunting. The further implication was worse—that she was not welcome in London. And that was not true.

Not exactly.

"Oh," was all Nicole could think of to say. She felt put

on the spot. She rarely went out into society—in fact, she hadn't in years. Did this woman know that? Of course she did. Everyone knew it.

"Of course you'll come," Stacy smiled. "Won't you?"

Nicole could not smile. She was being challenged. It was not her imagination. And her stomach was in knots. It had been so long. Certainly by now people would have forgotten.

"Well?" Stacy asked. She was still smiling.

Nicole disliked her. The other woman expected her to decline the invitation. Everyone knew she rarely went out. And they had not come calling in friendship, but only out of duty. It would be so terribly improper if they did not invite the Earl of Dragmore's daughter to such an important event. "Of course I'll come," Nicole said proudly, unsmiling.

Stacy looked shocked. But that was nothing compared to the expression on Margaret's face. "You will?" the blonde squeaked.

Anger filled Nicole. She still did not understand Stacy's motivation, but that did not matter. What mattered was the challenge. "Until Friday," Nicole said, standing.

When the two women had left, Nicole regretted letting them back her into a corner. But how could she refuse the challenge Stacy Worthington had thrown at her? And by now people had forgotten, hadn't they?

After the scandal, Nicole had been the object of much ugly gossip and speculation, and it had hurt. Her parents had been very angry with her, and even if she had wanted to hide at their London home, they would not have allowed it. But she was not a coward, and she had continued the season as if nothing had happened, holding her head high and ignoring all the gawking and gossip.

When the scandal began to die, Nicole bowed out. From the time of her debut, Nicole had not been impressed with the balls and routs, the soirees and supper parties, which she found endless, repetitive and quite boring. She enjoyed rising with the sun and spending her day on horseback, tending to Dragmore with her father and brothers. And to her, a good book was much more entertaining than most of these affairs.

The past four years had not been unhappy ones. Nicole loved her family, she loved Dragmore and she was content with the life she led. In fact, it was because she hadn't wanted to change her life that she had caused the scandal in the first place.

But . . . sometimes, usually when her younger sister Regina was in London with her mother, attending one party after another, dressed in fabulous silks and courted by handsome bachelors, Nicole missed her and felt alone, and she would suddenly wish that she were there, too. Regina was always the belle of the ball, the way Nicole had never been, and Nicole knew she wished for what she could not have. It was a small wish, a fleeting wish. Nicole reminded herself of the few times she had gone out with her family since the scandal, times that had not been fun, times where people looked at her and remembered, and sometimes whispered behind her back as well. She had only to remember those times and the wistful feeling would pass and be forgotten for weeks on end.

And now she was not only going out again, but she was going alone. Not only were her parents and Regina in London, her brother Ed was at Cambridge and her brother Chad was in France on business. She didn't have an escort. Ladies did not attend parties unescorted unless they were over thirty, which she was not.

Yet she would attend this masque, even without an escort. She would do so in high style and show up that snooty Stacy Worthington.

Draping herself in a fine red wool cloak, Nicole set off for Tarent Hall on Friday night. She was a jumble of nerves when she was finally on her way. Earlier that day she had given in to a few doubts about going without an escort, but she had finally laid them to rest by sheer willpower. She had been challenged and she was no coward—she was going to attend the masque, come what may.

She had a terrible feeling that she was going to regret this night. If she were sane, she thought to herself, she would forget all about Stacy Worthington and stay at home as a proper young lady should.

But it was too late now, Nicole thought, fingering the brilliant orange petticoat and vividly pink skirt beneath her cloak. She had never been proper, not really. There was a wild streak in her, and there always had been. She got it from her father's side of the family, or so her mother said, although the Earl insisted disregard for convention was a Barclay trait. At the age of twenty-three she was mature and honest enough with herself to recognize this outlandish side of her nature and accept it. It was this wild part of her that had accepted Stacy's challenge and that was even now propelling her forward without an escort against her better judgment.

Nicole had always hated the rules and conventions that bound all the women of her day. Fortunately, she was not alone, although she was in a quite radical minority, led by suffragettes and agitators like Elizabeth Cady Stanton and her aunt, Grace Bragg. Women were supposed to do nothing more than bore themselves with gentle womanly pursuits such as flower arranging and watercolors. When her tutor had tried to teach her those arts, the eight-year-old Nicole had flown into a rage. She would spend her days painting roses while Chad, Ed and her father rode across Dragmore, overseeing the tenants, the farms and the livestock? Never!

Of course, she was forced to learn such pursuits, which she did in a dismal fashion, but in her free time she haunted the menfolk of her family and was allowed to accompany them after her studies, a liberty unheard of for a well-bred young lady. Through childhood and adolescence she had been endlessly sorry that she was not a boy—another son. When she was not on horseback with her brothers and father, she could be found reading, everything from Byron's sensual poetry to John Stuart Mills' *The Rights of Women*. Her family never thought twice about her boyish inclinations until she was suddenly a full-grown woman, and then they did their best to ignore her unconventional ways.

They would drop dead if they knew what she was doing, or, worse, if they saw her now.

She had only had three days to find a fabulous costume, but she had solved the problem by scavenging in the vast attic of her home. Her mother, Jane Barclay, had been a popular stage actress, although she had given up her promising career to devote herself to her children, her husband and Dragmore a few years after her marriage. Acting was in her blood, for Jane had been following in the footsteps of her mother, the famous and incomparable Sandra Barclay, and there had been trunks of wonderful costumes in the attic.

Nicole chose a gypsy costume. Even she had to admit that, with her coloring, in the brilliantly colored clothes she had found, she looked like the real thing. Of course, the costume was daring. It was not exactly proper. The blouse fell off of her shoulders in a very suggestive way, and the skirts were only knee-length. But gypsies—or so the thirteen-year-old Annie assured her—went barefoot in short skirts. Nicole did not care. When Stacy Worthington and her little friend saw her, they would be set upon their ears! Nicole was certain that they did not really expect her to come at all.

She smiled as she sat back on the plush leather seats in the big black Dragmore coach, which was pulled by six greys and attended by four liveried footmen. Not only was she attending the masque in a very authentic costume, she was actually starting to become excited. It had been ages since she had been out among the set, and even longer since she had been to a costume ball.

The circular driveway in front of the Georgian brick home was already filled with coaches and carriages. A coach twice the size of the Dragmore vehicle had turned into the drive ahead of them. This carriage was also black, and so highly polished it gleamed in the moonlight. The coat of arms was brilliantly vivid, the lights of the carriage making sure that no one could possibly miss it, oversized and embossed as it was on two of the doors of the carriage. Two lions, one red and one gold, reared up against a black, red and gold shield, while another red lion snarled above it. Below the shield, the two rearing lions stood on a silver ribbon, bearing a motto that said simply, "Honor First." Such an elaborate coat of arms could only belong to the Duke of Clayborough.

Eight magnificent blacks pulled the coach, gold plumes waving from their bridles. Four footmen stood on the back running board, splendid in red, black and gold uniforms. A dozen outriders accompanied the Duke, all mounted magnificently on matching bays, all liveried in the Duke's colors. The coach was splendid enough for royalty, which, Nicole knew, the Duke was not.

They stopped in the drive, her carriage behind his, with Nicole straining to glimpse the illustrious guest of honor. She discerned only a tall, powerful figure in ebony tails, a black cloak swirling about his shoulders, lined in crimson, as he alighted. He had chosen not to come in costume, she noted, and there was no Duchess in tow.

She was helped from the carriage and hurried up the steps toward the bright lights of the mansion. The front doors were open, and a liveried servant took her cloak, not blinking once at her attire. She followed a footman to the entrance of the ballroom, her heart beginning to pound. When he asked for her name, she gave it automatically.

For just a moment, she recalled too many soirees, and too many failures. For just a moment, the daring side of her retreated, and she felt frightened.

She paused behind the Duke while he was announced. He was even taller than she had guessed, nearly half a foot taller than she, with massively broad shoulders. His hair was too long to be fashionable, as if he were too busy to bother with a barber. It was a dark, tawny color, and even in the interior lighting, she could see that it was heavily sun-streaked, as if he spent most of his time out of doors.

"Hadrian Braxton-Lowell, the ninth Duke of Clay-borough," the butler intoned. A long string of the Duke's various other titles followed.

The Duke paused, his posture impatient and careless, but the butler had barely finished the introduction before he was striding down the steps into the ballroom. Nicole moved forward, watching him as a splendidly attired woman, clearly the hostess, greeted him.

"Lady Nicole Bragg Shelton," the butler was saying.

Nicole did not hear him. Her heart was in her throat. She was suddenly overwhelmingly conscious of her bare legs and bare feet. She felt as if the entire crowd was staring at her, which they were, of course, because she had just been announced and, that, right after the Duke. A hush fell upon the crowd, and she prayed it was because of the Duke and not because of her appearance at this masque.

But he, too, turned and stared at her.

Nicole held her head high. Barefoot, as a true gypsy would be, bangles on her arms, her hair flowing to her waist, her skirts swirling above her calves, she gracefully descended the stairs. People started to whisper. Nicole had an awful feeling that they were talking about her.

She had been right, she should never have come. No one had forgotten, and her costume was too daring even for a masque.

Unfortunately she glimpsed Stacy Worthington standing in front of the crowd, clad in a white Regency gown, a perfectly proper kind of costume. Stacy wasn't on her ear. She was smirking.

Nicole forgot all about Stacy Worthington. The Duke was staring at her. He took her breath away. Somehow, she moved toward her hostess without falling dead away into a faint. "Lady Adderly," she murmured, curtsying.

The Viscountess blinked at her. Nicole felt the Duke's eyes burning on her. "Oh, yes, Lady Shelton, how good of you to come. And what a . . . charming . . . costume."

Nicole could not smile, she still could not breathe. But she was not sure whether it was because she was still being gawked at by a hundred guests, or whether it was because he stood so close beside her she fantasized she could feel the heat of his powerful body. "Thank you," she murmured.

"A magnificent costume," the Duke said, his voice carrying without any apparent effort on his behalf.

Nicole whirled and met his eyes. The floor seemed to drop out from under her feet.

He was handsome. Devastatingly handsome, devastatingly male. He nearly dwarfed her. His dark eyes seemed to command hers, and she was held enthralled in his power. "You are unique, Lady Shelton," he said abruptly, his gaze slipping down her body. "And I, for one, find it refreshing."

Just as abruptly, he turned his back on her, nodded to his hostess and strode off, leaving the two women standing there alone.

"Unique," Lady Adderly said, as if she could not believe it.

Nicole's heart started to beat again. A wild ecstasy filled her. She recognized his words as a compliment. God—that gorgeous man had praised her!

She found herself floating through the crowd. People still stared, but where once Nicole had hated being gawked at, today his words rang in her ears and she was oblivous to everyone around her. "A magnificent costume . . . You are unique, Lady Shelton. . . ."

Nicole found herself holding a glass of champagne. Her pulse was pounding rapidly and she felt overly warm. She scanned the crowd. She saw him instantly. To her shock, he was staring intently at her.

They were leagues apart. She could not clearly see his eyes, but she felt scorched by his gaze. She could see the intensity on his face. She could not look away from him, not until he lifted his own champagne glass, as if toasting her—or them.

Quickly, Nicole turned away. *The Duke of Clayborough.* How long would he be at Chapman Hall? Was he married? And what was happening to her? She was a mass of quivering nerves, and she could not take her eyes off of him! She found herself staring at him again.

He was listening to several lords and ladies, looking rather bored and as impatient as he had been when he had first entered the room. Stacy Worthington was beside him, gazing up at him adoringly. Nicole felt a stabbing of jealousy, deep and quick and hot. The intensity of it surprised her. And then, as if feeling her gaze, the Duke shifted and pierced her directly with his stare again. Nicole knew she should drop her eyes, but she did not—she could not.

An electric look passed between them.

"Dear Nicole, how long it has been!"

Nicole's attention was forced from the Duke, just as she saw his lips seeming to curve in a bare, sardonic smile. She recognized the gray-haired woman as the Marchioness of Hazelwood, and she tensed. This woman had been one of her biggest detractors after the scandal.

But now the Marchioness was smiling, as if they were old friends. "It is so nice to see you again, Nicole. My, can you imagine? The Duke says you are quite the thing!"

Nicole did not know what game the Marchioness was playing, but she would not be a part of it. "Yes, it has been some time, has it not?" Her voice was cool, for she had not forgotten how this woman had cut her four years ago. "Oh, I do believe it's been four years—since the soiree at Castleton. You do remember that little fête?"

The Marchioness surely had to remember how she had drawn her verbal sword and slashed Nicole to ribbons in front of a dozen of Castleton's guests, even going so far as to call her an Unacceptable, knowing Nicole could hear her every word. But now she smiled as if that night had never occurred.

"Oh, there are so many affairs," she sighed. She held up her spectacles, studying Nicole's costume. "Yes," she announced, nodding, "I can see how the Duke would find your costume quite unique. Please, do call the next time you are near Hazelwood, and give my regards to the Countess and the Earl." Patting Nicole's hand in a friendly manner, she turned away.

Nicole was stunned—and outraged. She was no fool. She knew that the Marchioness had invited her to Hazelwood only because the Duke had approved of her. She fumed inwardly. If the Duke had not been here tonight, or if he had not approved of her costume, would she have been the least bit friendly? Nicole was certain that the answer was no.

Nicole drank another glass of champagne, moving about, looking for the Duke discreetly, hoping to bump into him. To her amazement, many of the guests sought her out, extending invitations to her. She could not be pleased. But for the first time, she realized the extent of the power that someone like the Duke wielded. Tonight he had not tried to be her protector. His statement had been honest yet careless. Yet suddenly it was as if the scandal had never existed.

"You do not look happy, Lady Shelton," his deep voice came from behind her.

Nicole gasped. Spinning about so quickly to face him, champagne sloshed over the rim of her glass. He stood so close to her that her breasts, bound only in a thin chemise beneath her silk blouse, brushed his arm. Horrified, blushing, she stepped back wildly, spilling more champagne.

The look in his eyes, as he took the glass from her, was difficult to read. Their color, she saw, was not really dark brown, but the rich gold of sherry. She thought he might be somewhat amused. And his hand, taking her glass, touched hers, and seemed to caress her very soul. It burned.

"Let me replenish this," he said. He did not have to move, for a servant materialized from behind him with a tray of bubbling flutes. The Duke took one for himself and handed her another. "Why are you angry?"

Nicole quickly tried to recover her wits. "I am not exactly angry," she said carefully. Up close, he was even more stunning than from afar, and his impact was even more unnerving. She found herself staring at his mouth and wondering what it would be like to be kissed by him. When she realized the train of her thoughts she was horrified.

"You are certainly not angry now," he said, his gaze moving slowly over her.

There was something in his tone that wrung an instant response from her, something intimate that Nicole was too inexperienced to define. Nicole felt her breasts tighten as if he had actually touched her. "I am not angry now," she breathed.

His voice was husky, a low caress. "Good. I would not like you angry with me. Not now—when we have just met."

There were meanings there, vast meanings in his words, and Nicole was afraid to even guess what they could be. She wished his expression was less impassive, less controlled. His countenance was stern, inscrutable, and she had not a clue as to what he was thinking or why he had sought her out. But when his eyes held hers, her heart did somersaults. "I could never be angry with you," she heard herself say. Then she flushed, for she sounded like some coy, simpering miss, and it was exactly that type she could not tolerate.

"Ah, but there is the other side to consider, for I imagine your anger is like the rest of you, as novel and as stimulating."

She stared, speechless, for there was no possible reply

she could make to this, just as she could not quite fathom what he was driving at.

"Is it?"

"I—I don't know." She was thoroughly undone.

"I have no doubts," he said, and his voice dropped very low, "just as I have no doubts that your originality extends far beyond the public domain."

She thought of how she rode about Dragmore, dressed as a man. Here, at least, was safe ground. Her look was direct, and she breathed easier. "Yes, it does."

He drew in his breath sharply, his eyes suddenly blazing. Nicole had the distinct impression that he had not understood her and had, in fact, applied a meaning to her words which she had not intended. Unnerved by his searing regard, Nicole sought absolutely safe territory upon which to converse. "We are now neighbors," she said politely. "Chapman Hall is not far from Dragmore, not at all."

"How convenient," he replied dryly. "Then it would only be neighborly of me to invite you to my home, would it not?"

She was held captive by his golden eyes. She could not believe her ears. She smiled, and did not understand why he again drew in his breath. "I ride past Chapman Hall frequently," she said eagerly.

"I am sure you do. Then, the next time you are passing by, you must make sure to make a small detour and say hello." His words carried all the weight of a ducal command.

"I shall," Nicole cried passionately. "I shall!"

The Duke of Clayborough returned to Chapman Hall close to midnight, his mood more than irritated. He hated being fêted, having absolutely no delusions about why people catered to him. He was reclusive by nature, and his popularity was based only upon his title, wealth and power. He had little respect for the likes of the Adderlys, who fawned over him and made, in his opinion, complete fools of themselves by doing so.

He had never liked the endless balls and soirees which many of his peers seemed to revel in. He found them a waste of his time. His interests had always lain elsewhere. He had spent the past twelve years, since he was a youth of eighteen, running the vast Clayborough estates while his father, Francis, the eighth Duke, amassed a debt that finally reached the staggering sum of a million pounds. While Francis was indulging all his vices, his son was struggling to run the estates in an economic depression. The Clayborough estates ranged over nearly two hundred thousand acres and contained almost a hundred farms, the properties scattered about in Sussex, Kent, Derbyshire and even Durham. Like most of the peerage, the Duke had a wealth and livelihood based upon agriculture. Yet the British had been suffering severely in the past decades, unable to compete with the machine-reaped products America was exporting. Agriculture had been the crux of the Clayborough family fortune for hundreds of years, and it took more than discipline and hard work to fight the tide that had turned against it.

It took bold, innovative new strategies. While Francis spent his days in gaming halls and his nights God knew where, the shrewd young heir was investing in trade, London real estate and finance. But Francis' debts continued to increase and remained a terrible drain upon the estates.

Those days were now over. The Duke felt not one bit of sorrow that his wastrel father had died two years ago—in bed with someone other than his wife, and foxed to boot. The most sordid detail—that Francis' paramour had been a young man—had been effectively hushed up by his son before any more damage could be done. Not that his father's ways were a secret. The Duke had no delusions on that score, either. He was certain all of society knew exactly the kind of man the eighth Duke had been, just as they knew he was the exact opposite.

His father had relished all the weekend parties and hunts, the balls and routs, never retiring until after dawn and never rising before noon. The Duke was up at dawn, and usually retired before midnight. His business affairs demanded his constant attention, and he was known to work well into the night. It was not entirely discipline; part of it was a burning ambition that he was certain came from his mother's side of the family. The de Warennes were known for their shrewd business sense, which even the Dowager Duchess of Clayborough possessed in abundance. When the Duke had first become immersed in Clayborough's affairs, he had worked side by side with his mother, amazed at how she had been running the estates for the past two decades with no help at all from her husband.

He was irritated this evening because it was late and he had a full agenda for the morrow. He would rise as usual, with the sun. He was not inhuman, although many seemed to think he was, and if he didn't sleep soon, tomorrow he would be tired. And tonight had been nothing but a waste of his time and energy.

He entered Chapman Hall. His butler, Woodward, and his valet, Reynard, were awaiting him, and the head footman, Jakes, accompanied him. Woodward took his black, crimson-lined cloak without the Duke even noticing. "Will that be all, Your Grace?"

"Go to bed, Woodward," he waved at him dismissively. Tonight had not exactly been a complete waste of time, he thought, his pulse quickening. Her gypsy image loomed vividly in his mind. "Nor do I need you, Reynard. Thank you, Jakes. Good night."

Reynard and Jakes disappeared, but Woodward coughed and the Duke paused before bounding up the stairs. He lifted a brow.

"The Dowager Duchess arrived this evening, Your Grace. It was unexpected, but we made do and put her in the blue room in the west wing. It seemed to be in the best condition, Your Grace."

"Well done," he said. As he strode up the stairs, his brow furrowed. What was his mother doing here, for God's sake? He knew it was not a dire emergency, for if it had been, the Dowager Duchess would be up and waiting for him, pacing restlessly, no matter how late the hour. Still, the dowager estates were in Derbyshire, which was no easy drive to make, and if she had come from her home in London, it would have meant almost a half day's journey. She had not come merely to chat—something important was on her mind.

But it would have to wait until tomorrow. Tomorrow. His body tensed. Would the utterly seductive Lady Shelton "pass by?" A smile curved his lips, his first real smile of the evening, revealed only in the privacy of the master bedroom and shared only with the Borzoi thumping his tail enthusiastically in greeting to his master.

Clayborough stripped. He was still shocked at her admission that she was as original in private as in public, and again, for the umpteenth time, he imagined her naked in his bed, astride him, devouring him with her wild gypsy passion. In his imagination he was somewhat passive, as he had never been in his entire life. The fantasy aroused him unbearably, and he was not a man who succumbed to daydreams.

She was more than original; she was daring, and he guessed she was reckless as well. Of course, he knew she was somehow related to the Earl of Dragmore, whom he knew, admired, and respected. Nicholas Shelton was very much like himself: a hard, disciplined worker and a clever businessman. Was she his daughter-in-law? Some cousin, perhaps?

Obviously she was married, for she was no spring miss and her bold manners, especially coming unescorted in such a costume, confirmed this. The Duke was used to married women throwing themselves at his feet and doing everything they possibly could to get into his bed. Although he did not indulge himself in gambling, alcohol, or other wastrel pursuits, he had never been able to refuse a beautiful woman, although he rarely bothered to be the pursuer. He always kept a mistress as well, of course, but he tired quickly in these relationships and was continually changing liaisons. He was well aware that he had a reputation for being a ruthless womanizer, but it did not bother him—at least he was no sodomite like his late father.

It occurred to him that Lady Shelton would make a fine mistress. He did not know her well, but he sensed it. Unfortunately, as she was married, taking her as his mistress was out of the question and he would have to settle for an affair. Usually his interludes with married women were even shorter than his relationships with his mistresses. He rarely had time for the clandestine meetings a married woman required; usually a tumble or two sufficed. Lady Shelton interested him more than a bit—he did not think a couple of nights would do either of them justice.

He sighed, annoyed at the inconvenience it would cause him.

* * *

The Dowager Duchess was also an unfashionably early riser. Isobel de Warenne Braxton-Lowell had gotten into the plebeian habit in the early years of her marriage, when Francis had first come into his patrimony after the seventh Duke's death. It hadn't taken her very long to see that Francis had no intention of changing his rakehell ways. When the bills began to pile up, she had finally hired a chancellor to attend to them. It had been a rude shock to learn that funds were desperately scarce and the estates were withering, but nothing like the rude shock her marriage had been. And that had only been the beginning. Someone had to run the huge dukedom. Isobel had become that someone, and the more adept at it she became, the more angry with her Francis grew.

It was just past six in the morning and Woodward poured her tea from a silver-plated urn, which pointed up the plight of the previous owners of Chapman Hall as eloquently as the run-down grounds and worn oak floors did. No one of the Dowager Duchess' acquaintances used silver plate, especially not tarnished and dented silver plate.

Despite the hour, Isobel was dressed in an elegant blue day ensemble, the dress high-necked with wide leg-o-mutton sleeves, the waist exceedingly narrow, the skirt bell-shaped and pleated in the back. Isobel was fifty-four, but her figure was that of a woman in her twenties, and she watched it fastidiously. Likewise, except for the wrinkles at the corners of her vivid blue eyes and the character lines around her mouth, her skin was ivory smooth and, with the help of special creams, luminescent. Her face was a perfect oval, high cheekboned and partrician, the kind that wears well. She was still handsome and attractive. As a young woman she had been a great beauty.

Now, to match the costly blue silk of her dress, she wore sapphire ear bobs and one wide, stunning diamond bracelet interspersed with more sapphires. A large sapphire winged with two small rubies blinked from her right hand. She did not wear her wedding rings. In fact, she had been relieved to finally lay them to rest along with her departed husband.

"I thought I would find you up," the Duke remarked, striding into the room in tight-fitting breeches, boots and a loose white shirt. "Good morning, Mother." He went directly to her and kissed her cheek.

"Good morning." Isobel studied him as he sat down beside her at the head of the scarred mahogany table. No small amount of pride swept her as she watched him. He was her only child, and she had conceived him relatively late in her marriage, seven years after she had been wed, at the age of twenty-four. It wasn't just his striking looks that thrilled her, or his manly demeanor, but everything about him. For he was an honorable man, a son any woman would be proud of; as strong, solid and responsible as Francis had been weak, dishonest and irresponsible. Of course, knowing what she did, knowing the whole truth, she was saddened too, for even in the powerful grown man, she still glimpsed the grim little boy who never had the childhood he should have had.

"I am afraid to ask," the Duke said as Woodward poured him rich, black coffee. "But what brings you here?"

Instead of answering, Isobel said, "How was the affair last night?" Another servant brought them plates of eggs, bacon and kippers.

The Duke smiled slightly. "A damned nuisance, of course."

She regarded him, wondering what his small, satisfied smile meant, then thanked Woodward politely as he left the room. They were alone. "I am worried about Elizabeth, Hadrian."

At the mention of his fiancée, the Duke paused, fork lifted. "What is wrong?"

"Perhaps if you spent more time with her, you would not have to ask," Isobel said gently.

The Duke laid his silver down on his plate. "Clayborough cannot run itself, Mother, as you, of all people, should know."

"I do know. But your paths cross less and less, and I know it is bothering her. Even hurting her."

The Duke stared grimly. "Then I am remiss," he finally said. "For I would not hurt her, not purposefully. She is so busy in London with the social whirl, I thought it made her happy. It did not occur to me that she might—er—miss me."

"Of course she is happy in London, but you are her betrothed. In a few months you will be wed. People are beginning to talk."

"Is this what you have come to tell me?"

"No. I saw her the day before yesterday, Hadrian, and while she tries to pretend all is as it should be, it is clear that she is not well."

"She is ill?"

"I am afraid so. She is very pale, and she has lost weight. I finally asked her directly, and it took some prodding—for you know how Elizabeth is, never wanting to burden anybody, God forbid! But she finally confessed to being fatigued all the time, and although she is not eating any less, she has lost enough weight that all her gowns have had to be altered. I encouraged her to see a physician, but she laughed at me and said it is only fatigue and it will pass."

"Well, it does not sound as if she is in dire circumstances, Mother, or she would go to a doctor. I will be in London in a week or two, as soon as I have finished here. I will investigate, and if she is in need of medical treatment, you can be sure she will receive it."

Isobel knew he meant every word, for he never failed to carry out his intentions. Although he kept a mistress, as most men did, she knew he would be a good husband. When he was with Elizabeth he was always courteous, kind and respectful, and it was no game—it was his nature. He never denied her anything, not even a request to attend some function, although he dearly hated them and he was a busy man. He was not abusive in any way, and he kept his affairs most discreet.

Isobel knew he was fond of Elizabeth, for they were cousins. In fact, Hadrian had been twelve, Elizabeth two, when they were betrothed. Isobel knew that Hadrian felt no burning love for Elizabeth, caring for her as one might care for a sister, just as she was certain that Elizabeth did love him, and not as one would love a brother. That, of course, was not her business. The most important thing was that Hadrian and Elizabeth were friends, and that Hadrian would always honor and respect her. Isobel had seen enough of the world to know that friendship was not a bad basis for a marriage, for only a very few were ever lucky enough to experience love at all, much less to love their spouse. She was carried back to another time, to other shores, and she was sad. But the moment passed.

The Duke ate quickly, considering what his mother had told him. He was not alarmed, although Isobel must be or she would not have come all the way to Chapman Hall. His first order of business when he got back to London would be to discuss Elizabeth's health with her, and he would not be fooled if she were indeed ailing. Also he would go out of his way to accompany her to the theatre and other such nonsense. Once again, the Dowager Duchess was right, and he felt guilty. He had become too immersed in the affairs of his estates, and he had been neglecting his fiancée. It was unlike him, for if he had calculated correctly, he had not seen her in over a month. There was no excuse. Once they were married he resolved not to let such a pattern develop again.

The Duke excused himself to attend to the repair of Chapman Hall, which was in a sadly neglected condition. As he left the table, his thoughts once again turned to the brazen gypsy-like Lady Shelton. He had flirted with her last night like some shallow fop, and he was not a flirt, not ever. *He had actually pursued her.* He had invited her here, to Chapman Hall, and now he was sorry he had done so. Although Isobel would probably leave tomorrow, he absolutely could not allow her to meet Lady Shelton, a future lover; it would be the height of impropriety and disrespect. He hadn't been thinking very clearly last night, if he had been thinking at all. The realization unsettled him.

The Duke spent the morning finishing his review of the small estate, which covered a mere twenty acres, for it had been nothing more than a country home for its previous owners. He returned to the Hall in time for a dinner of minted lamb, which he took with his mother. Isobel had been out riding—she was an avid horsewoman—and she told him she would leave the next morning to return to London.

He shared some of his plans for Chapman Hall with Isobel, who, as always, was keenly interested in anything that had to do with the ducal empire. They were just finishing their meal when Woodward appeared, announcing a caller.

The Duke did not have to be told who it was—*he knew*. But Woodward gravely informed him that his visitor was Lady Nicole Shelton, although he barely heard. His mother was looking at him queerly, saying, "Lady Nicole Bragg Shelton from Dragmore, Hadrian?"

The slightest flush tinged his high cheekbones as he rose abruptly. "I have a riding date," he said curtly, his tone cutting off any further questions. He hurried out, leaving her gaping after him.

Woodward led him to the small parlor off of the slate-floored foyer. The door was open and the Duke's steps slowed as he saw her. A primitive need rose up in him; he became a stalking male. She was sitting on the sofa and she immediately stood, her gaze locking with his.

She was no wild gypsy today, but she was somehow more entrancing than she had been last night. She wore a bottle-green riding habit with a matching hat, her hair pinned up and out of sight. She held black leather gloves and a riding crop, twisting the former in her hands.

"I am glad you have come," he said low, halting in front of her. His gaze swept over her exquisite features, and yes, she was every bit as strikingly beautiful as he remembered. It had not been his imagination running wild.

She curtsied but he stopped her, lifting her back up. "Please, no formalities, I think that would be rather ridiculous given the circumstances, don't you?"

She blinked at him. Her eyes, he saw, were so pale that they were almost silver. He wondered if she had even heard him, or if she had even understood. Sometimes she perplexed him, with her blushes and confusion, as if she were not a lady of experience. Or perhaps she was as undone with the physical attraction that raced between them as he himself seemed to be.

"Thank you, Your Grace," she said, her voice low and husky.

He heard footsteps in the hall and he stiffened, knowing it was the Dowager Duchess. There was no graceful way out of the situation. He would have to introduce them. The Duke's jaw tightened.

Isobel entered the foyer, looking perturbed, her gaze going from his visitor to himself. The Duke thought he read disapproval in her eyes, and it disturbed him, just as her meeting Lady Shelton here did. "Lady Shelton, the Dowager Duchess of Clayborough," he said formally, his tone giving absolutely no indication that anything was amiss.

The two women exchanged greetings. Isobel said, "Won't you join us for tea, Lady Shelton? Woodward, please bring us some refreshments."

The Duke cut her off, taking Nicole's arm firmly. "I am sorry, Mother, but as I said, we have a riding date."

Before Isobel could insist they stay, and he saw from her expression that she would, he was leading his guest out of the salon and through the foyer. "It's a beautiful day, and it would be a shame if we did not take advantage of it," he remarked, thinking about how he would soon take advantage of what she was offering him.

"Of—of course," Nicole stammered, apparently unnerved by such an abrupt exit. She threw a look over her shoulder. The Duke had not a doubt that his mother was standing there on the porch, knowing exactly what he had in mind, and shocked that he would be so blatant about it.

But then, he was rather shocked himself. But that would not change his intentions. Not at all.

Nicole tried to look again over her shoulder, as the Duke led her firmly down the shallow steps and away from the house. The Dowager Duchess followed them out and was staring at them in shock and disapproval. Nicole's dismay rose. The Duke's mother was clearly displeased with her son's interest in her. She must know all about Nicole's sordid past, just as everyone did.

But then his words, with their husky, intimate tone, chased away all thoughts of the Dowager Duchess. "I had hoped you would come today, Nicole."

They were at the stables and he was ordering a groom to bring their mounts. Nicole's eyes were wide, riveted upon his striking features. He had called her Nicole. Everything was happening so fast, and it was like a dream come true.

Last night she had been unable to sleep, her thoughts swimming with his image, and she had recalled every word he had said to her at the masque. Nicole had never been interested in any man before, but now she understood the attraction between the sexes. And what she was feeling could be nothing other than love.

"I hope you don't mind my calling you Nicole."

"How could I mind?" she murmured, his tone and look sending tingles racing through her body.

"Good, then we shall dispense with all formalities, and you may call me Hadrian."

"Hadrian," she whispered, unable to look away.

The groom appeared with their horses, and the Duke stepped away from her to check her mount's girth. Nicole seized the opportunity to feast her eyes on him. Last night he had been dashing and undeniably male in his black evening wear, but today he was even more virile in appearance. His riding breeches, made of the finest, softest doeskin, fit his powerful thighs like a second skin. He turned back to her and she quickly dropped her gaze, praying he had not caught her staring so avidly—so brazenly.

They rode along a path through the fields. The Duke complimented her taste in horseflesh, admiring her blooded chestnut mare. Nicole usually rode her own horse astride, a hot-tempered thoroughbred stallion. But today she had ignored her own inclinations, for she dearly wanted to make a good impression. She was riding sidesaddle for his benefit. Just as she had had two maids help her to dress and do her hair, the entire toilette taking two long endless hours. She thought that he was pleased with her—it had been worth it.

Chapman Hall was far behind them now, lost behind a line of thick, tall oaks. The path meandered through the woods and ahead of them lay a glade, where a brook babbled by. "Let's walk," the Duke said abruptly, sliding lithely to the ground.

Nicole did not care what they did, and she halted her mare as he came around to her side. She slipped off—right into his arms.

She stiffened in surprise while his hands closed on her arms; their knees touched. He waited much longer than was proper before stepping away from her. Then he smiled, as if he hadn't been embracing her. It changed his forbidding expression entirely.

Nicole was breathless. How could such a man be interested in her? But he was, for hadn't he already told her that he had hoped she would come to Chapman Hall that day?

"Shall we walk?" he asked.

Nicole's tongue was tied. She managed to nod, hoping he would not think her a complete nitwit. She tried to think of a suitable topic of conversation, but he took her hand and all coherence fled from her thoughts.

A taut silence seemed to stretch between them as they strolled along the banks of the brook, the Duke having taken her reins from her and leading both horses. Nicole was more than speechless now, her heart was hammering. She had never in her life been as aware of a man as she was of the Duke of Clayborough. But she had to say something. Or he would begin to think her nothing more than a silly, besotted female idiot.

He must have sensed her distress, for he spoke, intruding upon the quiet of the afternoon. "You seem to be a very adept horsewoman."

She was much more than adept, but modesty was considered a virtue in a lady. "Yes," she agreed with him. She groped for something more to say. After all, if she could not expound upon the subject of horses, what could she discuss? "I . . . I am very fond of riding."

He slanted a look at her. "I am very fond of riding also."

His tone had changed and she swallowed. It was almost as if there were another meaning to his words. "I ride almost every day."

He was staring at her. "Are your rides docile, Nicole, or dangerous?" His tone was low.

She blinked. She could only think of how she preferred to ride at breakneck speed across the hunt course. "Dangerous." She could not fathom where this conversation was leading.

"Dangerous," he repeated slowly. He had stopped and so had she, for he still gripped her hand. "How dangerous?"

"I—I don't know." His look was unnerving her. As was his tone of voice.

"Do you find the danger exciting?"

There was nothing more thrilling than taking a four foot jump at a high speed. "Yes," she whispered.

His hand had tightened on hers. For a moment it

seemed that he could not speak. "You are so different from the others. I have never met a woman before who would admit she is attracted to the danger of her pastimes."

Nicole blinked at him. It was a compliment, or she thought that it was, though she could barely think at all. "Shall we go on?" she whispered.

"As riding partners?" he returned.

"R-riding partners?" she stammered, unable to believe her good fortune and not quite understanding him. "D-do you like hunting too?"

He stepped closer to her, taking her other hand. Nicole's eyes widened. His grip upon her palms was hard. She could not have moved away from him if she had wanted to—which she didn't.

"Not until today," he said harshly. "Just how good a rider are you, Nicole?"

Nicole could no longer think. He was reeling her into his arms, and she knew—*she just knew*—that he was going to kiss her. "V-very good," she whispered.

"I imagine you are superb," he said. His hands slid up to her elbows and their bodies touched.

Nicole had never been kissed before. In fact, she had never imagined what could possibly be appealing about a man covering your mouth with his—until last night. Last night she had dreamed of his kisses, wondering endlessly and shamelessly what it would be like, and now, dear God, she was about to find out.

"The time for pretense is over," he said. "I want you, Nicole. I want you very much."

Nicole could barely believe what she was hearing. Their thighs touched, her breasts brushed his shirtfront. And then his mouth covered hers, the kiss slow, gentle and delicate.

Rapturous longing filled Nicole as his mouth teased and seduced her. She strained against him, her ardor natural and even innocent, and his hands instantly tightened, nearly hurting her. The pressure of his lips suddenly changed, and he was devouring her.

Nicole gasped, pressed against him from toe to breast, his arms locked around her. His mouth was fierce, nearly brutal, demanding instant surrender. She opened for him and was shocked when his tongue thrust into her mouth. He pillaged there, while she was swept away by hot desire.

Filled with a sudden, desperate need, she touched her tongue to his. His response was instantaneous. He groaned, his hands moving down to her buttocks, grasping them firmly, lifting her up against the long, hard shaft of his manhood. Hungrily, shaking in his arms, Nicole began to fence with him. She was clutching the folds of his shirt, clinging, and pressing herself wildly against him.

Abruptly he laid her in the grass by the stream and covered her body with his. As he settled himself on top of her, his massive manhood against her loins, Nicole cried out in desperate, dazed pleasure. She felt him tugging up her skirts while she arched against him.

"Soon, Nicole," he rasped, "soon, I promise you, I will give you everything you want; I will ride you as you've never been ridden before . . ."

Nicole could barely think as his hand slid over her thinly clad knee, beneath her skirts and petticoats, then over her thigh. He moved his mouth to her neck, and she shifted, moaning, a stone abruptly digging into the back of her head. Her eyes flew open and sanity hit her full force. She was lying on her back, half in the grass and half in the dirt, and the Duke of Clayborough was treating her the way no lady should ever be treated.

She did not want him to stop. Even as her mind cried out a fierce warning, her hands dug into the thick, long tawny hair at his nape. Even as she knew she must not continue this endeavor, she moaned and thrashed as he stroked high up on the insides of her thighs, only the thin cotton of her lace drawers between her flesh and his. His hands came up and he began to unsnap the frogs of her riding jacket. This was the Duke of Clayborough, she managed to think frantically, and she wanted not just to make a good impression, but to be his wife.

That need was more compelling than any other need, and she grasped his wrists to stop him, crying out. "No, please! Not like this!"

Instantly he became still. He did not move for a heartbeat, but the moment was one of respite. Despite the delicious agony her body was in, despite the raging urgency in her veins, full coherence claimed Nicole. She knew, she had not one doubt, she had just gone too far. *No lady would do what she had done, or allowed what she had allowed.* Dismay filled her, chasing away all but her longing for him.

Abruptly he rolled off of her and sat up. He did not look at her. "You are right. I am sorry."

She had not expected that, and Nicole closed her eyes briefly in relief. She prayed that his apology meant that he would not condemn her as immoral. When she opened them he was standing above her, staring down at her, his expression inscrutable, which made him look even more forbidding than before. She tried to read his eyes, but they were dark and hooded and it was impossible.

He held out a hand, and Nicole, flushing, accepted it. He drew her swiftly to her feet.

She made a big show of brushing off her skirts, so as not to have to meet his gaze again. She was afraid to learn what he was really thinking, afraid she had just ruined herself in his eyes. How could it be otherwise? She, who had never really cared before what any man might think of her, had spent hours preparing for this meeting, only to ruin it all with her wildness. "It's not your fault," she said, swiping at her dress. She had the distinct urge to cry.

"I know better," he said calmly, still regarding her. "No lady deserves to be tumbled in the dirt like a dairy maid."

Astonished, she quickly lifted her gaze to his. Again, she found his countenance unfathomable. But hope filled her breast. "Are—are you angry with me?"

For a moment, she thought something flickered in his eyes. "I am not angry with you." He paused. "No man could be angry with such a beautiful woman."

Relief swamped her and she almost sagged. She was too relieved to catch the forced tone of his words. "You think . . . that I am beautiful?"

He suddenly appeared confused. Then he smiled, but it was nothing like the smile he had given her before, it was sardonic. "Of course I find you beautiful, my dear. If I did not know better, I would think you unsure of yourself." He laughed. "If you insist upon flattery, I will oblige you."

Something had happened, and Nicole was not sure what it was. She saw the cynicism in his eyes. She wasn't sure he was sincere, either, but then she remembered how he had kissed her—and there had been nothing insincere in that.

"Come to Chapman Hall tomorrow." It was no request. "In the afternoon. I will be expecting you."

Nicole nodded, wide-eyed, trembling, both dismayed and joyous. "I'll be there."

He dropped a quick kiss on her mouth. "You had better return to Dragmore now. I will accompany you until you are in sight of the house."

Nicole nodded, too bedazzled by him to do anything other than agree.

The Duke of Clayborough had a tight rein on himself as he returned to Chapman Hall, the same strict control he had been exercising since he had practically tumbled Nicole Shelton. He was perturbed, even disturbed. For he could not deny what had happened. He was a man of discipline, yet he had just lost his head—and every bit of iron control he had. He had almost fornicated with Lady Shelton in the grass. She had made him lose momentary control, and he did not like it. To make matters worse, he was filled with anticipation of their next rendezvous.

And the Duke was not a man who daydreamed about women, or anything else, for that matter.

Yet he was already planning to sever his relationship with his current mistress, Miss Holland Dubois, as soon as he returned to London. He had been bored with her this past month; he had only visited her a half dozen times. To ease the separation, he would shower her with a few jewels and a substantial amount of coin. He did not look forward to the task, for mistresses invariably were furious when the relationship was terminated, but she would have no trouble finding another protector, for she was very beautiful, very accommodating and very skilled.

Perhaps he would remain a bit longer at Chapman Hall. Instead of seeing Holland, he would be in bed with Lady Shelton. His jaw hardened again. Just thinking about what was to come aroused him, and he realized he was dangerously close to becoming infatuated with her. Severely, he shook his thoughts free of her.

He was shocked when, as soon as he had dismounted and handed his stallion to the head groom, Isobel flew down the steps of Chapman Hall and approached him with the strides of an angry soldier. "Hadrian," she said tightly. "Come inside, we shall talk."

He had not a doubt that he was about to get a rousing setdown for philandering *in residence*, and while he did deserve it, he was not in the mood to hear it. "Mother, may I remind you that I am not a boy of ten?" His tone was too polite.

"I do not need to be reminded of that, Hadrian," she snapped. Abruptly she headed back for the house, not waiting to see if he would follow.

The Duke sighed and decided to humor her. He had stood by and helplessly watched his father's callous and cruel treatment of her for too many years when he was a child not to concede to her in this instance, silly as it was. That abuse had finally stopped when he was fourteen. By then he was almost six feet tall, several inches taller than

Francis, and about the same weight. While their strength might have been evenly matched, Francis did not have the power of rage on his side, while Hadrian did. It was not the first time he had tried to prevent his father from abusing his mother. When he was a child he had tried to come between them, only to have the painful slaps Francis aimed at Isobel diverted to him. When he grew larger, his attempts at protecting his mother were met with a switch. When he was fourteen, all abuse had stopped, both that directed at his mother, and that he suffered when he tried to interfere, for Hadrian struck his father with one determined blow to his jaw, causing Francis to crumble at his feet. He proceeded to hit him twice more, until he was coldly satisfied that Francis would never dare to try and hurt his mother again. And he hadn't.

So now, as much as he resented her interference, he would hear her out respectfully and patiently.

Isobel promptly closed the door to the small shabby library, leaving them in absolute privacy. "Have you lost your mind?"

"To what, precisely, are you referring?" As if he didn't know.

"Hadrian! It's unseemly enough to have a paramour here, but, dear God! Nicole Shelton! How could you?"

A sixth sense warned him of imminent disaster. "I am afraid I am missing something of consequence."

"Have you ruined her?" Isobel demanded bluntly. "If you have, her father, Shelton, will kill you, regardless of who you are!"

"Mother," he said slowly, although his mind was racing, "I do not think we need to discuss my—er—indiscretions."

"Have you ruined her?" Isobel cried.

Anger reared within him. "Of course I have not ruined her," he snapped. "The lady is no spring maid, and I do not understand your interest."

"She is no spring maid but she is Shelton's daughter,

Hadrian, and it is not like you to—to—prey on innocents!"

He drew himself up. "Pardon me, but she is no innocent. I fear we are not discussing the same lady."

"We are discussing Lady Nicole Bragg Shelton, Dragmore's eldest daughter, and spinster or no, scandal or no, you cannot ruin her!"

He stared, the color seeping from his face. "Spinster?"

"Just what did you think?"

"I thought," he began, and stopped. "She is unwed?" He could not believe it.

"She is unwed! She was about to marry Lord Percy Hempstead four years ago, but she never showed up for the wedding, leaving the poor fellow standing there alone at the altar. It was a terrible scandal that, of course, ruined her chances for any other marriage. Any other decent marriage, that is. Of course, Shelton could buy her a husband, but what kind of man would he be? We both know Shelton, and I cannot see him compromising his standards in such a manner. Regardless, Nicole is quite an eccentric, or so they say. She is even more reclusive than you. She spends most of her time at Dragmore, rarely venturing out into society. And who can blame her? I saw myself how cruelly she was cut after that scandal. Have you ruined her, Hadrian?"

He was in shock. He was appalled at the terrible mistake he had almost made. He had come dangerously close to ruining a young lady. Yet she *had* responded to him as if she were a woman of experience, but now he could recall only too clearly those moments when her blushes and her confusion had made her seem uncertain and innocent. But how could he have known? She had attended the masque unescorted and daringly costumed, and hadn't she flirted with him? Or had he misread her every nuance? Had she purposefully led him on—or had he been the indiscriminate predator? "I have not ruined her," he said stiffly, and then he stalked from the room.

* * *

Nicole wished that her best friend Martha Huntingdon, the Viscountess Serle, would return from London, for she had no one to confide in about the Duke. It was so very nearly unbelievable. That she, too tall and gawky, a dismal failure when she had come out, then ruined by the scandal, should be courted by the charismatic, handsome Duke of Clayborough! For wasn't that what he was doing? He had invited her to his home, not once, but twice. And he had kissed her. He had told her that she was beautiful. Wasn't he as powerfully affected by her as she was by him? Didn't all of his actions indicate that he was courting her?

Nicole knew that she was highly inexperienced when it came to men, but she was almost certain that he would ask her to marry him, and soon. She dreamed of how he would propose, she dreamed of being his Duchess. She saw herself with his child in her arms, and saw him smile affectionately as he watched her and the baby.

And the small doubt she had, the tiny seeds of confusion, the dim memory of his sardonic smile and cool tone, she shoved into the recesses of her memory.

Her father and Chad returned that evening from France, having concluded their business. Ed, her younger brother, attended Cambridge, where he was studying the law. She greeted the Earl and Chad with a beaming smile and hugs, startling them both with her exuberance.

"What's happened to you?" Chad asked, his handsome face wearing a suspicious frown. "What are you up to now, little sister?"

Chad was almost thirty, with dark hair like their father, although he had inherited his fair coloring from his mother, the Earl's first wife. He was very handsome in a thoroughly patrician way, while the Earl's appeal was darker, more dangerous. Nicole scowled at him. "I am up to nothing, brother," she retorted. "After all, I am not the one who goes out in the evenings and does not return until well after dawn!"

"You are not a man," Chad pointed out blithely.

"Enough," the Earl said mildly, his gaze roving over his daughter with warmth. "You are glowing, Nicole. Is there something you want to tell me?" He posed the question casually.

Her father knew her too well. She was his first child with the Countess Jane, and she had spent more time on his knee than any other of her siblings. She was closer to him than either Chad, Ed or Regina. There was a bond between them that was hard to explain, although her mother had teased that it could be explained by the savage blood in both of their veins and the disregard for convention that ensued from it. Nicole had thought it a joke and had been amused by her mother's wit, but the Earl had seemed somewhat exasperated with his wife for her bald comment.

She had always been the apple of his eye and she knew it. He knew her too well, and he was too clever, besides. Nicole was certainly not ready to tell anyone in her family that she had a suitor, much less that it was the Duke of Clayborough. She dared not question herself too closely as to her motivations in keeping this affair a secret, when she had never kept secrets from her family before. She thought about what had happened today by the brook for the zillionth time and she blushed. "No, Father," she said as demurely as possible. "I am just happy you are home, I have missed you." Quickly, she hugged him again, but the look he gave her was doubtful.

The next morning, Nicole again had two maids help her to dress for her rendezvous with the Duke. Fortunately, both Chad and the Earl were out on the estate, tending to its affairs, so they would not remark on her unusual attire and wonder just where she had gone in her finery. She invariably accompanied them, but today she had managed to lie and say she had a headache. Both men had looked at her skeptically, and Chad had even burst out laughing.

"You?" he had said incredulously. "*You* have a headache?" Still laughing, he had ridden away with her father, and Nicole had wanted to throttle him.

She appeared at Chapman Hall shortly after noon, unable to wait another moment. Before she had even dismounted, a footman taking her reins in front of the house, she saw the Duke step out from inside the Hall, as if he had been waiting for her.

Nicole flashed him a blinding smile, but there was no response. His expression was stern. For an instant unease assailed her, but then she thanked the footman and slipped to the ground. When she looked up, the Duke was dismissing the footman and telling him that a groom would not be necessary, perplexing Nicole. If they were going riding again why had he not ordered his mount brought around?

She grew somber, her joy fading as she realized how hard and closed his face actually was. There was no warmth in his eyes as they finally settled on her countenance. "Has something happened?" she asked, her heart beating uncertainly.

"I am afraid so," he said firmly. "It appears that I am to be forever apologizing to you. I have made a terrible mistake, but not as terrible as it could have been."

"What—what mistake?" Her heart started to sink. He could not mean he had mistaken his feelings for her, she knew that he could not mean that!

His jaw clenched. "I did not realize you were unwed."

At first Nicole did not understand. He had not realized she was unmarried? So what? Then, horribly, the first inkling of comprehension began. *"What are you saying?"*

"I assumed you to be married, of course."

"You thought me married?" she echoed.

He said nothing.

He had thought her married. If he had thought her married, his intention had not been to court her. She stared at him, stricken. "But—you kissed me!"

He shifted impatiently. "Certainly you cannot be so naive as to think a man would refrain from kissing a woman just because she is married."

Her understanding swelled, horribly. He had thought her married—he had not been intending to ask her to marry him. He had thought her to be married, and not just to be married, but to be a certain kind of married woman, one of no morals. He had not been courting her; far from it. To use his own words, he had merely wanted to tumble her! She gasped, hurt, anger and dismay overwhelming her at once. He had been amusing himself at her expense!

Her dreams crumbled into the dust at her feet.

"I am sorry. I know I must appear a very low sort, but frankly, I am so used to married ladies offering themselves to me that . . ."

"I did not offer myself to you!" Nicole cried, crushed, devastated. Tears filled her eyes.

"I mistook your manner, then. Obviously, Lady Shelton, you may not come here again." His gaze held hers, dark and fathomless.

Nicole was in shock and hurt beyond words. "Obviously," she managed with a ghost of her old spirit, "I would be ten times the fool should I return here. You will certainly never see me again!"

She yanked the reins from his hand, and before he could assist her, she leapt into the saddle. It was made for riding sidesaddle, and she had no choice but to do so. It did not matter, the only thing that mattered was to escape him as quickly as possible. Tears of grief and humiliation blinding her, her breast knotted in pain, she spurred her mare into a gallop, and left him standing alone in a cloud of dust.

Nicole used the excuse of her headache to remain closeted in her room that afternoon and all that evening. She did not come down to supper. Both the Earl and Chad came to inquire after her and it took a supreme amount of self-control to hide her shattered heart from them. Not wanting to rouse more suspicion than she already had, she accepted the tray that Annie brought up, then gave its contents to one of the house cats.

Her misery deepened with the night. How naive she had been! How stupid! To believe in fairy tales when fairy tales did not exist, at least not for her, never for her. Foolishly she had fallen in love with the Duke; not with the man he really was, but with a man she had created in her own wild imagination. That man did not exist, and the Duke was nothing more than an immoral philanderer.

And just as foolishly she had thought him to be in love with her, too.

She was too hurt to hate him, at least for now.

She almost gave in to tears but she fought them. When she had first come out and had not been accepted by her peers, that had hurt horribly, too. At the time, it had been the most shocking blow of her life. She had grown up at Dragmore where she was accepted and loved by everyone from the lowest stableboy to her adoring parents. There had never been a day in her life—until her debut—that she had not felt secure. But her debut had changed all that.

For the fact was that Nicole was different from the other young ladies of society and they discerned this immediately. She had absolutely nothing in common with them. She had been raised to be active and to think for herself, and as a consequence, she was forthright and outspoken; they had been raised to be pretty, modest and demure, and they simpered with the men and gossiped with each other. Their predominant interests in life were the latest fashions and capturing a husband, and because Nicole honestly did not share those interests, she was an outcast from the start. She could not be forgiven for such sacrilege.

She had created the scandal herself, but Nicole had not expected society to turn on her as cruelly as it had. Actually, she had not thought much about what she was doing, knowing only at the last minute that she just could not go through with the marriage. She had never loved Percy Hempstead, never cared one way or another about him. Her first two years out she had shown no interest in any suitor, which was why her father had finally stepped in and offered her one prospect after another. They had fought. Nicole had begged not to be married off like some brood mare sent to stud, but he was deaf to her pleas.

"There are dozens of fine, eligible men for you to choose from," he had raged at her. "Yet in two years you've turned every one of them away! I will not allow you to ruin your future, Nicole, so now I am going to find you the right man!"

Nicole had run from him, furious and upset, yet knowing, too, that he was motivated by love for her, thought he was doing what was best, and also thought that one day, she would look back and agree that he had been right.

Percy Hempstead was a few years older than she was, good looking, pleasant, the heir to the Earl of Langston. Nicole wished she could summon up some interest in him, for he was clearly very nice, kind to everyone, including his horses and dogs, a true test of character.

He was also a hard worker, not a wastrel, and many young women had set their caps for him. Even Martha oohed and aahed over him, declaring how handsome he was with his dark hair and blue eyes and his finely sculpted features. Pressured by everyone, and liking Percy as a friend, she had finally agreed to the alliance.

As the wedding approached, her original objections to being wed grew stronger and stronger. She didn't love him. She barely knew him, he was practically a stranger. She didn't want to be married. She didn't want to be a wife—whose two primary functions in life were to be a beautiful ornament and to give her husband sons. She did not want to leave Dragmore. Panic filled her at the thought. She knew instinctively that Percy would never let her rise with the sun and ride beside him across his tenant farms. He would expect her to amuse herself with other ladies and proper womanly pastimes, always to be properly dressed, to be passive and obedient—to be, in short, the ideal woman. Terrible fear filled Nicole. Her life was about to be changed irrevocably, forever.

She could not go through with it. The night before the wedding, she ran away. She had a note delivered to Percy, begging his forgiveness, but she knew there was no reasonable explanation she could offer to him or anyone else for her behavior. She left another note for her parents. She did not run very far, for it wasn't necessary. It was enough to be missing on the day of her wedding and to have sent Percy the note. More than five hundred guests had been expected, and although she hadn't left Percy literally standing at the altar as the gossips later claimed, what she had done was ruinous enough. Percy never spoke to her again, and six months later he married a proper Victorian miss.

Her father did not speak to her, either, for almost a month after the first brunt of his rage had spewed forth. Nicole was desperately sorry that she had hurt Percy and she was just as sorry she had upset her parents, but she was *not* sorry she had not married Percy.

She had only a short week to recover from what she had done. In the following months, her parents had gone out as usual, and Nicole had accompanied them everywhere. "You will not hide at Dragmore," her father had said to her, the only words he'd spoken to her in a week. "You will face what you have done."

It had been awful, going to one ball or "at-home" after another, being stared at, being gossiped about the moment her back was turned. She knew her parents were suffering as much as she was, and in a way, she hurt for them even more than she hurt for herself. Nicole held her head high and acted as if nothing was wrong, but inside she felt like some strange species of animal in a zoo. After a few months her parents allowed her to do as she wished, but by then her appearance was no longer an event, and the gossip-mongers had found new fodder for their mills.

Now, lying on her bed, staring up at the gold pleats of the canopy overhead, she wanted to weep in a way she had never wanted to before. Her life had been perfect until she had turned eighteen and come out. Then it had been one disaster after another. She should have learned her lesson. But no, naive to the end, she had looked at the Duke, fallen in love, and stupidly thought him to be her knight in shining armor. Never would she be such a fool again!

She turned onto her side, dry-eyed. He had thought her to be married. He had never had an honorable intention towards her. Suddenly she clenched her fist, the beginnings of anger sweeping over her. How despicable he was!

That morning Nicole was up with the sun, as usual. She had spent a restless night burning with newfound anger. Her adrenaline gave her strength, and despite barely having slept, she was not tired. She joined her father and brother for breakfast, dressed in her breeches, determined to join them that day and continue her life as if nothing had ever happened. As if the Duke of Clayborough did not exist.

Both men looked at her. "You look like hell," Chad said.

Nicole ignored him, sitting on her father's left, across from her brother. She poured herself tea, feeling her father's regard upon her. "The headache lasted most of the night."

"I want you to see a physician," the Earl said.

"I'm fine now, Father, really," Nicole said, but she could not summon up a smile for his benefit.

"You are never ill," Nicholas Shelton said flatly. "I want you to rest today, Nicole."

She set her mouth firmly. "I want to ride with you and Chad."

"Absolutely not." He looked at her, and she knew better than to argue.

After she had eaten breakfast, Nicole felt tired and drained. When Chad and the Earl left, she returned to her bedroom and flopped on the bed, suddenly exhausted. The Duke's handsome golden image swam before her. She clenched her fists and closed her eyes. "Go away, damn you to hell!" It was the most shocking curse she knew.

A knock on her door brought her out of a heavy, much needed sleep. Nicole blinked, startled to realize that she had dozed for some time. It looked to be late morning, nearly noon. Groggily she sat up. "Yes?"

Aldric appeared. "I know you are not feeling well, my Lady, but the Viscountess Serle is here. Shall I tell her you are indisposed?" His kindly eyes were worried, although his tone was formal and impassive.

"Martha is here!" Nicole cried, delighted. "No, no! I'll be down in a moment!"

"Very well," Aldric said, looking relieved as he backed out.

Nicole flew from the bed and quickly washed her face, retying her hair into one long tail. Then she ran down the stairs. "Martha!"

The Viscountess Serle was a small woman, somewhat plump, with thick chestnut hair and ivory skin. She had been sitting demurely on the golden velvet sofa in the parlor, a cup of tea in her small hands, dressed in a green and pink striped ensemble. She set her cup down and leapt to her feet with a cry of delight. The two girls hugged enthusiastically.

"I have missed you so!" Martha cried.

"I am so glad you are back," Nicole returned, beaming.

Martha sat, pulling Nicole down beside her. Her smile faded as she stared at her friend. "Nicole, your eyes are puffy. Have you been crying?"

Nicole's expression turned somber. "No, although I thought I would."

"What happened?"

Quickly Nicole jumped to her feet and firmly shut the parlor door, turning back to face her friend. Suddenly she was overwhelmed with the urge to cry. Aghast, she covered her face with her hands and fought to stem the rising flood tide.

"Oh, dear," Martha gasped, hurrying to her. "Come sit down, tell me what has happened to upset you so!"

"I'm sorry," Nicole said, once she had a grip on her raw emotions. She looked at her best friend. "I am an utter jackass, Martha!"

Although Martha was used to Nicole's unconventional attire, mannerisms and language, she blushed slightly. "You are no fool."

"I made a fool of myself with the Duke of Clayborough," Nicole cried.

Martha gasped. "With the Duke of Clayborough!"

Nicole nodded grimly. "I went to the masque the other night at the Adderlys'. It was in his honor. I looked at him and my heart stopped, Martha. How stupid I was."

"He is very handsome," Martha said, her tone cautious.

"We talked. When he looked at me his eyes were like flames. He invited me to Chapman Hall."

Martha gasped. "He invited you to Chapman Hall! But that does not sound like the Duke of Clayborough, not at all! He must have been very taken with you."

Nicole looked at her, her eyes glittering like ice. "Oh, he was quite taken, let me assure you of that! He assumed I was married! He invited me there for a—a—a . . ."

Martha gasped again. "He thought you were married!"

"I thought he was taken with me." Nicole looked away, color rising. "I even thought," she stopped. "I thought he was courting me." She stole a glance at her friend, whose expression was stunned. "He kissed me, Martha."

"Oh dear," was all Martha could say.

"I liked it." Thinking about what had happened between them brought a deeper flush to Nicole's golden complexion. Worse, her heart began to hammer erratically, and she could feel his hot, hungry lips on hers as if he were kissing her again. "I kissed him back."

"Nicole," Martha began, but Nicole interrupted.

"Now I know why he hustled me out of the house and did not let me have tea with his mother!" Nicole cried, furious and humiliated all over again.

"The Dowager Duchess was there?" Martha moaned. "She saw you at his house? Nicole, you didn't have a chaperone with you, did you?" The question was hopeful.

Nicole shook her head. "Yesterday I went back to Chapman Hall—he had invited me to return. Somehow he had found out I was unwed, and everything changed. The bastard! He was as cold as ice, apologizing for his mistake, and telling me I must never come again. As if I would!"

"Oh, God!" Martha said, causing Nicole to widen her eyes.

"He thought I was some married trollop he would amuse himself with," Nicole whispered urgently. "Oh, I hate him!"

"Oh, Nicole," Martha took her hand, squeezing it. He didn't—he only kissed you—didn't he?"

Nicole flushed. She remembered how his body had pressed hers into the grass, how he had unfastened her jacket, how his hands had stroked up intimately along the length of her inner thighs. Her body began to throb in response to her vivid mental rampaging. "I'm still a virgin, if that's what you're asking."

"Then no harm is done," Martha said, patting her hand and sighing in relief. "Oh, you poor dear! Clayborough is a terrible rake, you know, and quite ruthless. No woman holds his interest for very long, it's said, not even his mistresses. And supposedly his mistresses are the most beautiful women in the realm."

"He has more than one?" Nicole asked, feeling hurt all over again.

"No, he keeps one at a time." Martha saw her expression and added, "But so do most men."

"Robert doesn't, does he?" Suddenly Nicole wished she had bitten off her tongue, for the question was too intimate to ask, even of her best friend.

But Martha smiled, her expression soft. "No, Robert doesn't, and I am very lucky."

Nicole knew how much Martha loved her husband and how he adored her. "You are very lucky," she agreed.

Martha looked at her. "I think Clayborough was taken with you, Nicole."

"He thought I was married."

"I still think he was taken with you. I see him from time to time in London, and he never shows any interest in any lady; they are always throwing themselves at him. Except, of course, for Lady Elizabeth Martindale."

"Lady Elizabeth Martindale?"

"The Marquess of Stafford's daughter." Martha made a face. "I do think he was taken with you. Oh, it's too bad they are engaged!"

Nicole froze. "He is engaged to her?"

"You didn't know?"

"I know nothing about him," Nicole said, the room suddenly very still around her.

"They have been engaged a very long time, since she was two—and she is just eighteen," Martha said gently, as if to soften the blow. "'Tis always been a fact that the Duke of Clayborough is unavailable, much to every young lady's dismay. She is to have her season, and they are to be wed this summer."

"I see," Nicole said stiffly, standing up. Her pulse began to roar, deafening her. A betrothal made between two such powerful families, one that had been sustained for sixteen years, was written in stone. He was as good as married.

Nicole saw red.

So he had not just thought her married, he was betrothed to another, and in seven or eight months he would be wed. He was more despicable than she had ever dreamed!

"Nicole," Martha stood, too, looking worried. "Sit down and drink some tea. Please."

Nicole looked at her, her eyes blazing. "I thought he wanted to marry me! Me!"

"Oh, Nicole!"

Nicole turned and strode toward the door, rage in every single one of her long strides.

"Nicole, where are you going?" Martha cried frantically. "Don't do something you shall regret! Please, don't!"

If Nicole heard her, she gave no sign. Moments later Martha saw her on her blood red thorougbred, riding astride, her nose almost buried in the stallion's black mane, galloping from the stables in the direction of Chapman Hall.

The Duke left the stable, the sounds of hammers pounding on wood following him. He was replacing the two back walls of the barn, which were sadly in need of repair. So far, he was satisfied with the progress the laborers he had hired were making.

He headed for the house with long strides, intending to take care of some correspondence before his midday meal. He had only taken a few steps, however, when the sound of racing hoofbeats made him pause, searching for its cause.

A magnificent blood bay thoroughbred was emerging from the woods at the far side of the ill-tended lawns, running all out. The stallion galloped across his lawn, his rider bent low over his back, and seconds later the animal came to a plunging, rearing halt beside him. The Duke was stunned at the sight of Nicole Shelton astride him.

He had never seen a lady astride a horse before, or any woman for that matter, and that was shocking enough. The sight of her long legs, encased tightly in men's breeches, powerfully gripping the horse, mesmerized him. Then he became aware of her stark, savage beauty, her eyes blazing and silver, her hair loose and windswept, flowing behind her. She was magnificent and he was frozen, both shocked by her defiance of every dictum of convention that existed and gripped in a barbarous desire.

Nicole leapt to the ground and strode toward him, her long legs straining the fabric of her breeches, leaving nothing of her form to his imagination. For another moment he could not tear his gaze away from her limbs, and it occurred to him that any woman who could ride a horse like that could certainly ride him equally well. Distracted, he only saw her raise her crop at the last possible moment.

"Miserable bastard," she hissed, swinging it furiously at his face.

Acting purely on reflex, the Duke caught her wrist just as the braided end flicked his jaw, leaving a stinging red welt. Anger quickly replaced his surprise. He took the crop from her, snapping it abruptly in two, and tossed it aside. She screamed, the sound one of pure rage, her hand flying up again, intent on striking him anew. He caught her arm and whipped her around too quickly and her back slammed into the barn. She dared to resist him, her other hand reaching for him, fingers curled, nails poised like claws. He caught that one, too, and pinned her to the wall, both of her wrists above her head, and in another scant moment he had closed the last few inches between them, pressing his hard, aroused body against hers.

What had just occurred was beyond belief, yet she continued to struggle wildly against him, like an animal caught in a trap, crazed. Her every movement fanned the fires in him, and he pressed more heavily against her, his manhood pulsing eagerly against her softness as he instinctively sought to subdue her. "Release me," she screamed. "Release me, you rotten cur, so I can give you what you deserve!"

Terribly graphic, sexual images danced in his mind. "And just what is it I deserve?" His breath fanned her lips, she went still. He knew it was that exact moment that she became aware of him and his virility.

"Ten lashes, not one!" she snarled.

"I do not think that is why you have come back."

"I came back to draw your blood!"

He trembled, both in response to her real savagery and to the idea of his drawing *her* blood. "Does spilling my blood excite you, Nicole?" he asked, very, very low.

"Yes! Yes! Yes!" She bucked wildly against him again, then froze, panting, when her gyrations only served to increase the intimacy between them.

"Beware," he said smokily, "if there is any more blood to be spilled today, it shall not be mine." He looked her in the eye, throbbing so strongly against her she could not possibly escape his meaning. Her eyes widened, and he was pleased that she understood.

"You would not."

"Right now, I would. Isn't that why you have come back?"

For a moment she was too stunned by his answer to respond, then she shrieked, twisting wildly and crying out at the pain she caused herself in his iron, immoveable grip. "Now you threaten me with rape?!"

"Threaten, no. Warn, perhaps. Rape—never."

"I will fight you until my last dying breath," she cried.

He saw her fighting him, then climaxing in his arms. His hold on her tightened, and he thought he might lose the last of his control. "You will like dying in my arms, Nicole," he promised softly. "I will make sure of it."

"Release me," she cried frantically. He knew she did not understand his meaning, but she sensed the danger she was in. "Release me, now, damn you!"

He had to. If he did not, he would cease to be responsible for his actions. His body was screaming at him, begging for its own release, so he turned his head away from hers, breathing deeply. "Do we have a truce?"

She laughed. "Never!"

He whipped his gaze to hers and saw the blaze of hatred in her eyes. "So you hate me, now, do you?"

"Oh yes," she spat. "For a moment I loved you, but now, how I hate you!"

He froze. That she had loved him, even if foolishly and for a short time, stunned him. Many women had fallen in love with him and he was well aware of it. But he had never really paid attention, and certainly never cared what they felt. Now, something seemed to prick him, and perhaps it was his conscience. "Love does not change to hatred so fast, Nicole," he said softly. Their mouths were very close. "Shall we test how much you hate me?" He did not know why it was so important to him to prove her wrong.

"There is nothing to test," she said, suddenly breathless. Her gaze moved to his mouth. "Don't."

There was no way he could prevent himself from kissing her, no matter how wrong it was, not now. Not when their bodies were pressed together from breast to toe, not when he strained against her femininity, not when she dared to declare her hatred of him. "I think that you want me more than you hate me," he murmured.

She opened her mouth to protest, but he covered her lips, not allowing any more words to escape.

She wrenched violently against him, but he merely pressed her harder against the barn, merely tightened his already painful hold on her wrists. She made enraged noises; he hungrily claimed her mouth, wanting to claim much more and knowing if he let this continue, he would claim all of her. She bucked against him and it was heaven, yet it was also hell.

As he had thought, she would fight him to the very end.

She spoke when his mouth moved to her neck, where his kisses left red crescent marks. "What of your precious Elizabeth!"

He became still. "What of Elizabeth?"

"You do not even pretend to be faithful to your betrothed!"

"So you have done your homework," he said, lifting his head to look at her. He saw the flaming anger in her eyes, and he wanted to change it to passion—for him. "Is that what this is about?"

"You are no different from a married man," she hissed. "Yet you are a despicable rake. Let me go, now!"

She was right, and because ultimately he had too much honor to ravish her, he released her. She screamed and leapt at him, trying to hit him again.

He caught her, this time around the waist, pinning her arms to her sides, stunned again at her savagery, and even more aroused. She whirled in his arms before he tightened his hold, trying to run from him. "Stop it," he snapped, shaking her once.

She was panting as if she had fought a great battle, and now he was pressed against her backside, which was no relief. Her breasts were full and heavy on his arms where he had wrapped them around her torso. She stopped trying to free herself, gasping great lungfuls of air, and he relaxed slightly, damning himself and his uncontrollable libido once more.

"I won't hit you again," she finally said harshly. "Just let me go."

"Why?" He breathed against her neck. "I don't think I embarrass you, Nicole. Or do I?"

She was very still, and he knew she was feeling him throbbing against her buttocks. He wanted to see her eyes, see her response. He felt her trembling in his arms. "You do not embarrass me," she finally said. "You only embarrass yourself."

Because his behavior was inexcusable, his tone was sardonic as he released her. "Touché. But it takes two to play this game, and if you had not come here, none of this would have happened."

She whirled to face him, backing up warily. He saw the glitter in her eyes for what it was, and while a part of him was appalled with himself, another part of him was triumphant.

"You are the one with no morals, you are the one who would stop at nothing to get what you want."

Anger flared. "Wrong. I warned you not to return here, and you did so at your own risk. If you did not come back for what I can give you, then why did you return?"

She gasped, crimson color suffusing her cheeks. "How arrogant you are! I came back to tell you what I think of you now that I know the truth!"

His hands found his hips, his mouth curved mockingly. "The truth. Oh yes, Elizabeth."

"You are as good as married, yet you chased me! I did not know, I thought you were eligible. You thought I was a married woman of no morals! So who does that make right—and who does that make wrong?"

Guilt pricked him, but he was not ready to face it. And he did not like being accused of wrongful behavior—he was not accustomed to being told that he was wrong. No one would dare. *Yet she dared.* And he did not like his own behavior—not before, and not now. Once again, she had incited him to anger and to an unwelcome lust. "You thought my interest in you was that of a bachelor courting a young lady?" His tone was mocking, hard, cruel.

She backed up, reddening. "I did not think you merely meant me to be a paramour."

"Just as I did not think you to be an unwed virgin."

She gasped.

He could not believe what he had just said.

"You are cruel!"

"You drive me to it!" Harshly, he said, "Let me tell you again. You are not welcome here, Lady Shelton, and you are not to come back."

She folded her arms tightly beneath her breasts. "I will never come back here, Your Grace. Unless, of course, it is to bring you and your bride a wedding present."

His smile was as sardonic as her words. "So the tigress has more than claws. Let me repeat—you are not welcome here, Nicole, and if you think to cause trouble between me and Elizabeth, think again."

"Do not worry, I have no intention of upsetting your precious Elizabeth!" Nicole whirled abruptly, running to her stallion.

His favorite wolfhound, the Borzoi, regarded him hopefully. Standing in front of a full-length mirror beside a red lacquer Chinese dresser, the Duke adjusted his silk tie, regarding himself expressionlessly. When he turned and was handed his black evening coat by his valet, Reynard, the Borzoi thumped his tail enthusiastically.

The Duke murmured, "I am going to supper, Lad, I'm sorry to say."

The Borzoi sighed and laid its head on its massive paws, resigned to an evening in front of the hearth.

"You do look fine, Your Grace, if you don't mind my saying so," Reynard said with admiration.

The Duke nodded his thanks curtly. "You may go, Reynard, I will be down in a moment."

He turned away from his reflection and paced to the butler's table, where he poured himself a cup of tea, blended especially for him. Grimly he stared at the contents of the delicate porcelain cup, which was dwarfed in his hand.

He should have refused Shelton's invitation. He had not even considered doing so.

A week had gone by since Nicole Shelton had galloped so recklessly into his courtyard and then galloped away—after their prolonged and heated encounter. Unfortunately, the mere memory stirred his loins painfully, and he knew damn well why he was going to Dragmore tonight.

What was happening to him? Was this the way of unrequited lust? He had never had a woman on his mind before. As callous as it sounded, all of his liaisons had been merely sexual, and as soon as the act was completed, his attention had turned to more significant matters. He did not want to have this particular woman on his mind now. Angry, he took a sip of the exotically fragrant tea, then threw the rest, cup, saucer and all, into the blazing fire. The porcelain popped and shattered loudly, making Lad regard him curiously.

He had released tension, but he had not erased Nicole Shelton from his thoughts. He was still somewhat shocked whenever his errant mind envisioned her as he had last seen her, astride a ton of spirited horseflesh, in men's breeches. And she had hit him with her crop. It was still unbelievable—it was still impossibly arousing.

The Duke paced. There was no way he could refuse Shelton's invitation now. But in truth, he did not even want to. He ran a hand through his thick, sun-streaked hair. He was playing with fire; he sensed it, he knew it—and she was the fire.

This last week he had thrown himself into the restoration of Chapman Hall with ruthless determination. He had risen earlier than usual and gone to bed later, not allowing himself a moment to rest or to think. Yet no matter how occupied he kept himself, she always lurked at the fuzzy edges of his consciousness, haunting him. Why was he so fascinated with her? Or was it obsessed?

Her striking looks were enough to drive any man insane, he decided, but it was her manner, her boldness, her savagery that was intoxicating. Most women—most *ladies*—were terribly boring. With the exception of his mother, whose intelligence and unconventional interest in business affairs set her apart from other females, he could not think of a single lady who was worth his time and attention. (Elizabeth was a different matter entirely, being his fiancée.) No woman he knew attended fêtes unchaperoned, unless they were over thirty, no woman rode about in breeches, no woman spoke as she did, no woman ever showed such a temper, not even his last mistress, who had been French and quick to anger. And no woman, *no woman*, chased a man down and struck him with her crop.

She was everything the women of his acquaintance were not, and it was for that reason, he decided, that he was so damn enthralled.

The problem was, he no longer trusted himself. He had behaved abominably toward her last week, even if sorely provoked. There was no excuse for forcing himself on her, for using his strength to assert his power over her, for kissing her, touching her. No excuse. Yet nothing could have stopped him then, and he was afraid that the next time nothing *would* stop him.

Next time?

He must make sure there was no next time. He could not live with himself if he ruined her, no matter that her reputation was already in shreds. No matter how she provoked him. Their last encounter had been a barbaric seduction. There would be no next time, he vowed.

He had lived his entire life honorably. Always, deep in the back of his mind was the knowledge of how dishonorable his father had been. His father, had he preferred women, would have taken Nicole that first day, in the grass by the brook. He was not his father. He had never been his father. He had never ruined any woman; the women he took to bed were already of highly questionable morals. Perhaps he had spent his whole life atoning for his father's sins, but it had been a life he could be proud of until now. Now he was in jeopardy, and it frightened him.

He was late. Unless he sent excuses, it was time to go. The Duke went.

Nicole lounged in bed, reading an essay by Amanda Willison, an American, on the need for the reform of education and dress for girls. How right this woman was, Nicole thought. There was a rap on her door, and Nicole set her book aside as her mother entered.

The Countess had returned home yesterday. It was no surprise to Nicole, for Jane never stayed away from her husband for very long, and Nicole knew that if Regina were not of age and imminently marriageable, Jane would not have adjourned to London at all. Regina had stayed at their townhouse on Tavistock Square, chaperoned by the widowed Lady Beth Henderson. Jane was intending to return to London the next day, and the earl planned to join her a few days later.

"You're not dressed," Jane said in surprise as she saw that Nicole was still clad only in a dressing gown, her hair damp from her bath.

"I'm sorry, I got so caught up in reading that the time escaped me. Is our guest here?"

"No, he is late. Let me call Annie, Nicole, to help you."

Nicole slid from the bed as her mother called for the maid, and pulled a gown at random from the armoire. Jane returned. She was small, slender and platinum blonde, strikingly beautiful at forty-one, and innately elegant. She frowned as she saw the pale blue gown Nicole had taken from its hanger. "That doesn't do you justice, darling."

Nicole shrugged. "Who is coming to dinner anyway, Mother, and why all the fuss? Cook was absolutely going mad this afternoon in the kitchens—the place looked as if we were to feast royalty."

"The Duke of Clayborough," Jane responded. "Why not wear your yellow gown? Or the green?"

Nicole froze. For one moment, she was certain she had misheard. "The Duke of Clayborough?"

"Yes. So will you wear the yellow? I had better go downstairs. He should be here at any moment."

Nicole nodded, not hearing a word. She stared at the door after it closed. Then she made a fierce, frustrated cry.

He would dare to come here? Here? It was too much, she could not stand it! She would not!

Nicole paced in a frenzy. How could she face him, after their last encounter? She did not regret what she had done, exactly, but she had shown him that she was everything the gossips claimed she was; in short, she had shown him that she was no proper, ladylike miss. Hot color rose on her cheeks. She had struck him once, he had kissed her in return. And the things he had said. . . .

She had never hated a man more, but she had never dreamed of anyone's kisses before, either, they way she dreamed of his.

It was disgraceful. It was shameful. She could not sleep at night, tormented by his striking golden image and the remembrance of the feel of his hot mouth, his seductive hands and his hard, powerful body. He was not only driving her insane, he was ruining her life.

She was frightened by her attraction to a man she despised, or a man she should despise. She remembered a conversation with her cousin, Lucy Bragg, from two summers ago. Far from soothing her, the memory touched off a sense of panic.

That summer, in 1897, Nicole and her family had gone to Paradise, Texas for the eightieth birthday celebration of her grandfather, Derek Bragg, a man who had been born in the mountains of Texas and had tamed the frontier, carving out an empire for himself and his family in the process. Nicole and Lucy had always been the best of friends, even though they only saw each other on alternate summers, when Nicole, as a child and adolescent, joined her American relatives for a month or two. Not only were Nicole and Lucy best friends, but they had shared more misdeeds than any two girls in the entire state, or maybe even in the entire United States of America. That summer, Lucy had made a shocking confession to Nicole.

The night of the birthday party, Derek's prized stud had been stolen, and a man had been murdered. One of the new hands on the ranch had been shot in the back, and it had soon turned out that he had been an escaped felon from New York. When Lucy had poured out her heart to

Nicole, that man, Shoz Cooper, had been in the local jail, recovering from his injury. Lucy had told Nicole that he had kissed her, more than once, and that she had liked it. Yet she had also told Nicole that she despised him.

At the time Nicole had been surprised, having never been kissed and in no way understanding how someone could like a man's lovemaking while disliking him. Yet remembering Lucy's confession did not alleviate her own fears now. For Shoz Cooper had not only turned out to be innocent, he and Lucy were now engaged and would be wed the following June. So Lucy had only thought she despised him—in truth she had loved him.

Nicole was not only afraid of how she yearned for the Duke's kisses, she was afraid that, like Lucy, her feelings went deeper, much deeper—and she refused even to consider how much deeper her feelings might be.

She could refuse to go downstairs, but that was the coward's way out. She had never been a coward, not even during the scandal, and she would not begin now. She would die before losing courage in front of the damn Duke of Clayborough.

Annie knocked just as Nicole decided that she would not only join their illustrious guest for dinner, she would dress for the occasion. "Annie, which is my most becoming, most daring gown?"

Annie gaped at her. "I don't know, mum, I'd have to look through yer things."

"Then let's look," Nicole said grimly, an idea forming.

The Duke was aware, from the moment he stepped into the foyer and handed his cloak to the butler, of every nerve in his body tautening with anticipation. He greeted his host and hostess and Chad, but was disappointed that Nicole was not present. He knew then that she would not join them for dinner. He should have been relieved, but he wasn't.

Shelton poured himself and Chad brandies, his wife a sherry, and had tea ready for the Duke. It was no secret that the Duke of Clayborough never imbibed alcohol. The Duke made himself comfortable in a large wing chair. Shelton took the one opposite. "So how is your work going at Chapman Hall?" he asked.

"I am almost through. I will be returning to London in a few days."

"You have restored her quickly. I recall the Hall being in a sorry state, indeed."

"Yes, it was." The two men began discussing some of the repairs the Duke had made at the Hall. A few minutes later, the door opened and Nicole walked in.

Shelton stopped what he was saying in mid-sentence, his eyes widening. Chad nearly choked on the sip of brandy he had taken. The Countess stared, barely refraining from parting her lips in a huge O. But the Duke did not see their surprise and amazement, for he was caught in the mad chaos of his competing senses.

Nicole smiled at her mother. "I am sorry I am late, Mother."

Quickly Jane stood, hurrying toward her. "That's quite all right. Please, come meet our guest."

The Duke rose to his feet. All of his good intentions fled, immediately forgotten. She wore a vibrant coral-colored gown, off the shoulder and daringly low-cut. It was more suitable for a ball than a meal at home, and it brought out the peach hue of her cheeks and the tawny rose of her lips. Her hair was swept up in the current fashion, and she wore pearls at her throat and in her ears. When she curtsied, he feared for one heartstopping moment that she was about to display all of her magnificent breasts.

Nicole straightened gracefully. "But we have met, Mother," she said, her eyes holding his. Her expression was bland, yet there was no way he could miss the sugary sarcasm in her tone. And there was nothing polite in her eyes, for they glittered with anger. "Have we not, Your Grace? Could you not even say that we are old friends—er—acquaintances?"

His jaw clenched, and every intimate moment they had shared flashed through his mind. "I do believe I have had the honor of an introduction," he murmured politely. His gaze was dark, dangerous, warning her to cease. For the battle lines had been clearly drawn, the gauntlet thrown—by her—and he did not trust her in the least.

"Where have you two met?" the Earl asked.

Nicole smiled, too wisely. "Perhaps His Grace should answer that."

Anger flashed in the Duke's eyes, for he was certain that she intended to do some damage to him—in whatever way she could—this night. He turned to his host. "At the Adderlys' masque, I believe."

"Oh, yes, I had heard that they threw you a party," Jane said, with a quick smile and an uncertain glance that traveled with lightning speed from the Duke to her daughter. Nicole still wore that strange, mocking half-smile.

"And of course," she said silkily, "we furthered our *acquaintance* at Chapman Hall, did we not?" She turned to him inquiringly.

Anger blazed in his eyes again at her daring, while he had no choice but to recall just how they had furthered their acquaintance—with him tossing her on her back in the grass. Silence filled the room. "It was very kind of you, and so neighborly," the Duke finally said, when he could find his tongue, "to call on me and welcome me to the country."

Nicole laughed, the sound rich and husky. "It was so kind of *me*." Her glance was pointed; they both knew damn well that it was Hadrian who had invited her to Chapman Hall for a seduction.

But Nicole wasn't through. "And it was so kind of His Grace to invite *me* to go riding with *him*." She smiled too sweetly. "He showed me the grounds. Fancy that," she told her parents and Chad. She looked expectantly at the Duke.

The Duke nearly choked. "One good turn deserves another," he said stiffly, thinking of how he would love to turn her over his knee and paddle her bottom, regardless that she was a full grown woman.

Nicole gave him a look that said she wasn't sorry and that she had no intention of ceasing her taunts. "We wound up by that sweet little brook, you know, the one that crosses onto our property. Not that we cared where we were, for what are boundaries between new *neighbors?*" She gave him another look, this one long and intimate, the look a woman who has been with a man gives him when she is interested in repeating the rendezvous. His gaze widened fractionally before he resumed his inscrutable expression.

But he was furious with her, and cursing her under his breath, knowing she would toy with him until she grew bored with the endeavor, knowing that this dangerous game of hers was some kind of misbegotten revenge for his callous mistake in thinking her married and attempting to initiate an affair with her. Tension crackled in the air, and he knew her family was growing perturbed as they sought to understand the barely hidden meanings behind her words.

It was time to play her game by her rules and teach her a lesson she had written. He turned a small, biting smile upon her. "You almost suffered great damage to your person, if I recall," he said smoothly.

A quick flush rose on Nicole's cheeks, her small, triumphant smile disappearing. She stared at him, eyes wide, dismayed.

"When your horse ran away with you," he added.

Her relief was transparent. "How I owe you," she managed.

"For saving you?" he asked silkily, thinking of how her virginity had just barely escaped him. "An honorable man could not have done otherwise than to extend himself in order to alleviate a lady's . . . er . . . distress." He recalled too clearly her physical *distress* when she had been in his arms and beneath his hot, aroused body. How he would have loved to relieve her agony!

"I cannot thank you enough." She barely got the words out.

"But you already have," he said. "For wasn't that the reason for your second visit?"

Her jaw tightened. "Of course."

He touched the side of his cheek where she had slashed him with her crop. Only the faintest pink scar was visible if one bothered to look closely enough. "You were very lucky," he said, remembering how her savagery had again incited his lust.

"So lucky," Nicole glared.

Chad broke the silence that followed their exchange, a silence where they stared at each other, eyes blazing. "Nicole is a very good rider. I cannot imagine her horse running away with her."

"Well, you see," the Duke said, unsmiling, recalling her soft body under his, "my mount was quite unschooled, with a mind and inclination of its own. It was my fault. Out of control, I rode right over her. I could not stop until the last moment, preoccupied as I was."

Nicole made a choked sound. He was terribly aware of her, standing by his side, a few inches between them, in her brilliant orange ballgown. Her breasts were heaving now, heaving with her fury. He wondered if she could control her savage nature, or if the volcano of her temper was about to erupt.

But she spoke sweetly, too sweetly. "I am *so* lucky I had the good fortune to be *ridden* over by the Duke, I mean, *by the Duke's mount*, am I not? It is not every day that one is so graced."

"You mean," the Duke gritted, "had I not ridden over you, your *mare* would not have shied—at the last moment, might I add?—and I would not have had the distinct honor of saving you." He found it hard to control his temper and his tone.

Nicole sputtered wordlessly.

The Duke smiled savagely.

The Countess exchanged a worried look with her husband. Quickly, before they could engage in any further verbal dueling, she said, "Why don't we go in and sit to supper?" Jane smiled too brightly. She glided forward and offered her arm to the Duke, but she looked at Nicole. "You never told me that you had met, darling."

"It never came up," Nicole said, and then her next words dared to mock him again. "The way some things always do."

As the guest of honor, the Duke was seated on the Earl's right. They were dining in the smaller of the house's two dining rooms, the one reserved for intimate or family gatherings. The Countess sat at the other end of the table, which seated twelve, with Chad on her right. Nicole sat across from the Duke on her father's other side. The Duke seated Jane, and returned to his own place in time to watch Nicole settling in her chair, dipping forward to reveal a generous portion of her breasts.

Purposefully? He was experienced enough to be sure of it. Their wordplay earlier, and her proximity, had already done dangerous things to his loins, kindling a fire he did not wish to entertain, not now or ever. Lips tight, he sat, resolving to keep his gaze off of her person.

Her last remark still stung. Had she truly meant what he had thought she had? Had she dared to refer to how easily he became aroused around her? He found his gaze upon her again, and she gave him a knowing smile, one that was infinitely seductive and infinitely infuriating.

She was teasing him, and if they weren't here, at Dragmore, he would drag her outside and show her what happened when she dared to play such a dangerous game with a man of his caliber. No woman had ever before dared to rouse his anger as she had, both this evening and the last time they had met. Was she a fool, or infinitely brave and equally reckless? Time would tell, he thought, startled to realize he anticipated some kind of continuation of their relationship. And that was not just impossible, it was out of the question.

She was staring at him and their glances locked. Although they were here at Dragmore dining with her family, his turn would come soon. He held her regard so long that it ceased to be polite, forcing her to turn away first.

"What do you intend to do with Chapman Hall?" the Earl asked as they were served their first course, a cold poached salmon in a delicate lemon sauce.

"I have not decided, but perhaps I will put it up for sale."

"So much work just to sell it?" Nicole asked, her tone provocative.

His hard brown gaze met and held hers, again. "Some endeavors demand labor, and the more labor, the greater the final reward." He could be referring to just about anything, but in this case, he was referring to her.

She smiled. "And sometimes there can be tremendous labor and *no* reward, *ever*." She met his stare.

How he would like to play this game to the end, he thought. How he would like to get her where she would be immersed in his power, helpless to deny him. "Such instances are very, very rare." Abruptly, he turned to her mother, not wanting to continue their banter, afraid they had already revealed too much. "The salmon is delicious, Lady Jane."

Jane could not restrain herself from darting her gaze between them. "I am glad," she managed weakly, finally catching her husband's eye.

Understanding her, the Earl began a more harmless topic: the state of the market. Although economies were not generally discussed in mixed company, as the head of the household the Earl could broach what subject he chose. However, both women seemed interested enough in the conversation to listen closely. The Duke responded to his host automatically, but his attention was elsewhere.

For Nicole continued to clash with him, this time by casting long looks at him from under her lashes, certain that there would be no consequences.

After the meal, they all adjourned together to the salon to enjoy after-dinner drinks. The Earl asked him if he minded the company of the ladies. Of course, by now the Duke was thoroughly irritated, having had to endure Nicole's seduction through the entire supper, and he would have loved to have had a cigar in quiet peace with the Earl and Chad alone. As a gentleman, however, he could not refuse.

But twenty minutes later, Nicole excused herself, with one last glance at the Duke. He watched her leave. Had she been signaling him? The look she had given him had been frosty, smug and somehow coy all at once. Had his turn finally come to even the score?

After five minutes he excused himself momentarily from the gathering. His host would assume him to be answering a natural need. As he walked down the corridor, leaving the salon behind, his senses stirred. He knew—he just knew—that she was somewhere nearby. And as he passed the library a glance within told him that he was right. He halted.

She lay on the divan, on her side, reading. The pose, intentional or not, was that of a classic Venus. Her hips were full and curved and lush, her voluptuous breasts spilling from her gown. She widened her eyes at the sight of him. He could not be certain whether it was an act or not.

He smiled, his first real smile that evening, and it was infinitely dangerous. He stepped into the library and closed the door.

Nicole gasped, dropping the book. "Whatever do you think you're doing! You can't come in here!"

"I can't?" He stalked toward her.

She sat up, although her feet did not drop to the floor. He watched the rise and fall of her breasts, enjoying the view. "You played," he said silkily, "and now you may pay."

With that, she leapt to her feet. At that moment, he pounced on her, making her cry out as he pulled her up against him. "Did you enjoy yourself tonight, Nicole?"

"Did you enjoy yourself?" she flung back defiantly.

"No," he said, "but I intend to now."

Certain of what was coming, she tried to wrench herself free of his grip. He refused to let her go, even though a part of himself was shocked with the disrespect he was showing for his host and with his blatant disregard for any consequences that might ensue. He ignored that part of himself and hauled her up against him and kissed her.

She made incoherent noises of furious protest, which he ignored. He kept a steel hold on her wrists, molding her mouth with his, his patience endless. She took a breath and he seized the moment, thrusting his tongue deep within her. She gasped as he proceeded to thrust into her mouth insistently, ruthlessly, and then she became still in his arms.

His relentless attack did not cease. He transferred her wrists to one hand and with the other caught her buttocks, pulling her against him. She became more pliant in his embrace, moaning softly. His own stance changed. No longer the enemy predator, he eased his grip and his hold became a sweet, intoxicating embrace. Their kiss became a mutual mating. It went on and on and on.

A noise intruded on his senses. Awareness of who he was, who she was, where they were and what they were doing was instantaneous. He thrust her from him.

She stumbled, flushed and panting. The regard she turned on him was unfocused, that of a woman in the throes of passion.

"My reward," he said huskily. Knowing he could not remain with her another moment, knowing that to be caught here would be the ruin of them both, he abruptly turned away and strode out the door, leaving her standing there, stunned.

He was halfway down the corridor when he heard her curse him, and then he heard the sound of glass shattering. He wondered what she had broken, but he could not smile. Victory was not always sweet.

Jane emerged from her own bedroom, which adjoined the Earl's, into his. She never, ever slept in her own suite, but she kept all of her belongings there, and occasionally she did sit in front of the fire with a novel. Now she paused in the doorway, clad in a blue silk dressing gown, her expression worried.

The Earl was stripped to his waist, still wearing his trousers, his feet stockinged. In his early fifties, he had the lean, hard body of a man who had spent, and did spend, much of his time in physical labor. He had learned to enjoy hard physical work as a boy growing up in Texas, and it was not a habit he had ever cared to break. To this day, if there were a stone wall to be built or a barn to be raised, he gladly pitched in, as his time allowed. Now, he met his wife's blue gaze, his own features grim.

She bit her lip, coming forward. "Whatever is going on between them, Nicholas?"

"So you saw, too?"

"How could I not see!? For all that he tried to hide it, the Duke was nearly seething, and Nicole, I would swear that she was teasing him, taunting him."

The Earl sat on a divan to remove his stockings. "I have never seen Nicole like this before."

Suddenly Jane's eyes sparkled with excitement. "Nicholas, she dressed for *him*. She is interested in *him*."

The Earl straightened, his unusually pale gray eyes sparkling. "You sound happy. Have you lost your mind?"

Jane stiffened, for her husband never talked to her in such a manner. "I assure you, all my faculties are intact."

"I am sorry," he groaned, instantly on his feet and pulling her small, slender body into his embrace. "I am upset, and I was taking it out on you."

She clung to him, loving the feel of his hard, powerful body, loving him even more than she had when they had first met when she was sixteen. A lifetime ago—a wonderful lifetime ago. "Nicholas, we should be worried, but . . ." She took a breath. "Can you imagine? Our daughter a duchess?"

Nicholas released her, incredulous. "Jane, you are not thinking straight at all! The Duke of Clayborough is betrothed."

"I know that. But betrothals can be broken."

Nicholas stared at her very grimly. "Not in this case," he said flatly. "I know Clayborough well enough. He lives by his family's motto, "Honor First". Even should he fall madly in love with our daughter, he will never, ever break his engagement. Instead, he will break Nicole's heart."

"Oh, dear," Jane said.

Nicholas turned away, running a hand through his thick black hair, streaked with gray. "So whatever is between them, it is now over. The sooner Clayborough returns to London, the better for us all."

"But you said he is honorable, and I am sure you are right. One merely has to look at him to know he is a fine, upright man. He would never do something untoward to compromise Nicole. We are worrying too much."

Nicholas turned, a wry expression on his face. "Jane, he is a man. That fact speaks for itself. Or have you forgotten that sometimes men of honor behave most dishonorably when the women they love are involved?"

They were both thrown back to another time, in this very same place, when she was sixteen and his ward.

"Now I am worried, Nicholas," Jane said, and she went into his arms.

Nicole pretended to oversleep, but the moment she heard hoofbeats outside her window she leapt from the bed to watch her father and Chad riding away from the stables. She bit her lip nervously, then ran to her bureau, pulling out a loose white shirt and breeches. Last night she had been furious but this morning she was strangely excited, almost elated.

Not that she wasn't still angry, of course. It was the height of arrogance for the Duke to come there for supper after what had passed between them, after his callous assumptions about her, his jaded interest in her, and his flat rejection of her. Much, much worse were the liberties he had dared to take in the library, with her parents just a few doors away. And if she had the courage to face the entire truth, there was the matter of her own response to his advances to consider—she had capitulated to him with nary a word! Just remembering brought anger, shame and humiliation. Had he intended to humiliate her by seducing her? Nicole would not be surprised, now that she knew of his scandalous reputation as a womanizer. Obviously the man had no morals and no sense of honor at all. Nicole intended to tell him exactly what she thought of his despicable behavior.

She dressed and flew down the stairs, knowing she would see no one other than the staff at this early hour; her mother liked to sleep in until almost eight—which was still unfashionably early for a lady to rise. Nicole's stomach was in knots of anticipation, so she did not pause even for a cup of tea. Instead she raced to the barn and with one of the grooms, saddled up her big, blood bay stallion.

She set off at a gallop. The early morning air was crisp and cold, promising fall's sudden demise. She galloped down the drive, then veered off across the lawns, jumping a stone wall effortlessly. In the next meadow she scattered the sheep and lambs, laughing in exhilaration, then took another wall in a soaring display of superb horsemanship. They flew down a path through the woods, stirring up the gold and brown leaves underfoot. A mile later Nicole pulled the bay up at the edge of his lawns, in view of Chapman Hall.

Her heart was pounding wildly in her breast amd her cheeks were flushed from the madcap ride. The stallion snorted impatiently, still wanting to run. "Later," Nicole said, stroking his warm neck. Eyes glittering, she urged the animal forward.

It was early, but the sound of carpenters came from the stables, their hammers ringing loudly. Nicole headed for the house, slipping off of the bay. She tied him to a post and trotted up the steps, banging the heavy brass door knocker.

There was no answer.

Nicole knocked several times, growing perturbed. The Duke might not be in, but surely his staff was there. Yet instead, the house seemed to be vacant, deserted.

Dismay rose in her breast. Nicole retrieved her mount's reins and strode determinedly to the barn. Perhaps he was there, inside the stables, overseeing his men. If not, surely they would know where he was. He had to be here, didn't he?

Leaving the stallion outside, she stepped within, her eyes adjusting to the dim light. The two men stopped their sawing and banging, turning to look at her. "I am looking for the Duke," she said, recognizing the laborers as men from the village of Lessing. Still, their blatant regard made her uncomfortable. She never came into contact with workers unless she was riding with her father and Chad. She was distinctly aware of her male attire and being unchaperoned and unprotected.

"He's not here," said the older man, squinting at her.

The young man straightened, leering. "He ain't here, but we are."

Nicole gave him a hard look that warned him not even to think nasty thoughts. "Where is he? And why is no one answering the door at the Hall?"

The young one, whose name she thought was Smith, sauntered forward. "Ain't no one there. That's why, miss."

"No one there?" she echoed.

"The Duke an' his staff has up an' gone," the older man volunteered.

"Now why are you so interested in His Grace?" Smith grinned knowingly.

Nicole didn't hear. "Gone? Gone where?"

"Back to London," the old man said.

"Back to London," Nicole repeated, barely able to absorb this information. "But when will he return?"

"He didn't say."

"But while you're waitin' for him to return, there's always me," Smith said, moving closer.

"Go to hell!" Nicole snapped, startling both men. She whirled and ran from the barn, still trying to comprehend that the Duke was gone. She mounted the bay, nudging him into a fast trot.

Gone! *He was gone!*

And there was no question about it, her heart had sunk right down to her very toes. She was absolutely deflated.

He had come into her life so abruptly, and just as abruptly, he was gone. One day there was only her family, her horses, her books and Dragmore, the next there was the golden, virile Duke. But now he was gone.

She should be relieved. She should be happy. She was neither of those things; she was deeply disappointed.

"What is wrong with you?" she said aloud. "Have you truly gone mad? He harbors only the worst intentions towards you, he is about to marry another, and you are mourning his absence!"

Logic did not vanquish her strange trembling, nor did it lift her spirits.

She slowed the bay to a walk when they reached the trail running through the woods. A few minutes later they came upon the racing brook, and Nicole was assaulted with the memory of how they had ridden here, and how he had kissed her, touched her. She stopped her mount, slipping off, and knelt by the stream, touching the icy water.

Life was not always fair. But she had learned that long ago, so why was she feeling so sorely now? Why had he returned to London so abruptly? Last night he had said he would be leaving in a few days. Last night—he had left because of last night!

Nicole straightened, certain that she was responsible, having pushed him too far. But he had started it by merely coming to Dragmore when he could have made his excuses. And she was not one to ever back down from a confrontation, and in this instance, she had eagerly risen to the occasion, relishing the battle.

What did it matter? He was not for her, and he never would be. The most she could hope for was more of his kisses, or worse, to sleep in his bed. At the thought Nicole blushed. Sex was a topic ladies never discussed but she understood the basics of the act, having been raised on the estate and having seen a stallion put to a mare once. It had been shocking but exciting. She had never seen a man naked, but she had felt the Duke's maleness when he had pressed himself against her, and she could imagine what he looked like. Imagine what it felt like inside her. Growing very warm, she blindly stroked her horse's neck, knowing she should be ashamed at the direction her thoughts were taking. But she wasn't ashamed, not at all, and that was the entire problem.

Of course, she was never going to sleep with him in such a manner, it was the height of fantasy to imagine what she was imagining. Nor would she ever have his kisses again, his dangerous, smoldering kisses. A lump rose up in her throat, a sense of choking panic.

She pulled herself together. "It is for the best," she told her stallion, who was nibbling on a patch of grass. She mounted abruptly, urged him into a canter, and did not stop again until she had reached the stable at Dragmore. There she handed her mount to a groom and hurried back to the house, keeping her mind blessedly and purposefully blank.

As she passed the dining room her mother called out to her, stopping her in her tracks. Nicole entered, surprised to see her mother up and at the table, for she usually had tea and muffins in her room while dressing.

"Good morning, Mother." Nicole came in, hesitating, instinct making her uneasy.

"Aldric says you've yet to eat," Jane smiled. She looked a bit tired, as if she had not slept well. "Sit down and join me, darling." Jane poured her a cup of tea, handing it to her as Nicole sat.

"I'm not very hungry today."

"Are you feeling all right?"

"Yes, I'm fine."

"I couldn't help but notice that you did not go out with your father and Chad today."

"I—I was tired from last night."

Jane nodded and buttered a warm muffin, handing half to her daughter. "Did you enjoy your ride this morning?"

Nicole flushed. "Sort of."

Jane set the muffin down, not having taken a bite. "Nicole, where did you go?"

Nicole could not hold her mother's direct gaze. Color flooded her cheeks. "Just around."

"To Chapman Hall?"

Nicole gasped. "What—what makes you think that?!"

"We had better talk," Jane said gently.

"There is nothing to talk about," Nicole cried, panicked.

"It is obvious that there is something between you and the Duke of Clayborough."

"Mother—you are wrong!" Nicole started to rise, but Jane restrained her.

"Then I am glad, for he is engaged, and soon he will wed his betrothed. He will never break it off, Nicole," Jane said gently.

Nicole knew that, yet hearing the words somehow hurt. "There is nothing between us," Nicole said stiffly. "I find him despicable, if you must know the truth. He is an arrogant and pompous ass."

Jane was visibly shocked.

Suddenly Nicole stared at her mother. "Mother, are you going back to London today?"

"Yes, this afternoon. I do not feel right leaving Regina there, even with Lady Henderson. After all, I should be sharing her season with her."

Nicole wet her lips. "I am going to go with you. I will pack now!"

Jane blinked. "But you never go to town. You hate London."

"I have changed," Nicole announced, standing. "I am bored with life here, I need to get out, meet people. Don't you agree?"

"It's been my and your father's deepest wish," Jane declared, surprised. "It isn't healthy to stay secluded in the country to the extent that you do."

"I'll be ready in no time," Nicole declared, flashing a smile and running from the room.

Jane watched her go, smiling as well. This was what her daughter needed, to get out again among the set, where she could still meet an eligible man, where she could still find love. And the fact that the Duke of Clayborough was here at Chapman Hall made it all the better that Nicole should join her and Regina in London. Still smiling, Jane reached for her muffin, her appetite restored.

The Duke arrived in London that afternoon and went directly to his residence at No. 1 Cavendish Square. Clayborough House was an imposing sight, taking up the entire block on the north side of the green. It had been built in the early eighteenth century for the first duke of Clayborough, and had since suffered a few additions. Six stories high, the entire front facade facing the street contained a hundred windows and three towers. The roof made the structure appear even larger, because of the three giant gables that soared by several additional stories into the sky. Each boasted the Clayborough coat of arms, awesomely oversized. The mansion was cordoned off from the street by an imposing and intricately designed stone balustrade, except for where the stone staircase, which was wide enough to accommodate a dozen guests should they choose to enter all at once, swept down to the street.

The Duke had sent a few of his staff on to London the night before after dining at Dragmore, and now Woodward greeted him at the door. The Duke motioned for him to follow, and they paced down a black and white marble-floored hallway and turned into a library that could accommodate half of Chapman Hall. He went to his desk, pulling one of his cards out of his pocket, and quickly penned a personal note upon it. He handed it to the butler. "Send this to Lady Elizabeth now."

"Will there be anything else? A bit of tea with your bath, Your Grace?"

The Duke nodded carelessly and hurried up the stairs.

His own suite also had marble floors, these gold and white. Once the room had been appointed as if to house royalty. Upon his father's demise, he had immediately removed all the furnishings except for a few and redecorated as he chose. Francis' tastes had been much too decorative and whimsical to suit his own, but more to the point, the Duke did not want any reminders of his father present, having enough memories to haunt him for a lifetime.

Now, dozens of Persian rugs covered the floors, providing warmth at night when the Duke enjoyed going barefoot. An old chaise and ottoman, reupholstered in a rich wine leather, faced the hearth, with a sixteenth century Chinese footstool nearby for the Duke to lay his papers and books on. Ever fond of Oriental antiques, Hadrian had selected for one wall a massive black lacquer Chinese screen inlaid with mother-of-pearl, designed with a floral motif on top and courting horses below. The rest of the furnishings were a somewhat eclectic collection of pieces which Hadrian had chosen strictly for comfort and utilitarian value. The only family heirloom that remained in the room was an eighteenth century mahogany secretary which he would not remove, knowing that his grandfather, the seventh duke of Clayborough, who had died several years before he had been born, had been terribly fond of it.

The room was rather different from the rest of the house, but it was his personal sanctum, and everything within it pleased him. He was sure Elizabeth would hate it the moment she saw it, just as Isobel had hated it, telling him bluntly that it was "awfully done," but he did not care. He knew Elizabeth well, and she would not defy him once he told her that not one inch of his suite was subject to change. In fact, she would certainly never broach the topic again.

His valet had already drawn his bath in the bathroom, which was also floored in marble, and as large as most country bedrooms. Accepting his tea, the Duke stripped and sank down into the sumptuous, sunken tub.

Presently he intended to visit Elizabeth, apologize to her for his neglect, and determine the state of her health. Yet his intention had *not* been to return to London today, or even tomorrow. Not until last night, that is.

His conduct had been scandalous. Her conduct had been equally scandalous, but that was no excuse. Obviously it was Nicole Shelton's character to defy convention. After witnessing her highly unusual and rather shocking behavior several times now, he could no longer be surprised that she had suffered a scandal of her own making some years past. A small smile suddenly tugged at his mouth. No one would ever accuse her of being boring. Conventionality was boring—it was why he so disliked the routine of parties, at-homes and social gallivanting that the rest of his class was so fond of. It suddenly occurred to him that in a way, he and Nicole were not so very different.

His smile abruptly disappeared.

He chased such a ludicrous thought right out of his head.

He was considered rather reclusive, his disdain for the social whirl was well known, but never had he triggered a scandal, and his behavior most certainly did not cause tongues to wag. With the exception of his extreme interest in business affairs, which was not considered appropriate for a nobleman of any rank, it was most certainly not his penchant to defy convention.

The Duke realized that far from relaxing in the hot tub, he was disturbed, and very nearly angry now. Recalling their verbal battle the night before, and their physical one—for how could he possibly forget it?—he was unsure if he was mad at Nicole, or at himself. Only one thing appeared to be clear. His iron control, his will and his self-discipline, were not what he had thought them to be, not as far as Nicole Shelton was concerned.

He grew more perturbed, and he lunged from the tub, water cascading down his naked, powerful body.

He decided that time would end his attraction to her. She was now at Dragmore, and he did not intend to return to Chapman Hall until his interest in her had subsided. Clearly he, who had never been untrustworthy in any aspect before, was untrustworthy where she was concerned. Was there actually something of Francis' despicable character in him?

He had been rubbing a thick towel slowly over his body, now he froze. The thought was chilling.

The Duke wasn't sure when he had first started hating his father, for he did not have a single memory of ever not hating him. It was as a very young child that he had first become aware of the distress his father caused his mother, and he had earned his first slap when he was four for trying to protect Isobel from him. The blow had hurt him but that had been nothing compared to the terrible fear that had followed. Not just fear for himself, but fear for his mother.

For upon seeing her child hurt, Isobel had flown into a rage, flying at Francis with the intention of sinking her nails deep into his face. Still stunned from being hit, Hadrian had watched his father easily prevent Isobel from mauling him, then he had seen him strike her and knock her down. Francis had left the room after laughing and calling her a whore. Hadrian had crawled to his mother, crying, but to his relief, she had sat up and hugged him, crooning to him that everything was all right. Once he saw that his mother was fine, Hadrian was filled with a burning hatred for his father that still endured to this day. He barely heard his mother telling him that he must never interfere again between his parents. He was too busy wishing his father would die, a wish that had not been fulfilled for another twenty-two years.

But he was not abusive like Francis, Hadrian thought, for never in his life had he hurt a child or a woman. He did not drink and he did not gamble. And he certainly had no inclination for boys.

When he was young, however, Francis had apparently enjoyed women, for it was not until he was older and jaded that he had turned to those of his own sex. A gentleman would have never accosted Nicole as he had done last night, but undoubtedly it was something his father would have done with no qualms whatsoever.

The Duke recalled their physical altercation outside of Chapman Hall, and how he had slammed her against the side of the barn after she had struck him with her crop. He had not meant to subdue her so roughly, yet he had.

He was afraid of the side of himself that he had unearthed, a dark side, that, until now, he had not known existed. No other woman had ever brought this side to light, and it was all the more reason for him to stay away from her.

He was engaged to Elizabeth, who was not only his cousin but a kind and sweet young lady, and he had known her nearly all of his life. He would never hurt her. He would never renege on his duty and violate his honor or hers. So why had he tempted fate last night at Dragmore? Had he and Nicole been found together he would have been forced to marry her and break off his engagement to Elizabeth. He had been, Hadrian decided grimly, temporarily mad.

An image of Nicole as his wife assailed him. She would make the worst wife, insolent, disobedient, forever provoking his temper. Unlike Elizabeth, who would devote her life to pleasing him. Why was he comparing the two, when there was nothing to compare?

Yet Nicole *had* wanted to marry him. Just as she now seemed intent on infuriating him—a misguided and very reckless form of payback. Suddenly he became very still.

Had she been setting a trap for him?

She was not the first woman to want to marry him, far from it. The Duke was well aware that every season many hopeful debutantes were determined to catch his eye and have him jilt Elizabeth. Of course, he ignored them.

But he could no longer ignore what had happened with Nicole. *She had thought him to be courting her, while he had intended only a brief affair.* Guilt claimed him. He had hurt her. For the first time since they had both learned the truth about each other, he dared to face this fact squarely. He clearly remembered her shock when he had apologized to her for mistakenly assuming she was a married woman. And now that he dared to recall this encounter, he could too easily remember the hurt and anguish in her eyes. Then, he had tried to avoid knowledge of what he had done, but now, he could not. He felt like a heel.

But she had recovered, swiftly enough, from any anguish he had unintentionally caused her. And last night she had been no hurt, brooding miss. Last night she had been a seductress, flaunting her beauty and daring him to meet her in a clash of verbal swords. Last night she had been fascinating. Last night, instead of retiring to the safety of her bedroom, she had lain upon the sofa in the library in a timelessly provocative pose. And when he had risen to the bait, stalked her, taken her in his arms, she had barely resisted him. Within moments, she had been moaning in abandon.

Had it been a trap?

He flung his towel onto the floor and stalked naked into his dressing room. Barely aware of what he was doing, he slipped on a dressing gown. Anger poured through him. She would not be the first who tried to seduce him away from his betrothal with her beauty, but she was the first he had succumbed to. He was certain now that she had sought to seduce him, to see herself compromised, to have them caught by her family. Why else would she have waited for him in the library? Why the hell else?

It was coincidence, but Elizabeth was seated with Isobel, the two of them enjoying tea and scones, when the message from the Duke arrived. Elizabeth accepted the card the butler handed to her, instantly recognizing the ducal crest. "It's from Hadrian," she breathed, a smile lighting up her small face and making her almost beautiful.

Isobel smiled too, thinking that Elizabeth was still so young and so transparent. "And?"

Elizabeth turned shining blue eyes upon the Dowager Duchess. "He has returned!" she cried joyfully. "He has returned and he is coming tonight!"

"It's about time," Isobel said. "Don't get too excited, dear, you know you were not feeling well today."

A rosy flush covered Elizabeth's cheeks. "How can I not be excited? It has been more than a month since I have seen him, and Isobel," the two were on intimate terms, "do not speak unkindly of Hadrian. It would be different if he were absent because of wastrel pursuits, but we both know how hard he works, and how seriously he takes his duties. If I do not chastise him, neither should you." The words were said gently and kindly, for Elizabeth was not capable of raising her voice at anyone.

"A mother is entitled to berate her son," Isobel said patting Elizabeth's small, pale hand. "But I am glad to see the color back in your cheeks. And I think it is time for me to leave."

Although Elizabeth was eager to run upstairs and fix her toilette, she protested sincerely. "You have just arrived! You can not go so soon, and really, I have time enough before he comes."

Isobel smiled and kissed her cheek. "I am leaving, dear, so run to your rooms and change your gown, as I know you wish to do."

Elizabeth smiled. Her own gentle mother had died when she was a young girl, and she loved the Dowager Duchess dearly. "I am so glad, at long last, that you are really to become a mother to me."

"And you have always been the daughter I have never had," Isobel said softly, hugging her once. And it was true, for Isobel had always been especially fond of Elizabeth.

Elizabeth beamed, hugging the card to her small breasts. She was a petite, slender girl, with an ivory complexion and fine, blonde hair. People said she was pretty, but Elizabeth knew that in truth she was rather plain, being much too pale and too thin, her hair too fine. She also had a sprinkling of freckles on her nose, which she covered with a fine dusting of white powder. Yet Elizabeth could not know that to many she was beautiful, and it had nothing to do with her actual physical appearance, but it had everything to do with her warmth.

So excited that she was short of breath, Elizabeth hurried up to her suite, calling for her maid. An hour later she had changed into a pastel green gown, her hair newly coiffed and coiled atop her head. Around her neck she wore a triple strand of exquisite pearls with a diamond clasp, a gift from Hadrian when she had turned eighteen two months ago. She had just finished dressing when the butler informed her that the Duke of Clayborough had arrived and was downstairs. Breathless, Elizabeth flew from the room.

The Duke rose the instant she entered the salon, smiling at her smile, taking her hand and kissing it. She had known him ever since she could remember. He had bounced her on his knee until she had gotten too big for him to do so, and then she had tested his endurance all through her childhood, tagging along behind him from the time she could toddle when he was a strapping and handsome, god-like twelve year old, until she suddenly became aware of her femininity when puberty pushed her into adolesence. He had even saved her life when she had slipped and fallen into a pond at the age of eight. He had been fishing there with his golden retriever, and, as usual, Elizabeth had been following him. She had not been afraid when the icy water claimed her, for he was her hero—she knew he would save her. Elizabeth could not recall a time when she had not loved him.

"I am so glad you are back," she said simply, after they had exchanged greetings.

Sitting beside her on the sofa, he apologized. "I am sorry I have been away so long."

"Do not apologize! I understand, I really do."

The Duke studied her. She seemed out of breath, but she did not look ill, for her eyes were sparkling with happiness and her cheeks were flushed. Yet she was thinner; it was all too noticeable now that his mother had mentioned it. "Mother says you have not been well."

Elizabeth's smile faded. "I am fine, really. It is true I have been tired, but Hadrian, I go to party after party and sometimes I do not get home until dawn. You know how the season is! Is it any wonder I am tired?"

She was right, and his mother was being foolish, although if there was one thing Isobel was not, it was foolish. "Then you must come home earlier if you tire so easily."

"I promise," she said, and he knew she meant it, just as he knew she would do anything he asked of her.

Nicole and Jane did not arrive in London until well after midnight, for they had not left Dragmore until that afternoon. Regina was still out with Lady Henderson. According to the housekeeper, one long-faced Mrs. Doyle, she had gone to the Barrington's ball. Both Nicole and Jane retired for the evening.

Nicole was up just after the sun had risen, unable to break her age-old habit and eager to see her sister, whom she had not seen in months. Whereas yesterday life had seemed filled with gloom, today the birds were singing outside her window and Nicole felt positively jubilant. For the first time in years, she was delighted to be in the city and looking forward to whatever festivities the day would bring.

She also could not help wondering if she would see him.

She took an early morning ride, accompanied by a groom for propriety's sake. Regents Park was deserted at this hour, which was considered ungodly by the fashionable set, most of whom had just gotten into their beds. By eight that morning she could restrain herself no longer, and she flung open the door to her sister's bedroom. Regina lay huddled in a ball beneath the covers, sound asleep. Grinning, Nicole tiptoed over, then yanked the covers from her.

Regina groaned in protest, flinging one hand over her eyes.

"Wake up, sleepy-head," Nicole cried, dragging Regina's pillow out from under her tawny-haired head and tossing it at her.

"Nicole?"

Nicole sat on the bed. "It's me."

Regina threw the pillow on the floor, wide awake now and incredulous. Then she gave a cry of gladness and hugged her sister soundly. "What are you doing here? I can't believe it!"

"I was bored," Nicole said, grinning. "You look awful. What time did you get in last night?"

Regina scowled, which did absolutely nothing to detract from her classic beauty. And in truth, the eighteen-year-old never looked awful. "At dawn. The Barrington's gave a rousing good ball. Everyone who was anyone was there! Oh, you should have come sooner!"

Nicole froze, then, to hide her expression, she retrieved the pillow from the floor. "Everyone was there? Who is everyone?"

"Do you want me to name names?" Regina was incredulous. "Tonight there's a crush at the Willoughbys'. You are coming?"

"Wouldn't miss it," Nicole quipped.

Fully awake now, Regina sat up, regarding her sister probingly. "Nicole, you seem different. What is going on? You hate London. Are you really going to come out and get into the rush of things?"

Nicole hesitated, wanting so much to confide in her sister, but afraid to. After all, what was there to confide?

That the Duke of Clayborough had harbored immoral intentions towards her? That she, the fool, had enjoyed his kisses? That she knew he was in London, and that maybe, just maybe, that was why Dragmore was suddenly so boring? That she was wondering if she would see him tonight? "I am tired of having nothing but sheep and cows for company," she finally said, hating to lie to Regina, whom she loved dearly.

"Well, I don't blame you!" Regina cried emphatically. From the time she could walk, Regina had always preferred lace and dolls to horses and climbing trees, no two sisters being less alike. "I am so glad you are here!" Impulsively, she hugged her sister, hard. "You just stay with me," she told Nicole seriously. "And I will introduce you to everyone and you will have a rousing good time!"

The grand salon at the Willoughbys' was already full when Nicole arrived with Regina and their mother that night. Smaller than a ballroom, the grand salon could accommodate a hundred people with ease, yet now it was crowded and warm. Guests were milling everywhere, sipping champagne and other drinks, while servants offered an exotic array of hors d'oeuvres. A trio was playing on a platform built for the occasion, but the strains of the piano, harp and violin were drowned out by the animated conversation of the glittering throng.

The salon was crowded, but not so crowded that Nicole wasn't immediately noticed and remarked upon. As she, Regina and Jane entered the room, she was aware of those standing closest to the arched entry turning to smile at her sister and mother—then gaping at her. And already her heart was in her throat.

While dressing for the evening, she had been stricken with a case of nerves. With a bit of probing, Nicole had surmised that the most upper of London's upper crust would be at this crush, for Lord Willoughby was not just the Marquess of Hunt but a confidante of the Prime Minister as well. Although Nicole had learned from Martha in their conversation at Dragmore that the Duke of Clayborough was apparently not fond of social gatherings, because of Willoughby's power and connections she thought that there was a good chance that he just might be there tonight. And even if he were not, she had not a doubt that his betrothed, Elizabeth Martindale, would be, not just because she was his fiancée, which in itself gave her tremendous status, but because she was a member of the de Warenne family, and its patriarch, the Earl of Northumberland, was one of the most powerful men in the realm.

Knowing she would see either or both of them had been enough to make her tense and nervous as she donned her turquoise moire ballgown. Yet still she avoided too close an inspection of her motivation in coming to London and attending this party. By the time she had left the house on Tavistock Square, her jitters had taken a turn for the worse. Although it was over a year since she had been to London, she had not been to an affair in the city since the scandal. The last real fête she had attended had been the Adderlys' masque, and that would have been a disaster if the Duke had not approved of her. Tonight, even if he were here, she was on her own. Nicole was very close to regretting that she had come.

A large group standing not far from the doorway all turned to look at her. "I say, isn't that Dragmore's eldest gel?" one fop asked, his voice carrying.

"It is," a matron answered, quickly removing her gaze from Nicole. "Did you hear about the costume she wore to the Adderlys'?" Abruptly, the matron lowered her voice, turning her back to Nicole and her family.

"They are all witches!" Regina cried loudly. She glared at the group furiously, her usually genteel step becoming hard and long.

Nicole grasped her gloved arm at the elbow. "It's all right, Rie. I expected some unpleasantness."

"I know exactly who is in that group, and I shall cut them sorely the next time my path crosses with any of theirs," Regina stated, amber eyes flashing. Then she looked suspiciously at her sister. "What kind of costume did you wear to the Adderlys'? And when was this?"

Before Nicole could answer, she was saved by her mother's interruption. "Are you all right, darling?"

"Truly, Mother, I am." Nicole managed a reassuring smile, although she was not exactly all right. She was also horrified because she was actually sweating. She would have loved to yank off her elbow-length white gloves, but did not dare.

Jane promptly maneuvered them to another group, this one full of personal friends of hers. While they expressed surprise over Nicole's presence, it was in a genuine way, without any rancor. Nicole was relieved, and for a few moments, she paused to chat with the Howards and the Bentons.

"Martha's here," Regina whispered, edging away from the group of older folk and taking Nicole with her. "Look." Regina waved.

Nicole smiled, thrilled that her best friend had returned to London. Martha hurried over, hugging both girls. "What are you doing here?" she exclaimed, her gaze penetrating.

Nicole shrugged, knowing Martha probably guessed the truth.

"Dragmore suddenly bores her," Regina answered, giving Nicole a shrewd glance. "What do you know, Martha?"

"Why, what do you mean?" Martha turned back to Nicole. "It is wonderful that you are here!" She gave Nicole a long look full of meaning which Nicole could not decipher.

"Lord Hortense is here," Regina suddenly whispered, excited. "Nicole, quick, look!"

Nicole followed her sister's gaze and found a dark handsome man in his thirties staring at them. She grew uneasy, suddenly wondering if Lord Hortense was staring at her or at her sister. Regina tugged her hand. "Isn't he handsome? He is rich, too, and his reputation and manners spotless! He has called on me twice! Nicole—I think he is courting me—I think he will ask Father for my hand!"

Nicole stole another glance at the handsome lord, and flamed at the bold look he sent her. This time there was no doubt of it and she quickly turned away. "You are still young, Regina. Surely he is not your only suitor?"

"Of course not," Regina said, yet Nicole's heart sank at the shining look in her sister's eyes. "But . . . I am in love with him, Nicole!"

Nicole bit her lip, exchanging a worried glance with Martha. She detested Lord Hortense with every instinct she possessed.

"I am going to mingle," Regina said breathlessly, and both girls watched her flit off into the crowd, moving, of course, in the direction of Hortense.

Nicole saw that he was giving her another long stare, and she quickly turned her back on him, furious. "He will break her heart."

"He is certainly giving you the eye," Martha said. "Normally I would not worry, for Regina is very popular and every week she is in love with someone else. But I think this thing with Lord Hortense is much more serious, Nicole. For two months now she has spoken about no one other than him."

"Oh," Nicole breathed. "Somehow I must warn her away from him."

"You must. Nicole, he is here."

Nicole froze. "The Duke?" she asked very softly, while her heart leapt wildly.

"Yes." Martha scanned the crowd. "I saw him some time ago, he must have just returned to London." She looked back at her friend. "Nicole, what are you doing?"

"Oh, Martha," Nicole cried, knowing exactly what she meant, "if only I knew! I just could not stay at Dragmore, I could not!"

Martha gripped her arm. "I see him."

Swallowing, Nicole followed Martha's stare. Her body tensed at the sight of him.

He looked utterly magnificent in his midnight black tailcoat and trousers. He towered a head above the crowd, splendidly handsome and utterly male. All the men around him seemed silly in comparison, their faces lily white in contrast to his bold golden coloring, their forms almost ridiculously slender next to his powerful build. His hair was still too long. It more than brushed his collar. Nicole smiled, thinking that he still disdained to visit his barber. Only a man like the Duke could get away with such an unfashionable inclination.

Of course, he was bored and restless, as he had been at the Adderlys', barely attending the words of some matron, his glance shifting about as he cocked his head towards the elderly woman. Finally he straightened to his full height, smiling somewhat painfully and nodding in agreement with whatever she'd said. And at that precise moment his restless gaze found hers.

He froze, his expression stunned and incredulous. Their gazes locked. Nicole could not turn her eyes away. There was quite some distance between them, but not enough to prevent Nicole from reading his every expression. The incredulity turned to flushed anger. A moment later his glance moved over her quickly, down to her toes and then back up again. It was not a polite perusal, it was not the look of a gentleman.

"He is furious," Martha gasped. Nicole had forgotten she was standing there, indeed, she had forgotten everything and everyone in those few moments, except for him.

"He despises me as much as I despise him," Nicole said unsteadily. She lifted her chin proudly, trying to appear careless, as if the meeting of their glances had been accidental. She was hurt by his anger, yet she shouldn't be. Instantly he turned away from her.

Nicole went very still. A small blonde woman had taken his arm, pressing it against her side. The Duke bent over her to listen to what she was saying, and she was smiling, laughing. When he straightened, he was smiling, too.

Nicole felt heartsick. "It's her, isn't it?"

"Yes."

Nicole turned her back to the couple. She hadn't gotten a good glimpse of Elizabeth, dwarfed as she was by the

Duke, but she had seen enough. She was petite and blonde and fair. Never had Nicole felt so tall and dark and awkward. And the Duke was fond of her, genuinely fond of her. It was so very obvious, Nicole realized, that tears stung her eyes.

"Nicole, let's go to the powder room," Martha said quickly, taking her hand.

Nicole's first reaction was to protest, but she bit it back. Instead, she managed a crooked smile and followed Martha from the salon.

By the time they had returned, Nicole had recovered from the impact of finally seeing the Duke with his fiancée. She mingled as Martha did, and was introduced to many people, all of whom were polite, for Martha was discreet and knew whom to introduce her to. And for the next two hours, Nicole always knew exactly where the Duke was.

Elizabeth rarely left his side, while he ignored Nicole. Twice more their eyes had inadvertently met, and he had quickly turned his back upon her, as if she did not exist, or as if she were beneath him. Such rejection was deliberate. Nicole was certain that he was as aware of her as she was of him, yet determined to avoid her at all costs.

She was sorry that she had no suitors of her own, for then she would hang on their arms the way Elizabeth hung on his. It was embarrassing. She was twenty-three, almost twenty-four, an old maid with no chance for marriage unless it was to some fat, old man. Elizabeth was just eighteen, blonde and perfect, betrothed to the Duke. Nicole disliked her, knowing it was uncharitable, but how could she not? The little chit had everything; she had her prince; she had Nicole's short-lived dream. It was impossible not to dislike her, just as it was impossible not to despise him.

By the time the clocks had tolled midnight, Nicole could stand the press no more. She slipped from the salon, seeking some air, certain that the Duke had left as well in the past hour with his precious betrothed, for she had not seen him in some time. She found the doors to a patio and quietly stepped outside. The night was crisp and cold, a welcoming contrast to the stuffy warmth of the salon. Clouds scudded across the sky, a few stars twinkled, and occasionally the waning moon showed itself. Nicole went to the brick wall and leaned against it, looking out at the well-lit gardens beyond. She realized that she was utterly drained now that he was gone, and that the evening had been nothing short of a disaster.

She should have never come to London. She had come because of him, she could face that now, and she was a fool. Somehow, her heart had broken again tonight.

She did not hear the doors to the patio opening and closing. She did not hear his footsteps. His voice, when he spoke, was low and angry. "What are you doing here?"

Nicole gasped, whirling around to face the Duke of Clayborough. Although the patio was dimly lit, she could see well enough to make out his expression, which revealed that she had not mistaken his tone.

"I am taking some air, not that it is any affair of yours."

"You know that's not what I mean."

"Do I?"

"Don't play games with me," he said ominously, taking a step toward her. "Why have you followed me to London?"

She gasped, not at his query, but at the accuracy of his suspicions. "How conceited you are! I have not followed you to London!" she lied, for she could never, ever admit that she had been lured to London by him.

"I do not believe you."

"That is your problem, not mine."

"No," he said slowly, "there you are wrong. It most definitely is *our* problem."

Nicole stood very still. She did not understand his meaning, not until his gaze slipped to her low decolletage, and then she drew in her breath sharply. Dangerous desire swept through her. It was a long moment before he spoke, their gazes locked. "I know you never come to London, Nicole. I know you have come because of me."

"You are arrogant, impossibly so," she retorted.

"And you are a liar."

"No!" she cried, trembling.

"Then why did you come to town when you never come—not since the scandal?"

Of course he would know about her fall from grace, just as everyone did, but that he should so openly allude to it distressed her. How sweet it had been to pretend that he had not known, or, even better, that he had not cared.

"Well? Can't you find a convenient excuse?"

Her cheeks flushed as she was reminded of the need to defend herself and lie to him. "I came to London last year—and that's the truth! Regina always begs me to come, just as she begged me now."

He took another step toward her. His smile was cold. "And to think that I thought you were an excellent actress."

Nicole backed away. "I am not acting."

"No? At this moment you are a terrible actress." He had taken another step closer, and again Nicole had moved backwards. "What's wrong, Nicole? Are you afraid of me?" he challenged.

Nicole instantly stood her ground. "Don't delude yourself!"

His smile was grim. "I didn't think so. You aren't afraid of me, are you? I know your game, Nicole. I am not a fool."

"I don't know what you are talking about."

He laughed, the sound disparaging. "Now this is acting!"

Nicole dug in her heels, furious with his mockery. "Think what you will. But I have no idea what you are raving on about!"

"You are stalking me, are you not, darling?"

"You *are* seriously deluded," she cried.

"Many women," he told her harshly, "have tried what you are trying. And none have succeeded in enticing me from Elizabeth. Do you understand?"

His words were like a slap in the face. She drew herself up, tears shimmering in her eyes. "I do not seek to entice you away from your precious Elizabeth!" she hissed. "And I suggest you return to her before she comes looking for you and finds you so intimately alone with another!"

"Elizabeth is at home."

"Warming your bed?" Nicole mocked.

He was stunned, but only for an instant. "The way you would like to?"

Nicole gasped. Her face flushed, but hopefully it was too dark for him to see. "That is the last place I would ever want to be."

"Really? Need I remind you of our past meetings?"

"Need I remind you that it was your behavior that was abominable?" she cried.

"I suppose it is first-rate for a lady to strike a man with her riding crop, not to mention ride about the countryside dressed as a boy."

Nicole drew herself up. "I'm leaving. I don't have to stand here and listen to your insults."

He caught her arm as she strode past him, whipping her around. She did not even try to pull away, knowing it would be useless. His face was too close to hers and she could not take even the shallowest of breaths. "Leave London."

"You cannot order me to leave the city!"

"You will not succeed in your endeavor, Nicole."

She jerked her arm free. "I am not trying to entice you away from Elizabeth! I have no interest in a philandering, immoral cad like yourself!"

"No?" He caught her chin in one large hand, and before she knew it his lips were very close to her own. "Really?"

"Don't do this! What do you seek to gain?"

They stared at each other. His jaw was clenched tightly. His fingers hurt her face. She waited for his kiss, expecting it, wanting it, afraid of it, and him. Suddenly he released her.

"It's what *you* seek to gain!" he said, his eyes blazing. "If you do not leave London, Nicole, I shall!"

"Good," she shouted back. "Good! Then go! Because you are not going to give me orders as if I were your precious Elizabeth!"

He stared at her, so furiously angry that he was shaking. For an instant Nicole was certain that he was going to strike her—or drag her into his embrace and ravish her. But the instant passed, and before she could blink he was striding across the patio, away from her. He flung open the doors and then slammed them shut.

Nicole sank down onto the hard stone bench in the corner of the patio, trembling violently. She did not see the stars overhead, she could not see anything but him. Then she covered her face with her hands, which still shook. What was happening? Why, oh why, had she ever had to lay eyes on the Duke of Clayborough?

Unable to fight her despondency, Nicole gripped the windowsill and stared outside into the bright, clear October sunshine. She heard footsteps behind her, but did not move, recognizing them as her sister's.

"Nicole, I am going driving in Hyde Park with friends. Charlie Ratcliffe has a new automobile. There's room for one more, why don't you join us?"

Nicole did not turn, not wanting Regina to see her face and ply her with probing questions. Although Regina had the innocent look of an angel, she was very clever, and she certainly knew Nicole as well as anyone, well enough to guess that something was seriously amiss. "I don't think so. I am going horseback riding this afternoon," Nicole said, although she had no such intentions.

Regina hesitated, then told her she would see her later and skipped out. Nicole sighed and turned away from the window, wandering aimlessly about the bright green morning room. Alone, she was haunted by the Duke's image, his words, their encounter. It was like being possessed by the devil, and how she hated it, how she hated him.

Aldric appeared. "My Lady, the Viscountess Serle is here."

"Don't bother announcing me, Aldric," Martha said, walking in. She took one look at her friend and turned to the butler. "Bring us tea, please, Aldric."

When he had left, Martha came forward to sit by Nicole on the couch. "I have never seen you like this,

Nicole, but somehow I had a terrible feeling that you would be down and out today. You must put him out of your mind. You must!"

"I cannot. Believe me, if I could, I would, but I cannot."

"There are other men in London, many other men. Please, let me introduce you to some of them."

"Oh, Martha, do not bother. My reputation precedes me."

"You can change your reputation, Nicole, if you try!" Martha said with temper.

"Perhaps I do not want to," she snapped back. Then she grabbed Martha's hand. "I am sorry, it is not you I am angry at."

"I know."

"Coming to London was a mistake, a big mistake. I am going home."

Martha looked at her for a long moment. "Running away? Like a coward?"

Nicole flushed.

"Will you let him chase you away?"

Nicole bit her lip. Martha did not know what had happened last night, but she did. Not only had he presumed to order her to leave London, he had actually challenged her by doing so. And he had dared to suggest that she was afraid of him! If she suddenly left, the Duke would think that he had succeeded in chasing her from town. He would also conclude that she was indeed a coward, and afraid of him. And apparently nothing was going to change his ridiculous assumption that she had come to London to *entice* him away from his precious Elizabeth anyway. She stiffened. That was a ridiculous assumption, wasn't it?

Had she secretly hoped to win him from his betrothed? What other possible explanation could there be for her behavior in chasing him to London?

Nicole trembled, dismayed with herself. She had never been more confused in her life. She would rather let him think the worst, which he was intent upon doing anyway, than let him win their private battle. And never would she admit, not to him or to herself, that she could have possibly harbored such foolish motivations in coming to London. "You are right. I must stay a little longer, then."

"Good! But you must not pine. This afternoon I am playing tennis at the club with several other ladies. We are missing a sixth. You are coming with us. It will be fun."

"I don't—"

"Nicole, you like tennis! You must get out and about and at least appear to have a good time, so he does not think you are pining for him."

"You are very clever, Martha," Nicole said, smiling reluctantly. "All right, I shall come."

They arrived at the Club-Near-the-Strand early that afternoon. Nicole rode with Martha in her carriage, and entered as Martha's guest. The attendant at the door obviously knew Martha, for he greeted her by name, checking her off of his list. Inside, they proceeded to find for themselves racquets and balls, then strolled outdoors to join the rest of their party.

Tennis was very popular these days, especially with young ladies. All of the courts were in play, except for the three that had been reserved for their group, and all of the players were women except for one pair of young men.

The rest of their party was already there, awaiting them. Five women sat around a table with a pitcher of lemonade, all clad in white shirtwaists and navy blue skirts, their racquets by their chairs. As Nicole and Martha approached, Martha murmured, "Oh, dear!"

Nicole missed a stride when she saw Elizabeth Martindale among the group. "You did not tell me she would be here!" And not only was the Duke's fiancée present, but sitting beside her was Stacy Worthington.

"I did not know. I am sorry, Nicole."

The ladies ceased their conversation abruptly as Nicole and Martha came to the table. "Hello," Martha said. "I thought we needed a sixth, and I brought Lady Shelton, but I see I have erred."

"So we can see," Stacy said. Her glance was contemptuous. "I brought my cousin, Elizabeth, to make the sixth." There was no mistaking her message that Nicole would not be welcome to play with them.

"I am sure we can work something out, Stacy," Martha said politely, although her eyes were daggers as she looked at the brunette.

"That's all right," Nicole said quickly, trying very hard not to stare at Elizabeth, for this was the first time that she was seeing her up close. The perfect little blonde sat quietly amidst the obviously hostile group. "I am tired anyway. I will just take your carriage and go home and send the driver back for you."

Martha gave her a look.

Nicole did not want to argue, and she gave Martha a look as well. Normally she would fight someone like Stacy, but Elizabeth's presence effectively quelled her natural inclinations.

"Perhaps that would be best," another girl said, a slender redhead wearing thin gold-framed spectacles. She glanced nervously at Nicole.

"I for one do not want to share my court time," Stacy said.

"Stacy!" Elizabeth reproved. She stood. "I do not believe we have met." Her smile was friendly. "I am Elizabeth Martindale, Lady Shelton."

Nicole was motionless for a long moment, staring at the proffered hand. Finally she remembered her manners and took it. "How do you do?"

"Thank you. Lady Shelton, I do not mind sitting out and watching. Really, I don't. You can play in my place. Actually, I am not overly fond of the sport."

Nicole's jaw tightened. The blonde's warm smile never slipped, and her blue eyes appeared genuinely friendly. Very coldly, Nicole said, "That is quite all right, Lady Martindale. You need not give up your court time for me."

"I really don't mind," Elizabeth said, only to be jabbed by her cousin, Stacy.

"If she wants to, let her go home," Stacy said.

Elizabeth pursed her bow-shaped mouth. "Stacy, we have enough time that all can play even if I choose to do so." She turned again to Nicole. "We can share court time, if you wish, but I warn you, I do tire easily." Her smile reached out to Nicole again, making her very uncomfortable.

"All right," Nicole heard herself say stiffly. "You may play first, though." She could not form a smile, could not even try.

All the girls took to the courts they had reserved while Nicole sat alone at the courtside table, trying to watch but still upset by Elizabeth Martindale's presence. The Duke of Clayborough's betrothed seemed to be a nice person. Nicole could not get over her apparent friendliness. But it had to be insincere, didn't it?

Nicole found herself ignoring all the players, except for Elizabeth, from whom she could not keep her gaze. She did indeed seem to tire easily, having no stamina or strength at all. She was the worst player on the courts, in fact, she could barely hit the ball. Was she, then, the kind of woman the Duke preferred? Some pale thin blonde? A woman too delicate even to play a passable game of tennis? A woman who had guileless blue eyes and an ever-ready smile? Nicole hated to admit it, but of all the girls she had just met, Elizabeth actually seemed all right. She was the only one who had tried to be friendly to her; even Martha's friends Julie and Abigail had looked at her cautiously and had not attempted to speak with her. Nicole knew that Martha felt badly for having talked her into coming.

Not even ten minutes later, Elizabeth walked off of the court, panting and perspiring and quite red in the face. "I told you I tire easily," she gasped, sinking down beside Nicole.

As much as Nicole disliked her, she quickly poured her a lemonade. "Are you all right?"

Unable to speak, Elizabeth fanned herself with a magazine left at the table, nodding. She drank thirstily. Finally she said, "Thank you. I just need to rest. I should not have come. I have not been feeling quite the thing these days."

"You probably have a touch of the flu," Nicole replied, twirling her racquet uncomfortably.

"I don't think so," Elizabeth said ruefully.

Nicole left her to join the others. For a while she played with Matilda, but it was a poor match, Matilda not even able to sustain a short volley. Stacy came over. "Let's you and I play," she said, rather snidely. "Matilda and Martha are more evenly matched."

Nicole agreed, making sure Stacy did not see her expression, which had darkened with determination. Stacy was the best player on the court and her intention was obvious; Nicole was certain the other girl hoped to trounce her. The girls moved to opposite sides of the court and began to volley. Nicole played often with her brothers at a public court not far from Lessing and she was a good player. Now she hit the ball easily to Stacy, who returned it just as easily to her. Gradually, both girls began hitting the ball harder and harder. Suddenly Stacy drove the ball furiously at Nicole, who managed to return it even more furiously, causing Stacy to miss it on the run.

Both girls were panting, eyeing each other with determination and dislike, and the play began in earnest.

Whack! Stacy hit the ball. Wham! Nicole returned it. Back and forth the girls volleyed, as hard as they could. Again Stacy missed, this time running right into the fence, unable to stop. By now the other ladies had paused and gathered to watch, with Elizabeth coming to stand at the fence as well. Stacy was panting; Nicole was not even breathless.

"Had enough?" Nicole asked sweetly.

"What they say is true," Stacy spat between great gulps of air. "You are no gentlewoman, you do not even play tennis like a lady!" With that, she stalked off of the court.

Nicole turned red with embarrassment and with anger, for Stacy had been trying to best her just as hard as she herself had been trying to win. The other ladies turned away, except for Martha and Elizabeth. Martha's mouth was pursed. Slowly Nicole walked over to them.

"Please forgive Stacy," Elizabeth said, touching Nicole's arm.

Nicole pulled her arm away.

"She is not usually so rude; I don't know what has come over her." Elizabeth's look was beseeching.

Nicole did not answer, and Elizabeth turned away.

"This was a mistake," Nicole said to Martha.

"I forgot that witch Stacy would be here, Nicole, and I am sorry, but you must consider that she is awful to everyone who is not in her charmed circle. Just because she is Northumberland's niece, she thinks the sun rises and sets at her whim. If she were not here, the other girls would have been more friendly, I am sure of it."

"Your friends were dismayed by my presence."

"That's not true, Julie and Abigail are just quiet and shy. Give them another chance, I promise you, you will see that they are very nice ladies."

Nicole nodded, and the two of them walked back to the group, now gathered around the table drinking lemonade. Elizabeth had pulled Stacy slightly away, and Nicole was shocked to hear her berating the brunette.

"How could you be so rude, Stacy? It was truly unbearable. You must offer your apologies to Lady Shelton at once."

"I? Apologize to that barbarian? Sometimes you are blind, Elizabeth, you see nothing but good in everybody!

Haven't you heard about her? She is an Unacceptable, and nothing will ever change that!"

"You are being very unkind, very uncharitable, and it is not becoming," Elizabeth rebuked. Then, seeing Nicole and Martha, she broke off. "Are you leaving already? Perhaps we should change partners, we still have court time left."

Nicole thought that it was incredible, this woman had defended her, a stranger, to her cousin, and now she was seeking, obviously, to salvage the afternoon for no one's benefit except Nicole's. "I have another engagement, I am afraid."

"Well, perhaps we will play another time," Elizabeth said. "It was so nice to meet you, Lady Shelton."

"And you," Nicole managed, unable to cut her.

She and Martha left and were soon ensconced in the Serle carriage in silence. After many minutes, Martha looked at Nicole. "What are you thinking?"

Nicole bit her lip, looking up at the roof with despair. "I am thinking that she is not only pretty, she is nice."

"Elizabeth is very nice," Martha said quietly. "There is no one who does not like her."

Nicole turned to stare out of the carriage without seeing Covent Garden, which they were passing. Is this why the Duke loved her? "Except me," she said sadly.

Martha had no response.

"Lady Elizabeth will be down shortly, Your Grace."

The Duke nodded, glancing once at his eighteen karat pocket watch and pacing restlessly about the small drawing room. It was unlike Elizabeth to be late, yet another fifteen minutes passed before she came down, dressed, he saw, not for supper and the theatre, but in a day gown. "Have you forgotten me?" he asked, surprised and teasing her somewhat.

Elizabeth sighed, coming to him. "I am so sorry, Hadrian, I did not forget. I fear I have made a grievous error."

She sank onto the couch and he sat beside her. "I doubt that," he said. "Are you feeling ill?"

"I am just exhausted. I played some tennis this afternoon and it fatigued me terribly. I should have sent you word then that I must cancel our engagement, but I so wanted to see you, and I did not want to disappoint you, either. I had hoped that a nap might restore my spirits, but I have only just awakened and I am still exhausted."

"Do not worry about me," the Duke said. "You should not have played tennis, Elizabeth, and I agree, you should return to bed for the evening."

She touched his hand. "You are not angry with me?"

"Of course not." Then his gaze softened. "But was it worth it? Did you enjoy your outing?"

She looked at him with dismay. "It was not very pleasant, Hadrian, indeed, I am still upset!"

"What has upset you?"

"Two of the ladies were terribly rude to another one, cutting her dreadfully—and one of them was Stacy."

"Stacy is not the kindest person we know."

"I felt just awfully for Lady Shelton, really I did. And there is no excuse for it! I know that apparently there was some scandal a few years ago, but that is in the past, and it is wrong to hold one mistake against someone forever."

The Duke was very still. "The woman they cut was Nicole Shelton?"

"Yes. Do you know her?"

He shifted. *She had not left town*. "Nicholas Shelton is now my neighbor, since I have come into possession of Chapman Hall. I dined with him and his family just before I returned to London."

"Well, she was terribly hurt by the whole incident, I could tell. She is very proud and she tried to hide it, the dear. I told Stacy just how disappointed I was with her."

The Duke cleared his throat. He was not merely uncomfortable with the conversation but with his past behavior and his innermost thoughts regarding the subject in question. It had been only the night before that Nicole Shelton had driven him into a nearly uncontrollable rage. It was only last night that he had been a hair's breadth from taking her in his arms and doing with her what he willed. It was very unseemly for him to be discussing Nicole Shelton with his fiancée, considering all that had happened between them. "Stacy needs to be told off now and again. If I do not see you tonight, shall we postpone supper until tomorrow?" *But why hadn't she left London? Did she still think to seduce him away from Elizabeth?*

"That would be wonderful. Hadrian, from what I understand, Nicole is not very welcome among the ton. And now that she is back in London, I think it is dreadfully unfair."

The Duke paused. If he dared to continue dwelling upon this topic he would have to conclude that he himself thought it was unfair, too, and worse, he did not approve of Nicole Shelton being cut today for a scandal long since dead. Nevertheless he did not want to discuss the matter, not with his fiancée, for to become her defender would be terribly inappropriate. "Life is rarely fair."

"That is not like you! I am going to invite her to join our poetry circle, and I will make sure she is accepted by all."

The Duke grimaced. On the one hand, what Elizabeth wanted to do was noble and right, but on the other, he was appalled at the thought of her becoming friends with Nicole Shelton. "Elizabeth, perhaps you will feel differently tomorrow. From what I have seen of Lady Shelton, she is a strong woman, and a few nasty gossips will not bring her down."

"I am determined, Hadrian," Elizabeth said matter-of-factly. "She needs friends like me, it is glaringly obvious, and I shall be her friend."

Very, very briefly, Hadrian closed his eyes. Could this coil possibly get worse? Nicole would not, could not, accept his fiancée's offer of friendship, could she? And why was she still in London? Was it because of him?

He should still be furious with her, but he wasn't. His anger had died last night. In fact, if he dared be honest with himself, he was very nearly elated that she hadn't left town.

The Duke had a terrible sense of impending doom.

Nicole was shocked the very next day when she received a prettily penned invitation from Elizabeth to join her poetry circle the following night at the Marquess of Stafford's. Regina looked at her curiously; the sisters were relaxing with tea and pastries in the green morning room. "What is it?" she asked.

Nicole reread the invitation, still unable to believe it was for her. "It is from Elizabeth Martindale. She has invited me to join a poetry circle."

Regina came to sit beside her sister. "You should go. How nice of Elizabeth."

Nicole carefully laid the invitation aside, her heart beating heavily. "Why would she invite me?" she asked aloud. "She barely knows me." But she couldn't help thinking of how ironic it was; the one lady in London to offer her friendship was none other than the fiancée of the man she had harbored a tendresse for.

"Because she is very nice. Undoubtedly she knows you are new to town, and is trying to include you in her set."

"You know her well?"

"We are friends. Go, Nicole," Regina urged. "You need to make some friends here."

Nicole bit back a reply. She could not possibly explain to her sister why she could not join Elizabeth's poetry circle even if she wanted to, which she surely did not.

Regina suddenly looked at the wall clock with a gasp. "Oh, I must go and change! Lord Hortense is taking me for a drive this morning!" She flew from the room.

Nicole could not even be distracted by her sister's ongoing infatuation with the miserable Hortense. Again she looked at the invitation. She knew there was no ulterior motive. Having met Elizabeth only once, she was certain of that. As Regina had said, Elizabeth was just being nice.

Abruptly, she crumpled the letter in her hand.

Why in blazes did she have to be so sweet? Why couldn't she be a shrew like her cousin, Stacy? And why in blazes did she have to pick on her, Nicole? Not only didn't she want her friendship, she didn't need it!

Nicole bit her lip hard. The terrible truth was that deep inside her heart there was a fragile part of her that would have loved to respond to the other girl's overtures. But of course that was impossible. They could never be friends. Not after what had happened between her and the Duke of Clayborough.

And because, in the darkest midnight hours, she still dreamed about him.

Quickly, before she could change her mind, Nicole penned a polite refusal and had it delivered that afternoon. She assumed that would be the end of it, for certainly Elizabeth would not continue to seek her out and befriend her. However, she was wrong.

Elizabeth came calling the following afternoon.

"Please sit," Nicole said rather formally.

"Thank you," Elizabeth smiled. She was rather breathless, a pale blonde vision in a tailored silver blue silk suit. "I am so sorry you cannot join us tonight, Lady Shelton."

"I am afraid I am already engaged," Nicole lied. She sat across from Elizabeth in a bergere, both of her hands clutching its smooth wooden arms.

"I hope you don't think that Stacy will be there, for she is not a part of our group, having no interest in literature." Elizabeth's eyes held hers.

Nicole was appalled that Elizabeth might think she was afraid to join the group because of her cousin. "Stacy is not the reason why I cannot come."

"Good." Elizabeth smiled. "As Hadrian pointed out, she has a tendency to be somewhat inelegant at times, and it is not just with you."

Nicole froze. "Ha—the Duke said that?"

"Oh, I was so terribly upset with her behavior that day, that when he came to take me to supper I could talk of nothing else. He approved of my having rebuked Stacy thoroughly."

Nicole swallowed hard, her face flaming. Elizabeth had sat with the Duke of Clayborough discussing her! Oh, how amused he must have been! It was too much! Absolutely too much!

"I have come to invite you to another affair, this one Saturday afternoon. I am helping Hadrian's mother, the Dowager Duchess, arrange it. Every year she holds an American-style picnic, an idea she apparently got from her Bostonian relatives. The young ladies bring a box lunch, which the gentlemen bid on. The winners, of course, sup with the ladies whose lunch they bought, and the proceeds go to a very needy charity—that of the poor orphans in this city." Elizabeth smiled. "It is always a big success, and a lot of fun. Everyone turns out. Won't you come?"

Nicole was aghast. If she put a lunch up for auction no one would buy it! She had not one doubt! "I am sor—"

Elizabeth was ahead of her, and she interrupted. "I didn't mean that you should bring a lunch, I understand why you would not want to. I only meant for you to come and enjoy the afternoon. In fact, I would be very surprised if your parents were not planning to attend, and I know Regina will be there."

"My parents," Nicole said stiffly, "are returning to Dragmore for the weekend."

"Oh."

Nicole was flushed, angry. Elizabeth had not intended to insult her by casually assuming she would not dare to bring a box lunch, but she had. She understood the humiliation Nicole would reap if she brought a lunch and no one bought it. Nicole's jaw clenched.

"I did not mean to upset you," Elizabeth said softly, worriedly. "It really is a good time, and not everyone is bringing a lunch. Being as I am one of the organizers, I am not, and you may certainly picnic with me and Hadrian."

"I am not upset," Nicole said as proudly as possible. "And whatever makes you think I would not come? With a lunch?"

Elizabeth's eyes widened briefly before she recovered. "Oh! I am so glad, then, that you shall participate!"

Nicole smiled grimly, knowing she had just foolishly committed herself to a course that could only result in disaster. But she was held in the throes of her own pride, and she could not back down, not in front of Elizabeth Martindale.

Saturday was a bright sunny day, an Indian summer day. The sky was cloudless, and the trees in Hyde Park all shimmered incandescently gold. Some two hundred noble ladies and lords had gathered for the occasion, all dressed in gay finery, their coaches and carriages lined up for miles behind them on the horse track that threaded through the park. Now everyone gathered around a platform that had been constructed for the festivity, one end of which was piled with picnic baskets all merrily painted and decorated in ribbons, bows, and lace.

Elizabeth clung to the Duke's arm, standing near the platform, facing the crowd, her eyes searching it. "I wonder if she decided not to come after all," she murmured.

"Who?" The Duke asked, shifting impatiently, unable to help himself from being bored. He had a weighty legal matter on his mind, and in a few hours he had a meeting at his home with several lawyers. His question was distracted, and he did not care about Elizabeth's answer, not, of course, until she responded.

"Nicole Shelton."

He froze, staring down at her. He had been relieved when Elizabeth had told him that Nicole had declined her invitation to read poetry. He had already decided that if Nicole accepted, he would seek her out and demand to know her intentions. But she had not accepted, and he had not had to seek her out. "I do not imagine she would come here," he said stiffly, although the thought of her actually being present made his pulse race.

"She said she would come, and she said she would bring a lunch." Elizabeth left off scanning the crowd. "I did not mean for her to participate in the auction, only to come and dine with us."

"You invited her to dine with us?" he asked incredulously.

"Of course. That was before she said she would bring a lunch. I assumed, so foolishly, that she would not, and how could I let her dine alone? But she knew I understood that should she bring a lunch, it would not be very popular, and it could be quite embarrassing, so she abruptly told me she would bring a lunch. She has so much pride—I admire her."

Hadrian's jaw clenched. "You need not admire her," he said, although he suspected he might, secretly, admire her too, although he was presently unwilling to admit it. He could also imagine how any gentleman here would love to buy her box and spend the afternoon with her in the privacy of a copse of trees, regardless of the scandal in her past. After all, they had eyes in their heads. He found he was distinctly displeased with the thought of Nicole Shelton sharing a picnic with some unnamed peer.

"But I do," Elizabeth continued. "I wish I was more like her."

"You are perfect as you are."

"Oh, Hadrian, you are being overly gallant. I must also confess that I have been worried that no one will buy her lunch."

"I am sure she has her admirers."

"Hadrian, you are a dear, but you are just not current, and how could you be when you are so rarely in town? I am not criticizing you," she added quickly, "for you know how proud I am of your skill in matters of business. But our set just does not forget. Sometimes they can be so cruel."

"I am sure you are exaggerating," he said, certain that the males present would compete eagerly for Nicole Shelton's company.

Elizabeth gazed up at him with a fond smile. "I hope you are right, but I have already taken care of the matter should it come to pass as I suspect it will. I asked our cousin Robert to bid on the lunch and he agreed, although he was not exactly charitable about it."

"Robert," the Duke echoed, thinking of Stacy's handsome, rakehell brother. He scowled, certain that it would not be long before Robert would have her flat on her back. "He is not trustworthy!"

Elizabeth gave him a curious look, surprised at his fierce expression. "Robert will behave himself, but I do not see him anywhere. Oh! Hadrian, she's here! She did come!"

Strangely breathless, the Duke turned slowly to follow Elizabeth's delighted gaze. Nicole stood with her sister, somewhat apart from the crowd, her head held high. She was a striking vision in a peach-striped suit and a straw hat adorned with one vibrant coral-colored rose. Her gaze met his.

He had forgotten to breathe, and he took a long, drawn breath. This circumstance was intolerable. How could he be standing here with his fiancée, whom he was genuinely fond of while lusting after another woman—one he could not have? This infatuation—this obsession—had gone on long enough. But how in hell was he going to end it?

Nicole wished she were anywhere but there. Regina was chatting gaily with two young ladies and their beaux, leaving Nicole momentarily excluded. She had been trying very hard not to look at him, but it was impossible.

Her glance stole to him again, and again she was frozen, for his regard was on her, too.

Nicole quickly looked away. She was trembling. Why did he have to be so magnificent? Why did she have to notice? Why did he have to be here, today, to witness what would surely be her humiliation? And why, why did he have to be betrothed to Elizabeth?

The bidding had begun. Nicole did not pay attention as one lady's basket, painted blue and white and tied with a pink ribbon, was sold to some young man for twenty-five pounds. Dread swamped her.

Even at the last moment, she should have backed out. It was the height of stupidity for her to have brought a basket lunch—no one would buy it. She silently damned her pride.

Several more lunches had been auctioned off, most of them for ten or twenty pounds. Nicole wondered if she could turn coward and leave now, before her box was put up on the block. She found herself staring at the Duke again.

For a scant moment, one that seemed to linger forever, their gazes locked. This time he was the one to look away, and when he did, it was to say something to Elizabeth. But Elizabeth had caught her eye and she waved gaily. Nicole did not know if she responded or not. She only knew that she could not turn tail and flee, not now. With a resolute sigh, Nicole turned to face the platform again.

"Have you seen Robert?" Elizabeth asked worriedly. "There are only a few lunches left, and I have not seen him."

The Duke was tense. "He probably tied one on last night and has forgotten all about his merry promise to you." It would not be unlike Robert, and in a way the Duke would be glad if the handsome bachelor never showed up to buy Nicole's lunch.

"Stacy!" Elizabeth called, seeing her cousin passing through the throng with her suitor, who had just bought her brightly decorated basket lunch.

Stacy came over, greeting her cousins. "This is Lord Harrington," she said, giving him a coy look. "He bought my lunch for thirty-five pounds!"

"How nice," Elizabeth said, pausing to greet him properly despite her distress. Then she took her cousin's hand and led her aside. "Stacy, where is your brother? Where is Robert?"

"Oh, I forgot to give you a message," Stacy said, smiling. "It slipped his mind that he has another engagement today, in Brighton, that he absolutely could not miss. He is very sorry."

Elizabeth paled.

Stacy laughed. "Don't worry, he told me about your scheme, and he didn't quite leave you in the lurch. He asked a friend of his to come to take his place."

"Who?" Elizabeth asked.

Stacy pointed. "See that redhead in the white linen suit? Standing next to the one in the plaid? His name is Chester something, and he will buy Nicole's lunch." She chuckled again.

Elizabeth stared at the disheveled young gentleman and his friend. Both of them were clearly foxed. "I will kill Robert," she said.

Stacy laughed. "I have to go, Elizabeth. Enjoy yourself!" She ran off with Lord Harrington so that they could watch the end of the auction.

Elizabeth returned to the Duke, stricken with anxiety, and told him what had happened.

Her lunch basket was put up for sale. Nicole's heart was in her throat and she wanted to die as the auctioneer held up the straw basket that was hers. She had known she should decorate it as Regina had done with hers, but she had tried, and the attempts had been dismal failures. Bows and ribbons had looked silly, as had lace and doilies. Flowers had seemed even worse, and finally, in disgust, Nicole had painted the basket a bright red. Everyone else had chosen to paint their baskets white or pastel colors, trimming them with ribbons and bows and other feminine fripperies. Nicole knew her basket was a terrible eyesore.

When the auctioneer held it up, his eyes widening, a chuckle escaped from the crowd. "Now what do we have here? Hmmm?" he murmured. "Whatever is in this unusual basket, it smells terribly good! Who's to open the bidding?"

Silence greeted him and Nicole's face burned. She tried not to look anywhere but straight ahead and at the plump auctioneer holding up her awfully colored basket.

"Come on, gents, let's start the bidding!" he called. "Who will start? Do I hear five pounds? Five pounds, gents . . ."

"Whose is it?" a man called out.

The identity of the girls who had made the baskets was no secret, but usually there was no need to ask which basket was whose, for the suitors made certain to find out beforehand. A few snickers rose at this question, the first of its kind that day. When the auctioneer looked at the small tag on the table and read her name out, Nicole truly wanted to die.

Silence greeted this announcement, and hundreds of eyes turned to focus upon her. Then someone said, "Ten pence!"

Laughter greeted the outrageously low bid.

Nicole was frozen. This could not be happening. They would make a joke out of her now!

"Ten pence," the auctioneer said, relieved to finally get a bid. "Do I have a pound? Do I hear a pound?"

"One pound," someone said, quite thickly.

Nicole's eyes, beginning to swim with tears, sought out this new bidder. He wore a white linen sack jacket and straw boater, and he was terribly drunk. Without realizing what she was doing, she cast an agonized glance at the

Duke and saw that he was furious, regarding the man in white as if he would dearly love to kill him. Then he turned to look at her.

The compassion she saw softening his face was too much to bear. It was the last thing she would have expected from him, and it threatened to be her undoing. Nicole took a deep breath, staring at the ground, using all of her willpower not to give in to tears. Suddenly someone took her hand. It was Regina. The bidding appeared to be stopping at a pound, which was as humiliating as if no one had bid at all.

"I hate them," Regina said. "We will go home."

Nicole could not answer.

"One pound," the auctioneer boomed. "Going . . . going . . ."

And then a deep, strong voice, one she knew so well, rang out, effectively hushing everything and everyone. "Five hundred pounds," the Duke of Clayborough said.

There was a stunned silence. Then the auctioneer beamed, slamming down his gavel. "Five hundred pounds!" he roared. "Do I hear five fifty? I have five hundred pounds . . . going. . . going . . . do I hear five fifty? And gone! Sold to the Duke of Clayborough for five hundred pounds!"

Elizabeth broke the astounded silence surrounding them. "Hadrian," she cried, "look at what you have done!"

The Duke winced. His gaze drifted past the top of Elizabeth's head and met Nicole's. She was wide-eyed, absolutely incredulous. During the bidding for her basket, his anger had flared at the mockery inflicted upon her by his peers. Grimly he had watched her trying to hide the anguish he could read behind her frozen, proud expression. He had wanted to throttle Robert's friend for his utterly ridiculous bid of one pound. And when he had realized that there would be no counter-offer, that Nicole's lunch would actually sell for such an embarrassing amount, he had come to the rescue with his staggering bid of five hundred pounds.

Nothing could have prevented him from rescuing her from the humiliation she was suffering, but he chose to think that he would have rescued anyone in a similar predicament. He would not inspect his motivations further than that. But would Elizabeth understand?

The Duke tore his gaze from Nicole, wondering just how long they had been staring at each other. "Elizabeth," he began awkwardly.

She clapped her hands. "How heroic you are!"

His eyes widened.

She clung to his arm, beaming. "How clever you are! Now everyone will know you have taken her under your protection, and no one will ever dare to make such fun of her again!"

"Do you not have a mean bone in your body?" he asked softly.

Confusion clouded her eyes.

He could at least reveal some of the truth. "It angered me to see her mocked so. I have always disliked any kind of abuse." He recalled, in a flashing instant, how his father had mocked his mother just as cruelly. And how Francis had mocked his own son, belittling the small boy at every turn, ridiculing every endeavor that child should have been proud of. That child . . . himself.

"I know, and that is why I lo . . . why I am so fond of you," she said, squeezing his arm. "People are waiting, Hadrian, you must go and get her basket." The auctioneer had begun the bidding on one of the last two lunches.

Even as he said the words, he felt a foolish disappointment. "I only bought her basket to save her from embarrassment, Elizabeth, not to share a picnic with her."

"Hadrian, you must! If you do not share her lunch, people will think I disapprove and am jealous. It will be a scandal, and you will have undone all the good you have just done. You must."

He was appalled. His own fiancée was sending him into the arms of another woman, one he coveted still despite his better intentions. Of course, Elizabeth could have no idea of how Nicole haunted his thoughts. "We will all dine together," he said firmly, even though he found this solution even more appalling than sharing lunch with Nicole alone.

"No, no," Elizabeth said just as firmly. "I am too tired. I have been here since early this morning preparing this event with your mother. If you intend for me to dine with you tonight, Hadrian, then I had better retire for the afternoon."

"I will take you home, then."

"And leave Nicole here, all by herself, to be a laughingstock? Don't be silly! I'll send your coach back." She gave him another warm smile, then turned to wave at the flustered Nicole.

The Duke made one last effort. "Elizabeth, if you leave now people will think you sorely put out."

Elizabeth laughed gaily, clearly in the best of spirits—as anyone could see. "To the contrary, they will know how much I trust you, and I shall shortly make it clear to all my friends how very pleased I am with how you have extended your protection to Lady Shelton."

Her words, of course, did nothing short of perturb him immensely. *How much I trust you.* How wrong she was.

There had been many women in his life. A gentleman was not expected to be faithful to a wife, much less a fiancée, and almost every gentleman kept a mistress. These other women were not of quality, so it did not matter. It was acceptable, even expected. And it was well known that gentlewomen were pleased that their husbands found comfort elsewhere, for ladies were too genteel to have to bear a man's appetites other than for the purpose of conceiving children. Yet dallying with Nicole Shelton was not acceptable. It violated not just Elizabeth's trust in him, but the code of honorable conduct all gentlemen lived by. Lady Nicole Shelton was another matter entirely, for she was of the aristocracy.

Hadrian walked Elizabeth through the throng, trying not to think at all. It wasn't easy. His heart was thudding heavily and his mind was not on his fiancée, not the way it should be, that is. He was too conscious of the tall, dark woman standing on the far side of the clearing. "I will see you tonight, Hadrian," Elizabeth said when they reached his coach.

The Duke nodded and helped her within, giving orders to his coachman. He stepped back as the coach moved off, and managed to smile as Elizabeth gave him a last wave of farewell.

Nicole watched them leaving, still unable to assimilate what had happened. Why had he bought her basket, and for such an incredible sum? How could he do something like that in front of Elizabeth, and did it mean something, portend something? She tried to warn herself not to be foolish, but her emotions were terribly raw, and the warning seemed trivial compared to how monumentally he had saved the day.

Now he was leaving. Nicole could not take her eyes from them, still standing beneath the thick, tall oak tree where she had stood since the auction began. Of course he was leaving, what did she expect? For him to come and claim her as all the other eager young men had claimed their ladies? Did she still harbor silly romantic fantasies about him? Did she still dare to be so foolish?

Regina gripped her arm, reminding Nicole that she still stood beside her. "I don't believe it," she whispered excitedly. "The Duke of Clayborough bought your lunch, oh, Nicole! This is a terrific sign! He has signaled everyone that you are not to be trifled with!"

Trembling, Nicole managed a weak smile. Is that what it meant? Or . . . could it mean something more? Hope leapt in her breast, although she tried to quell it. Regina did not know how many times she had been in his arms, and how nearly she had come to giving herself to him, fiancée or no. Maybe, just maybe. . . . "Lord Hortense is waiting for you. Go on, I'll go home and send the coach back for you." Nicole dared not complete her thoughts.

"Are you sure?" Regina asked, then she gripped Nicole's arm excitedly. "Nicole! Look!"

Nicole followed her sister's gaze and was startled. The Duke towered over everyone as he threaded his way back through the crowd, not approaching her, but the platform. Her eyes darted ahead of him. The auctioneer had long since stepped down and the only thing on the platform other than the cheerful white and green bunting and the array of hothouse roses was her vividly red basket. The Duke did not pause, heading unerringly for it. He picked it up. Then he turned, his gaze finding hers, and he began striding toward her.

Both girls were silent, each stunned for her own reasons. Regina broke the silence first. "I think . . . I think he intends to have lunch with you."

"I don't think so," Nicole said unsteadily, but her heart was fluttering like a hummingbird's wings.

The Duke approached. "Ladies," he said formally.

Regina came to her senses first, dropping into a beautifully executed curtsy. "Your Grace. I . . ." She looked from one to the other, fascinated by the intensity of their stares. "Lord Hortense is waiting for me," she managed breathlessly, then she turned and fled.

A silence fell between them, thick with a tension generated by the past and compounded by the present. Nicole broke it, wetting her lips nervously. "Everyone is staring. What are you doing?"

"Let them stare." He held out his arm. His expression was extremely grim. He had yet to smile or show any expression at all. "Shall we?"

Nicole blinked at his arm. "I—I don't understand."

His jaw tightened. "We are dining together, Lady Shelton, as I have bought your basket."

She lifted her tremulous gaze to his. "But . . . Elizabeth?"

"Elizabeth approves heartily, and had she not been so fatigued, she would join us as well."

A terrible disappointment which Nicole had no right to experience swarmed over her. "I see." She turned, but did not take his arm, having no intention of doing so. Her lips pursed tightly together as the secret bubble within her burst. Her fantasy balloon, filled with dreams, popped. What had she secretly hoped? That he had broken off with Elizabeth, here and now, so publicly? Broken it off to be with her? She was nothing more than a case of charity, for both of them, although the Duke's motives could certainly be more suspect.

Realizing Nicole would not take it, he dropped his arm, his eyes darkening. Together they strode across the clearing until they came to a spot shaded by three flaming red maple trees. Nicole glanced around as the Duke set the basket down. They were in full sight of everyone, but that was to be expected, as was the curiosity they aroused.

"Did you bring a blanket?"

"What?"

Roughly he repeated his question.

Nicole shook her head. The Duke shed his hunter green hacking coat, spreading it out for her. Nicole could not thank him, and instead of settling down upon it, she stared at it.

"I assure you, I do not have lice."

She whipped her gaze to his. "This is ridiculous. You really expect us to sit here and dine together civilly?"

"I don't just expect it," he said, eyes glaring, "I demand it."

Anger blazed in her eyes and she squared off against him. "I do not need your charity!"

"To the contrary," he said smoothly, "you certainly do."

"I did not ask you to buy my basket!"

"No, you did not."

"So why did you?" she cried, shaking.

He stared, the vein in his neck throbbing visibly. "Because it appeared that you had no other rescuers," he finally said.

"How gallant you are!" Nicole exclaimed, stung to tears. "I did not need rescuing, and certainly not by you."

"Perhaps you should let go of your pride for one moment, Nicole. How many times has it caused you to act rashly? How often has it created more problems than it has solved?"

"That is not your concern!"

"I suggest you sit down," he said, his own face flushed with anger. "Before we make a spectacle of ourselves and undo all that has been done."

"I do not need your protection," she said bitterly. "Go protect sweet Elizabeth."

"*She* does not need my protection, and fool that I am, I appear to have extended it to you, as ungrateful as you are. Now sit." Abruptly he pushed her down to her knees, and Nicole had no choice but to sit rather quickly upon his coat.

He dropped down on the grass beside her, and when Nicole was about to bounce up, he gripped her hand, keeping her anchored where she was. "We are still the focus of much attention and a fight will fuel the gossips. Haven't you had enough of gossip, Nicole?"

She closed her eyes briefly. "Yes."

He released her hand.

When she opened her eyes, she found him staring at her face intently. Nicole lifted her chin, blinking back the hot tears behind her lids. She could fight it all she wanted, deny it all she wanted, but she had needed his charity, she had needed him to rescue her, and now, if she were brutally honest with herself, she wanted even more.

There was no mistaking his strength. It emanated from him in a charisma no one could deny. If he were hers, she would go into his arms and weep for the past, which she could not change, and cry for a future she wished so desperately to have. He would be a haven, an inviolable refuge she so desperately needed, an invincible shield between herself and the rest of the world. But he was not hers, he belonged to Elizabeth; and this situation was nothing short of impossible.

He was still watching her, too closely, as if he could read her most private thoughts and feelings. Nicole found herself drawn in by his power, swept away by it. Once again, she was powerless to look away from him. She was afraid he knew her innermost thoughts. Afraid she was revealing too much. She did not want him to know, or even suspect, what she was afraid to acknowledge herself.

His anger had died. The telltale flush was gone. His eyes were again the rich gold of sherry, a tiger's eyes, dangerously mesmerizing. Nicole became still, lulled into utter motionlessness, anticipation overwhelming her.

He suddenly lifted his hand. There was no question that he was going to touch her. He reached for her face. In that moment, Nicole yearned for him desperately. And just as suddenly he dropped his hand and his gaze, reaching abruptly for her box lunch.

"Perhaps we should eat," he said.

A vast disappointment consumed her. She could not respond. She could only watch him open the basket and begin to remove the items within.

It had only taken that one instant for all of Nicole's turbulent, bruised emotions to congeal into one fiery ball of explosive desire. Although she sat motionless, determined to hide her response to him, she was trembling, her body tight and taut, almost painfully so. He had been about to touch her, she was certain of it. She could not seem to think of anything else.

His glance lifted and they stared at each other. The glitter of his gaze was as bright as hers, unconcealable.

Oh, dear God, Nicole thought, as violent desire crashed over her. In that moment, she did not care about anything or anyone other than herself and the Duke, for every leaf trembling above them, every sweet blade of grass around them, the festive crowd scattered through the park, the entire world, had just faded into oblivion. There was nothing and no one in existence other than herself and the powerful, virile man sitting opposite her.

Only her eyes moved, her body incapable of motion. They roamed over every exquisite feature of his face, lingering on his sensually sculpted lips, recalling the heat and power of them, the devouring hunger. They roved lower, over his broad shoulders and massive chest, clad in nothing but a simple white linen shirt, the top two buttons open and revealing just a glimpse of thick, dark chest hair. His long, powerful legs were encased in tan breeches, his high boots black and gleaming. Startled, her gaze flew back to his loins, where a thick rigid arousal strained the tight fabric of his pants. For a long moment she could not take her eyes away, could not move, could not breathe. Her body strained and quivered against the confines of her skin. Suddenly some kind of death seemed imminent, one that would take her straight to heaven.

He cursed. "Damn it. This is intolerable. This cannot continue."

Nicole wet her lips, shamelessly thinking about his kisses, about how it felt to be in his arms, and about another act no lady would even contemplate.

"I suggest," he said sharply, "that you think about something—anything—else."

Her most private desires revealed. She lifted her gaze to his and was consumed—gladly consumed—by the heat she found there. "I can't," she whispered.

He let out his breath harshly. "If you do not," he said roughly, "then we have a very long hour ahead of us."

She looked at him, his words drawing her attention away from her indecent thoughts.

"I think an hour will suffice, if we can endure it."

"An hour will suffice," she said slowly. "It is appropriate for us to share a picnic for an hour, and then, of course, you must return to Elizabeth."

"Yes."

The words were more effective than buckets of ice water thrown over her head, and she smiled almost sadly. How could she sit here and covet another woman's man, one who was practically her husband? It was terribly immoral, as immoral as her scandalous physical desire, and Nicole was ashamed. For a few brief moments, she had forgotten all about Elizabeth, and she would have done anything to be alone with the Duke, alone in an intimate way. But how could she have forgotten? She must not forget! This man was taken, he did not belong to her, but to another. She could never have him, and to sit here openly coveting him was the height of dastardly behavior.

"Let's not linger," she said abruptly, not daring to look him in the eyes. "Let's just go. You can tell all your wonderful friends that I was most charming, but I had a terrible headache. And you must thank Elizabeth, of course, for her gracious part in this rescue."

He was silent; she felt his stare. She refused to look at him. She felt like she was dying inside, bit by bit, a completely different kind of death than the rapturous one she had sensed was so near just minutes before.

"You are right," he said hoarsely, closing the basket and standing. He held out his hand, but Nicole knew better than to take it, afraid to touch him, although she wanted nothing more. Careful not to meet his gaze, careful not to let their hands brush, she handed him his jacket, waiting as he slipped it on.

Side by side, they walked across the park toward the long line of carriages. As they passed one picnicking group after another, the Duke nodded and said a brief hello, but Nicole did not look at anybody, too absorbed in her own ragged feelings. The sanctuary of the Dragmore coach could not come soon enough, yet a stubborn part of her wished to forestall their impending separation, for this time she knew it would be forever. On Monday she would return to Dragmore.

The coachman opened the door to the shiny black lacquer coach. Nicole was about to step in when the Duke grabbed her arm, restraining her. She had been careful not to look at him, but now her gaze flew to his. As their glances locked, an unnamed emotion, intimate and powerful, flared up between them both.

"Nicole," the Duke said huskily, "we must talk."

"Is there really anything to discuss?" she asked sadly.

His jaw clenched. Many seconds passed and he did not answer, apparently doing battle with himself. Then his grip tightened. "We will talk. My coach has not returned. You may give me a ride back to Clayborough."

"I will not do any such thing!"

But the Duke had made up his mind, and he was propelling her up the steps and into the coach. Nicole landed ungracefully on the back leather seat. Her eyes widened as his body appeared in the doorway. He sat down beside her, pulling the door closed behind him.

"Clayborough," he told the coachman. "And then you may take Lady Shelton home."

"Yes, Your Grace." The coachman disappeared and the carriage rolled forward.

"Why are you doing this?" Nicole cried.

He turned to face her. His eyes were blazing and Nicole responded immediately—her own turbulent desire had been roiling inside her since he had first approached her with her picnic box.

"What are you going to do?" he asked.

Had he sensed her intentions? Or was she so obvious—and he too astute? She managed a smile, but it was forlorn. "I am going to leave. I am returning to Dragmore on Monday!"

He stared at her. Nicole could hear her own racing heartbeat. The way he was looking at her and his proximity was making it nearly impossible to think, but she was almost hoping that he would protest her plans. He did not.

He turned his head away from her, revealing the hard taut line of his jaw, and he stared out of the coach's window. Disappointment claimed Nicole. She wanted to weep, and she wanted to lift her hand and reach out and touch the sleeve of his hacking coat at the same time.

She did not.

He faced her again. "Then this is goodbye," he said tightly.

"Yes."

Another pregnant moment filled the void between them.

"Nicole . . ."

She waited, waited for him to protest—or declare himself.

"You are unique," he said. "You are not like the others."

It was the greatest compliment he could have given her, she realized, and tears began to spill gently down her cheeks.

"Don't cry," he commanded, his fingers settling on her face. "Why are you crying?"

She shook her head wordlessly, her eyes locked with his. He leaned forward. She didn't move, even knowing as she did what was about to come, even knowing that she should resist. But this would be the very last kiss, and she wanted to remember it forever.

Cupping her face, he placed his mouth over hers.

It was a tender kiss, as if there were real affection between them. Then his hand slid down to her neck and tightened; his mouth moved more insistently, with sudden urgency. Nicole's tears had stopped.

She cried out in encouragement, gripping the lapels of his coat. Without hesitation she slid forward beneath his body; he came down on top of her. His arms were around her; her arms were around him. Their tongues mated in a fever of need, and she felt him settle the thick hard heat of his manhood in the cleft between her legs. He began moving against her with growing abandon, with insistence.

She did not want it to end like this. She did not want to let him go. She did not want to lose him to another woman, no matter whom she might be; she wanted him to belong to her.

He surged up against her body. Nicole clung to him, letting him do as he willed. The knot of tension within her was growing. At any moment it would explode, eclipsing her.

He stopped moving. He lay atop her heavily, panting. Nicole was also panting. She realized that her legs were wrapped around his hips. She wanted to die, but not of shame. At that moment, shame was the last thing on her mind.

"The carriage has stopped," he finally said, his words clipped. "It stopped some time ago."

Nicole closed her eyes.

"If I were a scoundrel, we would finish this here and now." The Duke moved off of her.

It was a good long moment before she could force herself to sit up. He sat rigidly beside her, watching her. "This is not why I took a ride home with you."

"I know."

"This is not what I intended."

"I'm not sorry."

He stared. The urge to succumb to the sadness came again with renewed intensity. And again she waited for him to tell her not to leave London.

"Goodbye," the Duke said softly. Abruptly he swung open the door and stepped out of the carriage, away from her.

Nicole had one last look at his face as he slammed the door shut. It was stern and impassive. Unforgettable. He was unforgettable. She hugged herself, trying to find comfort in the gesture, the space around her now empty and cold. Alone and cocooned by the dim light, she felt her eyes fill with tears.

The carriage began to move away; she thought that she could feel him watching her. And then, she thought she heard him.

"Nicole." Whisper-soft, urgent.

She did not dare look out the window, she did not dare. Instead, bravely, resolutely, she wiped her eyes and turned to face the darkness.

Martha followed Nicole upstairs and into her bedroom. She had not been at the picnic, having had other obligations, but of course, she had heard in precise detail what had happened. "Are you going to tell me," she began, then stopped, staring at Annie, the young maid, who was folding up garments from a huge pile upon Nicole's bed and packing them into her luggage. "Where are you going?"

Nicole told Annie that she could finish later, if she would, and turned to her best friend. "Where do you think? I am returning to Dragmore."

"But you can't leave London now!"

"Why ever not?"

"Because the Duke has accepted you, and soon others will extend themselves to you as well. Your life is about to turn itself around—you cannot leave!"

Nicole bit her lip, looking away. She had to leave, she knew that. Yesterday had been goodbye. It had been final. There was no other choice.

Yet Dragmore no longer seemed a sanctuary. Dragmore no longer lured her as it had; suddenly her home seemed terribly isolated. The temptation to stay was real and strong, and only slight encouragement would be needed to change her current resolve. Yet she must leave. They had said goodbye. To remain in London where the Duke of Clayborough was—with his fiancée—would be nothing short of self-inflicted abuse. "It nearly breaks my heart every time I am with him," she said softly.

"Oh, Nicole," Martha murmured, gripping her hand. "If you must know, I think he is taken with you, I do, and I am certain that is why he bought your lunch. But he is a man of honor and he will never leave Elizabeth. Everyone knows she is struggling with some kind of mysterious fatigue, and that she left the charity picnic because she had overexerted herself in its preparations. He took her to the theatre last night, although they did not stay long."

Nicole paced across the room, her back to her friend. "I know, Martha, and that is why I cannot stay. I must confess the truth to you, as well. I—I am afraid of what I might feel for him. I—I covet him, improperly, when he belongs to another. It is shameful." Nicole glanced at Martha, wondering if her friend could possibly understand exactly what she meant.

And if Martha guessed at the meaning behind her words, she did not let on, the subject being too intimate even for the best of friends. "In a way you are right, you should return to Dragmore, until you can get over him, but now the timing is ripe for your re-entry into society, and you *will* forget him sooner or later anyway. If you stay, you can find someone else. I am sure of it."

"I don't want someone else."

"Why should she find someone else?" Regina asked, standing in the doorway. "And where is Nicole going?"

"You should knock," Martha chastised.

Regina smiled sweetly. "Why? Does my sister have something to hide?" She closed the door and turned excitedly. "What happened yesterday? Nicole—you should have seen how the Duke of Clayborough was looking at you!"

Her sister's words tore at her, making her quiver hopefully when she knew it was hopeless. "How was he looking at me?" She hadn't wanted to ask the question, but she could no more hold it in than bite off her own tongue.

"As if you were the only woman in the world."

"Please, Regina," Nicole sat down abruptly. "You are mistaken."

Regina came to sit beside her, pulling up an ottoman. "And you fancy him as well, I could tell, it was so very obvious."

"It was obvious?" Nicole cried, turning crimson, utterly aghast.

"Obvious to me," Regina assured her. "Is it true that you took him home in your coach?"

"Yes, it's true." Nicole did not blush. And she remembered every single detail of what would be their last and final encounter, and she always would.

"Elizabeth is nice enough," Regina was saying, "but nothing compared to you. I am praying that the Duke will throw her over for you."

"Regina!" Martha rebuked sharply. "Do not give your sister foolish, impossible dreams. He will do no such thing."

"You have become an old fuddy duddy," Regina flung. "With love, anything is possible!"

Nicole got up and left the two girls to argue among themselves. She knew that Martha was right and Regina was wrong, yet the romantic in her secretly wished it were not so. She could not shake his golden image from her thoughts, nor their parting yesterday. She was certain, now, that he had indeed called her name, and that it had not been a figment of her imagination. Why had he called out to her? Had he really looked at her as if she were the only woman in the world? Nicole rubbed her throbbing temples. She must not listen to Regina who knew nothing of men and their ways!

Martha gained her attention. "You must not leave London, Nicole, I am begging you. The Duke never stays in town long, and he does not venture out very often among the set. Of course your paths will cross a few times, but no more, I am sure of it. If you leave now, you are resigning yourself forever to a life of spinsterhood in the country. Do not do it."

Nicole looked at Martha steadily, thinking about how the Duke had turned her entire life upside down. Before she had met him at the Adderlys', she had been content. There had been no foolish, painful yearning in her heart for what she could not have. She had loved her life just as it was.

No longer. Having met him just once would have been enough to never forget him. But it had been more than once and more than just an introduction. Like the sun, his aura was golden, powerful, blazing. Like the sun, it was an inescapable life-force. He had disturbed the pattern and harmony of her life irrevocably. For even when he was not present, like the sun, he was still there, he would always be there.

She could not imagine herself at Dragmore anymore, her life at the estate suddenly seemed unbearably lonely. She had never been lonely before, not ever. But now the feeling consumed her and she hated it.

"I don't know. I must think."

Regina also encouraged her to stay, but Nicole tried not to listen to her younger sister, who kept hinting at the possibility of love blossoming between her and the Duke. How naive and young her sister suddenly seemed, to believe in such adolescent dreams. Besides, Nicole had to face something else, something she could no longer deny. She could not dislike Elizabeth, no matter how hard she tried. She did not know her well, but she did not have to. She was one of the kindest people Nicole had ever met. Even if Regina were right, even if the Duke would leave Elizabeth and choose her, Nicole could never live with herself for inflicting such injury upon the other young woman. There was no possible happy outcome to this miserable situation, except, of course, to forget the Duke of Clayborough.

As if one could escape the sun.

The Duke entered the foyer of his London home, his hair tousled, his face ruddy from the brisk bite of the wind. He was returning from a long morning ride through the park and then along the Thames. He had ridden as if pursued by demons, hard and fast and reckless, in an attempt to escape his thoughts. He had been successful, for it had taken all of his attention to control the mount he had chosen, a particularly mean and dangerous brute of a stallion.

He had not eaten breakfast and a brunch of smoked salmon and whitefish was awaiting him when he entered the dining room. He was not surprised to see the Dowager Duchess there, for he had seen her carriage outside. Normally his mother's presence would be welcome, but not today, for he had not a doubt as to why she had come. His unshakeable ill humor increased.

"Good morning, Mother," he said, kissing her cheek and taking his seat.

Isobel returned his greeting, pouring him tea, which he drank black. "We raised one thousand five hundred and twenty-eight pounds yesterday," she said, her tone conversational. But her look was not.

Hadrian leaned back in his chair. "Does that include the five hundred pounds I contributed?"

Isobel's eyes settled upon him sharply. "Yes, it does."

"Please, I know you are dying to tear into me. Feel free."

"I do not know if I wish to tear into you or not," Isobel said, staring at her only child. "I was horrified to see her so embarrassed, and your rescue thrilled me. On the other hand . . ."

He raised a brow.

"Hadrian, please tell me there is nothing going on between the two of you!"

"Do you not think," he said firmly, "that this topic of discussion is most inappropriate between mother and son?"

"As your father is dead, I have little choice."

"There is always a choice, Mother."

"Hadrian?"

"I did seek to protect Nicole Shelton from further abuse. Let us leave it at that."

Isobel worried her hands in her lap. "Elizabeth loves you, Hadrian."

He winced. "And I am fond of her. I have always been fond of her. I was at her christening. I bounced her on my knee. As soon as she could walk she began following me everywhere. I am not going to renege on our engagement, Mother."

Isobel knew that now she could believe him completely, that he meant what he said. His words could not ease her anxiety. For she knew only too well how matters of the heart tended to take their own course, with no consideration for the consequences. And she was so terribly afraid that she could see it happening between her son and Nicole Shelton.

She was not one to judge, God knew, having once succumbed to such illicit passion herself, but it had been different with her. Francis had been a cruel, unfaithful husband. Hadrian's words jerked her from her thoughts. "I am worried about Elizabeth," he was saying. "I am convinced that you are right and that she is ill. She is still losing weight, and she tires even more easily than she did when I first arrived in London. I have summoned a physician to attend her."

"Oh, I am glad," Isobel said. "Does she know?"

The Duke looked at her grimly. "Not only does she know, this time she does not protest."

Mother and son stared at each other, absorbing the implication of this. Until this very day Elizabeth had kept insisting that she was fine, yet now, accepting a doctor was tantamount to admitting that something was, indeed, quite wrong.

Suddenly Isobel thought of Nicole Shelton, as different from Elizabeth as the night was from the day. Oh, she could understand Hadrian's attraction to her, for she was strong and intelligent, vibrant and healthy, the kind of woman that would be a lifetime mate for someone as powerful and dynamic as her son. If it were not for Elizabeth, despite the scandal, she would have heartily approved of such a match. Suddenly, she prayed that she had not made a terrible mistake, and she regretted the invitation she had sent that morning.

The Earl and Countess of Dragmore returned to London late the following day. Nicole had not left as yet, torn between returning to Dragmore, which she now dreaded, and staying in London, where she could hope for no more than a glimpse of the Duke from time to time. After supper, Jane invited Nicole into her rooms for a chat.

Nicole frequently spent time with her mother, but not at night, and not in her rooms. It was obvious that there was something her mother wished to discuss with her. She seated herself on a cherry red ottoman in front of the fire, regarding Jane expectantly.

Jane poured them both sherry and sat down near her on a small striped loveseat. "Darling, I've heard that you've been packing."

Nicole accepted the drink. "I had decided to return to Dragmore, but now I am not certain." She lifted her gaze to her mother's, wanting to confide everything to her but knowing she could not.

"Because of the Duke of Clayborough?" Jane asked softly.

Nicole restrained a gasp, her startled gaze flying to her mother's gentle expression.

"I also heard about the charity picnic," Jane said, reaching out to squeeze her hand.

"Oh, Mother." A lump had formed in Nicole's throat. She quickly averted her glance, studying her clasped hands.

"You can confide in me, darling."

"I can't."

"Nothing you will say can possibly shock me, and besides, I am certain I already know what you are feeling."

Nicole dared to look up at her mother. Of course Jane would be shocked if she knew what had passed between her daughter and the Duke. Nicole had no intention of telling her, but the rest of her burden was just too great. "You probably felt this way about Father," Nicole managed shakily. She was stunned when she had uttered the words, stunned with what they revealed, not to her mother, but to herself.

Jane was equally stricken, not having been certain until now just how strong her daughter's emotions were for the Duke of Clayborough. "I ran away from your father," she said, startling Nicole and causing her to spill some of her sherry. "He had agreed to marry me, but I was certain he had done it only because he had compromised me." She would not tell her daughter the truth, that she had, in fact, seduced the Earl, climbing into his bed when he was quite drunk. "I loved him so much I could not bear to be his wife unless he loved me as well."

"I think I can understand."

"Do you love him? Because that is what I felt for your father from the moment I laid eyes on him."

Nicole turned her face away, staring into the fire. For a long time she did not speak, afraid to answer, afraid of the answer. Finally, she said, "He does not love me. He loves Elizabeth, who is kind and good. And I like her, although at first I hated her. He merely . . . desires me."

Jane grimaced. "Love between two people is a rare and precious gift, Nicole. Rare and precious. I believe that if he really loved Elizabeth, he would not want you. But that is irrelevant. The Duke is a man of his word and he will never break his engagement. I am glad you see the situation so clearly, that you understand that. You are young and strong and I know you can forget him."

Nicole turned to face her mother, her eyes brimming with tears she refused to shed. "I will *never* forget him, Mother, *never*. But that doesn't matter at all."

Jane stood and embraced her daughter, comforting her as she had so many times when she was younger. When

Nicole was calm, she sat again. "How I wish I could help you through this."

"I am fine."

"It all will work out for the best, Nicole. Trust me. After what he did Saturday at the picnic, everyone now knows that the Duke has accepted you, and others among the set must do so as well. I know that right now you are hurting, but leaving London would be a vast mistake."

"That's what Martha said."

"I want you to stay," Jane said, gripping her hands. "This is your chance to regain acceptance into society, and to find someone who will love you as much as you love him. Don't shake your head! You will get over the Duke! You can either be a popular and much sought after lady here, or a lonely spinster at Dragmore. I had given up, and it has hurt me terribly to see you spending the best years of your life alone in the country, just as it has your father. We are both begging you to stay, Nicole, and take advantage of what the Duke has done."

Her parents rarely asked her for anything, and Nicole could not refuse them. Truthfully, she did not want to refuse them. The part of her that refused to forget the Duke did not want to leave London because of his presence here, did not want to return to Dragmore, where she would, if she were honest with herself, merely pine for him.

"Do you really think that I might gain acceptance and become popular?" She tried to envision the kind of future her mother wanted for her, a future where she held court among the bachelors until one of them, her Prince Charming, claimed her, but she failed. If she could forget him and have a life she had never before wanted, if she could be happy again, with such a life, then she must hope for such an advent, but she did not think for a minute that it was possible.

"I am certain," Jane said.

"I will stay."

A delighted smile crossed Jane's face. Then she hesitated. "If you are staying, I must tell you about an invitation I have accepted for us. It is for a hunting weekend."

"I love to hunt," Nicole said, momentarily brightening at the thought of such a weekend.

"The Dowager Duchess of Clayborough is hostessing it."

"Mother, I can't." Yet even as she said the words, Nicole's mind raced with the possibilities: She could hunt; the Duke would be there; and Elizabeth certainly could not hunt.

"I do not know the Dowager Duchess well, but I have spoken with her from time to time over the years and I admire her greatly. I think she feels the same way about me. We have always gotten on fabulously well. Only thirty families have been invited to this fête, thirty of the most powerful families in the realm. There will only be one or two eligible young men there, Nicole, but there are many eligible bachelors among these families. I want them to see you. That the Dowager Duchess has specifically included you in her invitation is a great act of generosity. As the Duke did Saturday, she is extending her protection to you as well. And Nicole, this is only the beginning."

It would hurt to go and see the Duke there with Elizabeth, yet her heart soared at the thought of seeing him again. At the same time, she understood exactly what it meant to have been invited by the Dowager Duchess of Clayborough to her home for such a weekend; it was an invitation that could not be refused. "Why has she done this?" Nicole asked, dazed.

"Perhaps because, like her son, she is a decent woman who cannot abide injustice," Jane said simply. "I know this is an awkward position for you to be in, and while I want you to go, if you are still too heartsore, I will respect your decision and we will say you are ill."

"If she has invited me directly, then I am going," Nicole stated. And she firmly told herself that she was going to begin a new life, one that would soon gain her many new suitors and great popularity, but her heart laughed back at her, and told her it was a lie.

It wasn't until the Monday afternoon following the charity picnic that Elizabeth was feeling better. Although the Duke had taken her to the theatre the evening of the picnic, they had had to leave the performance early so that Elizabeth could retire. She had remained abed for two days. Although she ran no fever, she seemed to be in growing pain and without the will to get up. The physician the Duke had summoned had not been certain what might be afflicting her, finally telling the Duke that she might possess a weak heart, in which case she must rest as often as she needed to, and forever avoid exerting herself.

"But then why does she now say that her body hurts her?" the Duke had demanded, irritated with the doctor's inability to tell him exactly what was wrong and exactly how to cure it.

"That I do not know, but perhaps it is a touch of the flu as well. You said that this is the first time she has been in any discomfort, have you not?" the physician asked.

"That's correct," the Duke replied. The doctor told him to give her some laudanum for her discomfort.

By Monday afternoon Elizabeth was sitting up and smiling and feeling much better. Tuesday she went out with her maid to do a little shopping, and it seemed that the doctor had been right, she had had a flu and her heart was weak, which explained why she tired so easily. The Duke was relieved.

Elizabeth's worsening condition had not just dismayed him, it had begun to frighten him. The Duke was a man used to being in control. He was a man with a will of iron and a strict self-discipline. Should business matters go awry, he worked ceaselessly to correct them, for as long as necessary, doing what had to be done with the utmost patience and perseverance. It had been many years now that he had run the ducal empire, and he was used to an extraordinary amount of power. In this instance, though, he was suddenly powerless. His fiancée's condition was beyond his control, but fortunately she had become better as mysteriously as she had taken a turn for the worse.

It seemed suddenly as if his entire life were tilting in a precariously topsy-turvy manner. The normal routine he was accustomed to, one predominantly devoted to hard work, no longer existed. And it was not just Elizabeth's illness, which seemed to defy explanation. There was also the matter of Nicole Shelton and his indefatigable interest in her. That, also, defied explanation, and exercising control where she was concerned seemed to be a losing battle. The Duke was not a man who had lost very many battles.

Although the Duke had many pressing matters with which to occupy his time in London, he made it a point during this short interlude to visit the Stafford home twice daily to check upon Elizabeth's progress. It would have been thoughtless and rude of him not to. But what was even ruder were his own thoughts as he looked upon his fiancée.

His thoughts came unbidden and unwanted. They consisted of an unseemly and surreptitious comparison. Elizabeth was unwell, so small and so fragile. Nicole Shelton's image formed in his mind. She was neither unwell, small nor fragile, but precisely the opposite. She was vibrantly healthy and vitally alive. On one particular visit, during which Elizabeth had fallen asleep as he sat beside her, it occured to him that he felt not the slightest bit of desire for her and that he never had. In fact, he had never even kissed her, except once on her eighteenth birthday, and then only because he knew she expected it. And it had been a chaste kiss.

He had done more than kiss Nicole Shelton. He had touched her intimately, with his mouth, his hands and his own loins.

Elizabeth was going to become his wife and he knew she would be an exemplary one. He was not sure how he would perform with her in bed, indeed, he had never thought about it until now, a highly inappropriate time to speculate upon such an event, but he assumed that when the moment came he would manage.

As he stood there looking down upon her as she slept upon the chaise in her sitting room, her face young and innocent, a niggling doubt arose. For the first time in his life, he questioned having been betrothed to his cousin while she was an infant and he a child. And it was because of Nicole Shelton.

Her intrusion into his life and his mind had become dangerous.

If he was a man obsessed—and it seemed that he was—his obsession had become worse.

He was sorry he had gone to the picnic the other day, sorry that he had rescued her. He wished like hell it could have been some other man. In the same breath, he knew he was lying to himself.

If only . . .

Shocked at where his thoughts were about to wander to, the Duke cut them off. Life was concrete. Circumstance begat circumstance, reality led to reality. Fantasizing about what might be was for the weak, the foolish and the romantic—not for someone like him.

He was glad she had left London, he told himself, glad and relieved. Her presence seemed to precipitate passions in him which he was not able to control, and he had been in complete control of himself since he was a very small child—he prided himself on his self-discipline. Now it would not be put to any further tests.

On Tuesday evening Elizabeth was well enough to join him at an at-home at the Earl of Ravensford's. It was a small intimate gathering. The Duke could not but be slightly dismayed when he saw that two of the guests were the Earl of Dragmore and his wife. They were two of the last people he wished to converse with, but to avoid them would be the height of rudeness. With some determination, he sought them out before supper.

He introduced Elizabeth and chatted with the Earl and Countess amiably. As he did so, he was aware that the Countess of Dragmore was studying Elizabeth discreetly. He had an uneasy feeling that she might know more than was appropriate about his relationship with her daughter, but he shook the feeling off as a foolish one, or, perhaps, a guilty one.

By the time supper was over, Elizabeth was looking pale. Quietly, before the men adjourned separately to their port and cigars, Hadrian took her aside. "Are you all right, Elizabeth?"

She gave him her fetching smile, the one that made her almost beautiful. "You worry too much, Hadrian, like some old fuddy duddy."

He had to smile. "Do you wish to go home? You look tired."

She hesitated. "I don't wish to appear rude and I do not want to interrupt such a pleasant evening."

"I will explain everything to our host," the Duke stated. While he did so, Elizabeth excused herself to attend to matters in the powder room. The Duke was in the hall awaiting her, alone except for a servant who held Elizabeth's fur-lined mantle. He was momentarily startled to see the Countess of Dragmore slip into the hallway.

And she was heading directly for him.

"Your Grace," she said, gliding towards him, "I know this is unusual, but might we have a word?"

It was more than unusual, but the Duke nodded. He wondered what she wanted, and wondered even more at her daring and disregard for convention. She was only ten years or so his elder, and still strikingly beautiful. Servants loved to talk, and the one holding Elizabeth's cape, pretending not to see them, would soon be spreading rumours about the Duke of Clayborough and the Countess of Dragmore. However, if she didn't care what might be said, then neither did he. It occurred to him that Nicole's disregard for convention might have come from her mother, who, he knew, had once been a stage actress. The Duke leveled his regard upon the butler. "Kindly leave us a moment."

The man disappeared.

"Thank you." Jane smiled softly. "My husband and I both wish to thank you for what you did the other day at the picnic."

The Duke was expressionless.

"You not only saved our daughter from a terrible embarrassment, you have made it possible for her to regain acceptance in society. We cannot thank you enough."

"Elizabeth is very fond of her. I could do no less." But as the Duke said the words, he wondered just how Nicole Shelton would regain acceptance in society if she had departed London.

"Nicole is fond of her, too. And I am glad she is better." There were no secrets in London.

"Thank you." Hadrian's expression did not change, but he was certain that Nicole Shelton was not fond of his fiancée. He would be stunned if she actually were.

Elizabeth appeared and greeted the Countess. "I couldn't help overhearing," she added. "I do admire your daughter terribly, Lady Shelton. Please, send her my regards and tell her I will call on her as soon as I am able."

"I shall." Jane smiled.

The Duke could not refrain from frowning. Nicole had left London, hadn't she? "Are you returning to the country, Countess?" he asked politely.

"Not immediately. Nicholas will be returning to Dragmore in a few days. But I must stay. After all, it is rare that I have both of my daughters in town, so I must take advantage of the situation, and of course, chaperone them properly."

"I see," the Duke said. *She had not left the city after all.*

He should be angry. Just a few days ago, her presence in London had infuriated him. But where was his anger now? It eluded him.

He wondered if she had deliberately lied to him, but instinctively knew that she hadn't. He had avoided thinking about the day of the picnic, but now he could do nothing but remember it. Something had flared up between them, something he was afraid to inspect too closely, something that was more than just passion. And it was because of that something that she had said that she would leave London immediately. It was because of that something that he had been relieved that she was going. Yet she had not gone.

Elizabeth noticed his change of mood instantly, and commented upon it in the imposing Clayborough coach as he took her home. "Are you upset, Hadrian? Have I done something to displease you? Did you wish to stay at the Langleys'?"

He found it hard to focus on his fiancée when his mind was spinning. "Of course you have not displeased me."

"I am glad," Elizabeth said with a smile. "As soon as I feel better I shall call upon Lady Shelton."

He was silent. The feelings rushing in upon him were overwhelming and turbulent, chaotic and nameless, impossible to escape. He did not want to identify them. He would not even try to. For just a moment he had the strangest sensation of being tossed about in the ocean by a rough wave, tumbling him every which way and making it briefly impossible for his feet to find the ground. And then the moment passed.

His senses sharpened and two potent, powerful images came to his mind. He saw Nicole at the Adderlys' masque, so inappropriately and daringly costumed as a gypsy. He had rescued her then, although at the time he had not dwelled upon it or his motives, yet any fool would have been aware of the undercurrents swelling in the crowd as they prepared to trounce her for her boldness. Instantly he had approved of her so no one would dare but do the same.

And he saw her as she had been at the charity picnic, frozen with humiliation and trying to hide it, so damned proud.

He did not want his fiancée calling upon Nicole Shelton. Yet he could not, would not, take away the chance he had given Nicole to be accepted by his peers. "That is very thoughtful of you, Elizabeth," he said.

Elizabeth smiled happily. The Duke did not.

The Sheltons arrived at Maddington, the home of the Dowager Duchess of Clayborough, Friday afternoon. Maddington had belonged to the Clayboroughs for more than five hundred years, and once it had been a vast estate that had been the cornerstone of the family's possessions in Derbyshire. Over the years the land had been sold off, and now it was a small estate of some hundred park-like acres. The manor still contained the original keep built in late Norman times, but so many additions, in so many different fashions, had been made to the original edifice that one had to be an architectural expert to discern when each part of the sprawling, turreted and domed structure had been built.

Upon arriving Nicole and Regina were shown to the room they would share, as were their parents. Supper was at eight, they were told, and they were asked if they would like hot baths drawn and tea served. Both girls replied in the affirmative.

While Regina flopped down on one of the four-poster beds, Nicole wandered to the tall windows overlooking a small balcony and the sweep of emerald-green lawns below. Her heart was in her throat and she was trembling nervously. She wondered if the Duke was already there.

In the middle of the week, when gossip held that Elizabeth was quite sick and bedridden, Nicole had thought that they would not come—and she had been disappointed. She knew it was the height of foolishness to want to see him, when she could not have his attention and when he would be with his fiancée. Yet she could no more rein in her emotions than she could a maddened, runaway horse.

But Elizabeth had recovered. Nicole had become an avid fan of gossip, pretending great interest in all the goings-on of the set, much to Martha and Regina's suspicion, while actually only seeking information about the Duke. She knew he had taken Elizabeth out twice this week; there was no reason the couple would not come to Maddington this weekend.

She sighed, aware of how foolish she was, watching a carriage pulled by six white geldings roll up the long, graveled drive, and not caring who it was because it wasn't his majestic black coach with the blazing trio of lions embossed upon the doors.

"What a beautiful home," Regina sighed lazily. "Lady Isobel is renowned for her elegance."

Nicole nodded, having barely looked at the room. The walls were covered in a blue and white fabric, the sofa in rose damask, the beds done up in mountains of white lace with blue and white pillows. One huge, cherry-colored Oriental carpet covered most of the floor, and as the room was large enough to accommodate two guests in separate beds quite comfortably, it was no small feat.

"She is also renowned for her skill in matters of business," Nicole remarked. Before meeting the Dowager Duchess she had heard of her. Who hadn't? Very few women ran several business enterprises as she did, and none of them were of the peerage. Nicole had known she was reputed to be attractive, but her reputation was more that of a strong, clever woman, and before Nicole had met her she had expected someone else entirely, someone more handsome and more masculine, not a woman of timeless feminine beauty and extraordinary kindness.

"Renowned? Notorious is more like it," Regina tossed. "They say she is named after an infamous ancestor of hers, a woman who had several husbands and was the mistress of a Turkish sultan and the king."

Nicole smiled, not believing such a tale. "A Turkish sultan? Which king?" she asked dryly.

"I guess it was one of the Conqueror's sons," Regina said. "It was ages ago."

Another carriage was rumbling up the drive, and Nicole quickly turned to the window. But it was not him.

"What will you do, if he comes with Elizabeth?"

"Of course he's coming with Elizabeth," Nicole said sharply.

"Maybe he won't," Regina said, ignoring her sister's tone. "Maybe he's so smitten with you he—"

"Regina, please stop it!" Nicole cried, wringing her hands. If her sister continued with her silly schoolgirl fantasies, she would drive her out of her mind—and feed the tiniest sparks of hope that Nicole was determined to douse. Nicole did not want to hope. Hoping was too painful.

"But she doesn't hunt," Regina said pointedly. "So why should she come?"

Nicole controlled her temper. "You are not hunting either tomorrow, and neither is Mother. Nor is Father, for that matter!" The Earl had pulled a muscle in his leg earlier in the week and was under strict instructions to recline whenever possible, and riding was out of the question.

"I guess you are right," Regina said, when a knock on the door interrupted her, signaling the arrival of their tea.

Gratefully, Nicole let the servant enter. She continued to keep a not-so-discreet watch on the driveway below. But by the time they went downstairs, the Duke of Clayborough had yet to arrive. And as it turned out, Regina was right. Elizabeth was not at supper that night. But then neither was the Duke.

The hunt was scheduled for nine that morning. Prior to that, all those participating attended a large breakfast, where spirits ran high. Nicole was as excited as the other guests. The night before she had been disappointed that the Duke of Clayborough had not been present and that he was not even at Maddington. She had not slept well. But now all traces of fatigue and disappointment vanished as her pulse quickened in anticipation of the upcoming hunt.

Most of those hunting that day were men, but several ladies were present, including the Dowager Duchess. She had the reputation of being an excellent horsewoman. Every year she had several fabulous hunting weekends, and invitations to these events were highly coveted and hard to obtain.

The Dowager Duchess' guests were always the creme de la creme of English society, and this weekend was no exception. Those eagerly awaiting the call to mount up consisted of several dukes, a half dozen marquesses, many earls and the Prince of Wales. There were a few foreigners present as well, including several royal members of the House of Hapsburg and two Russian ex-patriate noblemen. The one thing everyone had in common at these gatherings, other than power and blue blood, was their love of horses.

At the close of the breakfast meal, Isobel rang a small silver bell to gain everyone's attention. "Shall we?" she asked smiling, her eyes sparkling.

A rousing cry greeted Isobel's words as everyone lunged to their feet, including Nicole. She turned toward the doorway with an excited smile, her mind no longer on the Duke. But then she froze.

He stood there, dressed for the hunt in tan breeches, gleaming black high-top boots, a scarlet hunting jacket and a top hat. His gaze was fixed upon her.

Nicole had learned last night that, although he and Elizabeth had been invited for the weekend, they would not be coming. Elizabeth was ill again and confined to her bed. A maid told her that speculation ran rampant as to what, exactly, was wrong with the young lady, and the several physicians who had attended her could not reach an agreement upon what malady afflicted her. Seeing the Duke now was a distinct shock, but not an unpleasant one. Already keyed up, Nicole began trembling.

He swept his gaze away from hers and strolled casually to his mother, kissing her cheek and offering her a lazy good morning. He was promptly surrounded by many of the guests, all greeting him heartily and offering him sincere condolences for his fiancée's health.

Nicole left him responding politely to his mother's guests and followed those who were already gathering in the courtyard outside. Soon the rest of the group joined her as the grooms began bringing out their mounts. Everyone had brought their own hunters with them, including Nicole. Although she had wished to bring her bay stallion, that would have been foolhardy, for he was too much to handle riding sidesaddle, which propriety dictated she must do. She had brought a big black gelding instead, and now she went to him and stroked his neck. He snorted and shook his head, sensing her excitement, restlessly moving around her. But it was not the sixteen-hand hunter she was thinking about, it was the Duke of Clayborough.

He was here, he had come after all. *Without Elizabeth.*

Instantly she hugged her gelding's neck, her back to

the small crowd. Whatever was she thinking? It did not matter that he had come alone. Even though Elizabeth had not come, the few words they might share, the few moments, were only that, a few moments, and could not be more. Not ever.

She had to stop her errant thoughts, she had to. Not just because they were hopeless, but because hunting was a dangerous sport and she needed all of her concentration to participate in it. It was easier to focus on the hunt than on her heart.

But just when it seemed that she might successfully do so, he stopped behind her. She did not have to turn to see him to know it was he, nor did he have to speak to identify himself. She just knew.

"Good morning, Lady Shelton." The greeting was offered politely, yet Nicole thought that she heard more.

Reminding herself to be casual, reminding herself that no one but she herself could possibly know how rapidly her heart beat, she turned to face him. Their gazes met instantly. It was a moment of extreme intimacy even though the courtyard was a madhouse, filled as it was with two dozen restless horses, their excited riders and all the grooms. He could not seem to tear his gaze from hers, and Nicole felt the full force of his power, for he seemed to be attempting to reach into the depths of her heart and soul. In that instant, she knew that something had changed between them. She dared not consider what it might be. "It will be good sport today, the weather is perfect," she said as lightly as she could.

"Nevertheless," he said, moving to the black's side and checking the girth, "we have a large group. Hunting with so many riders invites accidents. Stay far to the back."

Nicole's eyes widened in surprised protest, for she never rode in the back, although that was where ladies were supposed to ride, and she had no intention of doing so now. Then it occurred to her that he might be worried for her safety. She had a flashing remembrance of how he had rescued her at the charity picnic. Was it possible? Did he actually care for her, just a little? She found herself staring up at him. The Duke stared back at her.

Very abruptly he held out his hands, cupped for her knee. Nicole allowed him to help her mount, hooking her leg over the sidesaddle and taking up her reins. "Thank you."

"Good hunting," he said curtly, turning away.

"Good hunting," Nicole echoed to his back. She watched him as he strode away to his own mount, a big black stallion with a bold blaze and two socks. Nicole exhaled, her senses running riot. Her hunter began to dance impatiently, sensing her mood, and Nicole had to concentrate on calming him.

Five minutes later they were off. The hounds had picked up the scent of the fox and were braying madly, racing across the first meadow. Nicole allowed herself to be jostled into the back with the other ladies as they started. Now, as the herd of horses and riders cantered across the rolling meadow, following the hounds, she couldn't help but be attuned to where the Duke was, riding far ahead of her at the front.

The group began to spread out as they approached the first fence, a low stone wall. Whoosh! Whoosh! Whoosh! A dozen horses cleared it, then a dozen more, some nearly in tandem. The group was stretching out as each rider found his own pace, the ladies falling back. Nicole moved forward, ahead of the ladies. She passed the Dowager Duchess whose first look of surprise changed to a smile.

The several gentlemen whom she then came abreast of were not so charitable. They were more than startled as she galloped by them, they were shocked. Only a Russian nobleman grinned at her daring.

A small stream lay ahead. Her hunter flew over it gracefully without breaking stride and Nicole laughed in sheer pleasure, caught up now in the thrill of the madcap ride. She passed another rider, recognizing Elizabeth's father, the Marquess of Stafford. He too looked rather stunned at her bold riding, but Nicole didn't care. Her hunter was in a controlled gallop and Nicole was steadily moving him into the middle of the pack. A large chicken coop blocked the trail. Ahead of Nicole, two bays took it, one after the other, the first horse catching his back hooves on the top rail and stumbling on the other side. The other rider was so closely behind the first that Nicole decided there might be an accident, and she urged her mount to veer slightly, already collecting him. They soared over the coop at an angle, and she was glad to see that the two riders had managed not to go down. A second later she passed them as well.

Two miles later, Nicole was behind the Duke and the huntmaster, who were by now far in the lead. A four foot stone wall loomed ahead and she had time to watch the Duke take it effortlessly, and admire him as he did so. Her hunter, eager to move to the front, was running hard now. Nicole fought to check him, the wall loomed, and they hurled above it. They landed smoothly and she let him run.

He stretched out into a full gallop, Nicole leaning as far forward as she dared without sacrificing her precarious balance. Her hunter's nose touched the flank of the Duke's stallion. He turned his head, saw her, and looked absolutely stunned.

Nicole laughed exultantly as she drew abreast of him.

"Get back!" he shouted as they galloped side by side, their two huge hunters tearing up the ground, their powerful hooves thundering loudly and nearly drowning out his words. "Dammit, get to the back!"

"Watch out," Nicole cried, still laughing. They were three strides from another four-foot hurdle, this one made of split logs. The Duke had no choice but to turn his concentration to his own mount. Both riders collected their horses simultaneously, and in perfect unison, they soared over, landing side by side and stride for stride.

Moments later he turned to her again. "I mean it, you fool!" he shouted, furious. "You will kill yourself! Get to the back now!"

"I always ride in the front," she shouted back defiantly. But Nicole was enjoying every moment of the wild ride—and his anger. Beneath her thighs, the horse was hot and powerful, a ton of horseflesh she controlled with only her skill and her body. And beside her, astride his own powerful, thundering stallion, the Duke had just as potent an effect on her senses, handsome, male, virile, and now, enraged.

"Slow down," he commanded, shouting above the braying hounds and the furiously pounding hoofbeats. "Ahead is a treacherous in-and-out."

Nicole only shot him a grin, letting her hunter move out even faster. Behind her now, the Duke cursed.

The in-and-out was treacherous, with only a stride between both fences, but Nicole was showing off and loving it. She took both fences a tad recklessly, yet faultlessly, too. Moments later the Duke moved alongside her again. One glance at his face showed her how angry he was, but stoically he was accepting that he could not make her slow down without interfering dangerously with her. They galloped together, the two hunters well-matched, running in tandem. They did not speak again. The sound of the animals' heavy blowing and the thunder of their hooves made it almost impossible. Nicole was overwhelmed now by the feel of the hot, wet horseflesh under her legs, by the physical sensation of being one with the racing, powerful animal, by the speed at which they were traveling—and by the Duke's proximity.

An hour later the hunt had ended and all the riders had gathered, the last few ladies included. Nicole had allowed herself to drop to the back of the group as they returned to the manor, holding her horse to a tight walk, ignoring the animal's protests. She understood the beast, for she felt the same way herself. Although tired from the long, difficult ride, she was too exhilarated to want to stop, and if it had gone on, she would have eagerly continued, too.

The Duke, of course, rode far in front. He had left her the moment it was over, tight-lipped, eyes blazing, apparently too angry even to speak to her. It was not his place to chastise her, yet she had a feeling he would. Nicole was still too exhilarated to be apprehensive. She had never enjoyed a hunt more!

She was so wrapped up in the afterglow that it did not register at first that the other ladies were regarding her quite coldly, with the exception of the Dowager Duchess, who was riding somewhat ahead of the ladies and was oblivious to their stares. When Nicole realized that she was the object of their disapproval she wanted to laugh in their faces. Because they could not ride as she did, because they did not have the courage to ride as she did, they condemned her for enjoying the sport the way a man would. Nothing could dampen the joy that she was feeling, not today. She slowed her hunter even more, not wanting their company and allowing them to move ahead of her. A moment later she realized her mount's gait was off.

Frowning, she pulled him to a halt and dismounted, patting his corded, wet neck. An inspection of his front left hoof showed her that a small stone was wedged there. Worried, Nicole pried it loose, afraid it had been there during the hunt, which could mean a serious, even crippling, injury to her mount. To her relief, an inspection proved that the pad was only tender; he had only picked up the stone recently and soon he should be as good as new.

"You were superb, darling," she crooned, stroking his soft muzzle. "So superb." The Duke's image filled her mind.

She turned and with a sigh saw that the riders had all

disappeared around a corner on the trail. No matter, she would walk the black the rest of the way. Taking his reins, she led him along the path.

The Duke of Clayborough was steaming with anger. His stallion felt it, skittering about and tossing his head restlessly. Nicole Shelton might be the finest rider he had ever seen, but she was a reckless fool. Right now he wanted nothing more than to put his hands on her and shake her until she admitted how wrong she had been.

No one attempted to talk to him for they sensed his mood, and Hadrian rode alone, off to the side of the group. Their laughter and chatter filled the quiet morning, echoing in the woods. The Duke heard nothing of what they were saying as they excitedly retold and relived the hunt. He was just too angry.

And the least of it was that she had defied him, although that was incredible too. He had ordered her to the back—and she had laughed at him and ridden to the front. In that moment, he could not think of a single person, male or female, who had ever disobeyed an express command of his.

She was lucky that she hadn't had a serious accident the way she had been riding, she was lucky she hadn't caused a serious accident. He had seen many terrible accidents resulting from careful riding in this sport, much less reckless riding. People broke their necks and were killed, and he had seen one young lad paralysed. One day she would become the sport's hapless victim too, if she continued to hunt like that. By God, it would have been bad enough if she had been riding astride, but she had been riding sidesaddle! It was lunacy!

He took a deep breath to steady his own raging nerves. His pulse was still racing, adrenaline still coursing through him. He could not shake her image from his mind as she had been during the past two hours. Nearly six feet of superb woman riding like a bat out of hell, exhilaration written all over her face.

He could still hear her laughter, wild and reckless. He could still feel her beside him as they rode like demons possessed on the straining, racing hunters. A surge of heat swept his body and he actually trembled.

She rode like a savage. She had been, he had to admit, magnificent. She would be, he knew without a doubt, equally magnificent in bed. In his bed. Suddenly, in that instant, he wanted her so much he was ready to drag her into the woods and do as he would, right then and there.

He took a few more deep breaths to ease the most agonizing state he had ever been in. Then, not at all assuaged, he turned to search for a glimpse of her. To his shock, she was nowhere in sight.

Abruptly he wheeled his stallion around and rode up to the ladies riding last in line along the trail. "Where is Lady Shelton?"

Looking surprised, they all turned to stare behind them. "I don't know, Your Grace," the Countess Arondale said. "She was behind us a moment ago."

Hadrian grimaced and rode off to find her, wondering what could have possibly happened now. Five minutes later he came upon her a mile down the trail, where it was still wooded and shady. She was walking her mount, in no hurry at all. He rode directly to her. She saw him and the air heated up and sizzled between them.

"What happened?" he said brusquely.

"He picked up a stone."

The Duke abruptly slid down from his black, trying to concentrate on the issue at hand. He handed his reins to Nicole without a word, but their fingers brushed. He cursed silently, kneeling beside the big black gelding and picking up its hoof. "It's not too bad, but he should be walked back." Finally, his gaze lifted to meet hers.

She stood very still. Her cheeks were flushed from the wind and the sun and her eyes were silver and bright.

"I will walk back with you," he said, handing her the reins and taking those of his stallion.

"You don't have to," she said, not moving.

He didn't answer. He was too aware of her. He moved ahead of her with long, purposeful strides, as if to outwalk her. He heard her following.

They walked in absolute silence, only the breeze in the trees making any noise. Yet Hadrian knew not only that she was behind him, but that she was just a few feet away and to his right. He could feel her presence and something else, something he was too experienced not to recognize, the heavy sexual tension that was enthralling her as much as it enthralled him.

Why did he want this woman so much? Was it because she was forbidden to him? Was it because she was so different? Was it because she was, on the one hand, so proud and strong, and on the other, so vulnerable? He wanted an answer, but knew he would not find one.

He was sweating. He wanted to rip his coat off but he was suffering from arousal and he did not want to expose it. To expose himself and his own sad lack of control. He closed his eyes briefly, telling himself that if he did not have control, he was nothing more than a beast. No more than Francis. He had managed to fight the temptation she offered these past weeks, he must not surrender now. While he fought with himself, he listened acutely to her: to her footsteps, to her soft, slightly shallow breathing. And finally it was Nicole who broke the silence.

"Why did you come back here?"

He stopped abruptly, but did not turn. His hunter pawed the ground restlessly. "It occurred to me that, after your performance earlier today, you might have done something else as reckless and as rash."

Nicole had paused too, abreast of him. "But why did you come back?"

He faced her. "Foolishly I thought you might be in some distress."

She smiled.

He grimaced.

"You came back to rescue me."

The Duke did not deny it. "Apparently it is a new habit of mine."

"I don't mind."

"You minded the other day."

She looked him in the eye. "No, I didn't. That was a sham."

They stared at each other. The moment was pregnant with too many possibilities. It was too intimate. The Duke shattered it purposefully. "You rode like a maniac today. Tell me, are you always so reckless? I begin to fear that you are."

Her chin came up. She had opened her jacket and her lush bosom heaved. He remembered that she did not wear corsets. "I did not. I am an excellent rider and I took no real chances."

"No real chances? You took every chance! One day you're going to kill yourself!"

Her voice, when it came, was whisper-soft. "Do you care?"

He was not able to answer, he refused to answer—refused even to inspect his own feelings. "There is a stream off of the trail," he said, breaking the silence that had fallen between them. "You must be thirsty. Let's water the horses and have a drink."

The stream was just a few minutes from the trail. Both horses were now cool enough to drink and they eagerly lowered their heads to the water. The Duke stood apart, unmoving. Nicole dropped to her knees and unabashedly began cupping water in her palms, drinking thirstily.

He watched her. Again he was struck by how she was everything the ladies he knew were not. She drank with abandon, spilling as much water on her shirtfront as she managed to imbibe. Then she splashed her face, briefly lifting it to the sunlight seeping through the trees. He was as unable to take his eyes from her as he was unable to stop wanting her. Suddenly aware of his regard, she stilled and looked up.

There was awareness in her gaze. Awareness and anticipation. He knew she would not refuse him, not today, not now. Hadrian found himself walking toward her. His heart was hammering, a dull roar in his ears that shut off any protest he might mentally make to himself. Slowly she rose to her feet.

His hands closed over her arms. "Tell me no."

She shook her head, denying his request. "Yes."

He covered her mouth with his, all of his resistance crumbling in that precise moment. There were no games, now, no pretenses, not for either of them, and Nicole instantly flung her arms around his neck, clinging. Hadrian embraced her as if she were something wild and precious which he had caught and which at any moment he might lose.

Their tongues mated in fierce abandon, a prelude to how they, too, would soon mate.

They sank down to their knees in the wet, loamy bank. He could not claim enough of her. His hands moved over her jacket, pushing it open. Her soft cries encouraged him. He pushed her onto her back, delving into her shirt and the chemise she wore below. He touched her bare breast.

He let her flesh fill his palm and overflow. He was a quiet, controlled lover, but now he wanted to groan like an animal, he wanted to express his profound pleasure. He did not, stroking her ceaselessly instead, aware of the feeling of explosive need—and heady jubilation—rising up in him.

Nicole gasped in pleasure as he ran his hands over her flesh, over her hard, tight nipples. When he pushed her clothes aside and lowered his face to her breasts, another groan escaped her.

He had to at least call her name, he had to. "Nicole."

She clutched at his longish hair, at his head. "Hadrian." It was a sigh.

He did not pause, teasing her distended, yearning flesh with his mouth and tongue. "Tell me to stop."

"No. Don't stop, Hadrian, don't ever stop."

He closed his mouth on one pink tip and at the same time closed his mind to the knowledge of what he was doing. Nicole arched off of the ground. He sensed how precipitously she hovered near her climax and his body went wild in response. Not being the kind of lover who freely murmured endearments and promises, he made his promises with his body.

Promises which, in a saner moment, would be impossible to keep.

Nicole began returning his caresses aggressively. Her hands were on his skin, beneath his shirt. His own hands were sliding up under her skirts, along her cotton-clad thighs. She cried out his name when he touched her. Never had his name sounded so wonderful before.

Determination to see her fulfilled in his arms swept him. He would do everything in his power, too, in order to achieve this. Sweat beaded his brow. "Die for me, Nicole," he commanded, touching her, kissing her.

Soon he was rewarded. She cried out, arching in abandon in his arms. He felt her spasms, strong and rhythmic and intense against his palm. And when she had stilled he felt an intense satisfaction which he had never experienced before.

She looped her arms around his neck. "Oh," was all she said.

That one word conveyed everything. It had been her first orgasm. She was not experienced. She was undoubtedly a virgin. She was certainly Lady Shelton. The Duke's gaze swept her, from her flushed face to her spread thighs, where her skirts were tossed up high on her waist. He had been about to reach for his trousers, to free himself, but his hand was frozen. Now was not the time for his conscience to intrude, reminding himself of who she was—and who he was. But it was too late. He closed his eyes, fighting himself. Thinking too clearly. He had given her her first climax, and if this continued, he would be her first lover. It was so very wrong.

Without a sound he wrenched himself away from her, flinging himself onto his back in the wet, muddy grass.

Nicole sat up. She was shaken to the core of her being. Although she was certainly more knowledgeable than most young women as far as the topic of sex went, she had never even considered the possibility that it could be an earth-shattering experience. Still breathless, she looked at the Duke of Clayborough.

He lay on his back in the muddy grass, as stiff and unmoving as a board, except for the fact that he was panting and out of breath. Nicole remembered how abruptly he had moved away from her and she understood that while she had experienced all that lovemaking could offer, he had not.

She trembled, her gaze sweeping over him. He was the most magnificent, virile man she had ever laid eyes on, and seeing him in such a state of raw desire fed her own hunger, a hunger she had thought assuaged. Something else swept her too, something sweet and aching and terribly tender. "Hadrian?" she whispered, love rising up and flooding over her in one swift, absolute tide. She touched his cheek.

He jerked away from her and was on his feet in one lithe movement. "Don't touch me!"

She recoiled, shocked by the anger in his tone, and by his rejection.

"And don't look at me as if I've just kicked you in the ribs!"

Nicole stiffened. "I'm sorry."

He ignored her, striding to the stream. She could not

help but notice that he was still aroused. He waded into the middle of the brook and plunged beneath the water's surface.

Nicole cried out. The water was frigidly cold. He was mad! "Hadrian," she gasped when he rose to his full height, shivering. "You will catch your death!"

"You will be my death."

She regarded him uncertainly. "Do you mean . . . the death you once referred to . . . what happened today?"

"No! That is not the death I mean!"

"Why are you so angry? What have I done?"

"Everything," he growled, his gaze sweeping over her.

That did not explain anything to Nicole, and she watched him submerge himself again in the icy stream. Slowly she got to her feet, terribly afraid that they would not be able to recover the warmth and intimacy which they had just shared, for a chasm leagues deep already seemed to be opening between them. She must do something to defuse his inexplicable anger and she must do it quickly. She picked up his jacket, and when he stood again, the water cascading down his lean, hard body, she said, "Come here."

The glance he gave her was rude, but he waded from the stream, shivering anew. Nicole placed his jacket on his shoulders, rubbing him as if it were a towel she held. He snatched the coat from her and removed himself from her touch. "Are you trying to seduce me?" he snapped.

Was she? "Would that be so terrible?"

"You are the only woman I know who would ever admit to such a thing. This is not right!"

"When we're together," she said, very softly, "nothing is more right."

He stared at her. His gaze was inscrutable.

Although her manner was bold, inside she was quaking, because so much was at stake. She approached him, touching him. This time he did not move away. "Why did you pull away from me just now? I am not a complete fool. I know that there is more. Don't you want me?"

For a long moment he did not speak, and Nicole was afraid of his reply. "I wish I did not want you," he finally said tightly.

He did not seem happy about the matter. Apprehension filled her. She touched him again, taking his hand. "I want you, Hadrian. I still want you."

He did not pull away from her, standing completely still. "You are merciless. Can you not see I am trying to be noble?"

"Right now I don't give a fig about nobility," she murmured, her hand tightening on his.

He pried her palm from his. "This is intolerable, it cannot continue. I take full blame for what has passed. Virgins are for marrying, not for this."

She was unable to keep the hope from leaping in her breast. He knew she was a virgin, was he implying that he should marry her? His feelings had seemed as intense as hers, surely there was more involved than just desire. Would he break it off with his fiancée now that he realized how he felt? Would he offer her marriage? "I cannot continue this way either. I cannot stand being apart from you."

"If you still think to seduce me, you are doing an admirable job."

Nicole stepped back. His words had the effect of a whiplash, physically hurting her. "Is that what you think? I thought . . . I had hoped . . ." She trailed off, realizing, in a way, that he was right.

He paced away from her. She watched him. He paced restlessly in a tight circle, back and forth, back and forth. Certain he would not agree to what she was suggesting, Nicole said tentatively, "I can return to Dragmore, and we can never lay eyes upon each other again. That is one solution."

He turned toward her. "That is the ideal solution!"

Nicole gasped.

"I had thought, too, that was what you were planning to do, the last time we spoke."

He wanted her to leave. He wanted her to leave London so he could not see her. It couldn't be possible, not after the intimacy they had just shared. Surely she was misunderstanding his meaning.

"Why didn't you leave?" he demanded.

Nicole's wits were scrambled, and he had to repeat the question. "I . . . I was going to. My parents asked me to stay." Horrified, she felt the heat of tears rising in her eyes. "They hope I will re-enter society and be a big success."

His square jaw tightened. "And is that what you wish? Do you now seek a husband?"

She looked at him, a golden god except that he was flesh and blood and mortal. She had wanted to marry him the moment she had first laid eyes upon him. "Yes," she whispered.

"Then I wish you all the luck."

He was not going to propose to her. He wished her luck in finding a husband—someone other than himself. Nicole reeled as if struck. The Duke moved to catch her, but she shrugged him off and hurriedly turned away so he would not see how devastated she was. How could he care so little, when it had seemed that he cared so much? Did she mean so little to him after all?

"I am nothing to you, no more than a passing amusement."

"I made it clear from the first that you could not have any expectations from me."

Nicole whirled. "Bastard!" she spat. It was the first time she had ever used such a dirty word, and she was glad to see that she had briefly shocked him. "Is that why you came looking for me today—to lift my skirts in the woods?"

"You know that is not true."

"Do I?" Her voice rose, she knew she sounded hysterical. She *was* hysterical. "I know only what has happened here today! You tell me I should expect nothing from you—yet you behave in a manner that leads me to expect everything!"

"I consider myself a beast." He did not take his eyes from her. "I am, after all, my father's son."

Nicole turned away, shaking in hurt and rage. "God, I hate you!"

"Then that makes two of us," he said, so softly that she was sure she had not heard him correctly.

"I am getting out of here," Nicole said, striding toward her mount.

His hand whipped out and he caught her arm. Angrily Nicole pulled herself free of him, daring him with her furious regard to ever touch her again.

"You can not return to the house like that," he said. "You look as if you have been tumbled in the dirt."

"But I was, wasn't I?" she said mockingly.

"Not quite," he gritted.

"Oh yes, however could I forget your *nobility!*" She started to mount, too angry and upset to think about her hunter's sore foot. The Duke caught her again and this time dragged her away from the horse.

"What are you doing?" she screamed, all of her emotions exploding.

He lifted her in his arms. "Not what you are thinking," he said coolly.

With a savage cry, Nicole writhed and tried to slam her fists into his face. He ducked, but he needed both hands to carry her so he could not defend himself, and one blow glanced off of his chin, "That is the third time you have struck my face," he said darkly.

"But not the last," Nicole replied furiously.

But just before her nails could rake his skin, he released her, and she plummeted into the icy water of the stream. She gasped, sinking like lead below the surface, managing to close her mouth before she swallowed too much water. Before she could react, she felt him hauling her up above the surface by her collar. She gasped air, air, sputtering, while he dragged her to the bank. She sank to her knees, and he began pounding hard on her back. She spat up the water she had swallowed.

Shc turned her gaze upon him. It was murderous. "Now I will kill you."

His arms were crossed and he regarded her with no emotion at all. "You fell back from the group and decided to water your horse. I came looking for you. Your mount shied, you fell in. I came in after you."

Her only answer was an inarticulate sound of impotent rage.

On their way back they were met on the trail by two grooms who had been sent to look for them. The Duke promptly told them what had happened, or rather, the story he had concocted. Since he and Nicole were wet, they took the boys' fresh mounts and left one of the grooms behind to walk back Nicole's injured hunter.

When they arrived at the house, several guests were still in the courtyard, discussing the morning's adventures. They were greeted with relief and concern. Again the Duke related the story he had invented and no one doubted a word of it. Not, of course, until they entered the house.

Isobel was hovering anxiously in the parlor that adjoined the foyer, and the moment the Duke and Nicole entered she hurried to them. Her glance went from Nicole to her son. "What happened?"

"Nicole's mount shied and she fell into a stream. I had gone back looking for her, and I went in after her," the Duke said matter-of-factly.

"But I am all right," Nicole said, managing a bright smile for the Dowager Duchess's benefit. She received no smile in return. Isobel regarded her speculatively, and Nicole was certain that she doubted every word her son had said. Shame flooded her, adding motivation to the compelling urge she had to flee, not just from the

Dowager Duchess with her too-knowing eyes, but from her son.

"You had better get upstairs and out of those wet things," Isobel finally said.

Nicole nodded, only too glad to leave, when her mother called out from behind her. Her heart sank as she saw Jane and her father descending the wide, winding staircase. "Darling, are you all right?" Jane cried, hurrying to her with her husband on her heels.

"I'm fine," she assured them, trying to hide her uneasiness. It was one thing to tell everyone else that she had fallen off her mount, it was quite another to foist such a tale off on her parents. Careful not to look at her father, she told Jane how she had fallen off her mount and how the Duke had rescued her.

"You fell from your horse?" Jane said disbelievingly. Her father stared at her.

"I thought I was alone," Nicole lied with aplomb. "And I was in that awful sidesaddle, which you know I never use. Hadrian startled not just my horse, but me! It was just one of those things." She darted a glance at her father. She saw from his stern expression that he knew damn well that she was lying through her teeth.

"You must get out of your clothes," Jane said firmly, pausing only to flash the Duke a warm smile. "Thank you, Your Grace."

The Duke nodded.

It was then that Nicole realized that she had just referred to him by his given name, and not as the Duke or "His Grace." Her heart stopped, and she darted a glance at the Dowager Duchess, who was staring disapprovingly at her. Another peek, this time at her father, showed that he was wearing almost the identical expression. Neither one of them had missed her terrible slip of the tongue, and crimson color flooded her cheeks. She did not dare look at the Duke, but she did not have to. She could feel his silent fury.

Only her mother was oblivious, and at that moment,

Jane led Nicole toward the stairs.

A silence descended upon the group left standing alone in the foyer. The Duke met Nicholas Shelton's stare, which was cold and angry. He flinched inwardly. Even before Nicole's disastrous faux pas, the other man had known that he and Nicole had not been innocently alone all this time. The Duke had sensed it the moment he appeared, and now Shelton's suspicions were confirmed.

When Nicholas Shelton spoke, his tone was as frosty as his pale grey gaze. "Perhaps His Grace would care to join me in the library? I should very much like to learn all about Nicole's fall from her horse."

The Duke almost winced. He had not a doubt that if he did not convince Shelton that his daughter had not been ruined, a disastrous clash would occur. "Nicole is very fortunate," he said politely. "Had I not taken the situation firmly in hand, she would not have been so fortunate. But I can assure you that she has not been harmed, and that she is in no way any the worse for what befell her."

The Earl of Dragmore's expression did not change. "I see," he said, his jaw tight. "Hopefully there will not be another incident of this nature." His gaze locked with the Duke's. "The consequences would be more than unpleasant, *I* assure *you*."

"Of course not," Hadrian said stiffly. The Earl was well within his rights, but the Duke did not like being threatened, regardless of how justifiable the threat was.

Shelton nodded and turned abruptly, limping slightly from the pulled muscle in his leg. The Duke watched him leave, finally allowing himself to feel the full brunt of his own anger, and practically all of it was directed at himself. The fact that he had very nearly ruined Nicole consumed him, as did how she had misconstrued his intentions.

"You had better start thinking about Elizabeth," Isobel said from behind him.

It was another warning and his temper exploded. "I am marrying Elizabeth in June," he snapped. "I have not forgotten that for a second. And then all shall be well, shall it not?"

Isobel looked at him sadly.

"For everyone shall be happy, shall they not?" His jaw clenched. "Or should I say—almost everyone?"

He strode away, his steps hard and angry. He had not meant to let his temper take over like that, but it had, and with it had come knowledge of his deepest, most secret feelings, which he did not want to confront. But it was too late. Everyone would be happy when he married Elizabeth. Everyone except himself.

For he was no longer looking forward to his upcoming marriage. Suddenly it loomed before him as nothing more than an ultimate act of self-sacrifice.

It was not until late that evening that Isobel was finally awarded the peace and privacy of her own apartments, her guests having finally retired to their beds. Alone at last, she was finally free to think—and to worry.

She stood in front of the vast, marble-mantled hearth in her sitting room, staring at the dancing flames. Gone was the convivial gaiety which had marked her expression earlier and in its place was grave concern. Her blue eyes were anxious and she worried the rose-colored sash of her silk peignoir.

Isobel was no fool. She had never been one, although, at one time, when she was young, she had been naive, innocent and gullible. Francis had changed that quickly enough—she had been introduced to life's unpleasant side with little ado, and she had learned and adjusted swiftly. Now she was in her mid-fifties and not merely a Dowager Duchess, but an educated, experienced and intelligent woman, and something of a businesswoman as well. Few women had experienced all that she had, and Isobel knew better than most that life forever dealt wild cards, especially when one least expected it.

Hadrian had fallen for Nicole Shelton and it was obvious. It was equally obvious that the poor young woman was wildly in love with her son. And they made such a striking couple, in ways that had nothing to do with their individually astounding good looks. Isobel was sad.

She was no stranger to illicit love, nor to heartbreak. She knew too well the overwhelming pain forbidden love generated. Although the pain would die a slow, lingering death, the sadness at what could not be would never die, at least, for her it hadn't. Her heart ached now for her son. She desperately wished that Hadrian was not in love with Nicole Shelton, to spare him the grief that was certain to be his fate.

And poor Elizabeth. It was a terrible triangle, for Isobel knew how dearly Elizabeth loved Hadrian. Hadrian would never jilt her, Isobel was certain of that, he was far too honorable. Just as she had been too honorable to run away from Francis. Like mother, like son. It was frightening.

Isobel sank onto a chaise, feeling the urge to shed tears. Her emotions were raw, as if she were in her twenties again, as if she were that young woman falling in love for the first time and tortured with her own illicit feelings for a man who was not her husband. His image loomed before her as if it were only yesterday that they had been together—tall and powerful, brown hair streaked gold by the sun, his face weathered and rugged yet compellingly attractive. Her heart clenched painfully. She realized that she was wrong—the pain never died.

She did not wish such an ill-fated love upon anybody, and certainly not upon her son or Elizabeth, nor even poor Nicole Shelton, who did not deserve all that her life had so far meted out to her.

Isobel knew only too well how love knew no bounds. Love did not submit to reason or to logic, it defied all attempts at being circumscribed. Hadrian was powerful, noble and honorable, but he was only a man. He would never intend to ruin Nicole, but having seen them together, having felt the tension between them, how much longer would it be before the inevitable happened? Hadrian would survive such an indiscretion much more easily than Nicole, and it was not Isobel's place to worry about the other woman, but she did. It wasn't fair, but then, life was rarely fair.

She closed her eyes, thinking of Hadrian—but not the man who was her son, rather, his namesake. Not for the first time, and not for the last, she wished desperately that she dared to tell her son the truth. Yet she, who had never been a coward before, was a coward now. She was afraid to witness his shock, worse, afraid of the revulsion he might feel, and she was afraid to lose his respect and his love. No, she could never tell him, not even when he had every right to know, and the truth had nothing to do with trying to teach her son so he would learn from her own past mistakes. Because had she the opportunity to go back thirty years, she would change nothing.

The Duke of Clayborough could not sleep.

He had stopped at the Stafford residence twice that day, as he had on his way back to London yesterday, but both times Elizabeth had been sleeping and he had not spoken with her. Even had he wanted to disturb her, he would not have been able to, for she had been dosed with laudanum for the pain that was suddenly and constantly afflicting her.

It was several hours past midnight. Alone in his high-ceilinged bedroom with only the Borzoi for company, Nicole's exotic image haunted him, and with it, Elizabeth's pale, delicate one. No small amount of guilt tormented him, and no small amount of confusion. He could no longer escape the truth.

No woman had ever haunted his waking—and sleeping—moments the way that Nicole did. No woman had ever created such enormous lust within him, and worse, no woman had ever caused him to behave as abominably and dishonorably as he had with her. He was furious with himself for responding to her the way that he had—for *allowing* himself to respond to her the way that he had.

Leaving his bed, the Duke slipped a velvet paisley robe over his naked body. He paced to the fireplace, where the Borzoi thumped his tail in a happy greeting. The Duke reached down to pet Lad's large head. "I no longer know who I am," he admitted to the dog.

Every meeting they had ever had replayed itself instantaneously through his mind. It was not the first time, but the zillionth. It was torture. His body was tortured.

Was he like his father after all? Had Francis been so obsessed by his young paramours that he could not help himself but to consort with them and cuckold his mother? Perhaps Francis had been tortured by his morals as well. Perhaps father and son were more alike than anyone knew.

If there was any reason to stay away from her it was this one, his own fear of turning out to be a replica of his father, a man he could still hate to this day with no remorse. Clearly he harbored within himself a dark side, one he had obviously inherited from Francis, one which he must, at all costs, subdue.

"Damn her," he said to the dog and the fire. Then he grimaced. "No, it is not her fault—it is *mine*."

Now Nicole Shelton sought to re-enter society and gain a husband. The Duke knew he should not be angry with her for such legitimate interests, but he was. Had she hoped he would be a suitor, despite Elizabeth? That he would throw over one fiancée, only to take another? He believed so.

His pulses had quickened disturbingly. The Duke paced faster, the Borzoi watching him with hopeful interest. The fire was dying to a soft glow. The Duke ignored the chill seeping into the room. He was determined not to question his own reactions. Absolutely not.

The Clayborough motto of "Honor First" was not just embossed on his coat of arms, it was emblazoned on his heart. No matter how he might now feel about his upcoming wedding, he would not—could not—break the engagement. But what about Nicole?

He closed his eyes. She wanted a husband. Every woman he knew wanted a husband, she was well within her rights. She hoped to re-enter society successfully. Now she could do so because he had extended his patronage to her. He could extend it even further. He could be even more than honorable, he could be charitable—he could encourage suitable prospects. *He could even find her a husband.*

It was the right thing to do. Somehow, Hadrian knew it in his heart. Yet the very idea was terribly distasteful. And the more aware he was of how bilious he found the role of matchmaking to be, the more determined the Duke became to aid her by finding her a proper husband.

The Duke had scheduled business engagements for all of the following day. Therefore he returned to the Stafford residence early the next morning, hoping that this time he might be able to visit Elizabeth. As it turned out she was awake and eager to see him, according to her father, the Marquess of Stafford. Hadrian had only to look at the man to know that she had not improved during the past few days. The Marquess was red-eyed, as if he had not been sleeping well and his face was drawn. In the few short weeks since Elizabeth had become visibly ill, he had aged twenty years. Hadrian exchanged a few polite words with the man, and was shown upstairs by the butler.

He stopped in the entrance to her sitting room, motioning the butler to leave. Elizabeth appeared to be sleeping. She reclined on a large chaise, covered with a heavy violet angora blanket. She was terribly pale and frail-looking, dwarfed by the chaise, which made her seem even more tiny and fragile. His heart clenched. She looked much, much worse, and for the first time since she had become so obviously ill, fear for her seized him.

Sensing his presence, or perhaps hearing him, she opened her eyes. The Duke came swiftly forward, managing a bright smile. It took her a moment to focus, then she smiled too. "Hadrian." With that one word—his name—she expressed all of her feelings for him and all of her pleasure at seeing him.

"Hello, Elizabeth, I did not want to wake you." He sat down on an ottoman, pulling it up beside her.

"I am glad you came."

He managed not to show his distress. Her voice was soft, breathless, barely audible. "Are you feeling better today?"

Her eyes shifted away from his. "A little."

He knew it was a lie. And Elizabeth never lied. His fear increased, chilling him. He took her hand. "Shall I tell you about the hunt?"

She nodded, the movement eager yet slight.

For a few minutes he proceeded to regale her with a description of the hunt. Her eyes almost shone as he described the more difficult fences he had taken. When he paused, she smiled. "It sounds wonderful. I'm so glad you went, Hadrian."

Holding her hand, looking into her adoring eyes, hearing her selfless words, he cursed himself for all the disloyal thoughts he had been having—and his disloyal behavior. Elizabeth did not deserve him, she deserved better, but she was engaged to him, and he owed her his loyalty. His determination to see Nicole wed increased.

"Hadrian," Elizabeth said, hesitantly. "What will you do if—if I die?"

Hadrian froze. "You are not going to die," he said, horrified. She was expressing the terrible fear he had and was too cowardly to face.

A slight sheen of tears appeared in her eyes. "I fear you are wrong."

He swallowed, gripping her hand. "You must not even think this way," he said firmly, but God, she looked like she was dying. No one had ever looked closer to death's door.

She blinked, turning her head away. "I don't want you to grieve," she said unsteadily. "I want you to be happy, I have always wanted you to be happy. You are young and strong and already you have waited far too long to get on with your life."

"Elizabeth," he protested, ashen.

A tear slid down her cheek. "Do you think that I don't know? I know that you are not really happy, Hadrian,

I have always known it, from the time I was a small child."

He could not speak.

More tears fell. "I wanted so much to be the one to bring happiness into your life. But it's not going to be."

He gripped her small hands.

"You need a son. You should marry quickly and have a son." Now she was crying. "I wanted to be your wife, I wanted to be the one to give you a son, I wanted to make you happy. But for some reason, God is not going to let it happen."

Anguish flooded him and he took her into his arms. She was as fragile and thin as an undernourished waif of ten. He held her gently, the only time he had ever held her since she had outgrown her pinafores, other than the one time he had kissed her on her eighteenth birthday. How could she talk like this?

"I don't like this kind of talk, Elizabeth," he managed. "You are young and you are certainly not dying. We shall be married in June, and you shall give me a son." He stroked her hair. "You are wrong, you make me very happy."

She leaned back to look at him and he saw that she was still crying, but silently now. "I don't want to die. I love you so. All I've ever wanted was to be your wife. Oh, Hadrian! It is not fair!"

He was stricken, he was aghast. And all he could do was hold her and soothe her as if she were a child. Now he could understand why the poor Marquess had been so red-eyed. It hadn't been from lack of sleep, but from weeping.

"You must sleep," he said, frightened by her increasing pallor. "I will come back later tonight, but if you are asleep I will only look in on you—I won't wake you."

Her eyes had drifted closed, but she was clinging to him with a surprisingly strong grip. The Duke gently disengaged his hand from hers and stood, trembling. He had exactly one thought—he must get a physician here immediately. He turned to go. Then he hesitated.

He returned and bent over her. She appeared to be sleeping. He touched her forehead, it was cool and dry. "Elizabeth," he murmured. "You mean so much to me." And he brushed her lips slowly with his.

And this time, when he looked back across the room before leaving at the door, he saw that she was smiling.

It was Regina who was the bearer of bad tidings.

Nicole had returned to Tavistock Square Sunday evening with her parents and sister, emotionally exhausted from the weekend and all too eager to leave Maddington. She had not laid eyes upon Hadrian since the fox hunt, or rather, since that uncomfortable incident in the foyer with the Dowager Duchess and her parents when they had returned bedraggled and wet from the stream. She had not known what to expect after Jane had shepherded her upstairs. She hadn't precisely expected Hadrian to leave Maddington immediately, but he had. For not minutes after she had changed out of her wet clothes, she had heard a commotion outside her window in the courtyard. With sudden intuition she had run to the window to see him entering the black lacquer Clayborough coach. The dozen liveried outriders awaited the vehicle, paired up in a motionless line like soldiers behind it. Just before climbing in, the Duke had paused and suddenly glanced behind him—as if feeling her watching him. But he hadn't seen her, and moments later he and his magnificent entourage were gone.

Since Nicole had arrived in London she had tried very hard not to think about the Duke and their last encounter, but it was impossible. She was no longer as angry as she was humiliated. His actions spoke for themselves—obviously he did not consider her a lady. Every time they met she wound up in his arms, eagerly. His intentions had not been honorable from the first, but why should they be? If she dared to be painfully honest with herself, she would admit that he was right in his assessment of her. A lady did not go to masques unescorted in scandalous gypsy costumes, a lady did not jilt her fiancé at the last moment, a lady did not ride about in breeches. And certainly a lady did not let any man, even her husband, touch her the way that she had let Hadrian touch her. If she were a lady like Elizabeth he would have never behaved toward her in such a scandalous manner.

Nicole was ashamed, too, that during the hunt she had completely forgotten Elizabeth's existence. When she was with Hadrian—and she wished she could stop thinking about him with such an intimate form of address—when she was with *the Duke* it was easy to forget everything. Nicole wished that Elizabeth were a horrible, mean person like her cousin Stacy, for then she would have no remorse or guilt for what she had done with Hadrian. But she wasn't like Stacy, she was kind and good, and one of the few people in this town who had gone out of her way to make Nicole feel accepted. Nicole did not want to betray Elizabeth, and was just as sorry for doing so as for failing to be a real lady herself.

And then Regina brought her news which made Nicole feel even worse.

"What has happened?" Nicole asked when her sister came running breathlessly into her room.

"It is Elizabeth Martindale," Regina gasped. "This past weekend she took a turn for the worse! She is so ill she cannot even get up out of bed, and the doctors say that she is failing."

Nicole stared, the color draining from her face. "Failing?"

Regina nodded, eyes huge, her complexion ghostly white.

"What do you mean, failing?"

"I don't know!" her sister cried. "The doctors say she is "failing"! I think that means she is dying!"

Nicole sat down hard on a chair, utterly shocked. *"Dying?"*

Regina sat down too, just as numbly. The two sisters stared at each other, speechless.

"I don't believe it," Nicole finally said. "Elizabeth is young—younger than either one of us! Young girls do not just suddenly die!"

Regina's mouth trembled and tears filled her eyes. "I cannot believe it either," she said huskily. "Perhaps it is not true."

"Of course it's not true!" Nicole cried, relief flooding her. "It is an awful rumor—and you know how the tiniest thing gets exaggerated by the time it's run the gossip mill!"

"You're probably right," Regina said, relaxing slightly. "She probably has the flu, a bad case of it, and that is all."

Nicole nodded, but she was still shaken to the core.

Nicole was still distraught when, an hour later, the Dragmore coach pulled up in front of the Stafford residence. Gossip was a terrible thing, true, but often where there was smoke there was fire. Nicole prayed that was not the case, in fact, she refused to believe it. Hoping that Elizabeth was merely sick, she wanted to pay her condolences to the younger girl who had been so kind to her. A coachman helped her from the carriage and a butler let her into the entry hall.

Nicole handed him her calling card, explaining that she understood that Lady Elizabeth was ill and she had come to express her best wishes, if possible. In one gloved hand she held a prettily wrapped box of chocolates, which she had purchased on the way over on Oxford Street.

The butler studied her card, but before he could speak, a furious male voice ground out, "Elizabeth is not receiving visitors!"

Nicole whirled around to see the Duke of Clayborough striding toward her, his expression positively black. He was only in his shirtsleeves, which were rolled up; he was not even wearing a waistcoat. His trousers, usually perfectly pressed, were creased and wrinkled. His dark regard was blazing. There were gray circles of sleeplessness and worry beneath his eyes. His hair, always too long, seemed longer and unkempt. Without taking his angry gaze from Nicole, he addressed the butler. "William, you may go."

William disappeared.

Nicole had not expected to see him here and his rage also took her by surprise. Instinctively, she backed up a step, but he kept coming. He grabbed her arm. "What the hell are you doing here?"

"I have come to see Elizabeth. I heard that—"

"You have come to see Elizabeth? Why? To see her condition first-hand?"

She tried to draw away, but he would not release her. "Let go of me! Please!"

He ignored her, shaking her roughly, drawing her closer so that her face was near to his. "Do you dare to think that if she dies, I will marry you?"

For one long moment, Nicole was stunned speechless. Then she wrenched her arm free. "How can you imagine I would think such a thing!" she cried.

"Then why did you come!" he retorted. "Why in hell would you come here?"

She was as stunned by his obvious distress as she was by the accusation he had just made.

"You are not welcome here!"

She managed to stand her ground and hold her chin high, but her eyes were glazing with tears. "You despicable man! I came to say how sorry I am that she is ill!"

"Why would you be sorry?" He laughed mirthlessly. "I imagine that you are the last person in England who would be sorry!"

That he should continue to slander her character so directly—that he obviously believed her capable of such cold-blooded emotions—managed to set a spark to her temper in mere self-defense. "She has never been anything but nice to me, when everyone else in this town—present company included—has been nothing but rude and insulting!"

"I find it very hard to believe that you came here out of a charitable spirit."

"What you believe, you have made more than clear." She stared at him, wanting to call him every godawful name under the sun, wanting to tell him just what she thought of him now, but she did not. But only because poor Elizabeth was obviously ill in this very house, and the servant was undoubtedly lurking around a corner, listening with fascination to their every word. Nicole was horrified to think that any gossip about her and the Duke might reach Elizabeth. "I no longer care what you think," she said stiffly, numbly. "If she is not receiving visitors, then would you kindly take her this gift and tell her how sorry I am?"

The Duke made no move to reach for the parcel she was holding out. Tears stung Nicole's eyes, and she quickly set the box of candy down on a chair. Abruptly, before he might discern how hurt she was, Nicole turned her back on him and strode to the door.

He stopped her. "I want you to know," he said, his voice cutting, "as soon as Elizabeth . . . recovers . . . I am leaving London."

Nicole shrugged her shoulder from his grasp, turning to face him. "Your schedule does not interest me."

"And Elizabeth will be coming with me. We are not going to wait until June to wed. We shall be married immediately."

She lifted her chin, meeting him stare for stare, when his words were more effective than any knife in wounding her. How could this man be the same one who had held her so passionately in the woods of Maddington—just two days ago? He acted as if he hated her. Nicole could not contain a shiver. Had she done something to turn his desire into hatred? Or did he blame *her* for what had happened at the hunt?

She might be hurt, but she still had her pride. Somehow she managed to hide her feelings. "Then I wish the both of you much happiness."

In that moment, while they stared at each other like the worst of enemies, a rapid series of images flashed through Nicole's mind, of them together, of her in his arms. She could feel his touch as if he touched her now. When he held her, she had thought he cared. But that had been her imagination running wild, for the man facing her now did not care at all for her—not in the least. If anything, he despised her.

And the Duke did not seem satisfied with her polite response, if anything, he seemed even angrier. Abruptly Nicole turned to leave.

William materialized to open the door for her, and Nicole again prayed no ugly gossip would reach Elizabeth. She had yet to cross the threshold when the Duke slashed his verbal sword one more time. "I meant it when I said that you are not welcome here. Do not return."

She stiffened, flushing. She had a hundred retorts, but not one of them was suitable for the butler's ears and the consequent belowstairs gossip. Certainly they had just generated enough of that. Then she decided that any reply she chose to make could not possibly make much difference in the face of the magnitude of gossip which would surely follow this exchange. "Contrary to what you think—and you seem intent on thinking only the worst of me—Elizabeth is my friend. She deserves happiness. No one I can think of deserves it more."

Nicole paused before exiting the door, now held open for her by the butler. "But the one thing she does not deserve is you. And *you* certainly do not deserve her."

The Duke was furious.

William, the butler, gaped.

And Nicole decided it was time to take her leave.

* * *

Elizabeth died that night. Her father, the Marquess of Stafford, found her the following morning in her bed. News of her death did not reach Nicole's ears until a few hours later, and by noon all of London knew that the beautiful, kind young lady had passed away.

Nicole was in shock. Elizabeth Martindale, dead? Sweet, kind, pretty Elizabeth? Elizabeth whom everyone liked? Elizabeth, who never saw the bad in anyone or anything? No one had deserved to die less—it was the height of unfairness. Nicole immediately retired to the privacy of her bedroom. She was in shock.

Now, perhaps, she could understand Hadrian's inexplicable temper and rudeness yesterday. Elizabeth had been dying, and although she herself hadn't known it, he certainly had. A man facing the death of someone he cared for—or loved—could not be expected to be polite, rational or pleasant. Nicole sank onto her bed, trembling. He must have loved Elizabeth very much. She had never been certain of the extent of his love for her, but his distress yesterday proved how deep it ran. Nicole's heart went out to him as she imagined his grief.

Elizabeth was laid out that night for three days. Nicole went to pay her last respects, accompanied by her family, with the exception of Chad who was at Dragmore. Edward came from Cambridge so he, too, could express his condolences. The huge Stafford residence was eerily quiet although it was full of hundreds of guests. Everyone moved about speaking in hushed tones, pausing to look at Elizabeth laid out in her finery in a handsome mahogany coffin. The Marquess, having first lost his wife and now his only child, was inconsolable. He could do no more than nod when the mourners stopped to speak with him, for he was incapable of speech.

Elizabeth looked serene in death. She even looked pretty, and someone had placed a smile upon her lips—or she had died that way. Nicole paused by the coffin, Regina at her side. She bit her lip as the urge to cry came over her. How could someone so kind and so young die before her life even began? Somehow, death was understandable when the deceased was old and had lived a full life, or was not a particularly nice person. But in this case it was shocking and sacrilegious.

"I can't look at her," Regina whispered, her voice husky with unshed tears. "I just can't." She hurried away.

Nicole took a deep breath and said a small prayer, hoping Elizabeth could hear her. She thanked her for her kindness, and wanted to apologize for having been intimate with Hadrian. But she just could not confess the latter, she could not. Perhaps Elizabeth would never know. She hoped not.

Dabbing at her eyes, she moved past the coffin. Her gaze lifted and settled on the Dowager Duchess of Clayborough.

For a moment Nicole was startled, remembering how the woman had looked at her in the foyer at Maddington, as if she knew that she and Hadrian had been up to no good. The Dowager Duchess was the last person she wanted to see, other than her son. Yet Isobel, although teary-eyed, managed a small smile.

Nicole had no choice then; she had to greet the woman. She moved to her. "I'm so sorry."

"We all are," Isobel said softly, her eyes brimming with tears. "Thank you for coming." Her voice broke.

Nicole nodded and slipped by her. She found Regina waiting for her outside the salon where Elizabeth lay in final repose. The two sisters exchanged looks of fatigue, distress and sorrow. "Father and Mother are speaking with the Marquess. They said we can leave in another half hour or so."

Nicole nodded, wanting to depart at that very minute, but knowing to do so would be impossibly rude. She and Regina huddled against the wall in the hallway, having no desire to move on into the larger salon where a buffet was laid out for the guests. Across the throng of people moving through the corridor into the salon, she glimpsed

Martha and her husband. Martha excused herself from the group she was in and made her way over to the two women.

"This is so terrible," Martha whispered after they had exchanged hugs. "I am in shock, I cannot believe it." Her eyes watered.

"None of us can believe it," Nicole answered.

"It is so unfair," Regina whispered. "How could God let this happen?"

The two older women turned to look at her for daring to express a thought which they were all having. Silence fell; Regina did not expect an answer anyway. Then Martha spoke to Nicole. "The Duke is here."

Nicole said nothing, but her heart tightened, with dread, with sorrow. Even though she could now understand why he had been such a monster the other day, it did not ease the pain he had inflicted upon her.

"Have you seen him?"

"No."

"He looks awful. I tried to speak to him but it was like talking to a wall. I don't think he heard a thing I said, but that is understandable."

The urge to cry again overcame Nicole. Hadrian must have loved her very much, more than she had thought, for him to have been so out of sorts the other day and to be so grief-stricken now. "He loved her very much."

Martha stared at her. "He knew her all her life. That's a long time to know someone, and they were cousins as well as betrothed."

"It's a long time to love someone," Nicole whispered tremulously. It was inappropriate, but insight hit her with the strangling strength of Jack the Ripper. He had really loved Elizabeth; he had never loved her, Nicole. He had lusted after her, which was something entirely different.

"He needs some time," Martha said, touching Nicole's hand.

If there was an innuendo there, Nicole did not want to entertain it. Fortunately, she did not glimpse him in the next few minutes, and shortly thereafter she left with the rest of her family. That night she cried, for Elizabeth, for Hadrian, and maybe, just a little, for herself.

The day of the funeral was particularly appropriate for mourning. The sky was a dark swirling gray, threatening rain, a northerly wind gusted incessantly, and by now, most of the huge oaks surrounding the Stafford crypt were bare, their gnarled limbs bleak and crooked. They morbidly reminded Nicole of skeletons—of the many skeletons which must be in this very cemetery. Nicole suspected that close to a thousand mourners had turned out for the service at the cathedral in London, but here in Essex, only a hundred or so had actually come to Elizabeth's graveside.

She stood between her mother and Regina, surrounded by the rest of her family. Chad had come for the funeral, and Edward, of course, had stayed in London so he could be present as well. Although they did not stand in one of the front rows, Nicole was taller than most of the mourners, and she had a clear view of the coffin being lowered into the dark vault beneath the Stafford chapel. She also had a clear view of Hadrian.

He stood on the far side of the tomb from where she stood with her family, clad in a black suit, hatless, head bowed. He had one arm around his mother, who unsuccessfully tried not to weep. Beside her was the Marquess of Stafford, who wept as well. The sound of a grown man losing the last of his control was terribly unnerving and distressing.

Beside them stood the family patriarch, the Earl of Northumberland, with his wife and immediate family. Roger de Warenne was Stafford's brother-in-law. He was a tall, thin man in his mid-seventies, his hair strikingly white. He was accompanied by his second wife, who was Isobel's age, and their three sons and their wives, including his heir, Isobel's half-brother, the Viscount of Barretwood. De Warenne had a dozen grandchildren from these marriages and they were all present, the youngest only five and trying to look terribly solemn. The Northumberland family could trace its power and antecedents all the way back to the Conquest.

Behind the de Warennes were their relatives— the Martindales, the Hurts and the Worthingtons. Included among this last group was Stacy Worthington, Elizabeth's cousin. She wept ostentatiously into a handkerchief.

Nicole couldn't help staring at Hadrian as the coffin was carried into the mausoleum. He looked terrible, and her heart clenched painfully at the sight. He was haggard and pale, his shoulders slumped in exhaustion. It was too far for her to see his face clearly, but she could feel, even from this distance, the grief he was suffering. How her heart went out to him.

Standing there as Elizabeth was finally put to rest, Nicole forgot all that had been between them. There was no more anger, no more shame, no more hurt and no more pride. On a day like this day truths were laid recklessly bare. She looked at Hadrian and wept inside for the pain he was afflicted with, and there was no doubt that she loved him completely and thoroughly. Had they been alone she would have gone to him and taken him in her arms as one would a child, to hold him, comfort him, heal him. But they were not alone, and she could only watch him and commiserate with him from afar.

His heart was broken, and in loving him, so was hers.

Three long days had passed since the funeral. Nicole had not gone to any social gatherings for she was in no mood to be gay. She had not known Elizabeth well or for very long, yet the shock of her abrupt death still lingered distressingly. And then there was Hadrian.

Her thoughts were consumed with the Duke, and for him she grieved. At the funeral she had felt his bereavement even though they had been physically separated by many yards, and his anguish was hers. How she wanted to comfort him. And even while she wanted to comfort him, to heal him, there was hurt too, of a different nature, in the realization of how much he must have loved Elizabeth. But the hurt she shoved aside, because his suffering was so much more important.

Nicole had to see him. She had to help ease his sorrow and offer what support she could, to let him know that no matter what, she was there for him. She knew it was not appropriate, not as far as superficial appearances went, yet somehow, it was highly appropriate, for Hadrian needed her. He had never needed her more. She was nervous, not knowing what kind of greeting she might initially receive, but nothing in this world could prevent her from calling upon him.

She knew from Regina and Martha, who had been out on the town since the funeral, that the Duke had refused all invitations and all callers. She was certain he would not refuse her.

The butler allowed her to enter the vast, domed foyer while taking her calling card. A heavyset, heavily jowled man, he studied it, then said impassively, "His Grace is not receiving visitors."

"So I've heard," Nicole said, taking a deep breath. "But I am a good friend of the Duke's—what is your name?"

"Woodward," he said, unimpressed.

"Please, Woodward, tell His Grace that I am here. He will not refuse to see me."

Woodward hesitated, then nodded and moved off down the corridor. Nicole expelled her breath. She realized that she was trembling.

The Duke of Clayborough was drunk.

Not obviously drunk, not stinking drunk, but drunk nonetheless. Hadrian had not imbibed spirits since he was a rowdy adolescent of fourteen, but on this day he had done so with determination. He had not slept in days. He needed to sleep and he would drink until he could. He needed to sleep so he could escape the emotions threatening to overwhelm him—the sorrow and the guilt.

The sorrow weighed down his heart as if he carried a heavy stone within his chest. He knew now, belatedly, that he had loved his fiancée. Not in a carnal way, never in a carnal way, but he had loved her, and now he missed her. He missed her sweetness and her smile. He missed her unfailing kindness, her unstinting generosity, her compassion and her grace. Memories haunted him. Elizabeth as a toddler, stumbling from one piece of furniture to the next, while he, at twelve, had watched with no small amount of amusement. Elizabeth falling off her pony at six and weeping in his arms. Elizabeth at thirteen, almost a woman, shyly offering him cookies which she herself had baked. Elizabeth at eighteen, dazed after he had kissed her for the first time.

It was too late now, but he realized that Elizabeth had been his best friend. His only friend. He was a man who kept to himself, a habit learned preciously early in his childhood. But never with Elizabeth. Perhaps duty had dictated his behavior toward her, but it had been so easy to be with her. And while he had taken their relationship for granted, she had been selfless. She had been constantly supportive of him no matter the circumstance—she had always been there for him. When he was not quite there for her, she had a hundred excuses to make for him.

If he could relive their relationship, he would. And everything would be different.

Hadrian was awash in explosive emotions that he did not want to face. For he had also learned in his childhood to carefully hide his pain, his anguish. To never reveal what he might be thinking or feeling. Not just from the perception of others—but from himself. And he had been successful for many years in doing so. Until recently. And now this, Elizabeth's death, was the final spark, and a conflagration of the heart threatened.

He did not understand why she had died. He believed in God, although he did not attend church very often, and her death made no sense. But then, much of life as he had witnessed it had made no sense. His father's cruelty to his mother had made no sense. Nor had his father's cruelty to him. Perhaps there was no God after all, or perhaps there was just no justice or mercy.

Perhaps he could have dealt with the sorrow if that was all there was to it. But there was more, so much more—there was the guilt.

He tossed down another scotch whiskey, scowling at the taste. He was in his library—he had not left it in days. He paced to the fire and poked at it, trying not to let his thoughts take their inevitable turn. But they always did.

Guilt festered. Nicole's image rose, still haunting him, with Elizabeth barely cold in her grave. Damn her, he thought, jabbing the fire viciously. Damn her!

Or should he damn himself?

These past months, while Elizabeth had been ill and dying, he had not spared her a thought, much less his attention. He had been too busy lusting after Nicole Shelton. Elizabeth had not deserved this from him; she had deserved so much more.

I am a bastard, a total bastard, a self-serving carnal bastard—not so different from my father at all.

He closed his eyes, but the vivid image in his mind would not go away. Nicole's vibrant and exotic face, laughing, sparkling, next to Elizabeth's pale lifeless one.

She was everything most beautiful in life; she was fiery energy, exotic beauty, untamable pride. Elizabeth had never been fiery, exotic or untamable, but rather the precise opposite. The contrast was unsettling, gruesome.

He had gone this far in a journey he was helpless to stop, despite the scotch whiskey; a journey deep into his darkest, most private inner self. And he did not want to take another step.

There was a wanting in him, a secret yearning, which he could not shake, and it was focused on Nicole.

A knock on the door snapped him from his reverie. Hadrian had told the staff he was not to be disturbed, but he would never take out his flaring temper on any of them. His tone civil, he said, "Yes?"

Woodward entered, looking as apologetic as he was capable of looking, given his well-schooled implacability. "Lady Nicole Shelton is here. She insisted I inform you, Your Grace."

Hadrian's heart slammed. The wanting, the yearning, choked him. "Send her away!" he snarled.

Woodward appeared shocked, but recovered instantly. "Yes, Your Grace."

"Wait!" Hadrian called when the butler was at the door. "I've changed my mind. Show her in."

Woodward nodded expressionlessly and disappeared. Hadrian paced, his blood boiling. Why had she come? Couldn't she even wait a decent interval after the funeral? Had she no respect for the dead? What did she want? How dare she!

He had meant what he had said the other day, just before Elizabeth had died, that he would adjourn to the country with his fiancée and that they would be wed immediately. Perhaps he had known she was dying and his intentions had been a form of denial. All that week as he attended Elizabeth on her deathbed, he had resolved to be loyal to her, both in deed and in thought—which meant he must end his obsessing over Nicole Shelton. Now, on the verge of a precipice which he had no intention of falling over, Hadrian was more determined than ever to get her out of his mind and his life.

Woodward showed Nicole in and Hadrian waved him away. His gaze pierced her. Why had she come? Why now?

As he stared at her he saw that she was distraught. Certainly not for Elizabeth. That would be utter irony. Her pale gray eyes seemed to be filled with compassion and concern. He wondered if he was drunker than he thought, for this empathy could not be for him. Could it? This was not the savage harridan he knew so well, this was not the woman who had practically confessed that she sought to seduce him.

"Hadrian? Are you all right?"

He leaned back against the fireplace, ignoring the heat of the flames behind the screen, which were dangerously close to his body. "Oh, I am all right," he said, his tone mocking and belying his words. "After all, one's fiancée's dying is an everyday event."

A vast silence greeted his words. Her expression dissolved into even greater sympathy while he was shocked at what he had done—he had put himself forth nakedly and revealed his grief. As if he wanted her to react—which he did not.

"I am so sorry," she cried, but he cut her off.

"I should not be surprised at this visit, should I? You have always defied propriety. But I confess that I am."

She did not move, standing behind the sofa, facing him, her gloved hands holding her reticule. "I could not stay away," she said softly. "I had to be certain you were all right."

"You have come here out of concern for me?" he asked incredulously. He did not believe her. Or did he? The soft caring look in her eyes tortured him. Tested him.

"Why else?"

"I can think of other reasons," he said crudely, his gaze sliding over her. "I meant what I said the other day—I did. It is over, Nicole. Whatever was between us—it is over." Anger washed over him with frightening intensity. Anger at her, at himself, at the world.

"I understand."

"If you understood you would not be here."

"It is because I understand that I am here, Hadrian," she said softly. "You should not be alone."

"I want to be alone!"

"If that is true, then why did you allow me in?"

He stared at her, unable to deny more of the stark truth. He didn't want to be alone—he wanted to be with her. "Get out. Now. Before it is too late."

She did not move. Her eyes seemed softer, more caring. It could only be an illusion.

He was furious now. "Didn't you hear me?" he roared. "I told you to get out! Out of here, out of my life!" He hadn't been aware that he was still holding his whiskey glass, but the next thing he knew, he had thrown it as hard as he could, not at her, but at the door behind her. It whizzed past her head and shattered explosively against the rich wood.

Nicole flinched slightly.

He was panting. A cavern had opened up inside of him. It was black, but deep in the abyss was a kaleidoscope of swirling colors, his blood, his guts. So many feelings. At all costs, to be avoided. He hated it, hated her. "You are a fool. I almost hurt you."

"But you didn't," she whispered. "And you won't."

He turned abruptly away from her, shaking.

"I know you are hurting," she murmured. "I know you are striking out at me because there is no one else to strike out at. I don't mind. I, too, think it horribly unfair. How could such a thing happen? To someone so kind, so sincere?"

"Don't." He was facing the fireplace and its blazing heat was becoming painful on his thighs and stomach. He closed his eyes. She was everything Elizabeth had never been, and in being here now, so alive and vital and vibrant, it struck him painfully. So painfully. And Elizabeth's image was receding, eaten up by the choking yearning. In its stead was Nicole.

"I am going to ask Woodward to bring us tea," she said finally. He listened to her leaving and felt a moment of panic when he knew he should be relieved. He tried to summon back Elizabeth's face, but only succeeded in gaining a hazy, indistinct image. He took a deep breath to gain control of his emotions. He must fight himself, he must.

Nicole entered. His heartbeat became erratic the moment she did. "You look very tired, Hadrian. Please, come and sit. Woodward will be here shortly with hot tea. Have you eaten anything recently?"

He turned slowly. His gaze met hers and held it for a long time. He hadn't been imagining it, the expression in her eyes. It was genuine. It was for him. He was afraid to go near her. For, in that moment, desire slammed violently over him.

"Hadrian?"

His answer was to turn away from her, to lean on the mantle and stare at the flames in the hearth. No matter how hard he tried, he could no longer see Elizabeth's face clearly in his mind.

Woodward knocked and entered with the tea. He listened as the butler set the tray down and asked Nicole if she wanted anything else, but he did not turn around. He was afraid to move, afraid of himself and what he might do.

The door closed. Silence fell across the library. It was broken only by the ticking of the tall grandfather clock on one wall, and the snapping and popping of the flames. He heard Nicole get up and walk over to him. He tensed.

She stood behind him so closely he felt her warmth. "Hadrian? Don't you want to come sit down?"

"No."

"Would you like to go upstairs to bed? It frightens me to see you like this."

It frightened him to be like this. He didn't move, clutching the stone mantle. It was his intention to tell her again to leave—to order her to leave. Instead, he said, "I cannot sleep, Nicole. If I could, believe me, I would not be here like this."

She made a small sound of distress. Hadrian almost jumped when he felt her gently touch his back. He closed his eyes, barely hearing what she was saying, desperately wishing she would put her arms around him and hold him as if he were a child. But she did not.

He could not fight anymore.

"Hadrian, maybe if you try now, you will be able to sleep. I can see how exhausted you are. Let me call Woodward."

Her palm trembled on his back. He let out a long breath. Unthinking now, except for the one word screaming at him inwardly. *Danger!* "Don't call Woodward," he said harshly.

Nicole bit her lip, then with both hands began to knead his neck. Hadrian went very still, becoming even more tense. As her hands dug into his muscles, he felt himself beginning to shake. He couldn't stand it. *He had lost.*

"Nicole," he cried, turning abruptly and enveloping her in his arms.

She froze, but she did not attempt to push him away. Her eyes were wide but not frightened. He hugged her to him and felt an answering quiver in her body. He buried his face in her neck. The vibrant colors swirled over him, fast and hard, too many to identify.

"It's all right," she quavered. She stroked his hair, his back. "It's all right."

He was aware that he was crushing her, perhaps hurting her. But as if he were in a trance, he could not ease his hold. He held her for a long time. The waves of color kept crashing over him. Joy, despair. Grief and pain, so much pain, and a strange exultation. The panic had gone. Instead, there was pulsing desire.

And in his arms, Nicole was warm and wonderfully alive. He could feel the beat of life in her, pulsing through her, its heat, her heat. She was strength, she was sorrow and compassion, joy and triumph. He rocked her. She clung to him.

Tears stung his closed eyes. He was shocked at how he needed her. If the need weren't so strong he would confuse it with physical desire. But it was that strong, and the feelings intensified each other.

Her hands came up to hold his face. "Always," she whispered, pulling back so she could look into his eyes. He saw tears in hers, as well. "I will always be here for you." Slowly, almost chastely, she covered his mouth with hers.

It was too much. Hadrian exploded. His hand anchored itself in her nape, abruptly loosening her unswept hair so that it spilled down her back. He tilted her face up for his kiss. For one scant instant their gazes met, hers wide with both surprise and anticipation, his blazing. Then his mouth covered hers.

Hard and hot. Wet. Their tongues entwined recklessly. Mated with abandon. Mewling noises escaped from Nicole's throat. Hadrian sank down to his knees, taking her with him. When she was on her back, he rained desperate, hungry kisses all over her face—on her eyelids, her forehead, her cheeks and temple, on her jaw, mouth and neck. Nicole sobbed.

"Nicole," Hadrian whispered, his thick, hard body coming down on hers. There were words which wanted to gush forth, but he was so overwhelmed, he could not find them, did not dare express them.

Nicole clutched him fiercely, kissing him back wildly. Hadrian pulled her skirts up, found the slit in her drawers, and grabbing the fabric with both hands, he ripped it apart.

Seconds later he had freed his massively engorged phallus and was thrusting ruthlessly into her. She stiffened at his onslaught, but it was too late, he had forgotten she was a virgin, he had forgotten everything. He tried to slow his rampaging thrusts, tried to stop the madness that possessed him, and failed.

A moment later it was over. He collapsed, shuddering, on top of her. She held him, caressing him. His pulses subsided and eventually his mind began to function.

The colors were still there. Bright and strong, vivid. His expression uncharacteristically soft, relaxed, Hadrian smiled. "I'm sorry."

"Don't be sorry," Nicole said vehemently, stroking his damp hair. "Don't ever be sorry, not with me."

He was groggy now with a fatigue induced not just by physical release, but by the whiskey he was unaccustomed to and the days he had not slept. Nicole's soothing caresses were impossible to fight. He felt the heavy cloak of sleep descending and could not resist. He tightened his hold on the woman in his arms. His last waking thought was that he no longer wanted to resist, not her, and not himself, and he dreamed of brilliantly hued rainbows.

Hadrian awoke in darkness. For a moment he was completely disoriented. He turned his head, wincing at the stab of pain behind his temples, and saw the dying coals of the hearth. The burgundy drapes on the tall windows on that wall were open, revealing a heavy darkness outside. It was very late in the night. Total recall hit him. He was on the library floor, where he had fallen asleep. After making love to Nicole Shelton.

Another fierce stabbing lanced through his skull at the thought.

It all came back to him as he slowly, tentatively, rose to a sitting position, pushing the blanket to his hips. She had come there with sympathy in her eyes and on her lips, and he had been overpowered by a need he had never before felt for any human being.

For an instant, he was frightened by the memory. Just as quickly, he regained control and the unruly feeling vanished.

He remembered her warmth as he embraced her, just holding her; then he remembered how furiously and crudely he had driven her to the floor and penetrated her. He could feel a dull, hot blush of shame covering his cheeks, shame that competed fiercely with his anger. He had not only been as callow as a vigin schoolboy, he had been as precipitous.

How could it have happened?

Very grim and very shaken, Hadrian got to his feet, adjusting his clothes. He had long ago added electric lighting to his homes, and finding a switch, he flooded the library with light. He moved behind his desk and sat down hard.

What the hell had he done?

Head in his hands, he was swept up with sensations as if he were experiencing them anew. Too many sensations, too many feelings. He shook them off with a tremendous effort. It was easier—safer—to concentrate on the facts.

No matter that she had come here, and she shouldn't have, he should have refused to see her. Instead, he had lost a battle he had been waging since he had first laid eyes on Nicole Shelton, one against himself and his own desires. He had lost, it was done. A fait accompli. There was no point in dwelling upon what could not be changed. And now, of course, there was only one course of action open to him. He would marry her.

With Elizabeth barely cold in her grave. At this rude thought, he moaned, his head throbbing steadily now. Yet the festering guilt was gone. He did not know why, and did not bother to speculate upon the answer. It was enough that that particular source of torment had dissipated.

His gaze lifted and he became aware of the two pillows on the floor with the blanket. Had he woken up, he would not have continued to sleep on the floor, much less fetch those items for himself. Woodward would never dare. It had to have been Nicole. He tensed as he imagined her covering him with the throw and placing pillows beneath his head. Damn it! He did not want to feel tenderly toward her!

Yet she was going to be his wife. There was no reason to avoid her any longer, no reason to be so angry, except perhaps with himself. He could not help but be aware that he was not really displeased with the notion of Nicole becoming his bride. In fact, his mouth had softened into a bare smile.

Quickly Hadrian lunged to his feet, pacing. He was not choosing her for a wife, he told himself harshly. This was not a matter of choice. Had it been a matter of choice, he certainly would not choose Nicole. He could not imagine her being a proper wife, much less a Duchess. No, she would most definitely not be his choice.

This was a coil of his own making and he would do his duty. That was all, there was nothing more to it. He needed a wife anyway, sooner or later, and due to the circumstances, it would just be a little sooner than he had anticipated. Tomorrow he would speak with her and settle the matter definitively.

And should there be a life after death, he hoped fervently that Elizabeth would understand.

Nicole had spent half the night awake, unable to think about anything other than Hadrian and what had just happened—and what might happen now.

At first she had been in a state of ecstasy, daydreaming about him as the clock struck midnight. The intimacy they had shared thrilled her and she did not regret it for a moment. Nothing could be more wonderful than having Hadrian in her arms with no anger and no defenses, baring his soul to her. Of course, she hated seeing him so anguished, but he had turned to her for comfort, comfort she would readily give him again and again.

But as the night deepened, some of Nicole's elation lessened. She wondered what Hadrian would think about what had happened, she wondered what he would think about her. She knew better than to be too hopeful. He certainly would not be lying in his bed with a smile on his face, dreaming about her. She knew him well enough to think that he would not take it in stride. In all probability, he would be angry. And most likely he would be angry with her.

Nicole was no longer smiling dreamily.

And what about Elizabeth? Nicole sobered completely. As far as the dead girl went, she was ashamed. She hoped, fervently, that Elizabeth was already in heaven and had not seen what they had done. But. . . . Nicole had a feeling that even if she had, she would understand. Elizabeth had never harbored a grudge against anybody in her short life, and she had always sought to see the best in people. Surely she would understand how Hadrian's grief had led him astray, and how Nicole genuinely loved him and just could not fight her love for him any longer.

Thoughts of Elizabeth were more than sobering, they shattered the last of her pleasure abruptly. Hadrian was grieving. How could she forget? He was grieving for the woman he loved. And it was terribly obvious, after seeing him yesterday, how much he had loved his fiancée. She should not be dismayed, for Nicole already knew of his feelings, but she was. How could there be so much sorrow where just moments ago there had been so much joy?

It was too late for regrets, but Nicole wished that at least a few weeks could have gone by before she had gone to console him. Or a few months. She recalled now how Martha had said that Hadrian needed time. Of course he did. Eventually he would live fully in the present again. And she would be there, waiting. Hoping that he would be able to love her, just a little, once he was over Elizabeth.

Nicole hugged a pillow to her bosom. How could she have forgotten, even for a few minutes, that she was only an object of his passion, not of his affections? But didn't she have enough love for the two of them? Could that not change? Could he not, one day, come to care for her?

Yet how could she compete with a dead woman, a paragon of the female sex?

Nicole did not know how she would survive the days until she saw Hadrian again to judge his mood and his feelings toward her. She was certain that she should not be the one to visit him, that she should wait for him to come to her. But she was terribly afraid that he would not call upon her. Elizabeth suddenly loomed between them with more force than she had when she was alive.

Late that afternoon, when she was changing out of her riding habit into a simple dress for supper, Regina flew into her room without knocking. Nicole paused, regarding her curiously, while Annie buttoned up the back of her silk dress with dexterous fingers. Regina's eyes were nearly popping from her head.

"What is it?" Nicole asked.

"You have a caller! You won't believe who it is."

"I am in no mood for guessing games," Nicole said. All day long her humor had been foul—she felt as if she wanted to tear her hair out or jump right out of her own skin. She could not stand the unknown, the waiting.

"It is the Duke of Clayborough!"

Nicole's mouth dropped. "Hadrian? I mean, the Duke? But—what does he want?"

"I don't know! It's astounding—what with Elizabeth just buried and all! Mother is with him, for Father is not back from his meetings yet. What could he want?"

Nicole began to tremble. That exact question was echoing in her mind. It made absolutely no sense that he would come here after what had occurred yesterday, unless he was so angry that he had come to rage at her. Only raw fury would bring him here in complete disregard of convention and propriety. If only a little more time had elapsed so that he could calm down!

Nicole fidgeted while Annie and Regina pinned up her hair, then thanked them breathlessly and hurried down the stairs. She skidded to a halt before she came to the door of the tea room, caught her breath, and gracefully stepped in.

The Duke sat beside her mother on a sofa with a cup of tea in his hand and scones on his plate. His head turned at her entry and his gaze fixed upon her. Nicole expected to see blazing wrath, but she saw nothing in his expression at all. He rose to his feet.

Nicole flushed, remembering everything, curtsying unsteadily. "Good day, Your Grace."

He returned her greeting perfunctorily. Jane poured her a cup of tea and Nicole sat opposite them on a small, straight-backed chair. Her hands were too unsteady to hold the cup and saucer without rattling them, so she set them down. "This is very unexpected," she said.

His expression was enigmatic. He did not look as well as usual, but he did not look as he had yesterday. The circles were gone from beneath his eyes, although they were still bloodshot. His face was grim, the lines around his mouth strained, yet he was cleanshaven and impeccably dressed in a tan sack jacket, a darker necktie and brown trousers. "Is it?"

Nicole's flush deepened. She knew exactly what he was referring to, and she very nearly wanted to die. An awkward silence fell when he did not continue. Jane, looking from one to the other, attempted to ease it. "Now that you have come out, will you be attending the Fairfax ball this weekend?"

"I do not anticipate doing so," Hadrian said, turning his attention to the Countess. "I am not exactly in the mood for dancing, eating and making merry."

"Of course not," Jane replied. "I cannot help but be surprised, also, Your Grace, that you would come here."

"Perhaps if you give me a few moments alone with your daughter, all matters will soon make sense," he returned, unsmiling.

Jane nodded, giving Nicole a speculative glance before rising to her feet. "I do have some letters I must answer," she said. "It should take about fifteen minutes." She left, leaving the door open behind her.

Bless her mother, Nicole thought, for she could not imagine any other lady leaving her daughter unchaperoned with a gentleman caller, even with the Duke of Clayborough. Nicole shifted as he continued to stare at her. He was making her exceedingly uncomfortable.

She clutched her hands, waiting for him to speak. He seemed content to just sit there and stare. Today he was a different man from the one he had been yesterday—it was as if he were another person entirely. *Or had yesterday been some wild figment of her imagination?*

It was not just that he was sober. There was no grief for the public to see, no desolation, no despair. His face was a mask. But she knew he must still be feeling all of those things—she could not have imagined the depth of his grief. "Are you all right?" she whispered unsteadily, wanting to reach across the small table and touch his hand. She knew instinctively that he would reject such a gesture on her part immediately.

"That is a question I should be asking you."

She blushed. "I am fine."

Now he seemed uncomfortable. "Is my visit really such a surprise?"

"Yes."

"Did you think that after yesterday I would not come?"

She blinked, sitting up very straight and very still. Did he mean what she thought he meant? That he had come because he wanted to see her? She gave him an uncertain smile.

"I have come to rectify matters, Nicole."

"To—to rectify matters?"

"I would like a word with you in private," the Duke said abruptly, rising to his feet. He crossed the room with hard strides and shut the door soundly. He turned back to her, arms crossed. "The one thing I am is honorable. I live by my honor, or I try to. Yesterday I failed dismally."

Nicole's hopes plunged downward. "You are angry at me."

His face tightened. "There is no point in anger. You are not to blame. I am to blame. My actions speak for themselves."

"I do not blame you," she whispered, wanting to cry. He regretted what had happened, he regretted what they had done—what they had shared.

"Whether you blame me or not is irrelevant. The consequence of your visit is what is important, nothing else."

Nicole wet her lips. "The consequence?"

"You are no longer a virgin, and you could be with my child."

"I don't care about the first, and as for the second . . ." She trailed off. Nicole hadn't thought of that, purposefully.

"Only you would respond like that." He seemed grimmer. "I have come to make certain you understand that I would not leave things between us as they are. That would be even more intolerable than my behavior yesterday. We shall be wed."

Her mouth dropped open.

"Normally we would wait one year," he said, his gaze piercing, his tone commanding. "But being as there could be a child, we shall be wed immediately. I will speak with your father when he returns this afternoon."

Nicole was stunned. For a moment her head was spinning and she could not sort out her thoughts. Yet even though she could not, there was no jubilation, just the dawning of darkness, of despair. "You don't wish to wed me."

He paused. "What I wish is irrelevant. My actions yesterday have decided your fate—and mine."

"I see."

"You look distraught," he remarked, striding across the room and pouring her a sherry. "I did not mean to be so blunt."

"You could not have been more blunt," she said. Nicole felt tears brimming and furiously batted them away with her lashes. "You have made it clear that you seek to wed me out of duty and honor."

He handed her a sherry—she refused it. "You speak as if my intentions are those of swine. It is my duty to marry you."

"Just as it was your duty to wed Elizabeth," Nicole said. "Yet her you loved."

He did not respond.

"You do not really want to wed me, do you, Hadrian? If you had a choice—"

She saw his anger for the first time. "There is no choice! What I want is inconsequential!"

"Not to me."

Silence fell.

"What does that mean?" he demanded.

Nicole was about to confess all, but she stopped. He had come here to do his duty, "to rectify matters", as if she were some business affair that needed adjusting. How noble he was. How very noble—when yesterday he had been as near tears as a man of his caliber could be—over another woman. He loved another woman. The one thing Nicole had left was her pride. "If you do not know, then I shall not tell you."

He turned and stared at her.

Proudly, mouth pursed hard, she lifted her head. "I cannot wed you, Your Grace."

He was shocked.

Finally she could read his expression, and it almost made her change her mind. He looked as if she had struck him a painful and unexpected blow across the face. Nicole looked away, at her hands trembling in her lap. She wanted to marry Hadrian and be his wife more than almost anything—but the one thing she wanted even more was his love. She did not have it. He loved and grieved for a dead woman. He did not want to marry her at all, he would do so only because he had taken her virginity. How could she accept his offer on these terms? How could she give him her heart—while all he gave her was a cold gold ring?

He had already broken her heart too many times to count, and being an unloved wife would be worst of all.

"Did I hear you correctly?"

"I will not marry you," she said, more firmly. "Elizabeth is not even cold in her grave and—"

"As I said," he ground out, "we will be married immediately. I have already had my solicitors begin drawing up the documents and they are procuring a special license."

Nicole was on her feet, furious with his presumptive actions. Anger was a refuge she welcomed. "My mind is made up. I think you should leave—now."

He did not move. "You are the rashest woman I know. I suggest you think this through very clearly."

"There is nothing to think about. And if you do not go, then I am afraid I shall have to be the one to leave."

A long moment stretched between them while he stared at her and she looked anywhere but at him. Finally he said, "I do not believe this. I do not believe you. There is not a single woman in Great Britain who would refuse me."

She looked at him sadly. "There is one."

"You will not have to leave," he said, striding across the room. He flung open the door and was through it before she could blink. "Good day, Lady Shelton. Forgive me my audacity."

Her anger died instantly. She opened her mouth to call him back—and shut it abruptly. Nicole watched him with anguish. She watched him until she could see him no more, and listened until his footsteps had faded away. "Good bye, Hadrian," she choked.

Hadrian returned directly to No. 1 Cavendish Square. Shaken. Angry. Yet there was so much more behind the anger, so much more.

She had refused him.

He could barely believe it. Yet he recognized a will of steel when he saw it, and Nicole had not been coy. As resolved as he had been to marry her and rectify the situation, she was equally determined not to marry him.

He locked himself in his library. The Borzoi was sleeping there under his desk, and upon seeing the Duke, he rose eagerly to greet him. The Duke was so preoccupied that he did not even notice. The question echoed, screaming inside his skull. *Why did she not want him?*

Was it possible, after all the passion they had shared, that she truly did not want him? Hadn't she wanted to marry him the moment they had first met? What could have happened to change her mind? Something had happened, that was very clear. For why else would she reject him, the Duke of Clayborough? Hadrian was not vain, not at all, but he was astute enough to know that with Elizabeth's death he was now the preeminent catch in the land. So why now this rejection?

This rejection which was searing.

The Duke was no fool. He was well aware that he was catered to because of his position, wealth and power. He was well aware that he could—and did—do as he pleased solely because he was the Duke of Clayborough. It had nothing to do with his being Hadrian Braxton-Lowell. He was eagerly sought after by his peers only because he was the Duke of Clayborough—and if he were not, he would not be popular at all. In fact, his reclusive nature and his penchant for business would be loudly frowned upon—he would most likely be considered somewhat odd.

But Hadrian did not care. He had never cared about what others thought about him. He had stopped caring about what others thought about him long ago.

With women it was no different. Many women had fallen in love with him. Women competed fiercely with one another for his attention. They competed fiercely for the honor of jumping into his bed. Many had hoped to win him away from Elizabeth. Many had wanted to marry him. But it was not because he was handsome, virile, smart or honorable that they wanted him. It was not he himself that they wanted, it was the Duke of Clayborough.

Women even competed to become his mistress, although such efforts had no bearing at all upon whom he chose. And it was not because of his prowess in bed, or how excessively he inundated them with the fripperies they desired, or how lavishly he kept them. His current mistress was the stunning Holland Dubois. She gained a definite stature from being the Duke of Clayborough's mistress. When she went out to the theatre, restaurants or the fashion houses, wherever she went publicly, she was catered to, her every whim instantly met. She gained vast power from her liaison with him, more power than she could gain from any man other than royalty. She had a degree of power that could only be surpassed by his wife, should he one day take one.

He had proposed to Nicole Shelton. He had intended to marry her, to make her his wife, to make her the Duchess of Clayborough. Never again would society dare to criticize her. She would, finally, irrevocably, be accepted. For the power and position and wealth that were his would become hers.

Yet she had turned him down.

And she had meant it. She did not want the trappings of his position which he offered—and she did not want him. Something had happened to make her dead set against him. It was obvious what that was. His own behavior. His behavior yesterday, in the library, his behavior every time their paths had crossed.

He was no different from Francis, and she recognized this.

Hadrian gasped, turning to stare at his face in the mirror over the mantel. Did she know of his father, of the dissipated, perverted creature he had been? Had she learned of his antecedents? Had she glimpsed these same traits in him?

"I am not like Francis," he said harshly. "I have spent my whole damned life living honorably—I am not like him!"

He saw the pain in his own eyes. He saw the doubt. For a moment he was stunned by himself. And then the expression he had cultivated so carefully, for so long, was in its place, one perfectly bland and perfectly impassive.

But the truth mocked him. The truth hurt. She had rejected him. It hurt the way he had hurt before—a hurt he had thought was long since dead.

A hurt he was determined to bury now.

The truth was history, a history he had chosen to carefully forget, and indeed, he had been successful in the endeavor. Until now. Until her. Now the truth was in the present, as vivid as if it were today, not years of yesterdays ago. The truth was a very small boy, crying and frightened, alone in his bed, alone in his room, at Clayborough, in the darkness of an endless night.

He thought it was his earliest memory. He thought he was no more than four years old. He was going to be the next duke, so he was supposed to be a man, but he was not a man. He was afraid. He tried to stop the tears, but his sobs woke his parents up. "Darling what is it?" Isobel murmured, quickly entering his room and embracing him.

Trying not to cry, trying not to be afraid, he told her about the monster that had been chasing him in the darkness. She soothed him and he felt better, until he heard his father's voice in the doorway. Even before he understood the words, he tensed. "You spoil him. Leave him be. What a coward he is!" Francis laughed. He understood and was stricken with pain at the cruel statement. Was he, really, a coward? His father was staring at him, smiling in a nasty way. "Sissy boy," he jeered. "Afraid of the dark! Dukes are never afraid of the dark, but then, you will never be a real duke, will you? You will never be a real duke!" Isobel was on her feet, in a rage. He huddled into himself, already knowing what was to come, already afraid. He knew it was his fault, what was happening. "Stop!" she shouted, flying at Francis. "How dare you! How dare you . . ." "I dare what I will," Francis snarled. He caught her and jerked her violently into the hall. "Leave the sissy alone! Do you hear me? Leave your sissy boy alone!" They fought. He watched them fight, knowing his mother was being hurt because she wanted to protect him—a sissy boy. He cried. He could not help it. He did not know how long he watched before, despite his fear, he got up and tried to help his mother. But he was small and not very strong, and his two little fists only enraged Francis and made him turn his slaps to him. His mother was dragged from the room. His father ordered that he be left in darkness, and his door was locked from the outside. He crawled into the bed, hurting, miserable, still afraid. It wasn't his first realization that his father—that tall, blond, handsome god-like man, the Duke—did not like him. Did not love him. He could not remember how long he had been aware of that. Forever, maybe. He curled up under the covers.

The truth. Hadrian stared at himself in the mirror and regained control of himself. God, that had been so long ago, and he had thought that particular memory dead. He had thought the pain dead. The pain of his father's rejection had somehow become tangled up with the pain of Nicole's rejection.

He told himself that he was being a fool. But it was too late, he had already faced raw, naked emotions and taken one step off the precipice. Yet there was still time to step back.

He could dwell on the hatred which had never died. The hatred he felt for Francis still gave him strength. And power. Francis had given him his strength, even though he had meant to make him into a weakling. Francis had been the sissy after all, and because he was a weakling he had victimized those who were weaker than himself, especially his wife and son. It was so easy to understand now—it had been impossible to understand then.

He would not brood about Francis—and he would not dwell upon Nicole's refusal of his suit. Francis was dead, the past was dead. He was proud of who he was. If she thought he was like his father, then she was wrong—and he would prove it to her. He would reach deep inside himself for even more strength. And the beast which had been revealed would never surface again.

Calmer, he could now consider Nicole without emotion. It did not matter what she thought about him, or what she thought she wanted. She was rash, reckless, unconventional, and in this case, foolish. He knew better. She did not want to marry him but it would not stop him from doing what he knew was right.

And that meant making her his wife.

Not even an hour later, the Duke returned to Shelton's home on Tavistock Square. He was ushered inside by the butler, to whom he gave his draped coat and gloves. An inquiry assured him that the Earl was in residence and Hadrian was shown to the Earl's study.

He was, of course, circumventing etiquette. Especially in an instance like this, he should have sent a formal note requesting an interview at the soonest time convenient to

Shelton. But Hadrian felt he must settle this matter as soon as possible.

Nicholas Bragg Shelton greeted him informally, and Hadrian knew that he had forgiven him whatever trespasses he suspected he had taken with his daughter during the hunt. The man was about to be shocked. There was no avoiding it. Hadrian hoped his honorable intentions would diffuse what could be a terribly unpleasant situation.

"Hello, Hadrian. What brings you calling like this?"

"Nicholas." The two men shook hands. "I must apologize for calling without notice," he began, but Shelton cut him off.

"You should know me better than that. I don't give a damn about propriety and I never have. Shall I send for that damned tea you prefer?"

Hadrian shook his head, wondering if Shelton's attitude explained Nicole's defiance of convention. He sank into a lush emerald-green wing chair opposite the Earl. "I'll get right to the point, Nicholas. I want to wed your daughter."

Shelton sputtered, recovered, and stared. "Nicole?"

"Yes."

"I am afraid that you have taken me completely by surprise."

"Somehow I had thought I would," Hadrian murmured.

Shelton leaned forward, his regard piercing. "Elizabeth is barely cold in her grave."

"Unfortunately that is true."

Shelton's gaze had hardened. "Why are you coming to me now? As you damn well know, Nicole is not deluged with marriage proposals. There would be little to fear if you had waited another six months before asking me for her hand."

Hadrian grimaced. There was a possibility that waiting six months could be disastrous, but he did not wish to point that out, not yet.

Shelton stood abruptly. "Is there a reason for haste?"

Hadrian also rose to his feet. "Unfortunately, there is."

Shelton was motionless.

"My behavior has been indiscreet.

For an instant there was another silence. "How indiscreet?"

"There could be a child."

Shelton drew in his breath.

Hadrian said nothing, giving the man a moment to absorb this information.

Shelton kicked back his chair and paced to the floor-to-ceiling windows, gazing out at the mansion's spectacular gardens.

"I see," he finally said, the words clipped. "Now I understand your offer." He turned to stare at Hadrian, his gray gaze as sharp as steel, glittering. It was a look that would make a lesser man cower. "I would very much like to take my fist to your face, Hadrian."

The Duke said nothing.

"But I am not a fool, even if my daughter has allowed herself to be used as one. Despite that unhappy fact, both you and I know that this is the best thing that could ever happen to her."

Hadrian nodded, relieved that the worst had passed. "I will send my lawyers over first thing tomorrow morning, if it is convenient, to draw up the marriage contracts."

"You do not wish to haggle over the details now?"

"If your daughter's dowry consisted of one pence, I would marry her anyway," Hadrian said flatly.

"Of course," Shelton returned. "*Honor first*. But perhaps you should have recalled your family motto before you ruined my daughter."

"Touché," Hadrian said with another grimace. "I can only apologize. I am truly appalled by my own behavior and I take full blame for all that has happened."

Shelton eyed him thoroughly. "Maybe you had better direct your apologies to Nicole."

"She refused to accept them. Perhaps you should know, she is not keen on the idea of our wedding one another."

"Why?"

"I do not know."

"Do not worry about Nicole," Shelton said firmly. "While I do not relish the idea of forcing her again to the altar—surely you have heard what a disaster it was when I arranged for her to marry Percy Hempstead—she will do as she is told this time."

"I assumed that you would feel that way."

"Have you thought of a date?"

"Yes. I have already begun the proceedings to procure a special license so that we can be married immediately. Does the second Sunday from today meet with your approval?"

"That kind of haste will cause a scandal. People will guess why the two of you are marrying."

"I will take care of the gossips. There will be no scandal, not the kind you are thinking of. I shall make it abundantly clear that I am besotted with Nicole, a man so in love that I could not wait a moment longer to wed her. Because of Elizabeth I shall be condemned—not Nicole."

An expression which Hadrian could not read crossed Shelton's face. "All right. I thank you for sparing my daughter any further hurt."

Hadrian's jaw tightened. He did not think he had misunderstood the Earl's reference, and he could not let it pass. "I am sorry if I've hurt your daughter, Nicholas," he said, very softly. "And if it will ease your mind, when we first met she did not know I was engaged and she wanted to marry me. So much has occurred since then, but in time things will straighten themselves out between us, I am sure of it."

"But the question really is how you will feel in time."

Startled, Hadrian took a moment to answer, and when he did it was honestly. "I do not object to taking Nicole as my wife."

Shelton stared at him, his gaze searching. Hadrian felt an embarrassing tell-tale blush.

Shelton suddenly smiled. "Yes," he said, just as softly, "I think you are right. I think, with a little time, things will work out very well indeed."

"Aren't you ready, yet?" Regina asked.

Nicole sat on her bed in her underclothes. She glanced at her sister, who was a stunning golden vision in yellow chiffon, and sighed. "I wish I hadn't promised to go."

"Nicole! You have promised, and unless you claim you are sick, Uncle John will be terribly hurt if you do not come!"

Nicole knew that Regina was right. Although John Lindley was not actually her uncle, he was her father's best friend and she had known him since she was a toddler. When she was a child, he never failed to arrive at Dragmore with gifts for her and her brothers and sister. Nicole could not have loved him more even if he were her uncle.

But she had not recovered from that afternoon. From Hadrian's wretched, so-honorable proposal. She would never recover. How could she? When she wanted to marry him so much it hurt—and when to marry him would pain her even more?

Regina approached, her skirts whispering around her as she moved. "Nicole, what is it? I have not seen you so up and down since you have come to London." She sat beside her sister on the bed, her amber eyes registering their concern. She lowered her voice. "It's him, isn't it?"

Nicole nodded, meeting her sister's gaze.

Regina took her hand. "He likes you, Nicole, it's so obvious. Once he has ceased mourning for Elizabeth, you shall see. I am sure he will come forward to court you. And you must encourage him—I will teach you how."

Nicole almost burst into tears. She said, "He has already proposed marriage to me."

Regina gasped. "What!? Why, that is stunning!"

Nicole shook her head. "I refused."

"You what?!"

"I refused."

"Are you insane?"

Nicole gripped her arm. "He does not love me, he loves Elizabeth. He has given his heart to a dead woman. He only offered to marry me because he has kissed me . . . improperly." She blushed. She did not dare tell her sister the truth. "Intimately."

Regina stared, confused. "What do you mean, intimately?"

Nicole closed her eyes. "Hasn't Lord Hortense kissed you?"

"Of course."

The way Regina responded told Nicole that she had no idea of how a kiss could be intimate and shameless—open-mouthed, hot, tongues touching.

"What did he do, Nicole? What do you mean, he kissed you intimately? A kiss *is* intimate."

"There are kisses," Nicole said softly, "and there are kisses."

Regina was perplexed—and more than a bit curious. "Aren't you going to tell me?"

"All right!" Nicole nearly shouted. Tears swamped her. "He kissed me so hard my mouth is bruised! For ages and ages and ages! Our tongues touched! He touched me—where he shouldn't! Does that satisfy your curiosity?"

Regina was shocked speechless.

"Don't ever let Lord Hortense—or any man—take such liberties with you!" Nicole cried. "Or you will find yourself in my position!"

Still clearly stunned, Regina managed, "You must wed him."

"I will not. I cannot! He admitted that he was asking for my hand out of duty and nothing more."

Her sister's eyes widened again. Finally she found her voice. "All right, so it's not ideal. But he is the Duke of Clayborough. You must say yes."

"I cannot!" Nicole said again. "He treats me hatefully! I love him—and he has not one shred of love in his heart for me! Don't you understand? I could not bear to be his wife, loving him, while he feels nothing for me, while he runs to other women—to his mistresses. Can't you understand this?"

"No," Regina said bluntly. "All men have mistresses, Nicole. We are talking about the Duke of Clayborough! You are stupid if you don't marry him—especially when you love him!"

"I don't care that he is a duke. I care about how he feels about me. And all men don't have mistresses. Father doesn't have a mistress," Nicole fired back. "Neither does the Viscount Serle!"

"They are exceptions," Regina stated. "And you are being exceedingly foolish."

"If you marry Lord Hortense, will you be so blithe when you learn that he keeps a woman, too?"

Regina colored slightly. "I will not be surprised."

"Then you do not love him!" Nicole lunged to her feet to pace in a flurry of silk petticoats.

"I do!" Regina cried. "I am madly in love with him!"

"If you loved him, you would not be able to so casually accept his womanizing."

"Perhaps I am a realist and you, Nicole, are a romantic!"

Both sisters stared at each other. The very notion seemed absurd. Anyone who knew them would swear it was the other way around, yet in that moment it appeared that Regina was right. A knock on the door saved Nicole from responding.

Jane poked her head in. "Nicole, when you are dressed could you join your father and me in the library?"

Nicole was uneasy. "Whatever for, Mother?"

"There is something your father wishes to discuss with you," Jane said, her mien serious.

Dread overwhelmed Nicole. *It was about Hadrian.* She was certain of it. Had they somehow found out about her visit to Clayborough House yesterday? "What is it?"

"Just join us in the library, please." It wasn't a request. Jane smiled and closed the door.

Nicole realized how nervous she was when Regina touched her arm, making her jump. "You had better dress," she said. Her expression, usually gay, was grim. "And you had better change your mind—quickly—and tell the Duke you will accept his proposal!"

"Please shut the doors."

Nicole looked from her father, standing in front of his desk, to her mother, seated on the sofa. She closed the mahogany doors behind her. "Have I done something I don't know about?" She tried to smile.

Neither one of her parents smiled back. Her father was very grim. The feeling of dread rose again, washing over her. Especially when her mother got to her feet and came to her, looking so terribly anxious. "Oh, dear," Jane said softly.

"What is it?" Nicole asked.

"The Duke of Clayborough was here today," Nicholas said. "He has asked for your hand and I have agreed."

For an instant, Nicole thought that her father was referring to Hadrian's visit when he had proposed to her in the parlor. It took her a moment to comprehend just what he had said. The Duke had returned to Tavistock Square after that and gone directly to her father with his suit. "What?"

"Our lawyers are meeting tomorrow morning."

"No!" she cried violently. "I won't marry him!"

Jane's grip tightened on her arm, but before she could speak, Nicholas was striding toward her. "I believe that you have no choice."

Nicole froze, pinned by the look in her father's eyes. *He knew*. Hadrian had told him. She moaned.

"It's a little late for regrets," he said, staring at her. "And because of the possibility that you are with child, you shall be wed the second Sunday from today."

"*I'll kill him*," Nicole cried.

"There will be no crying off, Nicole. If you were so set against marriage to Hadrian, you should have considered that before allowing him to take you to bed."

Nicole spun out of her mother's grasp and rushed to the window, trying to get a grip on her hysteria. She was furious, furious with Hadrian for going to her father and telling him all, not only humiliating her but insuring that Nicholas would accept his suit and accept it with resolve. She was also filled with panic.

"Darling," Jane said, breaking the terrible silence. "It cannot be so bad. Hadrian is a fine man. He will be a fine husband. And I know you have feelings for him. Even if you think you no longer love him, in time, I am certain your feelings will return."

Nicole whirled. "He loves another woman! He loves Elizabeth!"

Jane and her father stared as the implications of her emotional outburst sank in. Jane came to her. "Elizabeth is dead."

"That makes it worse. Can't you see? I could not have competed with her when she was alive, but now, now I will be forever haunted by her memory!"

"You do love him," Jane said softly, touching her daughter's cheek.

Nicole jerked away. "You ran away from father because you loved him! And that is precisely why I cannot marry Hadrian! Surely you, Mother, of all people, can understand!"

"I was a fool," Jane said. "The best thing that ever happened to me was your father finding me and forcing me to marry him."

Nicole's jaw clamped into a hard line. "I am not marrying him. I am not."

Nicholas spoke, reminding them both that he was present. "I have accepted Hadrian's offer and you will not change my mind. Or have you forgotten the possibility that you are pregnant?"

Nicole winced at the blunt terminology.

"Yes, Nicole, pregnant," Nicholas said crudely. "I am not going to allow you to bear me a bastard grandson."

Tears filled her eyes. She had never known her father could be so cruel. "If we wait, maybe—"

"No. Enough is enough. Apparently you love the man anyway. You—"

"I don't love him!" she shouted, and in that moment she did not. "I hate him!"

"Regardless," Nicholas said harshly. "My decision stands."

"Darling, it will work out," Jane said consolingly.

She was panting. Again she shook off her mother's touch. "There will be a scandal. Father—I cannot bear another scandal."

"There will be no scandal. The Duke is prepared to take all the blame for your hasty marriage. He will make sure society thinks him a lovesick fool. No one will suspect the circumstances, or if they do, they will be in doubt."

"He is going to *pretend* to love me?" She could not bear it!

"He is protecting you from scandal," Nicholas said.

"You will force me—again?"

"Yes."

"Don't you remember what happened the last time?"

Her words hung in the air. Nicole instantly regretted them. Nicholas stared at her. "Are you threatening me, Nicole?"

For the first time in her life she was afraid of her father, but she held her ground. "Don't do this to me!"

"I will not let you run away," Nicholas said fiercely. "Not this time."

"You will have to tie me up and carry me to the altar!"

"If you wish to create the scandal, so be it."

Nicole sucked in her breath. Jane cried out at her husband in protest. For Nicole it was just too much. There was no changing his mind. With a small sob she fled the room.

Nicole was in a panic. Her father and the Duke of Clayborough were the two most powerful men she knew. If the two of them had decided that she was to wed Hadrian, then it would happen. She had caught her father by surprise the last time by running away at the last moment. In truth, she was ashamed of what she had done—but she had had no choice. She would never regret running away from Percy Hempstead. Yet she had never fought against that marriage the way she would fight against this one. And this time her father was forewarned. Nicole shuddered. He had meant it when he had said he would not let her run away—he had implied he would tie her up and carry her to the altar if need be! He was so set upon her marrying Hadrian that nothing was going to change his mind.

She paced her room in a frenzy. Once her father had been her greatest ally, her best friend. How could he do something like this? How could he force her to marry against her will? It was as if she were chattel. As if she were a slave—to be sold to another human being at whim. Although other women were given no choice in marriage, although other women did not even expect to be given a choice, Nicole had not been raised like other women. She had always had a shocking degree of freedom. Nicholas had not raised her to be a mindless and dainty porcelain doll set upon a pedestal. She had not been raised to be an ornamental wife and nothing more. He had approved of her knowledge of farming and breeding and mathematics, he had approved of her unconventional education; indeed, he had always been interested in her opinion on matters ranging from Dragmore to politics. And he hadn't cared less about how she dressed when she was at Dragmore with the family. He had thought her breeches most sensible for riding. He had certainly agreed with her that painting watercolors when one had no talent and singing when one had no voice were silly and useless pursuits, much to Nicole's relief. He had been proud of her unusual achievements and her intellect.

Yet now, now he did not care how she felt. He was marrying her off despite her deepest protests. He was making a decision about her and her life, changing it completely, against her will. He was no longer her greatest friend and ally. He was set against her. Hadrian had come between them—Hadrian had done this.

Thinking about the Duke and what he had done enraged her. Nicole's temper exploded. How dare he interfere in her life! How dare he ruin her relationship with her father!

There was a soft rapping upon her door. Nicole recognized her mother's knock and stiffened. She did not ask her to enter. Jane had taken her father's side against her, and Nicole could not be forgiving.

Jane entered anyway. Nicole turned her back on her. "Do not be mad at me, or at your father," she said gently. "We love you so much. We only want the best for you."

"If you really loved me you would not force me to marry him."

"In time you will feel differently, and understand what we have done."

"I doubt it."

Jane hesitated, still speaking to her daughter's back. "We are going to John's. I will tell him that you are ill."

"Why? I am not sick—just mad!"

"It's better that you do not go," Jane responded calmly. "Nicholas told me that the Duke was on John's guest list.

I doubt that he would be there, but if he should be, I think it best you do not meet until your temper has abated."

He was the last person Nicole wanted to see. "I heartily agree," she gritted.

Her mother left the room. A few moments later, Nicole went to the window and saw the Dragmore coach rolling down the drive and onto the street. She stared after it.

The first thing that Nicole saw when she stepped into the red salon at John Lindley's home was the Duke of Clayborough. The second thing she saw was Stacy Worthington.

She had decided to come. Why should she sulk in her room? Maybe he would think she was avoiding him. He was the last person she was avoiding. In fact, she had a few things she would love to tell him.

But she had not counted on this scenario.

She took a sherry from a tray being passed around by a servant and sipped it quickly. Her heart was beating erratically. Stacy Worthington was flirting with Hadrian. Nicole could not take her eyes off of them.

She laughed at everything he said. She pressed close to his side, gazing up at his face with a look of rapture. She appeared to devour his few words. She clung to him.

Not that Nicole cared. *She did not care*. She did not care that yesterday she had been in Hadrian's arms, that today he had proposed, and that they were supposedly engaged. If he wanted to make a fool of himself with another woman—a slender, beautiful woman—that was fine with her. In fact, maybe he would decide to make Stacy his wife! Nothing could suit her more!

Who was she kidding?

Nicole was upset, more upset than she had been all day. She realized she was staring at them, and finishing the sherry in a very unladylike manner, she turned away. Misery etched itself onto her heart.

She looked around the crowded salon, wishing she had not come. She ignored her parents. She saw Regina laughing with Martha and her husband, and was glad to see that her best friend was present. She smiled at them from across the room. Then she became aware of how she was standing alone in the midst of all the chatting clusters of people. Suddenly she felt awkward, and she would have loved to join one of the groups, but she did not know anybody. She was aware, too, that the two ladies besides her were looking at her, although they were attempting to be discreet.

Nicole's stomach clenched, and for a moment she forgot about the Duke and Stacy. She had been out of the social whirl for years and she had only arrived in London recently, so she told herself that it was not surprising that these ladies would be interested in her. Yet whom was she fooling? She was still considered something of an oddity and an eccentric despite all the years that had passed since the scandal. Would it never change? Would she always be an outsider?

She weaved her way toward the Serles and Regina. She was very careful not to even glance at the Duke. But the moment he spotted her she was aware of it. She could feel him looking at her.

"Martha," Nicole said, with no small amount of relief.

Martha hugged her while her husband pecked her cheek. He excused himself to leave them alone to their gossip.

"Nicole," Regina said once he was gone, "if I were you, I would go and talk to the Duke. That little witch Stacy Worthington has her eye on him—and if you're not careful she'll get him, too!"

Nicole looked at her sister frigidly. Thankfully Regina had not yet learned of the arrangements made between the Duke and her father. "I do not care."

"He came alone," Martha said. "But Stacy is definitely after him."

"Good. She can have him." Nicole took another glass of sherry from a passing tray. Ladies never had more than one drink, but she wasn't a lady, was she? She recalled lying in Hadrian's arms upon his library floor yesterday and felt heat rise in her cheeks. She knew he was staring at her. Perhaps he was remembering, too. Unable to control herself, she turned to look at him. Their glances locked.

Stacy was trying to talk to him, but he did not appear to be listening. Nicole thought about how he had imperiously decided her fate. About how *he thought* he was going to become her husband. About everything he had done. She gave him a very angry glance. He nodded politely. It was then that Stacy noticed where his attention was, and Nicole was satisfied to see her become a livid pink. Nicole turned away.

"You can lie through your teeth all day, Nicole, but I know how you feel," Martha whispered.

Nicole saw that Regina was about to speak, and she gave her a quelling look. Regina smiled somewhat smugly.

Just then two gentlemen paused beside them, politely greeting Martha. Introductions were made all around, and Nicole realized with a start that Lord Glaser was interested in her. "How are you tonight, Lady Shelton?" Glaser asked.

Nicole replied politely after recovering her senses. It had been a long time since a man had sought her out in society. What had changed? She had not been out since the charity picnic, excluding Elizabeth's wake and funeral. Was she suddenly considered acceptable because the Duke had extended his protection to her? No one, of course, knew of their engagement yet. And no one ever would, she thought resolutely.

She caught Glaser casting a glance at her person—the kind of look that Hadrian had sent her way a hundred times. He quickly redressed his gaze, but Nicole was uncomfortable. She didn't like to think it, but Hadrian's avid interest had never bothered her.

"I must say, I am pleased you are here tonight, Lady Shelton. You brighten up things considerably."

She had no choice but to thank him.

"Will you be staying in London for the rest of the season?"

"I doubt it," Nicole said awkwardly. He was interested in her, and she didn't know whether to laugh or cry.

"You must stay," Glaser said.

"I haven't decided yet," Nicole said. She saw that Hadrian was watching them. She had never been a flirt, and in truth, she didn't know how to be one. But she was suddenly overwhelmed with the urge to try, even though she had always been scornful of women who would stoop so low in order to make their beaux jealous.

She smiled at Lord Glaser and looked him directly in the eye. "But, perhaps you can persuade me." The moment the words were out, she knew they were too suggestive to be coy. Martha looked horrified. Glaser was briefly stunned.

"I mean," she blushed. "I mean, I am enjoying myself so, and . . . oh, excuse me!"

She broke free of the group, pushing through the crowd. She hadn't meant to be suggestive like that, she hadn't meant it at all. She had only meant to flirt! But flirting was for fools like Stacy Worthington! And now she was the one who had acted like a fool!

Outside the salon the corridor was empty, but she did not stop until she came to the powder room. Fortunately it was empty and she hurried in, locking the door behind her.

Oh, what a faux pas! She turned to regard herself in the mirror and saw that she was still red with embarrassment. Could she have possibly made a worse blunder?

Nicole swallowed and wet a washcloth and moistened her face. When she was composed she left the powder room, resolving to avoid Lord Glaser for the rest of the evening. She stepped outside, and there he was, waiting for her.

He was a handsome man and he was smiling. Nicole was frozen. "You should not have run away," he said.

"My lord," she said, "forgive me my slip of the tongue. I did not mean it the way it sounded."

"Of course you did not," he smiled again. She could not tell if he believed her or not. He touched her gloved wrist lightly. "There is a ball Friday night at the Abbots'. Would you care to accompany me?"

She was stunned at the invitation. But she was not given a chance to answer.

"She will not accompany you, Glaser," the Duke of Clayborough said. "And if you don't take your hand off of her arm, I will remove it myself."

He had come up behind them silently. Nicole jumped. Glaser was puzzled. "I beg your pardon, but did I hear you correctly?"

"You heard me correctly."

Nicole stared at Hadrian. His handsome face looked as if it was carved in stone. Yet his eyes were blazing as he gazed pointedly at Glaser's palm, resting so lightly upon her arm. Glaser's grip tightened. "I am not allowed to invite the most beautiful woman in London out? See here, you may be a Duke, you may outrank me, but that does not give you special rights."

"I have every right. My future wife will not be going with you to the Abbots' ball."

Glaser suddenly dropped his hand. "I had no idea, Your Grace," he said quickly.

The Duke's smile was cold. "Of course you did not. The engagement was only made today. The announcement is in tomorrow's papers."

"Excuse me again," Glaser said, nodding at them both. He hurried off.

Nicole was gaping. "How could you!"

She had hoped against all odds to get out of this engagement before it became common knowledge. She had no doubt that Lord Glaser would be spreading the news within seconds. By tomorrow morning all of London would know of their engagement, making a graceful and private break-up impossible. Once again the Duke had irrevocably set events in motion, affecting her life and her future, purposefully and without her consent.

"How could I what? Rescue you from an unwanted admirer?"

"Who said he was unwanted?" she flung heedlessly.

He gripped her arm. "He had better have been unwanted, Nicole."

She tried to shake him off and did not succeed. "Let go!"

He complied when it suited him. "I see you are upset."

"Upset? Hah! That is an understatement—Your Grace!"

"Are you upset because I have chased away a handsome but currently illegitimate suitor?"

"You know damn well why I am upset!" She hoped her curse would shock him.

It did not. It only angered him. "The moment someone enters this corridor, we shall be a spectacle."

Nicole laughed. "We are going to be a spectacle the minute our engagement is announced! Rather—a scandal!"

"I will not allow you to be the brunt of any scandal. I shall take the full brunt of any repercussions."

"By *pretending* to love me?"

For a moment he did not respond. "Trust me."

"Trust you?"

He blushed. Yet he set his mouth in a hard, grim line. "There is no point in beating a dead horse," he warned. "I have already said I take full blame for yesterday's incident."

"Yesterday's *incident?*" Tears abruptly came to Nicole's eyes. This man facing her was as cold as ice—not the passionate one who had held her and loved her. But that was just it—he hadn't loved her, not really. And now he was going to *pretend* to love her. "I am glad you blame yourself. We shall let bygones be bygones. But I am not marrying you!"

"You are very foolish, and besides, at this point, no one is asking you."

"How right you are!"

"I did ask you," he reminded her grimly.

"And I said 'no'!"

"You made your feelings abundantly clear. Why do you insist upon this argument?"

"My whole life is being decided without my consent and you ask me why I argue with you?"

"Nicole," he said tiredly, "you may argue until you are blue in the face, but the matter has been decided. We are getting married the second Sunday from today. And that is final."

Nicole lifted her chin. Tears filled her eyes. Her back was to the wall and she knew it. It was hopeless unless she did something terribly drastic, but she had not even dared to think that far ahead.

"Hadrian!" A woman called. "There you are—I was wondering where you had got to!"

Nicole stiffened and the Duke released her arm. She blinked away her tears of impotence and fury. Stacy Worthington smiled sweetly at the Duke, ignoring Nicole. "Shall we go back inside?" she asked.

"My dear," the Duke said, taking Nicole's arm. He shot her a warning look which Stacy could not see. His thumb stroked her gloved wrist. "Shall we?" he asked, giving her one of his rare smiles. It softened his features, and for a moment Nicole stared, mesmerized.

Stacy was staring, too.

Nicole could drown in his golden eyes. With an effort she realized that this was a game, that it was all pretense. Her heart turned over. She tried to pull away, but his grip tightened so quickly that she could not move an inch. In fact, she was pressed against his side.

She did not want to be pressed against his side. She did not want to be anywhere near him. She did not want to be the recipient of such an intimate and tender look. But there was no choice.

"Stacy," the Duke of Clayborough said. "I believe you have already met Lady Shelton?"

"Yes."

"Lady Shelton has done me the great honor of agreeing to become my wife," he continued, giving her another too-warm look.

Nicole told herself fiercely that she would not burst into tears, she would not.

"Hadrian!" Stacy gasped. "B-but . . . Elizabeth!"

The Duke looked at his cousin. "Elizabeth is dead," he said. "And I am marrying Nicole in less than two weeks time."

Nicole closed her eyes, but not before seeing the other girl's wrath.

His arm moved and slipped around her shoulder in a warm and intimate embrace. "I am afraid I just cannot wait," the Duke said.

Nicole left Lindley's immediately, begging a ride with the Serles, who were also preparing to depart. She was distressed from her encounter with Hadrian and she knew it showed. Martha, however, would never question her in front of her husband, and Nicole had been counting on this. She practically leapt from their coach when they stopped at Tavistock Square, mumbling her thanks and hurrying into the house. Once within there was no need for pretense. Aldric's expression was openly worried as he watched her rush through the foyer. "My lady," he called after her. "Are you all right?"

"No, Aldric," Nicole cried wildly, already flying up the stairs. "I am not all right!"

Her room was no sanctuary. Not many minutes later, she heard her parents and Regina in the hall outside, saying their good nights. Nicole quickly turned off the lights in her room, wanting to maintain her privacy. She heard her parents moving down the hall. A moment later there was a wild pounding on her door. She groaned. By now, her own head was pounding as well.

Regina did not wait for Nicole's response and barged abruptly in. "You look as if someone has died!" Regina exclaimed, her own enthusiasm not dimmed in the least. "Is it true? Is it true that you are to become his wife? Several people asked me just as you were leaving Uncle John's! They said he said you were engaged! Nicole! Are you to be the next Duchess of Clayborough?"

"Please." Her headache had just increased.

"Oh, God, it is true!" Regina cried. "What happened? I thought you refused him!"

"I did!" Nicole said crossly. "The wretch went to father. Father accepted without my consent."

Regina beamed. "That is wonderful!"

"I am not marrying him."

Regina's smile vanished. "I hope you're joshing me."

Nicole gave her a dark look.

"Father has arranged it! He is the Duke of Clayborough! What is wrong with you? You told me yourself you're mad about the man!"

By now, Nicole had no idea how she felt about Hadrian Braxton-Lowell, although she genuinely suspected her feelings had turned. "Not any more, I'm not."

"You're a fool if you don't marry him."

"Then I guess I'm a fool."

Regina huffed, fists clenched. "You're going to fight this, aren't you? You're going to fight Father, aren't you?"

"I am. Why are you upset?"

"Why am I upset?" Regina looked as if she were on the verge of tears. "Well, Nicole, I'll tell you why. Because you're being bloody selfish!"

Nicole had never heard her sister curse and she was shocked. "I'm selfish?"

"I've never complained before. But if it weren't for you I'd already be married! *Bloody hell!* I'm almost nineteen and they've been making me wait hoping that one day you'll get an offer so you can marry first. Well now you've got an offer—a good one! But you're too stupid to be reasonable. And I'm sick and tired of being an old maid. Bloody hell!"

Regina was so distraught that tears pooled in her eyes. Nicole was aghast, having had no idea that her sister had been so distressed. "Please try and understand. I can't marry him, I can't."

"I don't understand—I'll never understand! You are being selfish and stubborn and just plain stupid!" Regina ran from the room, slamming the door behind her.

Nicole was trembling. She and her sister were very close. Although they'd had plenty of spats, they'd never fought like this. How long had Regina felt this way? How long had she blamed Nicole for being forced to wait to marry? Nicole suddenly felt as if her sister was right and that it was her fault that Regina was still unwed. She felt as if she had wronged Regina. She loved her little sister; she wouldn't hurt her for the world.

But Nicole also felt as if her sister had abandoned her. And that hurt her. Now, when she needed her sister desperately as a friend and ally, Regina had deserted her.

"Nicole, we must talk!" Martha cried.

It was teatime the day after Lindley's at-home. Nicole was immensely glad to see Martha. All day she had been confronted with the wedding preparations now madly under way. Apparently, despite the haste, or because of it, the Duke was determined to have the grandest society wedding in years, and Jane was immersed in a whirlwind of planning.

Nicole did not care what they planned. But her mother made sure she was kept informed of the more important details. Jane had also sent for a seamstress from one of the top fashion houses, and Nicole had been forced to endure that woman's attentions for many hours as her wedding gown and trousseau were chosen, fitted and refitted. In fact, it was going to be a week of endless fittings.

Nicole grew angrier and angrier.

It was apparent from Martha's distraught tone that she had learned of the impending nuptials. "It's all over town! I didn't believe it! But when I walked in here and saw Mr. Henry—the best chef in town—and Madame Lavie—the most creative and expensive designer in town—I realized it is true!"

Nicole was in her undergarments in her bedroom, Madame Lavie having just left. She paced away. "It's true."

"And you didn't tell me!" Martha cried, hurt.

Nicole whirled. "Everything happened yesterday! Only yesterday! Ohh! That bastard has made sure that there is no way out!"

"You had better tell me everything," Martha said, instantly concerned.

Nicole sat and did so. When she had finished Martha looked shocked—for Nicole had not hidden the real reason for the marriage. Yet she reached for Nicole's hand to hold it comfortingly. "I know this is not how a woman dreams of being married, but this is what you wanted from the first. And there could be a child, Nicole. Of course you must marry him. Why are you being so stubborn and foolish?"

Nicole stood. "I am tired of being told the same thing by everybody I love—by everybody who is supposed to be on my side."

"Do there have to be sides, Nicole?"

"He has turned this into a war," she said darkly. "If he had only waited . . ."

Martha looked at her inquiringly.

Nicole grimaced and refused to speak aloud her unfinished thoughts. But they were there. *If* he had waited, then maybe, in time, all of this might have happened the way it should have. *With him seeking her hand in earnest.*

"You poor dear," Martha said softly.

"The last thing I want is your pity. How am I going to get out of this now?"

"You can't!" Martha cried, horrified. "Everyone knows of the engagement and that event alone is unseemly enough!"

Grimly Nicole sat down facing her friend. "How unseemly? I may as well know all of it. What are the gossips saying now?"

Martha hesitated.

"They're saying the worst," Nicole guessed, pained even though she had known it would turn out this way—another scandal with her at the center.

"It's that bitch Stacy Worthington," Martha declared

heatedly, her vulgar language shocking Nicole and causing the older woman to blush. "I heard her myself this afternoon at Sarah Lockheart's."

"What is she saying?"

Martha hesitated. "That there is only one possible reason why the Duke of Clayborough—a man of honor—would wed you so shortly after his fiancée's death."

"And she's right," Nicole said. "So much for Hadrian's pretense!"

"What pretense?"

Nicole told her how he planned to play the lovesick fool to remove all suspicion about the reason behind their abrupt wedding.

"There is that gossip, too," Martha said eagerly. "Sarah's the one who said she heard that Clayborough is absolutely mad about you and *that* is the real reason for such haste."

"Who would believe that?" Nicole asked sadly, her heart wrenching anew.

"I would."

Nicole jerked. "Now you're being foolish."

"Time will tell all, won't it?"

The possibility that, in time, the Duke might come to love her flooded her with such fierce yearning that Nicole choked. "He is a cold man," she whispered, but she remembered him in the library, embracing her as if she were a phantom that might disappear at any instant. Embracing her as if he needed her desperately. As if he loved her. She closed her eyes, not wanting to remember—not wanting to hope.

Martha suddenly smiled. "This won't be like the last time, Nicole. Scandal cannot hurt you now, not as the Duke's bride. Not as his wife."

Nicole took a breath, composing herself. "I must face it, musn't I? I am going to marry him—and in a week and a half's time. There is nothing I can do to avoid it."

Martha stared at her solemnly. "You ran away from Percy. You could always run away again."

Nicole gazed back at her dear friend. How could she possibly explain to Martha that she would not even consider jilting Hadrian in such an awful manner, when she could not even explain it to herself?

Martha smiled. "But you won't, will you, Nicole? And it's not because the Duke won't let you."

Wisely, Nicole did not respond, for she had no plausible response to make.

Hadrian returned to Clayborough House in a black humour. His lawyers had spent the day with Shelton firming up the marriage contracts, and several hours ago he had signed them with a flourish. Then he had dressed with unusual care to pay a proper call upon his bride. He had no illusions; he was certain she would be in a fine temper—as fine a temper as she had been in last night. He was prepared to hold his own responses in check, and he resolved not to be goaded by anything she said or did.

He had not seen her. Upon arriving at Tavistock Square, the butler had informed him with expressively dismal eyes that Nicole was indisposed. Although the man's face was impassive, it was clear he was lying for his mistress and was distressed at denying the Duke. Shortly afterward the Countess appeared. She apologetically informed him that Nicole was ill and confined to her bed. Hadrian could guess exactly how ill she was, and just what the cause was of her malady.

He pretended to accept Jane's excuses, inquired politely after Nicole's health, and informed the Countess that he would return on the morrow, and hopefully, Nicole would be well enough to receive him then. Yet once he was ensconced in his coach, the civil facade he'd worn dropped.

He strode into Clayborough House, so irritated and preoccupied that he did not even see Woodward, who was waiting for him to hand him his coat. He slammed the doors of the library resoundingly shut. He did not need this pretense of hers to know that she was unhappy with the arrangements. She had already made her feelings very clear when she had rejected his suit out of hand herself.

This game would end soon enough, he thought grimly. The Countess had understood his veiled warning that Nicole had better receive him on the morrow. If she insisted upon being so openly opposed to their union, how was he going to save her from scandal? He was trying to protect her, yet her actions were going to undo all that he sought to accomplish.

Yet he should have known better than to expect her to demurely accept wedlock to him when it was arranged without her consent. There was nothing demure or passive about Nicole and there never had been. Hadn't he secretly admired her more than once for her daring disregard of convention? Yet now was not the time to contravene the social codes. That reckless streak that so attracted him—and he assumed that this was the lure she possessed—would make his intentions to protect her that much harder to fulfill.

But fulfill them he would.

She was going to become his wife, and as such, she would gain not just his name, his title and his wealth, but the respect that was due her as well. He had never given a damn before about what his peers said about him. He had always known that they were not just in awe of him, but secretively harbored some degree of doubt about him, as well. But now there would be no more doubts, not about him, and not about his wife.

He would make sure of it.

Isobel arrived at Clayborough House that evening dressed for supper in a magnificent crimson gown, the skirt beaded elaborately along the hem. Although Isobel's figure was still shapely enough that she could get away with the most daring of current fashions, she was realistic enough to know that at fifty-plus one she did not have the skin of a twenty-year-old and her gowns were more modest than revealing. To match her gown she carried a dark red reticule beaded in jet, and she also flashed rubies on her ears, at her throat and on her wrists.

By now she had heard the gossip. She did not doubt it. Not after the tension she had witnessed between them. She intended to ask her son directly if he was marrying Nicole Shelton in less than two weeks time.

Woodward greeted her with a smile that was reserved exclusively for her. Isobel suspected that he had fallen in love with her when she first married Francis, but wisely, she had always pretended ignorance of his emotions. "Hello, Woodward. How are you this evening?" She had always been familiar with the staff—even when Francis mocked her for it.

"Fine, thank you, Your Grace. His Grace is in the red salon awaiting you."

Isobel smiled, handed him her mink wrap, and allowed him to escort her to her son and announce her formally.

Hadrian greeted her warmly, although he seemed disturbed. When they were alone and seated with drinks, tea for him and white wine for her, Isobel looked at him directly. "I have heard gossip, Hadrian."

He grimaced. "Which gossip?"

"All of it, I suspect. Are you marrying Nicole Shelton?"

"Yes, I am. I am sorry you had to find out this way, before I could tell you."

"Is the rest of the gossip true, too?"

He stood restlessly. "If you mean am I madly in love with her, no."

Isobel eyed him.

"I intend to circumvent any unsavory rumours by appearing absolutely lovestruck," he stated.

"I see." She had to smile. "I cannot imagine you acting besotted."

"All the more reason my behavior will be credible."

"Hadrian, do you mind me asking? Why are you marrying Nicole Shelton so soon after Elizabeth's death?"

He flushed. "Because she could be with my child."

"I see. So there is truth to the rest of the gossip, as well."

His face darkened. "So that is the talk, is it? I shall nip it in the bud quickly enough! I shall find out the perpetrators of this gossip and make my displeasure unequivocally known."

"I'm sure you will stop the rumours in no time," Isobel said softly. She, too, stood, and placed her hand on her son's arm. "How are you feeling?"

He tensed and moved away. "I will always miss Elizabeth, but she is dead." He paced to the tall picture window and stared out of it.

"I mean about your marriage. About your bride."

He turned, his smile polite. "I am taking full responsibility for my behavior, Mother. What more would you have me say? That I really am in love with Lady Shelton? I assure you, I am not."

Isobel smiled. "I see."

"May I have your approval?" he asked. "I know she will not make the best duchess, but I imagine with time she will manage well enough."

"To the contrary," Isobel said, still smiling. "I think she will make a fine duchess and a wonderful wife."

Hadrian stared. He grew somewhat red and coughed, loosening his necktie. "I am glad you think so."

"She is a fine woman. I like her. I admire her resilience and her independent thinking."

Hadrian sighed. "You would. Mother, she is dead set against this marriage. Her 'independent thinking' is already causing me grief."

Isobel laughed. "I imagine it is. Hadrian, you are too straight-laced by half. A little impropriety in your life will do you good."

"A little impropriety in my life will do me good?" he echoed. "You make no sense, Mother. Obviously I am nowhere near straight-laced enough."

Isobel sobered. "Darling, we all make mistakes. You are not the only conscientious man to succumb to his passion for a woman. Believe me when I tell you that a good dose or two of Nicole Shelton's independent thinking is just what you need."

"One dose of Nicole Shelton is the equivalent of a hundred doses of any other woman! Nicole does nothing by halves, Mother. When she is daring, it is in full form. Are you accusing me of being too proper?"

"Am I?"

"Would you rather I be like dear Francis?"

Isobel was instantly somber. "Of course not. You are *nothing* like him, Hadrian, *nothing!*"

"Really?" He was cool, pacing to the butler's table and pouring himself another cup of tea. "Perhaps Lady Shelton thinks differently."

Isobel started. "What does that mean?!"

"I fear she finds my behavior somewhat reprehensible. In truth, it has been reprehensible. There is more of Francis in me than I ever suspected."

Isobel was white with anger. "That's not true!"

He lifted his gaze to her. His expression was mocking. "We all have a dark side, Mother. For some, it is just darker than others."

Isobel was speechless.

"I did not mean to upset you," the Duke said quickly. "This topic is too morbid. Shall we discuss the wedding plans? I decided that all of London should attend, to see that we have nothing to hide."

"Hadrian." Isobel came to him and touched his arm. "You are not like Francis. It upsets me when you speak like that. You are not at all like him!" Guilt was lodged in her chest for denying her son the truth.

"I should have never brought it up." His face was closed, and she knew he would not discuss such a distasteful—and intimate—subject with her again.

Isobel turned away. Her heart was pounding and her palms were clammy. Francis had been dead and buried for two years now. She had thought him out of their lives. But another quick look at Hadrian's brooding face told her that he still haunted not just her, but her son. Oh God! She must tell him the truth!

She resolved that she would. She had not realized that Francis still affected Hadrian, even dead and buried as he was, that her son was accusing himself of being a monster like Francis, and that he thought Nicole found him just as dishonorable. Hadrian was the most honorable man she knew—and as such, he had every right to know the truth.

Isobel trembled. The time had never been more right. After all, he was about to marry, soon he would have his own son. She would tell him everything. She must.

"Mother, are you all right?"

"Just a bit faint," Isobel managed.

"Let's go in to eat," Hadrian said, quickly coming to her and taking her arm. His sherry-colored gaze took in her features with vast concern.

Isobel wanted to cry. For the same dilemma that had confronted her for years still loomed before her. What if, by telling him everything, she sacrificed his love and his trust? Hadrian was the most important thing in her life and she could not bear it if he turned away from her, she could not. Somehow she had to reach deep within herself to find the strength and the courage she needed to reveal what she must to her son.

Isobel was born in the spring of 1844. She was the Earl of Northumberland's first child. Her mother, Lady Beatrice, died giving birth to her. It was fifteen years before Roger de Warenne remarried. In the ensuing time, there were just the two of them—father and daughter.

From the very start she was a blonde, blue-eyed beauty. Her father adored her and doted upon her, as did the entire household and all of her aunts and uncles as well. In consequence she could not but be somewhat spoiled, but by nature Isobel was not manipulative, and her precocious ways were endearing. The Earl proudly noted that she was by far too clever for a lady, even a young one.

The Earl was determined to arrange the best marriage possible for his daughter. The de Warennes were one of the premier families in the realm. They claimed as fact their belief that Rolfe de Warenne, who had come to England with William the Conqueror, was one of his greatest generals and closest advisors. He had become the first Earl of Northumberland in 1085, and every earl since had been a power behind the throne. It was a family tradition of sorts. Roger was no exception; he was a confidante of the Prime Minister's and he exercised great behind-the-scenes power in the affairs of the country.

He was also close friends with the seventh Duke of Clayborough, Jonathan Braxton-Lowell, another extremely influential man, although in those days he was with the opposition. Politics aside, both men were not only well-acquainted, but they genuinely liked, admired and respected one another. It was one fateful night at their exclusive James Street club that they decided to wed their children to each other.

Of course, for two such men there was much more than friendship involved in forming such an alliance. Roger de Warenne did not know the details, but he guessed the facts from the marriage contract that the two men agreed upon. Isobel was one of the greatest heiresses in the land, but Jonathan insisted she bring a great deal of sterling into the Clayborough dukedom as well as two very productive estates. Roger could only surmise that Clayborough was cash-poor. That did not disturb him, not in the least, for Northumberland was very very rich.

Francis was one of the most sought-after bachelors in Britain, so it was not surprising that Roger chose him for his daughter. One day he hoped to have a legitimate son to inherit his title, his wealth and his power, but Isobel was his first child and he loved her dearly. She had wealth already by being a great heiress. As his daughter she held the complimentary title of "Lady." She could have any man she wanted, but it was not up to her to choose. Roger wanted more for her, much more than what was obviously attainable. By marrying her to the future Duke of Clayborough he achieved much more, for one day she would be a duchess, her rank surpassing even his. One day her son would be the ninth Duke of Clayborough. Roger exercised great power, but his grandson would have—unbelievably—even more.

Roger was too shrewd to take any chances on his vision of the future. Because Jonathan was so desperate for the sterling, he succeeded in maneuvering him into a corner. Should Francis die before Isobel, with no issue from their union, Isobel would inherit Clayborough. De Warennes lived long lives, so Roger had not a doubt that Isobel would outlive Francis, and should they be unlucky enough not to have a child, Clayborough would revert to the de Warennes. And should they have a child, his surname would be de Warenne Braxton-Lowell. Either way, Roger had won for his family what he wanted.

The contract was signed, sealed and delivered. But the friendship between Roger and Jonathan was never the same. The Duke of Clayborough could not forgive the Earl of Northumberland for what he had demanded.

Isobel was sixteen, and for the first time in her life she was unhappy. The year before her father had married a woman not much older than she was and their relationship had changed terribly. His new wife, Claire, was a widow in her early twenties, a stunning, dark beauty whom her father could not seem to be apart from. Suddenly Isobel was no longer the focus of his universe. Suddenly he was barely aware that Isobel existed.

Isobel was thrilled when the Earl announced her betrothal. She was eager to escape her home—and her father. She was so eager that she demanded her wedding be moved to an earlier date instead of waiting until after her first season, and her father agreed.

Without even having met Francis, she was already in love with him. She knew all about Francis Braxton-Lowell. He was twelve years her senior and considered *the* catch in all of Britain. He was blond and dashing and had every female who met him swooning. When Isobel met him she was not disappointed. He was beautiful, and his cool disdainful arrogance only made him more attractive.

In May of 1861, on Isobel's seventeenth birthday, they were wed.

And her illusions were promptly shattered.

Prior to their wedding night, Francis had always been the perfect gentleman. In fact, he had never even kissed her, never even offered her any of the flowery flattery Isobel was so used to hearing. Not that she cared. He was the prince of her dreams and he could do no wrong. It was his sophistication, she assured herself, which made him aloof—and exciting.

She vaguely knew what to expect on her wedding night. Her grandmother had explained to her in some detail what her husband would do. Isobel had been shocked—yet titillated. She could not imagine a man having an appendage that grew big and hard which he would put inside her. Thinking about the kisses which her grandmother assured her would proceed the momentous event excited her even further. How she had been yearning for Francis' kisses!

Francis came to her with a cold glint in his eyes, unsmiling, offering no comfort, no tenderness, and no words of love. "Are you ready for me?" he asked, his tone mocking. His gaze swept her as he leaned against the closed door of her bedroom.

Isobel felt a moment of panic. She was clad in a sheer, beautiful nightgown, her hair down and flowing to her waist. Yet he seemed unimpressed, even indifferent. "Yes," she managed to keep her voice firm, she managed to smile.

"Such a brave lass," he mocked again, approaching her. "Will you still be brave in another moment?"

Her eyes widened, she could not respond. She had the distinct impression that not only didn't he love her—he didn't even like her! But she had to be wrong.

He tossed aside his dressing gown and Isobel was treated to her first sight of a naked man's body. Francis was slender, but all lean muscle, yet she could not focus on that. What did draw her attention was the appendage her grandmother had referred to, and it seemed huge to her innocent eyes and suddenly she was very afraid.

He laughed, coming down on top of her. "Not so brave now, are we?"

"Francis, wait," she cried, panic engulfing her.

He ignored her and kissed her.

Isobel instantly gagged. His breath reeked of cigarettes and whiskey. His kiss was wet and slippery—she did not like it at all.

"Frigid little bitch, aren't you?" he murmured. "Spread your legs."

Isobel froze at his words. Before she could react he was opening her thighs for her—and then he was ripping her apart. Had she known the pain would be so great she would have been prepared and she would not have screamed. But she did not know, she wasn't prepared, and she did scream. Fortunately, Francis spent himself quickly, and just as quickly he left her.

But not before a cruel parting word. "I do hope your attitude improves."

After that, Isobel hated him. She had never been abused before, not physically and not verbally. And she was not a woman who could hide her feelings. Francis was amused. She quickly realized that he was glad she hated him and he liked hurting her in bed.

Fortunately he did not come to her bed very often.

Although Isobel despised her husband, she had been born to nobility and she took to being a future duchess with ease and aplomb. They entertained at least once a week, and she was an outstanding hostess, soon considered one of the premier hostesses in the realm. She received more invitations than she could accept, and she was out every night of the week, without Francis, who went his own way with his own friends.

Isobel also got on famously with the Duke and Duchess, whom she grew extremely fond of. The Duchess was a stern, aloof woman, but when she gave praise she meant it, and she approved of Isobel. The Duke was warm, hearty and kind, and he doted on her. Isobel could not understand how two such people could have had a cruel son like Francis.

She soon heard the rumours. It became apparent to her that Francis spent all his time with a wild crowd of young men, most of whom were bachelors. They devoted themselves to gambling, racing, drinking and the hunt. Isobel also learned from one of the women in her social circle that Francis kept a beautiful dancer as his mistress.

She was furious. She knew men had mistresses, but it had never occurred to her that *her husband* would be like other men. Indeed, she had never dreamed a marriage such as hers could even exist! It was the greatest insult to her pride that Francis spent most of his nights with another woman—even though she did not want him at home with her. And the worst part of it was that the whole world knew of his infidelity.

"Someone told me that you keep a mistress, Francis," she said furiously. "And apparently it's common knowledge. Is it true?"

There was no hesitation. The blow came before she could even see it coming. He struck her across the face so hard that she fell to the floor and saw stars. When she began to focus dizzily, her face throbbing in pain, Francis was bending over her. "Don't you *ever* speak to me in such a manner again, Isobel. What I do is *none* of your affair. You have one purpose in my life—do you understand? And that is to give me my heir."

Wisely, Isobel did not answer and she did not move. He strode away from her, leaving her on the floor. Then she sat up. Despite the pain, which brought forth hot tears, her eyes blazed.

There were no more illusions to shatter, no more innocence to lose. She was not yet eighteen.

Isobel could not conceive a son. Francis came to her bed less and less frequently, which did not help matters. Yet the more time that went by without her becoming pregnant, the more he accused her of being barren and worthless and the quicker he was to find an excuse to strike her.

Four years after they were wed, the Duke of Clayborough died. Isobel was deeply saddened by the loss of the man who had become such a friend to her, almost replacing her father, and she wept at his funeral. Francis showed no remorse. If anything, he took up the title of Duke eagerly enough. He remained isolated in mourning for less than an entire week.

Isobel was furious with him. She was careful to ignore him and say nothing, however. She had learned to not only avoid her husband, but to refrain from criticizing him. Besides, everyone knew that Francis was an alcohol-addicted wastrel, she knew that now.

It was during this time that her father came to see her without Lady Claire. He came to comfort her, yet Isobel was cool. These past few years he had begun a new family; Claire had given him two sons. Isobel had rarely seen him, and that he no longer seemed to love her as he had hurt her more than anything.

"I know how fond you were of Jonathan," he said heavily, suffering his own grief over the loss of his friend. "I, too, shall miss him."

He had always seemed immortal to Isobel, yet suddenly she saw him as a man of his age. Suddenly she realized that he was not much younger than the Duke of Clayborough had been—and the Duke was dead of natural causes. Fear swept her. No matter what had happened since he had married that woman, he was her father—and she loved him. "Father, we must spend more time with one another," she said firmly.

He looked suprised, and pleased. "I am always willing to make time for you, darling," he said. "But you are always too busy."

"Me! You are always with Claire and the boys."

"Since your marriage I have invited you repeatedly to join us in London or in the country—and you have always refused. Yet I know you and Francis go separate ways. I assumed you have such a busy and important social schedule that you have no time for your father."

Shocked, Isobel realized he was hurt. She went into his arms. "I thought you were too busy for me," she murmured. "It appears we have misunderstood one another."

After that, she began accepting his invitations, and soon found that she adored her half-brothers. Claire wasn't really so bad, in fact, she went out of her way to befriend Isobel. And her father always managed to find time so that the two of them could be alone. Isobel realized that she had been a foolish young girl to turn away from him all those years ago. It was obvious that he was content with Claire and that he worshipped his boys. She was happy for him.

Six months later the first of Francis' debtors came knocking upon her door. He was exceedingly nervous and apologetic, but he had a note that was four months overdue—for twenty thousand pounds. Isobel was shocked, and when she told Francis, having put the man off, he told her to mind her own business. In the following month several more debtors appeared. Isobel did not pay anyone, telling them they must speak with her husband, who was very adept at avoiding them. The astounding amount Francis seemed to owe was a hundred thousand pounds.

He finally told her that he did not have the money.

The debtors kept hounding her. Francis merely laughed, shrugging off the entire affair. Finally one of the debtors threatened to take Francis to court. Isobel hated Francis, but she could not allow that to happen. She pawned her family jewels.

Unnerved by what had happened, Isobel was determined to appraise for herself the family's state of affairs. She took it upon herself to go through his desk. To her shock, she found a great many bills unpaid, all of which were owed by the estates. Several managers of Clayborough's different holdings had come to her requesting funds recently, and she had put them off, too. Now Isobel sought out the manager of their ancestral home and questioned him closely. She learned that while there were managers for the various Clayborough holdings and estates, they had always been in charge of day-to-day operations while the purse strings and general supervision had been left up to the Duke. Jonathan had been dead for nine months now, yet Francis had not taken up his responsibilities. Isobel was appalled.

She knew what she wanted to do. She thought that Francis might be displeased. Yet she had long since stopped caring about what he thought.

She traveled from one holding to the next, inspecting every inch of Clayborough property, poring over the books and holding meetings with the managers. When she had a firm grasp on the situation, she went to their bank and had a bank draft drawn up. She then presented it to Francis.

"There are many bills which have not been paid, Francis," she told her husband one morning when he returned home disheveled and unshaven from the night of revelry before. "I have gone over all of the accounts thoroughly and I need access to eighty thousand pounds to pay our debts. Our banker has drawn up this check. Would you kindly sign it?"

He grabbed the draft. He saw that it was payable to his wife. He tore it up. "If we had eighty thousand pounds in the bank, do you think I would let you spend it?"

"But Mr. Pierce was only too glad to draw up the cheque."

"You fool! He would gladly lend us the sum—with interest!" Francis stormed out.

Isobel thought for a long time. Then she met with the Clayborough solicitors. She went back to Mr. Pierce. Her father went with her. A loan was arranged—in her name only. All of the estate's bills were paid off and they began running smoothly again, under Isobel's close supervision.

She was now running the vast ducal estates with all their affairs. Although she was a novice, she was clever, and she had the solicitors and her father to aid her. When the first small profits came in from her farmlands in the south and from timber sales in the north, Isobel felt a tremendous sense of satisfaction as she signed a draft and sent it to Mr. Pierce. It would be a long time before Clayborough would be on an even footing again, but with prudent management, she intended to make it happen.

And the more successful she was, the more Francis taunted and mocked her—the more he hated her.

* * *

In the fall of 1867 Isobel took her first voyage to America. It had been three years since Jonathan died, and the Clayborough estates were holding their own despite the bad economic times. Isobel had made some investments that she hoped were wise, including one in a mining company. She had leased them vast tracts of land as well as undertaking a partnership with them. In the future she hoped to see sizeable profits—she was gambling on it when she did not have the means to gamble at all.

With the end of the War Between the States, she, as well as many others, saw the possibilities for gain that would come with the rebuilding of the South. Isobel was on her way to Virginia to invest in land that was now burned out and dirt cheap, but that would one day be worth a fortune. Of course she did not have the funds to buy, but Mr. Pierce had been only to glad to give her what was now her third loan.

It was no secret that she was running the Clayborough estates, and that she had undertaken several business ventures. The peerage had been shocked, even scandalized. *That she, a woman, a duchess, had gone into business*, was beyond their belief. The peerage disdained business as a matter of course, and could not believe a lady—*a duchess*—had actually and actively immersed herself in such a pursuit. They still disapproved. Yet as the Duchess of Clayborough, Isobel was too powerful to be shunned; no one would ever refuse one of her highly coveted invitations, no one would ever leave her off of their guest list. Indeed, hostesses prayed she would attend their affairs. No one dared even look askance at her. Isobel knew she was the height of gossip and she found it amusing. Francis did not shock anyone (except for her) with his new found penchant for young men but she shocked everyone with her obvious intelligence and resolution.

Francis was not amused. Not by the gossip, and not by her. He had never thanked her for rescuing him or his home, and he never forgave her. He also never failed to mock her as a barren, sexless bitch of a woman.

Isobel did not care as long as he left her alone. She supposed he was right, that she was barren, for they still had no children. Yet he had not come to her bed in over a year, as if he had given up, too. Isobel knew that he was too involved with his current paramour to find time for her. And while Isobel was relieved, she couldn't help but also be sad. She was intelligent enough to know that to want a child was foolish, not with Francis for a father, but she did. It was not, she realized, going to happen. She was only twenty-three, but she felt as if she were fifty and well past her child-bearing years.

The Sea Dragon was sleek and white-masted, one of the fastest clippers on the ocean. She normally did not carry passengers, but once Isobel decided to make this business trip, she wanted to get to America as quickly as possible. Knowing his employer, her secretary arranged her transportation on the Sea Dragon by paying an exceptional fee.

Isobel saw him before she even boarded. She stood on the wharf with her maid and a single trunk, unable to move. Her heart was lodged in her throat.

She could not even see him clearly. The sun was behind him, obscuring her vision. She only saw an impossibly tall, powerful figure of a man, in high boots and breeches and a carelessly worn linen shirt. She heard him shouting orders. Her blood raced. Her body quivered. He was impossibly male. What was wrong with her?

He stepped out of the blinding sun, then froze, turning his head slowly toward her. His chestnut hair, tarnished with gold, carelessly brushed his shoulders. It framed a strong, compelling, fascinating face. With sharp eyes he searched the dock until he found her.

Isobel could not look away. He stared at her for what seemed to be an eternity, an eternity she had waited for her entire life, and then he smiled. The smile was direct and intimate. It was meant for her and her alone. Isobel blushed.

"Go," she urged her maid, Bessie. "Go find someone to carry on my trunk." There was relief in focusing her attention elsewhere, but she knew he was still staring. Just as she knew with every fiber of her being that she should not board this ship—his ship. She didn't have to be told to know it was his. Just as she also knew she would not—could not—turn back.

"Who are you?"

"Isobel."

It was sunset. They had been sailing all day. It was the first word he had spoken to her. He had come up behind her silently, but she was not startled. She had been standing alone at the rail for some time, expecting him. Waiting for him.

"Isobel."

She turned to face him fully.

The impact he had on her was just as powerful as before. He left her breathless, senseless.

"My name is Hadrian," he said softly, his gaze sweeping her face. Studying it, memorizing it. "Hadrian Stone."

"I know. I asked."

They stared at each other. Isobel's heart was pounding wildly, almost in fright. But it was not fright. And she knew she should be frightened. For it was desire. Desire which she had never ever in her life experienced before, not even in the slightest degree. Wild hot tormenting desire, desire that pooled between her thighs.

He wasn't quite handsome. His face was hard, his jaw too strong, his nose a touch too large. His eyes were amber, a blaze of gold. He had stubble on his face, and his hair was too shaggy, too long. He towered over her by a half a foot at least. He was big, he was powerful. She thought if he touched her, she would die.

He inhaled long and slow. "God damn it," he said. "You are the most beautiful woman I have ever seen—and all day today I kept telling myself you were a dream—that you couldn't possibly be real. But you are real—aren't you?"

"I'm real," she whispered, wanting desperately to touch him.

He lifted his hand. Isobel waited, suspended in agony. His fingers brushed the high curve of her cheekbone. She closed her eyes, praying that he would take her in his arms. She did not care who would see.

Abruptly he stepped back from her, cursing. Her eyes flew open and she saw that he was angry. She could not guess why. He turned on his boot heels and strode away without another word.

After a moment, Isobel followed him.

"Stop," he said in the corridor below decks. A muscle in his neck bulged. "Stop right there."

She knew without being told that his cabin was behind the door he guarded with his back. She wet her lips. She was nervous, as if she were sixteen again. "I can't," she whispered.

His face hardened. "You're a lady," he said. "And from the look of that ring, a married one."

"Yes, I am," she said sadly.

"Is this so damn easy for you? Do you do this all the time?"

She was aghast at what he thought. "No! Never, never have I been unfaithful to my husband in the seven years we've been wed. Until now."

He gripped her arms, practically dragging her up against him. "Are you telling me the truth?"

The truth was in her eyes. "Yes."

His grip tightened. It hurt. Isobel didn't care. "Don't you see?" He was almost shouting. "I don't want one night from you. I would rather not have you at all."

It was too much, Isobel sobbed. She clutched his soft white shirt and found her fists pressed against his rock-hard abdomen. "Hadrian! I don't want one night either!"

He crushed her body with his, down into the hard mattress of his spartan bed. Isobel still wept, with need. He understood, sweeping her skirts and petticoats away, ripping apart her drawers, touching her hot, slick flesh.

She cried out wildly, attaining her first climax instantly in huge, unbearable waves. He held her as she rode it out.

"God, Isobel," he gasped, ripping open her bodice.

The tears of joy shone in her eyes. "That was the first time," she whispered, and then she started to cry in earnest.

He didn't understand, but he sensed the change in her. He swept her up into his arms and held her hard in his embrace while she wept. She wept for herself for the first time in her adult life. She wept for all the hurt she had suffered in Francis' hands, for lost innocence and shattered illusions. She wept for meeting Hadrian when it was too late. And she wept because, for the first time in too many years, it was safe—for at long last she had found her haven.

"You must think me mad," she said finally. A long, long time had passed. Later Hadrian would tell her that she had cried out her grief for hours.

He still held her, she in her torn clothes, half naked and snug against his side. "I have never seen a woman with such heartbreak," he said softly. He stroked her hair, loosening it. "Do you want to tell me about it?"

Isobel smiled, sadness and joy intertwined. "No. Not now. Maybe never. The heartbreak is gone. You chased it away."

He smiled, kissing her forehead gently. "I am glad."

If only Isobel had realized how wrong she was. The heartbreak wasn't gone. It was only just beginning.

She watched him disrobe. Her breasts were heaving from the many caresses she had endured. She lay amidst her torn clothes on the single blanket he slept with. That now-familiar heat was already burning between her thighs. She stared with mouth-watering longing at his massive, naked chest.

He stared back, a fierce wanting in his eyes. "I am proud you look at me like that," he said.

"You are so beautiful," Isobel returned.

He laughed, the sound raw, shaky. He shed his pants. Isobel moaned at the sight of his long, hard powerful legs. Then she saw his huge straining phallus. "I may explode just watching you," she whispered.

He made an inarticulate sound, instantly coming down on top of her. She reached for him wildly. Their mouths fused. He was already settling between her spread thighs; she was already locking her legs around his waist. He thrust into her. They both cried out.

"Dear God," he said. "Isobel, Isobel—is it possible I am already in love with you?"

She clutched at him fiercely as he rocked her with his strength and his power and his love. "I hope so. How I hope so!"

She never told him about Francis. He asked, but when she made it clear that it was not important, not to them, he respected her wishes and withdrew. Isobel knew he loved her as much as she loved him. She did not want Francis to intrude upon their happiness. Nor did she wish to think about the future.

But as they approached the shores of America, he would not let it be. "When are you going to tell me that you are the Duchess of Clayborough?"

Isobel lay naked in his arms in his small, bare cabin. She gasped. "You know! You've known all along!"

"Yes, I know. Did you really think I wouldn't make inquiries the moment I saw you standing on the wharf?"

Isobel was angry—and relieved. "You could have told me that you knew."

"You could have told me who you are."

She was silent, sitting up; he was silent. They gazed at each other. "Not now," she finally said. She touched him, stroking his chest. "Not now, Hadrian."

He sat up, gripping her hand and stopping her from deferring their discussion. "Yes, now. I know you don't love him. I know you love me."

"I will always love you."

He smiled, satisfied.

She did not smile.

He grew uneasy. "Isobel, I've never wanted to marry before. Until you. I want you, not just here in my bed. I want you as my wife. I want to give you children—little sons and daughters." He was intense.

"Maybe you have. Given me one, at least." She could not smile either. A sense of panic enveloped her.

"You're not going back to him." It wasn't quite a statement, it wasn't quite a question.

Isobel whimpered. "How can I run away?"

He was shocked. "You love me! That bastard—and I don't know what he did to you—but I know he's broken your heart! You can't go back to him!"

"But run away?" She was shocked with the very idea, an idea she had avoided at all costs.

"Was this a game, then?" he shouted, furious and on his feet.

"No! It was never a game! I love you! But Hadrian, I am a de Warenne."

"You mean that being a goddamned duchess means more to you than I do, is that it?"

"No! It means that de Warennes do their duty—as painful as it may be. A de Warenne does not run away from her husband and her life. She does not."

"Oh my God," he said, when he realized that she believed what she was saying with all of her heart. "You are serious? You are serious?"

Isobel closed her eyes. She was a de Warenne. She had always been a de Warenne. And now she was a part of Clayborough. It wasn't that she loved Clayborough—although she did. It was that she believed in loyalty, duty and honor. If she did not, then she was not Isobel de Warenne Braxton-Lowell. If she did not, then she was nobody.

He left the room abruptly, his face white with the realization of what he would never have. What they would never have.

* * *

Isobel stayed in Virginia for three months with Hadrian Stone. It was bittersweet. They both tried not to think about their parting, they tried desperately to only live in the present. Never had Isobel loved more. And the day she had to finally leave America, she had never hurt more.

By now he knew her as only a man can who truly loves a woman. He did not bring up her leaving Francis again. He knew how much she hurt. He took her to the dock.

Isobel was resolved not to cry, because if she started, she knew there would be no holding back the storm of her emotions. She refused to entertain her doubts, too. It would be so easy to stay with him, to turn her back on who and what she was, if she even dared to contemplate doing so. At all costs, she had to close her mind down to the option which did not—could not—exist.

His hands closed over her shoulders. Beyond them, another clipper, not the Sea Dragon but an insipid imitation, bobbed at her moorings. Above them the sky was flawlessly blue. Spring was in the air everywhere, except in their hearts.

"I love you and I respect you," he said finally, staring into her eyes. "That's why I'm letting you make the most important decision of your life. If this is what you feel you must do, then I support you."

She could no longer contain the tears. They flooded forth copiously.

"I will always love you," he said harshly. "And I will always be here. If you change your mind—next year, the year after—or in ten years, I shall be here. There will never be anyone else, Isobel, never."

"I don't want you to wait for me," she tried to tell him, but it was a lie and they both knew it.

"There will never be anyone else," he said again. "I love you, Isobel."

Isobel boarded the ship, blinded by her tears. She was bedridden with her grief. She left America, and with it, her heart. For that belonged to Hadrian Stone, and it always would. She returned to England, but she was never whole again.

He was sure he had not heard correctly. "I beg your pardon?"

Isobel was white, whiter than any ghost could be. "Hadrian . . . I should have told you long ago. Francis is not your father."

The Duke of Clayborough stared.

They had just finished supper and retired to one of the more intimate salons so the Dowager Duchess could indulge in an after-dinner port despite the fact that ladies rarely drank anything stronger than sherry. No sooner were the two heavy, gleaming teakwood doors closed behind them, than Isobel had asked her son to sit down. Bemused, he had complied. And then she had stated that Francis was not his father.

"Is this some kind of poor joke?" he asked. But his heart was thundering so loudly he could barely hear his own words.

"It is not a joke. Francis," and she swallowed nervously, "is not your father."

Hadrian was carved from stone. The impossible pace of his pulse increased. His mother's words roared in his head. *Francis is not your father*. It was impossible, it was unbelievable; it was a dream come true for a man who never dreamed at all.

"Are you all right?" Isobel asked anxiously. "Here, sip this." She was hovering over him, offering him her glass of port. Her hands shook.

Hadrian gripped her wrist with unthinking force. "He is not my father?"

"No."

He was on his feet, still holding his mother's arm. "Then who is?"

"You're hurting me," Isobel gasped.

Hadrian saw the pallor of her face and the tears in her eyes and instantly released her. "Dear God, forgive me, Mother. I did not realize what I was doing."

"There is nothing for me to forgive," she said sadly.

"Who is my father?" Hadrian demanded again. His senses were still reeling.

"His name is Hadrian Stone. An American from Boston. A ship's captain."

The Duke stared. He wheeled away and paced to the mantle, staring at the leaping flames within. Long moments passed before he could begin to assimilate this information. Francis was not his father—thank God. His father was an American named Hadrian Stone. A sea captain. It was so bizarre he wondered if he might, after all, be dreaming.

"Are you all right?"

He slowly turned. "I would like to hear the entire story, Mother."

She nodded, wringing her hands.

Hadrian stood in front of the hearth, immobile. And finally, at long last, the truth was revealed.

It was incredible, he thought. Although he appeared calm as Isobel finished her tale by telling him of her decision to leave Virginia and Hadrian Stone to return to Clayborough, he was far from it. "This explains everything," he said into the heavy ensuing silence.

Isobel's face was still an unearthly pallor. She sat on the edge of the sofa facing her son, her hands worrying the folds of her dress in her lap. She stared at Hadrian anxiously, searchingly, but he barely saw her.

"No wonder he hated me—and you."

Isobel bit her lip. "He hated me before I ever met your father. He hated me when I took over the responsibility for these estates which should have been his—and his hatred grew every time I bailed him out of debt."

"Yes, that I know." He was standing, now he paced. "Jesus," he finally said, and when he turned back to his mother, his eyes flashed with anger. "You should have told me years ago!"

"I know," she whispered. "You are angry."

"I am trying not to be. I am trying to understand how you would want to keep your affair a secret—even from me. But good God! Shouldn't I have known before now that that bastard was not my natural father?"

"Yes."

"God, Mother, I wish you had told me!" He wheeled away. Agitation appeared in his every long, restless stride. Suddenly he whirled back to face her. He was too self-absorbed to notice how close his mother was to tears. "What happened after you left Virginia? Did you ever hear from him again?"

Isobel's heart, already pumping madly, began an erratic, frightened beat. "What are you thinking of?"

"I must find him, of course. If he is still alive."

She sat very still.

"Well?" he demanded sharply.

Tears finally filled her eyes. "Yes, I did hear from him—for a while. But it's been twenty years now—with no word."

"Can you please explain?" He was impatient.

"After I returned to Francis he sent me a note. A short, brief, impersonal note. It was an inquiry after my well-being. For several years he continued to do this. It was always clear from the postmark where he was at the time. His address was in Boston. When I met him that was where his home was."

"And then what happened?"

Isobel's heart lurched. The memories were too painful, as was her son's abrupt interrogation. He hadn't said anything, but he was angry—he was angry with her. And after the anger, then what would follow? His disdain? Very softly, she spoke, trying to keep the tremors from her voice. "I know that, in the beginning, he wanted me to know where he was. It was his way of telling me that he was still there, waiting for me, if I changed my mind. But then the letters stopped." Her voice broke and tears spilled. "Maybe he is married. Maybe he is dead. I do not know."

Hadrian stared, eyes wide as comprehension struck him. "You still love him!"

Isobel found a handkerchief and dried her eyes, quickly and desperately regaining a semblance of control. Her tears were as much for her son as for his real father—and for herself.

Suddenly Hadrian moved to his mother's side and laid a hand awkwardly on her shoulder. "I know this is difficult for you. But Mother—this is of the utmost importance to me. I must have that address in Boston."

"Of course," she managed forlornly.

Hadrian turned away. To the room at large he said, trying to control the rush of excitement flooding over him, "I shall write him a letter immediately. I will hire investigators. I will send one of them to Boston. If he is alive, I shall find him."

Isobel swallowed, preparing to deliver the coup de grace to her son. "Hadrian, he doesn't know."

Hadrian whirled.

"I never told him. He has no idea that he has a son."

The revelation was shocking. That night after his mother had left, Hadrian sat up alone in the library with the Borzoi, staring into the dancing flames of the fire without seeing them. He could barely assimilate what he had learned, that Francis was not his father, that his mother had had an affair with a man named Hadrian Stone and that *he* was his father.

Anger swept him. He was angry with his mother—very angry—although he was trying hard not to be. He was trying to understand her motivations, although for the life of him, he could not. Not only had Isobel not told him the truth years ago when she should have, she had not even told Hadrian Stone the truth.

When he had demanded to know how she could have kept the truth from his father, as well as him, she had been so distressed she could not answer.

He could not stop thinking about the mysterious American who was his actual father. Hadrian Stone. Isobel had named him after her lover. What was this American like? He was a sea captain. Hadrian could not imagine his mother with a sea captain, and in his mind's eye he could not get past an image of a stocky, stubbled, gray-haired man in a striped shirt and navy blue pants. Although he had pressed her repeatedly, Isobel had refused to answer his inquiries. Although he had known he was upsetting her by asking her about his father, he could not, would not, stop. Did he not have a right to know something—anything? She had finally said that Hadrian Stone was everything Francis was not, and with that, in tears, she had fled the room and his house. Momentarily, Hadrian had been remorseful for what he had done, but then his mind had again seized upon the fact he could not get over, the fact of his paternity.

He laughed out loud. Now he could curse Francis to his heart's content with no remorse, and more importantly, now he could understand why Francis had despised him. For that had been the question which had haunted him his entire life, and finally, it was laid to rest.

Hadrian called upon his fiancée the following day. Although he was overflowing with the hope of finding his father alive and well, and he had hired runners the very evening his mother had told him the truth, one of whom was already Boston-bound with a letter, his wedding was rapidly approaching. He had not slept at all the previous evening, and by dawn's first light he had finally been able to come to terms with the astounding fact that a man named Hadrian Stone was his father. Other than to wait for some results from the investigation he had initiated, there was nothing more for him to do. But as far as his future wife was concerned, he had plenty to do. For he had a future to secure for them.

Hadrian intended to continue with his plan to protect Nicole from the scandal that was trying to take root over their impending wedding. In order to do so, they must venture into society so he could assume his role of a madly lovestruck swain. Hadrian had not lost any of his resolve to quench the malicious gossips from spreading tales that were too damned close to the truth to be of comfort. If anything, he was now more determined than ever to protect his bride and gain for her the acceptance she deserved.

The immense black Clayborough coach with its trio of lions emblazoned larger than life upon its doors pulled up in front of the Shelton residence on Tavistock Square. The Duke alighted. His strides were always lithe and agile, but today they were particularly effortless. In fact, when Aldric responded to the doorknocker, he could not help but gape at the Duke, who greeted him with an uncharacteristic smile. Hadrian knew that he was probably grinning like an idiot, but he could not dampen his good humor even if he wanted to.

But as he waited for Nicole in the morning parlor his pleasure began to fade. She did not appear. Fifteen minutes became a half an hour. A half an hour became three quarters of an hour. Hadrian's pleasure turned to annoyance, which turned to anger. How could he have forgotten for a moment, despite the incredible turn of events, that his bride was more than reluctant? The last time he had seen her was at Lindley's, and she had been furious with him. Yesterday she had managed to avoid him. Had she not received the veiled warning he had given the Countess? Did she really think to avoid him again? Could she be so foolish?

He left the parlor and found a clearly anxious Aldric hovering in the foyer.

"Your Grace! May I bring you more refreshments?"

"Where is her room?" The Duke demanded.

Aldric froze. "Your Grace . . . er, Your Grace . . ."

"Might I assume it is up those stairs?"

"On the second floor," the butler breathed, eyes wide.

The Duke of Clayborough waited.

"Fifth door on the left," Aldric whispered.

The Duke was already gone. He took the steps effortlessly and two at time. He rapped sharply on the fifth door twice, and without waiting for an invitation that he doubted would be forthcoming once his identity was known, he barged in.

Nicole was in her underclothes. There were piles and piles of silks, chiffons, taffetas, velvets, tulle, wool, cashmeres and even furs upon her bed, while plumes, ribbons, lace, and other accessorizing items were scattered about the room. Boxes of hats, all opened, and gloves, were everywhere. The floor was barely discernible, for wrapping tissue had been strewn haphazardly about. There was a pile of reticules in all sizes, shapes and colors imaginable, on the floor by the sofa. The renowned seamstress Madame Lavie was on her knees, measuring the hem of Nicole's bright gold silk petticoat. Two other young women were seated in the room, sewing madly. As one, everyone froze and gaped at the Duke.

Nicole was the first to recover. She shielded her breasts, popping as they were from her lace-covered corset, with her arms. "Get out!"

It had taken Hadrian all of a split second to realize she had had no intention of coming down to see him at all. "Everyone leave. *Now.*"

In another second, the room was empty except for the Duke and his bride.

Her arms still crossed against her chest, Nicole backed away, trodding upon the mountains of fragile tissue. "You cannot be in here. You are worsening what is already a scandalous affair!"

"A scandalous affair?" He mocked. "They will say it is a scandalous love!"

"Oh! How could I forget the game you are playing?"

Hadrian smiled, not pleasantly. Although she covered her bosom from his view, he had already seen the ripe flesh straining against her corset, had already glimpsed dark red nipples poking against the fine gold lace. "How long did you intend for me to await you downstairs, Nicole?"

"Forever!"

He smiled again, the expression ruthless. "Not a very wise course of action." His gaze swept her again. His body pulsed with awareness of how alone they were, and where they were—in her bedroom with her bed not a foot away from them.

"You must leave. There will be more talk already because of your coming into my room like this." Her voice had become breathless.

"Good," he said, taking a step towards her. A tight, hard step—as tight and hard as his big body. "They will say I am so mad about you that I chased you into your bedroom, losing all sense of any sort of chivalrous conduct."

Nicole quickly moved to the other side of the bed. "You are mad!"

"And you, my dear, are a coward," he said softly, stalking her.

"I am not a coward," she gritted, gripping one of the fat, intricately carved bedposts. Her breasts heaved in fury. "You are the coward—to steal behind my back and ask my father for my hand, after I had already refused you!"

He froze. Then he was upon her, grabbing her by the arms and dragging her from the bedpost. She shrieked. He shook her. He watched with angry interest as her breasts burst free of her corset. "To the contrary," he said in her ear, his tone strained, "anyone foolish enough to marry you is the bravest of men."

Nicole wrenched free of him, reaching wildly for one of the lavish fabrics littering her bed and clutching an opaque red chiffon across her chest. "Then feel free to cry off!" She shouted. "I won't take offense."

He told himself, even as he accosted her, that he was only acting out of the need to shut her up before she ruined his intentions of protecting her and added more fuel to the gossip he sought to avoid. Even as he thought this, even as he dragged her up against his body, even as he pulled her up against the length of his straining manhood, he knew it was a half-hearted excuse. The fact was that he was sick and tired of these games, of these protests. "Then your sensibilities are stronger than mine. I am warning you, Nicole, I am quickly becoming offended." With a hard smile that wasn't a smile at all, he covered her lips with his.

She struggled wildly, trying to strike him and almost succeeding; he caught her wrists and pushed her down into the heap of luxurious material covering the bed. "I can see the hurt in your eyes! Why not admit your vulnerability? Why do you push me so hard? How is it that you make me forget myself?"

"It's all my fault, of course!" she cried, but she was motionless, lying on her back on the bed, his heavy weight pinning her there, his legs between hers.

He did not respond. Not verbally. Very deliberately, he yanked the red chiffon she was holding from between them. Her eyes widened and she bucked, but he did not release her wrists and kept her pinned to the bed.

For a long moment she did not move, except for her naked breasts, which were heaving beneath his crisp shirtfront. "Can we cease with all this nonsense?" he demanded.

Her gaze had drifted to his mouth. Quickly it flew back to his eyes. "My future is at stake. I do not think that is nonsense!"

"Our future is at stake," he replied. "Our future."

She jerked against him again. "How dare you do this to me," she whispered.

His gaze flickered to her naked breasts. He thought that she referred to both his manhandling of her now, and his decision to marry her despite her protests. "Give up, Nicole. You have already lost. Accept what is going to be. Accept the fact that in a few days you are going to be my wife."

She strained against him again. He knew he must be hurting her, for he would not lesson his grip on her wrists, and he knew she was as achingly aware of him as he was of her, his massive hardness buried as it was in her groin. "I will never accept that," she gasped.

He didn't laugh. There was nothing amusing about her continuing to resist his will. Only she could ignite his temper so easily, as she had done from the moment they had met. "You never learn," he said. Sweat beaded his brow as he fought with himself, and lost. His body began to shake. The enormity of his need was terrifying.

Their gazes continued to remain riveted together. Just as he knew he must surrender to the passion raging in him, he felt her resistance snap. With a small cry, Nicole closed her eyes, arching her body up against his.

He did not need any encouragement anyway. He kneed her thighs apart and took her mouth with his. His kisses were explosive. Nicole heaved against him eagerly, seeking out his tongue with hers. Ruthlessly he pumped his loins against her.

There was a determined knocking upon the door.

Hadrian leapt to his feet instantly. He yanked up her corset. Nicole gazed at him out of glazed, passion-drugged eyes. "We have company," he whispered urgently, pulling her to her feet. She was like a mannequin, a dead weight. He shook her once and was relieved to see the focus returning to her expression. Leaving her, he tucked in his shirt and straightened his tie as he went to the door. He opened it just as there was another knock.

It was the Countess. Hadrian had not a doubt that she was not fooled by them, although her smile was pleasant. "Your Grace, hello. I thought perhaps I should bring you more refreshments while you visit with my daughter."

"How thoughtful," he murmured, glancing at Nicole. She stood with her back to them, staring out of one of the tall windows, clad now in a green print dressing gown. He was relieved at the interruption although his body was not. He had not intended for things to get so out of hand.

Jane placed a tray upon a glass table. For a few moments they exchanged pleasantries. When she departed, she left the door wide open. Hadrian turned to his bride. By now she was scowling at him; clearly the past few minutes had not improved her mood.

"I hope you are satisfied," she flung heedlessly.

"I am far from satisfied."

She colored. Her arms were again defensively crossed in front of her chest. "Why have you come? To throw salt on my wounds?"

"What wounds?" he asked dryly, turning from her. Now that they were alone again, even though she was covered by the robe, the hot ache in his loins was building anew. He poured them both cups of tea, hoping to distract his body from its intent.

"You know what wounds," she snapped. "Why do you insist upon this ridiculous marriage? I heartily agree with what you said—that you are a fool to marry me."

"I did not say that, Nicole."

"I am not the sort to be a duchess, as you well know," she said, as if she hadn't heard him.

"Perhaps you sell yourself short."

Her eyes widened.

He calmly sipped his tea, but he never took his eyes from her.

She recovered. "Hadrian—why do you insist that we wed? If what happened between us doesn't matter to me, then why the hell does it matter to you?"

He winced, but not at her crude language. Could she possibly mean what she had just said—that what had happened in his library several days ago was of no importance to her? "You know why. You may be with my child."

"If I am with child, I can have it without being wed to you. I am used to scandal—what difference will a little more make?"

He was grim now. "If you think you can change my mind, think again. I am unmovable."

"Then you will have a very reluctant duchess on your hands," she said coolly.

"Dare you threaten me?"

"I do not threaten. I advise."

"And you lie," he said with a calm he did not feel. He set his cup and saucer down. "We both know in reality just how reluctant you are—the proof being obvious not just five minutes ago."

She flushed, but whether with anger or embarrassment or both, he could not tell. "Perhaps I am not reluctant when it comes to matters of the flesh, but I am reluctant when it comes to marrying you!"

Her barb struck him with unerring accuracy and he did not like the wound it left. She had not softened one bit towards the prospect of marrying him. She could not know that Francis was not his father, if indeed that had been a concern of hers, but he was too proud to tell her, and more importantly, he did not trust her with such a secret. Not yet. He could not risk his mother's reputation. "Am I truly so odious?"

She stood very still, her face pale, some of the anger leaving her eyes. When she responded, it was with the utmost care. "Whether or not I find you odious is not the issue."

"Do you find me odious?" he demanded.

"No."

Now he was motionless. It was very hard for him to prevent a smile from forming on his lips. "So I am not such an ogre." His eyes sought hers.

Her mouth trembled. "Do not force me against my will!"

"Nicole, it is too late."

"It is not too late. You can cry off. People will only say that you have recovered your sanity!"

He could not miss her desperation, and any smile he might have entertained was gone. For whatever reason, she was as opposed to him now as before. "I suggest you change your will," he said coldly.

"I do not want to be sacrificed to your noble idea of duty."

"You have made yourself abundantly clear," he gritted. "In fact, I am damned tired of hearing this refrain. The truth is, *I do not care what you want.*"

"*Damn you,*" she hissed. "You only care about yourself. You are cold and heartless, just as everyone says!"

Hadrian smiled, not pleasantly. His feelings were hurt, and he was angry that he could be vulnerable where she was concerned. "I had intended to invite you to accompany me out tonight, but I can see that would not be wise."

"It would not be wise," Nicole agreed fiercely. "I would refuse. I have no intention of going anywhere with you."

He was furious, and only controlling his fury with the greatest of wills. He would not force her to accompany him to the ball. She would only cause more tongues to wag with her animosity towards him so evident. For it would be a miracle if she would bow to appearances and behave as a bride should. "I will see you at the cathedral." He was already heading for the door, but her next words stopped him in his tracks.

"You hope!" she cried.

He turned slowly. There was no hiding his emotions now. "I am not Percy Hempstead," he said, very slowly and very distinctly. "Let me make that fact very clear."

She did not move, did not even appear to breathe.

"I am not a twenty-two-year-old boy; I am not a besotted fool. If you think to jilt me, think again. For I will not turn tail and run the other way as he did, oh no. I will find you, and I will drag you to the altar on your back if need be, no matter how you might be screaming. No matter how scandalous it might be."

She still did not move.

He smiled dangerously. "And no one would condemn me for my behavior. Because I am the Duke of Clayborough—and because I am a man. While you, you are nothing but a woman—and an eccentric one at that. One whom, they will say, needs a firm male hand and perhaps a beating or two."

Nicole gasped.

"My actions will be applauded," he finished ruthlessly. "Yours will be condemned."

"I despise you," Nicole managed.

His smile was twisted. "If you choose to create this kind of scandal, so be it. I will wash my hands of the affair and leave you to stew in your own juices. My generosity in protecting you only goes so far."

"Get out."

He did not answer. He was too angry. He strode from the room.

The Duke of Clayborough was nervous.

It was his wedding day.

He had not seen Nicole in the past ten days, not since he had last visited her with the intention of inviting her to the ball. It was a deliberate course of action. Once again she had made her feelings for him perfectly clear, arousing his own emotions, which were too explosive around her in any case. It was safer, much safer, to keep his distance from her until after they were wed.

And he dared not think about the battle that would ensue once she was his wife.

The Duke had remained in London this past week and a half. In that short space of time he had attended three at-homes, two balls, one regatta, and one lavish soiree. The fact was, and it astonished London, that he had accepted more invitations in one week than he had in the past year. And not only had he appeared at these various functions. He had actually stayed for several hours, mingled with the other guests, and had been, in short, most charming. This kind of behavior was so uncharacteristic of the reclusive and rather unsociable lord that the Duke had become the most popular topic of conversation among the set.

But Hadrian's nature had not changed. He was no more interested in the social life of his peers than he had been before. He was, in fact, champing at the bit to get home to Clayborough, where various affairs awaited his personal attention. He had stayed in London only because of Nicole.

He was making a new beginning for them both. He had never been unpopular, of course, he was too powerful not to be a coveted guest, but he had not been overly popular because of his blatant indifference to the social whirl. By the end of the ten days, he had, indeed, become popular. And his popularity would soon be his wife's.

The ugly rumours were no longer circulating in London, either. If any gossip about the ill timing of his and Nicole's wedding lingered, it was in the throes of a slow death. The new gossip was exactly as he had contrived. At every function Hadrian attended, when congratulated upon his engagement, he was appropriately enthusiastic. Any open display of emotion from the Duke was so unusual that this might have been enough to do the trick. However, word had spread like the worst firestorm of his advent into Nicole's bedroom the other day. And this time the gossip was favorable.

Everywhere Hadrian went, people were talking about them. Just the night before, at the Avery soiree, he had overheard two matrons and one single lady, all acquaintances of his.

"Shocking," Lady Bradford declared. "He actually chased Madame Lavie out so they could be alone!"

"Scandalous," Lady Smythe-Regis responded fervently. "He must be completely mad about Lady Shelton to forget propriety like that!"

"Can you imagine being the object of such interest on the part of the Duke?" Lady Talbott said dreamily. "It must be love!"

Hadrian quickly turned away before they could spot him eavesdropping. He was more than pleased.

He wasn't pleased, however, on the afternoon that he decided to make an appearance at his club on James Street. Upon entering the den he favored, he was aware of all quiet conversation stopping. Usually he was greeted politely and then ignored by the other members, all of whom knew his preference for solitude. Grimly he wondered what had caused this change in his cronies' reaction to him. It would be too hopeful to think that it did not have something to do with his bride and himself.

He shortly found out. The Earl of Ravensford, whom he knew better than most of the other lords, approached him. "Do you mind if I join you for a moment, Hadrian?" Jonathon Lindley asked.

Surprised, Hadrian agreed. It quickly became obvious that the Earl had something on his mind. "Just what is it that you want to tell me, Jonathon?"

"You won't be pleased," Lindley warned, keeping his voice down.

Hadrian gestured for him to continue.

"Nicole is like a daughter to me, so I must tell you what I have just learned. Two members of this club have made a wager."

The Duke stiffened. "What kind of wager?"

"The kind of wager that needs redressing. Lord Hortense and Lord Kimberly have a bet that your bride will bear you a child within nine months of your wedding."

Hadrian did not move. Although his face was as still as chiseled granite, fury swept over him in one hot wave. When he could speak, it was to thank Ravensford for the information. A moment later he took his leave.

He found Hortense that evening at his home as he was preparing to go out. The interview was short and to the point. One well-placed blow loosened several of Hortense's teeth. The threat which followed was taken to heart. Hortense was very apologetic.

Lord Kimberly met with exactly the same fate.

More gossip, more scandal, but all of it was in the Duke's favor. He had acted honorably in defending Nicole's reputation, while the other two gentlemen had never been known to be anything but rogues. Besides, the ladies whispered, it was just so romantic!

The only thing which did not go well that week was an interview with the Marquess of Stafford—Elizabeth's father.

Hadrian had gone to call on his friend himself, hoping to somehow explain what would be unexplainable to the desolate man. Stafford was still locked up in his home in an inconsolable state of grief. Because he had seen no one since the funeral, he did not know of Hadrian's engagement. And because Hadrian had been like a son to him, as well as his daughter's betrothed since childhood, Stafford received him when he was not receiving callers.

"I will not ask you how you are, George," Hadrian said quietly.

"Do not." Stafford was gaunt, thin and red-eyed. "I cannot stop grieving. How I wish I could."

"I know it is trite, but in time, you will be able to remember her without so much pain."

"No," Stafford said. "You are wrong. This pain is never going to die."

Hadrian was silent. He was terribly uncomfortable, for how could he tell this man that he was marrying another woman on the heels of Elizabeth's death? Yet he had to inform him personally, before Stafford should learn of the engagement himself. "George, I too, miss Elizabeth. I always will."

Stafford began to cry. With a great effort he regained control. "I know."

Briefly Hadrian closed his eyes. In truth, as much as he had cared about Elizabeth, and as saddened as he was by her death, it was distinctly hard to visualize her now. "She is happy, George. She is at peace when she was in so much pain. For if there is a paradise, she has found it."

Stafford started to weep again. Hadrian handed him his handkerchief, wondering if he should, after all, depart and let Stafford learn of the nuptials after the fact.

"Yes," the Marquess finally said, trembling, "Elizabeth is in heaven. No one deserved heaven more."

After a few minutes had passed and the Marquess was more composed, Hadrian spoke. "George, I am terribly sorry that I have come to personally inform you of something and the timing is most inappropriate. If there was any other way, believe me, I would not intrude upon your grief now."

"Hadrian, dear lad, you are always welcome here."

Hadrian trembled. For a moment he felt a guilt he had not felt since he had consummated his passion with Nicole. And suddenly he saw Elizabeth with crystal clarity, as if she stood before him in the room behind her father. She was smiling and looking at him with love. There was no accusation of betrayal upon her face. The Duke's eyes widened and he sat straighter, but it was a figment of his imagination—a ghostly hallucination—for the image was gone. And so too, miraculously, was the guilt.

With difficulty Hadrian began. He felt he owed it to Stafford to be honest with him, and although he knew he would be upset, he trusted the man's honor and was certain the truth would be safe nevertheless. "In my own grief, I turned to another woman in a moment of passion."

Stafford looked at him. Then he said, "I understand. What does it matter? You are a young man. Do not blame yourself."

"I do not think you understand, George. The other woman was not my mistress, nor was she a whore."

Stafford was puzzled.

"She was a single young lady, one whom I now must wed."

Stafford stared, unable to immediately comprehend what he was being told.

"I am marrying Nicole Shelton in a week."

Stafford still stared.

"I am sorry," Hadrian said.

Stafford lunged to his feet. "*You are marrying some other woman next week*?"

Hadrian also rose. "I am sorry."

"How could you!? Dear God, how could you do this?" Stafford shouted. "Elizabeth barely dead, not even cold in her grave! How can you do this, how?!"

"It is a matter of honor," Hadrian said, only outwardly composed. "Elizabeth is dead, and I have ruined Nicole. And of course there is the need for haste."

Stafford was red-faced. "How dare you come here to tell me you are marrying another woman next week! Damn your cold heart, Hadrian! Damn you! Damn you to hell! Oh—you did not love my daughter, I see that now! You never loved her! How glad I am that she is not marrying a cold heartless bastard like you!"

"I am sorry."

"Get out!" Stafford screamed. "Get out! Get out, get out, get out!"

The Duke of Clayborough arrived at the church early. The ceremony was to take place at St. Martin-in-the-Fields on Trafalgar Square. A small chapel had originally existed on this site in Norman times, and by the twelfth century a church there had its own parish. It had been rebuilt several times, most recently in the early eighteenth century. It was now a magnificent piece of architecture—a large rectangular building with an imposing portico straddled by a high steeple, with a dashing statue of Charles I in the foreground.

Hadrian entered through a back entrance, leaving his mother, the Earl of Northumberland and Lady Claire, and the Earl and Countess of Dragmore to greet the guests, which numbered nearly a thousand. Because of the circumstances surrounding his wedding, he had decided to make it the wedding of the year, at the least. He was determined that no one of any importance be left off of the guest list—and that no one think he and his bride had anything to hide. Isobel had agreed, as had the Sheltons and his grandfather, Roger de Warenne. Thus the guest list included not only the most important aristocracy in the land, but many influential politicians and businessmen as well, and even Queen Victoria herself.

Hadrian chose to brood alone in a small antechamber. He was exceedingly nervous and he could not fathom why. He was struck with an unpleasant image—of himself standing alone at the altar, waiting for his bride, who never came. He paced, filled with tension. Nicole Shelton would not dare; the idea was ludicrous.

After what seemed like hours of waiting, there was a knock on the door and his grandfather walked in. Roger de Warenne, the Earl of Northumberland, eyed him thoroughly. "You look a bit green about the gills, lad."

"I feel green," Hadrian returned. "Is she here?"

"She's here. She didn't run out on you."

Hadrian scowled, but despite his best intentions, he felt relief. He told himself that no man could possibly relish the idea of dragging a furiously unwilling bride quite literally to the altar in front of a thousand guests.

The Earl of Northumberland laughed. "Nothing like a challenge, is there?"

The Duke's jaw clenched. "I am amazed you approve of her." The moment he had decided to wed Nicole, he had gone to his grandfather to apprise him of his intention. Of course he could do as he chose at this stage of his life, but it was a matter of respect to seek out Northumberland's approval. He had expected some amount of opposition. There had been none.

"I don't know yet if I approve of her," the Earl of Northumberland said bluntly. "I approve of her family and I approve of a timely marriage. I am not interested in having a bastard grandchild."

Hadrian had not told him the reason for the marriage and at the time his grandfather had not asked. He lifted a brow, knowing that he should not be surprised at Roger de Warenne's insight.

"You may be able to fool all of London, lad, but you can't fool me," Northumberland said.

"Indeed."

"Your necktie needs straightening, Hadrian."

The Duke began to fumble with it and preoccupied, he did not see the Earl of Northumberland's satisfied smile.

Nicole sat very still, barely breathing. Her sister was with her, and unfortunately Regina was as nervous and frightened as if it were her own wedding. Martha sat beside her as well and held her hand. She was the only relatively calm one in the room—yet even her palm was damp. "Relax. You look as if you are going to your funeral."

"Aren't I?"

Regina cried out. "Will you persist in being a fool even now?"

They had barely talked all week. Regina was obviously thrilled with the match, making Nicole even more angry every time their paths crossed. Their relationship seemed to have deteriorated completely from friendship to hostility.

"I will feel exactly the way I want to feel," Nicole snapped.

"Why not let the whole world see how unhappy you are!" Regina shot back.

"I intend to!"

"Stop it!" Martha cried, standing. "Dear God, now is not the time to fight. And Nicole, if I were you, I would think twice about humiliating the Duke in front of all his guests!"

Nicole opened her mouth to respond that Martha was, fortunately for her, not Nicole, but she stopped abruptly. The strains of the music which had been filling the room for the past half hour had ceased. Her parents had been greeting the guests as they arrived; by now all of the guests must be seated. Everyone froze, listening to the silence. It had been Nicole's adamant decision that there would be no procession, just the bridal march to the altar where the groom would be waiting with his grandfather. Regina pulled a white kerchief out of her glove and wiped her brow.

Nicole trembled. It was about to happen. She was marrying the Duke of Clayborough. Oh God.

"Here," Regina shoved the kerchief in her hand.

Nicole took it, not seeing the sympathy on her sister's face, for her eyes were suddenly full of tears. She did not even know why she was crying.

Regina looked at Nicole and Martha. "Where is Father?" Panic filled her voice.

Maybe something has happened, Nicole thought desperately. Maybe some crisis had occurred—and there would be no wedding.

Her father entered the room. "Are you ready?" he asked his daughter. He glanced at the other two girls. "You had better go and take your seats."

Martha grabbed Nicole's hand and kissed her cheek. Regina hesitated, then quickly kissed her sister as well.

When they were alone, Nicole rose unsteadily to her feet. Her relationship with her father had also been destroyed by the advent of her wedding; she could not look at him without feeling betrayed—and lost.

Nicholas' gaze swept her. "You are so beautiful," he said, his voice broken. "I am so proud of you."

It was Nicole's undoing. What had he to be proud of? She had scandalized society since she had come out, she was only marrying now because she had been unchaste, she had not spoken to him since he had arranged this marriage. Tears welled. "Father . . ."

"I love you very much, Nicole. Believe me, I have dwelled long and hard on whether I have done the right thing in accepting Hadrian's suit. And I am convinced that I have. Please forgive me for doing what I think is best for you."

She could not continue this fight with him, not here, not now, on her wedding day. She came forward, wanting to be his daughter again so badly—yet the hurt he had caused her would not go away. She looked at him, wanting to say so much, wanting to ask him how he could do this to her, wanting to tell him she did forgive him—

that she did love him. She opened her mouth to speak, saw the hope in his eyes. But no words came out.

The wedding march began.

They regarded each other for a very long moment. Nicholas held out his arm somberly. Unable to speak at all now, Nicole took it.

A thousand guests were waiting.

The Duke of Clayborough was waiting.

The Duke of Clayborough was furious but it did not show. However, it was unlikely that he deceived any of his guests. And if his bride continued to so openly display her ill will towards him, he thought, he might forget public appearances and all the good he had done this past week and a half and openly strangle her.

They were at the reception, held at his own residence on Cavendish Square due to the huge number of guests that had been invited to the wedding. It would have been a beautiful ceremony. The cathedral was a splendid work of architecture and vast enough to hold their thousand guests. And Nicole had been a ravishing bride in her silver gown; yet she had been an angry one, as well.

Her veil had been transparent. Delicately spun of silver tulle, it hid nothing. Her expression—her anger—had been obvious for everyone to see. She had not made one attempt to appear a happy bride, indeed, the reverse seemed to be true.

The moment Hadrian had seen her coming down the aisle, he had been stunned senseless. The fiercest emotions he had ever experienced had welled up in him, and for one heartstopping instant he had known that he was, somehow, in love with her.

That instant had passed immediately. Her countenance became clear as she approached, her beautiful, silver-eyed, dark countenance. There was no mistaking her emotions. She dared to humiliate him—and herself—in front of their thousand guests.

She avoided looking at him as she approached. In fact, she kept her chin high, her mouth set in a grim, mulish line. Nor would she look at him when she paused beside him at the altar. When it was time for her to say her vows, she had actually been silent. Hadrian had taken her hand and squeezed it very, very hard—a warning that he would force her to his will even if she so stupidly made more of a spectacle of herself now. She had then, finally, to his relief, spoken. But it was too late to quell his anger.

Now they were man and wife.

And there was not one soul at Clayborough House who did not comprehend that the bride was reluctant, to say the least.

The Duke's polite smile had long since fallen by the wayside, a cold unyielding mask slipping into its place instead. He had had enough. He did not care that they had been at their own reception barely an hour. The longer he remained seated beside his stony-faced bride, who refused to eat, drink or even speak, the more dangerous his anger became. And he was trying so very hard to control it.

"We are going," he told her abruptly.

"Now?"

"Now. This minute." He rose, and because he held her hand, he pulled her up with him.

"Then let me change."

"Interested in propriety now? It's a little late, don't you think so—Madam Wife?"

She stiffened. "They won't cut the cake for hours."

"I don't give a damn."

"That is apparent," she said, looking at him meaningfully.

"Your double-entendre escapes me. Why do you seek to delay? You are obviously not having the time of your life."

"Because staying here is better than leaving with you."

He laughed coldly. "Ah, now we get to the bottom of things. You seek to delay the inevitable. Are you afraid of being alone with me and betraying yourself?"

"I am not afraid," she said tightly. "I merely wish to delay what shall be exceedingly unpleasant—our future."

"If you continue to rile me this way, it will be more than unpleasant."

Her eyes widened. "You threaten me?"

"Take it as you will." He grabbed her arm again and propelled her along with him. She started to struggle, and he turned on her in tightly controlled fury. "Haven't you made one scene too many today? Must you make another?"

"You are the one making a scene," she hissed, but she stopped fighting him.

Hadrian ignored her. They paused to say good bye to their families. In the process of departing, however, they were waylaid again and again by well-wishers, many of whom could not disguise their lurid interest in the cool groom and hostile bride. The Duke nearly jettisoned his wife into the Clayborough coach once they were outside.

She scrambled into the opposite corner and sat there. Hadrian climbed in across from her, ignoring her as best he could, though he was so angry with her that he wanted to throttle her. He signaled the driver to begin their journey.

Neither one spoke. Hadrian was furious with her for her behavior on this day, in front of the cream of British society. He had worked hard to quell any gossip about them, wasting his precious time on stupid fêtes and silly balls, charming insipid ladies and fawning gentlemen, acting like a lovestruck fool. No doubt everyone now thought him the biggest sort of fool—besotted with a bride who openly despised him. In just a few hours Nicole had undone all that he had achieved in the past ten days—all that he had achieved for her sake.

"I hope you are pleased with yourself," he said.

"Why should I be pleased with anything on this day of all days?"

She was sitting as far from him as possible, in the corner on the other side of the coach. As angry as he was, he could not help but notice how spectacular she was in her silver wedding gown with her ebony hair flowing loose. He stretched out his long legs in a casual manner which belied the tension rising in him. "I suggest you begin to change your attitude. You are now my wife. That circumstance will not change—not until I am dead. Or do you enjoy creating scandal?"

She glared. "You know I do not."

"To the contrary, I think you truly enjoyed making one scene after another today." And he certainly knew that she had enjoyed humiliating him. Another surge of anger rippled over him. He fought it admirably.

"You forced me to the altar. Did you think I would come meekly? With head bowed, in submission? If you thought so, then you thought wrong."

"There is only one place where you submit to me, Madam." His glance skewered her. "Perhaps that is the one place where I should keep you. For both our sakes."

Nicole had flushed at his reference to her unfortunate passionate nature, now she gasped at his suggestion. "I hope you are jesting," she muttered grimly.

"The idea has vast appeal."

They stared at each other. For Nicole, the coach was too small. Hadrian was too near for comfort. His proximity had been disturbing since the moment she had approached him at the altar. His proximity was always disturbing. She could not help but think about the impending night—their wedding night.

It was impossible to believe, but she was now his wife. Once she had wanted that with all of her heart, but that seemed to have been a lifetime ago. She was his wife, he had done his duty. And now he expected her to accept her position—and, she suspected, his advances. She clenched her fists. He could not force her to marry and expect her to be docile, he could not. And if he really thought that tonight she would accept him with open arms, then he was insane.

But what about all the nights after this one? Even if she successfully refused him tonight, how long could she succeed in rejecting him? Nicole did not have to think too long to know that her cause was hopeless. For she rejected out of hand the idea of an anullment, and would not even examine her reasons.

But he must see that he could not force her to his will this way, he must.

However, her heart was beating too rapidly and she was too aware of his regard upon her. It was bold and blatant—his intentions were obvious. Nicole wished she could not remember what it felt like to be in his arms, what it felt like to be the recipient of his kisses. Unfortunately, her memory was perfect.

Nicole turned away from him to stare out the window. The winter evening was approaching with undue haste, yet despite the chill in the air, and the fact that her silver fox cloak was open, she was not cold. Far from it. She was suddenly seized with an inexplicable panic, suddenly feeling trapped, boxed in. She clutched the fox closer, for comfort.

Hadrian broke the silence between them. "I did not make any plans for a honeymoon."

"Good."

He continued calmly enough. "I have some pressing matters to attend to at Clayborough and at several other estates. I will have disposed of these matters within three weeks. We can travel then—if you wish."

She finally turned to face him, the panic still there, its partner despair. "I do not wish! I do not want to go anywhere with you! I do not wish to be your wife!" Her voice broke. "I do not!"

"Again, your feelings are no revelation. In fact, I am tired of hearing them. Please keep your distress on the topic of our marriage to yourself."

Nicole turned her teary gaze from his hard, glittering one.

"I have no wish to honeymoon with a shrewish bride, anyway," he said.

It shouldn't have hurt, because she did not want to go abroad with him. Honeymoons were for lovers, not antagonists. She knew without a doubt that if he had married Elizabeth, they would have enjoyed weeks and weeks alone together on the continent. But it did hurt. She snuggled deep into the fox cape, fighting tears of exhaustion, hysteria and perhaps, defeat.

They arrived at Clayborough Hall five hours later. It was dark now, a starless, dismal night, and Nicole could not really see the palace which, she had heard, rivaled that of even the royal dukes. Hadrian helped her from the carriage. Nicole let him, having no choice, but the moment her feet touched the solid ground she quickly withdrew her hand from his. She heard his breath hiss in displeasure.

There were so many servants lined up in the vast entry to greet her that Nicole froze in surprise and a touch of fright. Perhaps a hundred members of the staff were all waiting to meet their new mistress—her. She pulled her silver fox cape more firmly about her shoulders, her only movement. She realized that Hadrian was addressing them.

"It is late. You may meet the Duchess tomorrow at noon. Please return to your duties."

Everyone disappeared.

Duchess. *You may meet the Duchess tomorrow*. It hadn't really registered. Nicole still did not move. *She was the Duchess of Clayborough*. It was amazing, it was terrifying.

"This is the housekeeper, Mrs. Veig. Tonight she will show you to your rooms."

Nicole managed to nod at the stern-faced, uniformed woman who stood silently by the stairs. Hadrian then asked her if she would leave them for a moment. Mrs. Veig also vanished.

Nicole became aware that the room they were standing in—the foyer—was larger than most ballrooms. The ceiling was several stories high. The floors underfoot were green and gold-flecked marble. Huge white pillars rose to touch the ceiling. Naked angels were carved at their tops. This was Hadrian's home?

This was now her home?

"I will give you a tour of the house tomorrow," he said.

She turned to look at him.

"Because it is late, we will eat in our rooms—later."

Nicole stared at him, still trying to adjust to the idea that she was now the Duchess of Clayborough—one of the premier peeresses in the realm.

"I shall be up in a half an hour," he told her. "I expect you to be ready. Is that enough time?"

All at once what he was saying struck her and her eyes widened. She realized that he was watching her closely, attempting to read her thoughts. Before she could tell him not to bother intruding upon her on this night, he called for the housekeeper, who instantly appeared. Without another word, the Duke strode abruptly away.

"Are you ready, Your Grace?" Mrs. Veig asked. Her voice was not as stern as her expression.

Nicole was shaken by the circumstances, including the fact that this was her wedding night and she was not about to submit to Hadrian again. She managed to turn to the housekeeper. "Yes, please."

Mrs. Veig's face softened. "Come this way, then. Your bags have already been brought up the back way."

Nicole followed Mrs. Veig, apprehension freely filling her now. How would she manage a home like this? And this was just one of the many fantastic residences he kept! How could she possibly oversee such a huge staff? Why, she wouldn't even know where to begin! Suddenly she regretted that her education had not been more conventional—that she had refused to bother learning about household management except in its most rudimentary aspects.

Nicole's gaze roved ahead of her, up the endless flights of curving stairs, her hand running along the smooth teak railing. A red runner trimmed in gold covered the stairs. Huge paintings, some landscapes, some portraits, many done by masters, gazed down at her from the walls.

They did not pause on the second landing. "There are more apartments here, but His Grace's suite—and yours—are on the third floor," Mrs. Veig explained.

The housekeeper's words jarred Nicole back into the present and the crisis about to confront her. In a half an hour Hadrian would be at her door. Her stomach turned over nervously, yet her pulse leapt, too. If only she could be confident that she could, indeed, control her desire for him. But she had no confidence at all, for as furious as she was with the events surrounding this day and with Hadrian, she could never deny that he was the most spectacular male she had ever laid eyes on.

But she would die of shame if he had his way with her tonight.

Nicole finally entered her bedroom through a grandiose sitting room done up in pink and white tulle fabric. There was a study to the left, the walls papered in a cherry stripe, and two vast walk-in closets and her dressing room. Again, the theme everywhere was pink and white; even the marble floors of the bathroom were a pale rose. It flashed with sadness through Nicole's mind that pink was probably Elizabeth's choice of color. It occurred to her that every time she entered these apartments she would be reminded of the dead girl—and Hadrian's love for her and his grief. Hadrian, who was now her husband—but not out of choice.

Nicole suddenly despised pink.

Five maids were madly at work unpacking her things, including her own thirteen-year-old Annie. Already only two of her five trunks remained unopened. The rest of her belongings would be coming later in the week.

More than apprehension was filling Nicole now. She trembled, feeling desperately sad. "Thank you," she said to the maids and housekeeper. "This is fine. I can do the rest later." She wanted to be alone.

Everyone turned to look at her in shock with the exception of Annie, whose eyes had been as big as an owl's since she had first entered the palace. The housekeeper finally spoke, her tone gentle despite the admonishment. "We've plenty of staff to be doing that, Your Grace. When you want anything, just pull the bellcord."

Nicole nodded.

Mrs. Veig dismissed the maids, except for Annie. "Is there anything else you'll be wanting?"

"Just a bath."

"It's drawn," she said. "Good night, then."

Nicole felt disoriented, dazed. She sank down on the bed, a huge upholstered, canopied and curtained affair that looked as if it dated back several centuries. The coverlet was a pale pink velvet, smooth to her touch. Then she saw her sheer white bridal nightgown laid out neatly on the bed. In less than half an hour Hadrian was going to come here, intent on claiming his rights as her husband!

"Are you all right, mum?" Annie asked, still wide-eyed. Then she blushed. "I mean, Your Grace?"

"Please, Annie, the formality isn't necessary." Nicole was on her feet. She went to the heavy white drapes and pulled them back, but she could see nothing. The night was pitch black and foggy. Only a few lights illuminated the circular graveled drive, which glistened like polished shells in their glow.

"Annie, I wish to be alone," Nicole said. She was still trembling, more now than before. She had to think—and quickly.

Annie nodded and hurriedly turned and headed for the nearest door. She opened it only to find herself in the sitting room. Blushing, she found the door to the hallway and shut it quietly behind her.

Nicole turned to stare at the pink and white bed.

She stared at the wispy nightgown laid out there, one

designed to inflame a husband's sexual appetite.

She remembered his kisses, his touch.

Nicole's trembling increased. She was suddenly aware of being exhausted to the point of feeling faint. She sat down hard on a red chaise, wishing she had more time, wishing she could think clearly. But she could not think at all, her thoughts were confused, a jumble. She only knew that after all that had transpired today she must not allow Hadrian to trample over her and claim his conjugal rights, not tonight. And tomorrow she would think about the future and how she would handle it and him—and herself.

She wondered if she dared to lock Hadrian out of her rooms. Nervously Nicole approached one door, aware of the loud ticking of the clock on the wall to her right. She did not think there was much time left before Hadrian would knock upon her door. She did not feel up to another confrontation with him. She was so tired. She knew he would be angry if she did lock her doors, but it would be so much easier to lock him out and face him in the morning than to let him in and fight him tonight. Quickly Nicole turned the lock on the door that she had entered her bedroom from, then she went to the one that opened on the hallway and locked that, too. Her unease heightened as she backed away into the middle of the room.

This was not the way to begin a marriage, she realized. It was probably the worst possible way to begin a marriage. Before she could take a step back to one of the locked doors, he knocked.

Nicole froze. Not already! She prayed it was a maid and not her husband. "Yes?" Her voice was unsteady.

"It is I," Hadrian said.

Nicole hesitated, debating unlocking the door. A sudden cowardice assailed her. If she let him in . . . it would be easier to keep him on the other side of the door, so much easier. She tried to think of something to say to him and could think of nothing that was soothing.

"Nicole?" he asked. There was impatience in his tone. "May I assume that you are ready?"

"No," she blurted. "I am not."

There was a short silence. She strained to hear what he was doing, but she heard nothing. Then he tried the knob, saying, "Do you again seek to delay? That would not be wise." He stopped.

She imagined his expression, stunned to find himself locked out of her room. She wrung her hands. "Hadrian," she began. "I am very tired. I think—"

"I begin to understand," he said softly.

At his tone, Nicole froze.

"Open the door, Madam."

This was one great big mistake! "Hadrian," she cried, regretting such a foolish strategy of trying to bar him from her room, "I am very tired—tomorrow we shall talk."

There was no response. Seconds ticked by. Nicole was amazed when she realized that he was actually walking away! Her ploy had worked!

Shaking wildly, she slumped down onto a small, plush sofa in front of the gleaming pink granite mantle. She had an inkling that she had just escaped a very harrowing confrontation—maybe she had even escaped with her very life.

Her heartbeat, still erratic, finally began to slow. She laughed, the sound a bit shaky. She clapped her hand over her mouth, as more laughter, much of it hysterical, threatened to burst forth. God, she had chased him away. And it had been so easy!

Suddenly a click focused her attention on the door. It glided open, revealing the Duke's powerful, rigid body, a key in one of his clenched hands.

For the first time in her life, Nicole almost swooned.

"Don't you ever lock me out again," he said. His tone was much too calm.

Nicole stood absolutely motionless. Her heart was beating in a frenzied, frightened rhythm. Hadrian filled the doorway and she could feel the heat of his anger emanating from him in thick, undulating waves. He was clad only in a velvet-lapeled dressing gown. His calves and feet were bare. It dawned on her that he was naked beneath the robe, and she began to back away. His expression was fiercely angry.

"Do you understand me?" he ground out. A vein pulsed in his temple. His eyes were black. Nicole saw that his fists were clenched at his sides. She watched him slip the key into the pocket of his gown.

"You have no right," she said in a bare whisper, her courage almost failing her completely.

"I have every right. And if you wish to start our marriage on this note, then so be it." His gaze swept her hard. "You are a very reckless woman, Madam."

A dozen responses and a dozen pleas coursed through her mind. "You were forewarned. It is you who are reckless. To take me as your wife when I distinctly refused you!"

His eyes widened. A pregnant silence hovered between them.

Nicole wished she had responded in any way but the one she had chosen.

Hadrian could not believe his ears. He was so furious he did not trust himself to speak for a long time. He stared at his frightened yet wildly hostile bride. If he were less of a man he would turn her over his knee as if she were a wayward child and deliver a few hurtful wallops. Of course, he would never be so abusive.

It was the humiliation that had finally gotten to him. First the humiliation in front of all of society: he could imagine the gossips now, their glee as they discussed how madly in love the poor Duke was with his hateful bride. But the final blow had yet to come. For he had had to go to Mrs. Veig in order to get a key for the lock to his bride's room. By now he was certain that every servant in his employ was speculating upon why the bride had barred the groom from her rooms on their wedding night. A flush tinged the Duke's high cheekbones. There would be gossip about them even in the privacy of their own home! It was time to put a stop to this nonsense once and for all.

"You made yourself quite clear the first time, when I proposed directly to you. Do you have a death wish, Madam? Did I not distinctly ask you to *keep your distress to yourself?*"

"Do you think that will make it go away?"

He had truly had enough. Exercising great will, he turned with outward poise and closed the door behind him. He turned back to face his wary, watchful bride. "You have precisely one minute to shed your wedding gown, Madam, and if you do not, I shall remove it for you."

"You would rape me?"

He smiled coldly. "I have no intention of raping you. Or should I remind you *again* of a certain avid aspect of your nature? I suggest you begin with the buttons. You have forty-five seconds left."

She drew herself up straighter, her voluptuous breasts heaving hard. "I won't, Hadrian. I won't share a bed with you tonight."

"I am not giving you a choice."

"How stupid of me to think that you would! Your Grace! How stupid of me not to realize that such an all-powerful lord as yourself would not even consider giving a woman—his wife—a choice! You did not give me a choice as far as marrying you, so why would you give me a choice now?" Her eyes snapped with anger, but they also sparkled with tears.

He could give in to this argument or not. He chose not to. "Thirty seconds, Madam."

Nicole looked as if she would scream incoherently with frustration. Abruptly she threw her hair over one shoulder, rage in her every movement. She tore open the top buttons on the back of her dress, the small pearls breaking free of their threads and scattering across the floor. No woman could unbutton her gown herself, under normal circumstances, but his wife was so mad that she had nearly superhuman powers. He watched her yank violently on the beautiful fabric, popping off all of the rest of the buttons. Wisely, Hadrian did not make a comment.

Nor did he move. During their confrontation, lust had been the last thing on his mind. He was only pursuing this because of the struggle for power between them. He was determined to make Nicole his wife in every sense of the word and end this ridiculous resistance of hers once and for all. Now his body responded instantly, aggressively, to the sight of her ripping off her own gown. It was a sight he would not forget for a long time, if ever.

Nicole wrenched her torn dress down over her hips, and down her long, endless legs. She stepped free of it, kicking it at him. Panting harshly, she raised her wild gaze to his.

He had not moved, watching her unblinkingly.

But she was not through. Already she was shedding her many tiers of petticoats and kicking them away with her silver high-heeled shoes until the room around her was littered with frothy, sensuous silks and chiffons. With the same kind of superhuman effort, she pulled the top laces at the back of her corset free and wrenched it from her body. She threw it directly at him. Reflexively Hadrian caught it.

They faced each other. Nicole was still in a frenzy and her heavy panting filled the room.

"Are you finished?" Hadrian asked quietly.

"Are you satisfied?"

Again, Hadrian thought it wiser not to respond.

The silence lengthened. Nicole's frenzy diminished. Hadrian watched the sanity returning. He watched her panting slow and ease until her naked breasts merely trembled. He watched her straighten. He watched the awareness come into her gaze, watched the tinge of pink cover her cheeks. Unable to help herself, she crossed her arms to cover her bosom.

He could have made a comment, but he did not. He held out his hand. "Come here," he said softly.

Nicole raised her gaze to his. He saw more tears glistening there. Instead of giving him her hand—in surrender—she turned her back to him, clutching herself. She shivered.

He approached her silently from behind. "It does not have to be this way," he said gently.

"Does it not?"

His hands closed on her naked shoulders. Her skin was smooth, silky, warm. "No, it does not." He leaned forward as he brought her back against him. She tensed at the contact with his body. Hadrian lowered his mouth to the crook of her neck.

She was motionless. His lips played delicately over her skin, yet there was nothing delicate about the way his phallus strained against her buttocks. "Oh, God, don't," she moaned.

He ignored her. He pried past her crossed arms to cup her breasts. He pressed fully into her. He continued to kiss her neck from behind.

Nicole gasped, but it was almost a sob. It was a moment of surrender and Hadrian knew it. He turned her swiftly and lifted her in his arms, carrying her to the bed. Just before he came down on top of her, their eyes met. Here were still wet with tears, but he saw the sparks of desire, too. He kissed the wetness from her lids, still deliberately holding himself in check—the most difficult act of willpower he had ever experienced in his life.

Nicole's head slipped back into the abundant luxury of silk and velvet pillows and she arched up into his body. "Hadrian," she whispered, her hands suddenly twining in his hair.

It was the moment he had been waiting for—for his entire life. His passion exploded. He clenched her in a rock-hard embrace, his mouth on hers, devouring and demanding. Nicole opened to him completely.

Their tongues rushed at one another. Her thighs locked around his hips. Hadrian's hands coursed down her long, curved body, seeking out the heat and the wetness—the welcome—of her femininity. She greeted him with a rapid thrusting of her hips. Suddenly he was temporarily insane. He lifted her hips and buried his face in her heat. Never in his life had he done something so outrageous before. She gasped and he began to worship her with his mouth, kissing her intimately, wildly, and then his tongue was stroking over and between and into every fold of delicious flesh he could find.

She climaxed violently and he felt every shudder against his face. She climaxed a second time, gasping his name, as he continued to nuzzle her. Hadrian rose up over her powerfully. The muscles in his shoulders, chest and arms bulged and strained. He grasped her face with both large hands. "Look at me!"

Her eyes flew open. They were dark and hot with desire—and still moist with tears. Their souls met. Hadrian entered her.

Their bodies heaved and bucked frantically on the pink velvet bedspread. Silk and satin and brocade pillows spilled to the floor. The posters of the three-centuries old bed groaned, the salmon pink canopy shook, the tasseled trim leaping madly. And almost as one, their cries, male and female, split the night.

Nicole tried not to cry. But a few tears slipped down her cheeks. She did not know if they were tears of despair or tears of joy. Was it just sheer emotional exhaustion?

She turned her head to watch her husband. *Her husband*. Her pulse quickened at the very idea. She lay naked atop the pink velvet of her bed; he was stoking up the fire in the hearth. He was also unclothed. His back was to her, and unwilling yet mesmerized, she leaned upon one elbow to openly stare at him.

He was magnificent. A sigh she could not contain escaped her. The muscles in his broad shoulders and his sinewed arms rippled as he added wood to the flames. His back was long, slabbed with more glistening, chiseled strength. His buttocks were high and hard and powerfully male. Her gaze slipped curiously. He straightened and turned instantly, his glance meeting hers.

He knew what she had been doing. A blush crossed her features. Hot awareness thickened in her veins, ran to her loins. She shifted restlessly.

"Do I meet with your approval?" he asked quietly.

Nicole gazed into his eyes. The fire leapt behind his bare, golden body. It was an illusion, wasn't it, the warmth she saw there? With a volition of its own, her gaze slid over him again, over his broad, thickly hewn chest, over his trim hips, over his heavy, large manhood, now flaccid and damp. "Yes," she heard herself whisper.

He moved to her. She tried to keep her eyes away from his, but it was impossible. Their glances were locked together. He sat down on the bed beside her. To her surprise he slipped a hand in her thick, wavy hair, stroking it. For the second time in her life, she almost swooned, but this time, with heady pleasure.

She tried to read his thoughts, tried to penetrate and comprehend the warmth—for surely it was warmth—that she saw in his eyes. She was so afraid she was seeing what she wanted to see, but the hope was impossible to chase away. And then, as he bent his head down to hers, it ceased to matter. Not at that moment. She waited an eternity for the feel of his lips. When it came, she sighed. She sighed, and she surrendered.

Nicole awoke, too exhilarated to be tired, despite the fact that she had barely slept at all—due to her insatiable husband. She stretched with satisfaction and glanced at his side of the bed, only to find that he was gone.

She sat up. She was still naked and it felt glorious, despite the fact that she was also terribly sore from so much excessive passion. But she smiled. She smiled and smiled and smiled.

Oh what a fool she had been! She knew that now. She had been utterly stupid to resist marrying Hadrian. To resist marrying the man she loved so much that it hurt.

It was better being with him than being apart from him. Much, much better!

Slowly, she got up from the bed. She saw that it was past midmorning—she had slept shamefully late. She found her robe on the floor and slipped it on, then went to the drapes and pulled them open. A heavy gray day greeted her. Winter was on its way.

She wondered where Hadrian was.

She wondered how he would act towards her now.

She moved into the marble bathroom and began to run the water. Thoughtfully, she sat on the side of the tub. She must not delude herself, she knew. Just because they shared such a splendid passion for each other's bodies did not mean that he loved her. She could not forget that Elizabeth was not even dead a month. Yet, in time, his grief would lessen. And she, Nicole, would still be here, his wife.

If they shared so much passion now, might he not one day come to love her?

She tried to remind herself that he had married her out of duty. It no longer seemed quite so relevant.

Nicole's hands trembled. She should have never resisted this marriage. She should have never openly displayed her anger in front of all their guests. She should not have attempted to lock him out last night. Oh, how she hated her pride today! She realized ruefully that she probably did not have any left. He had seen to that, last night.

And she did not care.

There was a rapping on her door. Nicole got up to answer it and found Mrs. Veig with Annie. The housekeeper was looking anxious and holding a breakfast tray in her hands. "Your Grace, I would never presume to bother you, but I could not help hearing the bathwater." And she shot Annie a disapproving stare.

Nicole smiled. "I am about to take a bath."

"You have staff to prepare your bath, Your Grace," Mrs. Veig stated. Then her regard became dark and accusing as she glared at little Annie. "Get in with you, girl! Go and see that the bath is exactly as Her Grace likes it!"

"Yes'm!" Annie fled.

Nicole blinked. She had forgotten the extent of her new circumstances; she was no longer Lady Shelton, she was the Duchess of Clayborough. And duchesses, she assumed, did not dare prepare their own baths. "I'm sorry," she said.

But Mrs. Veig did not hear, or she pretended not to, entering the room and setting the tray down on the delicately wrought glass table in front of the hearth. A fire crackled there, and the housekeeper turned to attend it, stoking it. Nicole wondered if Hadrian—her husband—had made the fire for her before he left her bed at dawn. "Did someone—Annie—come in this morning to tend to the hearth?"

"No, Your Grace." Mrs. Veig was shocked. "I would never allow anyone to disturb you unless you gave explicit orders to the contrary. Do you want your maid to stoke up the fire at first light? She can do so quietly, without awakening you."

Nicole wondered if Hadrian would share her bed again tonight. "No, no, that's fine. I'm a light sleeper, I would rather not be disturbed."

Mrs. Veig nodded, moving towards the bed.

Nicole sat down somewhat dumbly on the chaise, staring unseeingly at the tray of muffins, jam and tea. Hadrian had left the fire for her. Such a small gesture. And she was moved to tears!

"Annie," Mrs. Veig called sharply. "As soon as you finish in there, take these sheets to the laundress, and then you may make the bed."

Nicole looked at Mrs. Veig. The woman turned away, moving to the draperies on the other windows and opening them automatically. Nicole's gaze widened as she stared at the bed. There was a dark red stain right in the center of it and it looked like blood.

She could not believe her eyes.

Nicole descended the stairs slowly, uncertainly. This was her home now, but she felt like a stranger, not like its mistress, and certainly not like a duchess. She had no idea of where she was going, or what she should do, or be doing.

She was Hadrian's wife, the Duchess of Clayborough. It was still incredible. But she smiled, unable to forget being in his arms last night, or the look of warmth in his eyes. And today, today he had stoked the fire for her. It was such a little act—yet for Nicole, it was terribly significant.

She was his wife. It wasn't so bad—it wasn't bad at all. Maybe it could even work out, with a little effort on her part. She was going to do her best to recoup the disastrous start. She was going to do more than accept being his wife. She was going to try and be a good wife—she was going to try and please him. *And win his love.*

In case he was about the house, she wanted to appear as a duchess should. She wanted to avoid her own penchant for committing faux pas. She wanted to be proper. She had exercised the utmost care in doing her toilette that morning. Annie had been there to assist her, but the young maid knew about as much as Nicole did about proper attire, and Nicole had not a clue as to how a duchess should dress in the mornings. She was determined to dress properly. Fortunately, Mrs. Veig had been with them, hovering about Annie, wanting to make sure Nicole's every need was met.

Nicole's only need had been to know what to wear. She did not want to appear ignorant, and she had very casually asked Mrs. Veig what her preference was—if she liked this gown or that. Flattered, the housekeeper had chosen a beautiful yellow and green ensemble, the jacket tight-fitting and flared at the hip, the skirt draped elaborately in the back. It was as Nicole suspected. Duchesses dressed. She wasn't too happy with having to wear such finery so early in the day, but she would do it.

As she crossed the second floor, she passed a bevy of maids busily cleaning in the corridor, on the landing and in the fantastic ballroom just off of the landing. Its doors were flung wide open, revealing gleaming black and white marble floors, white plastered columns, and a frescoed ceiling. Everyone swiftly curtsied to her with the same chipper chorus, "Good morning, Your Grace."

Nicole slowly continued her descent. She was a bit shaken by such deference; it was incredible. She was even more shaken at the notion—and hope—that Hadrian might be somewhere in this palace, and that she would see him. Her heart was already beating with excitement.

On the ground floor she paused. What did a duchess do with her time? Mrs. Veig had informed her that dinner was at one, *if* that met with her approval, and Nicole had said it had. It was only half past eleven. At some point she had to decide upon the evening's supper menu, for Mrs. Veig had asked her what she would like to have that night. Nicole could not care less what the chef prepared, but it seemed to be important to Mrs. Veig that she determine the fare, so she would do so.

But first she must find her husband. Didn't wives always greet their husbands with a cheery "good morning?" Even duchesses? She hesitated somewhat nervously on the first floor. Two liveried male servants stood ahead of her in the foyer keeping vigilance upon the massive front doors. Nicole quickly approached them. They both greeted her as all the other staff had that morning.

"Would you happen to know where Hadrian is? I mean," she flushed, "where His Grace might be?"

The men were impassive, not cracking even the slightest smile at her blunder. The elder answered. "He has not yet gone out, Your Grace. You might try his study, or the green library."

"And where are those rooms?"

"His study's down the hall, tenth door on your left. His library is upstairs on the third floor, the door before his suite. There's a library on every floor," he explained kindly, seeing her questioning expression.

Nicole set off for his study. The two gleaming red doors were closed. She was trembling now, and a fantasy assailed her, one in which Hadrian rose from behind his desk to embrace her eagerly as she entered his domain. How silly she was being. She knocked.

Inside, the Duke had been trying to attend to the matter of several accounts, without much success, all that morning. Usually he spent the mornings out on his estate on horseback. This morning, after leaving his new bride snuggled up beneath the velvet bedcovers, he had chosen to do paperwork in his office—and await her.

He was an early riser, and today, despite last night, had been no exception. Indeed, he doubted he had actually slept more than an hour or two. But he was not tired. To the contrary, there was no mistaking the exhilaration flowing in his veins.

And it was because of his wife.

His wife.

All morning he had tested that phrase, silently, with no small amount of satisfaction. He was surprised with the intensity of the satisfaction he felt, and the possessiveness that went with it. Nor could he stop thinking about her. His obsession had magnified a hundredfold, not decreased. But what did it matter? For now she was his. He could be as obsessed with her as he damned well wanted to be.

Would she have softened after the incredible night they had shared? His heart leapt at the thought. Or would she, with the morning light, be her old recalcitrant, prideful self? Would they do battle—or would they establish a truce?

At the soft rapping upon his doors he lunged to his feet, knocking a stack of papers from his desk. He bent to retrieve them hastily, knowing it was Nicole who stood outside his door and knowing too, full well, that she was the cause of his blundering. Deciding to sort out the mess later, he placed the stack haphazardly on his desk—his desk which had never been less than neat and tidy. He strode quickly across the study and opened the two doors.

Her cheeks flamed when their gazes met. For one instant, neither spoke, both gazing at each other, perhaps assessing each other's humor.

"Good morning," Nicole said.

"Good morning," he replied politely. It was hard to keep emotion out of his voice, emotions he dared not analyze. *But the colors were there, rainbow-hued, and they had never been so bright.*

When he realized she was standing in the hallway, he quickly stepped aside. "Please, come in."

"Thank you."

He closed the door behind her, thinking that she was the most gorgeous creature he had ever seen, and that yellow—bright vivid yellow—was a magnificent color on her. Topazes, he thought. He would buy her topazes.

She strolled into the center of the room. He watched her. She turned, smiling deliberately, uncertainly. He managed to smile back. Neither one of them were wearing their hearts on their sleeve, he realized. But he also saw that she was not a shrieking hussy. Today she was trying to be as cautious and polite as he was. That in itself declared some sort of existing truce.

"Did you sleep well?" he finally ventured into the lengthening silence. It was impossible not to think of her physically, not to be aware of her physically. He was warm, the room was warm. He wondered what her reaction would be if he swept her into his arms and made love to her on the sofa.

"Yes. No. Not really." This time a small bubbly laugh escaped her.

This time his smile, in response, was genuine.

Their glances locked.

Nervously, Nicole turned away first. "I just wanted to say hello."

"I'm glad."

Her head whipped around, she stared.

He felt himself flushing, so now he turned away, too. What if she should guess the truth? That he wanted her to be acquiescent to him—that he wanted her to be more than acquiescent? "Would you like to meet the staff?"

"Oh, yes," she said eagerly.

He gestured to her and she moved to him. He opened the door for her and allowed her to precede him out. "After the introductions are made," he said, again, acutely aware of the sexual tension between them, "I must leave to take care of matters I have neglected for far too long."

"Oh."

Was she disappointed? He hoped he wasn't being a fool to think so—to hope so. "Mrs. Veig serves a luncheon at one. If you do not care for the schedule, change it as you would."

"One is fine."

It was very hard to walk beside her and not accost her, he realized. Last night's complete abandon made it even worse. He knew he was being utterly selfish to even contemplate how he might discreetly and deviously cry off his responsibilities and take her back upstairs. She was probably in no shape to entertain her lusty husband this morning. Still, he could not get the notion out of his mind.

The introductions took an hour. The staff that maintained the residence of Clayborough numbered one hundred and ten. In addition, there was the rest of the staff to consider, the gardeners, the gamekeepers, the park manager, the stableboys, the grooms, the stablemaster, the trainer, the kennelmaster, the kennelmen, the coachmen, the footmen and the outriders. There were also two masons and four carpenters, for, as the Duke explained, there were always repairs to be made to such an old home.

He walked her back to the house, if such a sprawling palatial residence could possibly be called such. At the front door he turned her over to Mrs. Veig and Woodward. "Enjoy your dinner, Madam. I am sorry I cannot join you." His tone was formal, but his regret was sincere.

"I understand," Nicole said, her eyes upon his booted feet. "What time will you be back, er, my lord?"

His brow shot up and he smiled at the careful form of address she chose. But it had been the proper form of address, just as she had appeared the picture of propriety this entire morning. Had his wife decided upon more than a truce, had she had a change of heart? And was it wise for him to be so pleased with the prospect—with her?

"I intend to return by six-thirty. If you care to, you can meet me in the red salon for a sherry before supper, at seven-thirty. Supper is at eight. Unless, of course, that does not meet with your approval."

"No, that is fine," Nicole said, flushing a little.

"You may change anything you like, Nicole," the Duke said softly, so only she could hear. He wanted to make it perfectly clear that her position as his wife and duchess gave her a power, in her domain, commensurate with his. And perhaps, obliquely, he wanted her to know that he himself was trying to please her. "You only have to tell me, or Mrs. Veig or Woodward, what you wish to have done."

Nicole nodded, her eyes wide upon his face.

He hesitated. There was so much in her gaze, so much he was afraid to even consider what he saw. His jaw tightened as the absurd thought of kissing her good bye welled in his mind. It would not be a polite peck upon the cheek, either. It would be a rousing display of passion. With great difficulty, he restrained himself.

But he regretted it all day.

They rapidly settled into a routine.

Nicole would awake at an indecent hour, only to find that Hadrian was gone. Nicole would not see him again until they met in the first-floor library before supper. She learned that he rode out on his estates shortly after sunrise. Although he did return in the afternoon, he secluded himself in his study, and Nicole thought it wiser not to invade his sanctum, although she dearly would have loved to.

Thus Nicole had the day to herself. After a leisurely bath—there being no need to hurry—Nicole dressed with Mrs. Veig's unwitting guidance. She then descended from her suite to meet with the chef to discuss the day's menus. This seemed to be of the utmost importance to everyone. After that task, it did not seem as if there was anything else that required her attention. Mrs. Veig and Woodward ran the staff and the house with the utmost efficiency. Had Nicole wanted to intervene, or supervise, she would not have known where to start. Her only other duty seemed to be to decide what clothing to wear for the evening meal and to inform Annie, so she could inform Mrs. Veig, who would then have the appropriate maid put it in the press so it would be wrinkle-free when she was finally ready to dress.

Her circumstances were too new for boredom to set in. The house was so vast that Nicole continued the explorations she began on her first day. These explorations were time-consuming. In the space of the several hours that remained until dinner was served at one, Nicole could not even cover an entire floor, and the mansion had seven.

It occurred to her that she might have to spend the rest of her life exploring.

It also occurred to her that it would be nice to join Hadrian as he made his rounds of his tenants and agricultural and livestock operations.

She dashed such thoughts from her mind. She did not have to ask to know that duchesses did *not* indulge themselves in estate management. They probably didn't spend all of their time exploring their own homes, either. But for the life of her, Nicole could not figure out what they *did* do.

At one o'clock, she dined alone. That first day she had been served her meal in the formal dining room. The experience had been somewhat unnerving. The room was the length of two tennis courts—and so was the dining table. She had sat at its foot, being served a seven course meal by a bevy of servants, with Woodward hovering over her to see to her every wish and whim. Unfortunately, Nicole was not a big eater and she had no whimsical fancies. After that, she had requested she take her midday meal in the music room, which was bright and cheery and, in comparison to the monstrous dining hall, cozy. Hadrian had said, after all, that she could do as she chose.

In the afternoons she rode. The stablemaster was a gruff, short Irishman named William O'Henry. He first insisted that she ride with an escort of six liveried servants. Nicole had been dismayed at such a prospect. And because her husband had made it quite clear that she might change anything that did not meet with her approval, she insisted she ride alone. Mr. O'Henry had been aghast. Finally they had compromised, but only because he insisted the Duke would have his head (and dismiss him forthright) if he let her ride about the estate unattended. O'Henry himself joined her. Nicole soon found she did not mind. The older man was a true delight, not just being a master horseman, but a rather witty fellow as well. He regaled her with tales of horsebreeding, racing and hunts, and had more than a few amusing anecdotes to relate about several exceptionally personable horses he had cared for in his long lifetime.

Nicole made sure to return by five so that she would have plenty of time to dress for supper. That first night she had Annie play the spy. The little maid had discreetly discerned that the Duke did not dress for supper. To Nicole's relief, Annie informed her that His Grace's attire was relaxed in the evening, consisting of no more than a smoking jacket, trousers and slippers.

Very eager to see Hadrian again after the night they had spent together, Nicole chose her attire with care. She donned a casual gown of midnight blue, and carefully debated whether to adorn herself with pearls or diamonds. Not wanting to appear too formal, she finally decided against any jewelry except for a small pair of earbobs and a cameo at her collar. She applied a light sweet scent to her throat and wrists, and allowed two maids an hour to put up her hair in a style that seemed artless and uncontrived.

The Duke was awaiting her in the library. He seemed restless and impatient, but surely that could not be, for Nicole arrived exactly at seven-thirty, although she had been ready a half an hour earlier. To her complete dismay, she found her husband formally dressed in a double-breasted black suit and tie. Somehow she had misunderstood, or Annie had been misinformed. Nicole hoped that Hadrian would not think her appearance terribly deficient.

The next evening she was determined to be a proper duchess right down to the very last inch of her tall frame. She wore a daringly low-cut and straight-silhouetted evening gown that was the latest fashion and the height of sophistication. She wore it with all of her diamonds, with sateen high-heeled shoes, and a matching evening bag. Her hands were gloved and she carried a small, exquisite silk fan. Her hair had taken two hours to do—and this time it was contrived. She would not make the same mistake twice.

To her shock, Hadrian greeted her in none other than his smoking jacket and slippers!

"It appears we are at cross-purposes, Madam," he had commented dryly. But his eyes were gleaming with frank admiration.

"Last night you dressed," Nicole said breathlessly, unable to find the situation amusing, not when she was the recipient of such a very male look—one laden with promise.

"Madam, last night you chose *not* to dress."

She blinked. Suddenly they both smiled. He came towards her. Even in his paisley smoking jacket, the Duke was the epitome of a virile male. His strides were long, restless. A highly charged sexual energy seemed to ripple visibly over his body. He handed her a sherry. "Perhaps we should discuss this," he said. His tone was not casual. It was low and suggestive.

Nicole wet her lips. She would never again be immune to his nearness, his heat, his intent. "What would you like me to do?"

"Ahh, need you ask now?"

She flushed, recalling the things he had guided her into doing last night, their second night of ecstasy—things no decent woman should ever even suspect were possible between lovers.

He came to her rescue, one forefinger touching her cheek. "Forgive me. You distract me, Madam Wife."

Nicole was faint with pleasure.

"Would you like me to go upstairs and change into more formal attire?" he asked, serious now.

She shook her head. "I much prefer you like this."

He smiled, she smiled. They had their first understanding.

They dined each night in the formal dining room. It was a conversationless affair. The table seated eighty. Nicole had counted the chairs the very first time she had taken a meal there. Separated from her husband by such a vast space, she could not even hope to carry on a conversation with him. The most she could do was steal discreet—and not so discreet—glances at him, or be the recipient of his stares, which became increasingly heated as the meal progressed. By the end of the week Nicole decided it was time to insist they adjourn to a smaller room for their supper. Hadrian was surprised at her request, but he also seemed, she thought, pleased by it. Thereafter they dined in one of the smaller salons on the first floor. And although conversation was now more than possible, there was little of it. There was just too much tension between them.

For they both knew what awaited them after dinner. A night of heated passion, of decadent indulgence.

Towards the end of the first week, Nicole was thrilled to have her mother, Regina and Martha come calling. Jane had sent a note asking Nicole if it would be all right to do so, and Nicole had quickly reassured her that a visit would not be an unwelcome intrusion. Martha's presence with her sister and mother was a wonderful surprise. Nicole refrained from greeting them herself at the front door as she would have liked to do. She was too aware of her changed status now, and too concerned with being proper. Woodward escorted the trio into the airy music room, and moments later Nicole made her entrance.

She was dressed in what was casual attire considering her status, but the gold gown was the most expensive moire with a lavishly scrolled contemporary motif, and it was in the latest silhouette, which was quite straight and altogether daring. She also wore the gift which Hadrian had given her the night before, a stunning ensemble of diamond-encrusted topazes, and her hair was piled high in a very elegant fashion. Her three guests gaped at her, speechless.

Nicole swept forward, beaming and ecstatic to see everyone. "Mother! Regina! And Martha! How glad I am that you have come!"

They exchanged hugs. Martha recovered first, her gaze moving slowly over Nicole, and then the furnishings. "My, my," she said, smiling. "Being a duchess becomes you."

Nicole flushed with pleasure. "I suspect that I must maintain appearances." She gestured at her gown. "So far, there has been no one to see my efforts, though, except for the staff."

"And your husband," Martha said.

"He rises with the sun and is gone shortly after. He returns sometime in the afternoon and locks himself in his study until he must change for supper." But it was not a complaint—she was smiling as she spoke.

Jane suddenly smiled. "Have you had a change of heart, Nicole?"

"What a fool I have been!" Nicole cried passionately. "How could I have been so stupid to resist this marriage!"

"You are happy, then?"

Nicole bit her lip. "I have no pride left. I will admit the truth. I am more than happy, I am ecstatic!"

Martha rose and rushed to embrace her. "I am so glad!"

"Dear, I am so happy for you!" Jane cried excitedly, also hugging her daughter.

Regina waited, wide-eyed.

Nicole sombered.

"I am happy for you too," Regina said, tears welling up in her beautiful golden eyes.

"Oh Rie!" Nicole cried. "I hated fighting with you, I did!"

"I was being selfish, not you," Regina said quaveringly. "It was not your fault that Father was making me wait to marry."

"But I should have known how you felt," Nicole protested. They gripped each other's hands tightly.

"Are you in love?" Regina whispered.

"Yes," Nicole whispered back. "Yes, I am!"

Smiles wreathed the two sisters' faces, and they hugged enthusiastically.

More embraces were exchanged all around. When everyone had sat again, Nicole turned to Jane. "Mother, how is Father?"

"He is fine. And he shall be thrilled when I tell him how happy you are!"

"I am so sorry we fought. He was right—as he usually is—in making me wed Hadrian. It is the best thing that has ever happened to me!"

"Why don't you tell him that?" Jane asked, pleased. "He misses you, darling. And he has been so worried that he did not do the right thing."

"Before you leave, I shall write him a letter," Nicole decided. "Please ask him to come visit me soon."

The ladies began to talk excitedly about Nicole's marriage and about the duties of a duchess. Nicole finally said, "I think, in time, he might truly come to care for me. And even if he doesn't, I think we will at least be friends. He is kind and respectful. He is attentive. In fact, I think he is trying his best to please me." She flushed again with pleasure.

"Just as you are trying to please him," Martha pointed out, still unable to believe Nicole's elegant appearance and subdued manner.

"Yes, I am," Nicole said. This time her blush was brought on by graphic memories of how she attempted to please him in bed. There was no question that she had been successful in that endeavor. She was rapidly becoming as skillful as a courtesan, she decided. Last evening she had finally had the courage to do what she had wanted to do from the very first night—to worship his body with her hands and her mouth as he had worshipped hers. And afterwards Hadrian had held her very tightly for a very long time.

"I cannot wait until the two of you begin to go out," Regina said with satisfaction. "I cannot wait until society sees you now! If I were you, I would cut *dead* everyone who has *ever* cut you!"

"It won't be like the last time, will it?" Nicole said rather ruefully. She hated even thinking about her behavior on her wedding day and how she had humiliated Hadrian in front of all of his guests. It was amazing that he had not been angrier with her than he was; it was amazing that they had privately recovered from her reckless disregard for public appearances.

"I should hope not!" Martha exclaimed. "The poor Duke has been the butt of a few good laughs, but once people realize you have come around—more than come around—they will no longer be making jokes."

"Jokes? What jokes?"

Martha blinked and quickly looked at Jane, who was curious and apparently ignorant of the ridicule, and Regina, who was not. "Oh dear, of course you do not know. It's not important, Nicole, what is important is that you and he are getting on famously."

"Tell me." Her jaw was set stubbornly, grimly.

Martha was reluctant.

Regina was not. "She should know! If it were I, I would absolutely want to know!"

Martha sighed. "The week before your wedding he was the most charming and amiable of men! Everyone could not help but notice the change in him, for in the past he made no secret of his indifference, even boredom, with the social whirl. Remember how he promised to play the lovesick fool? Well, he did his job too well! It was all the talk—how madly in love the Duke was—and how you must have been responsible for such a dramatic change in his personality. While everyone agreed such haste to wed was scandalous, it was also the consensus that it must be love."

"Oh, no," Nicole said when Martha paused.

Martha sighed again. "Unfortunately, your anger with the Duke was all too obvious at your wedding. Afterwards, the consensus changed. They said it was true love all right—on the part of the Duke. Clearly you did not reciprocate his feelings. It was the height of conversation."

Nicole was angry, angry at the gossips, and even more angry at herself for humiliating Hadrian in such a way. Their wedding could have been the worst scandal imaginable if the nasty rumors hadn't been stopped. Yet he had done more than stop them, he had actually made their precipitous marriage acceptable, more than acceptable if Martha's tone was any indication. He had protected her as he had promised—while she had undone all that he had done in one fell swoop, striking back at him brutally, if unintentionally. She silently vowed to rectify matters immediately. The next time they went out, she would make certain that there was no doubt in anyone's mind that the Duke's bride was madly enamored of her husband.

"I did not mean to upset you," Martha said.

Nicole did not answer. A new thought struck her, mesmerizing her. She had forgotten about the blood on her sheets the morning after her wedding night. She had not been able to think of any plausible reason for the bloodstain, except that Hadrian must have cut himself somehow. Now a stunning idea occurred to her. Had he been trying to protect her again? Had he contrived the bloodstain upon her sheets so that no one would know she was not a virgin on their wedding night? Servants gossiped terribly belowstairs. Had there been no stain, everyone at Clayborough would have known of it shortly thereafter. Soon a maid would tell another female servant who was employed elsewhere. Eventually it would reach the ears of her mistress. By then it would just be a distant rumor—but it would be all over town.

Nicole was certain that Hadrian had stained her sheets. To protect her. There was no way he could have cut himself while in bed with her. Her heart swelled impossibly with her love for him.

* * *

Nicole's guests spent the night. Everyone passed a wonderful evening with much laughter and good humor, even the Duke, who could not help but enjoy the camaraderie the ladies shared. The Countess, Regina and Martha left early the following morning. After their departure, Nicole donned her breeches and boots and hurried from the house. By now, no one so much as blinked at her attire. On the first day that she had gone riding, however, not even giving her costume a thought, everyone she had passed had apparently been stunned. The maids had regarded her out of popping eyes, the doormen had gaped, Woodward had gone white and the stableboys had blinked and quickly looked away. Yes, she had been uncomfortable. But she had recovered—and so had everyone else.

She supposed, ruefully, that duchesses were expected to ride sidesaddle in fashionable riding habits. However, Hadrian had told her she could do as she pleased—and riding her blood red stallion astride was doing exactly that. After that first time, she did not give it another thought.

The stablemaster was waiting for her. Nicole waved as she approached, smiling. He smiled back. O'Henry too wore breeches and boots, but his were stained and well-worn, while his hunter-green hacking coat had definitely seen better days. "Good afternoon to ye, Yer Grace," he said, leading out their mounts. "I thought ye might not be comin' on this foin day."

"Miss riding Zeus? Never!"

They mounted and set off. Nicole was in high spirits, for her world had become just about perfect. All it needed to be complete was her husband's love, and she was growing more confident that that was, indeed, a real possibility.

An hour later they crossed a meadow and clattered onto a country road. No one was about, and Mr. O'Henry turned to her with a grin. "Ruffian here is wantin' to run. Think ye can keep up, Yer Grace?"

Nicole laughed. Mr. O'Henry now knew she was a superlative rider, and he no longer worried over her as he had the first few minutes of their first ride together. "Can you keep up with me?" Nicole challenged, and leaning over her bay's neck, they were off.

They leveled out into a hard gallop, the two stallions thundering side by side, stretched out for all they were worth and relishing it. They raced neck and neck for a mile or two, until both riders saw three men walking down the road towards them. Of one mind, Nicole and O'Henry reined in their mounts, not wanting to cause an accident or kick up dirt in the faces of the pedestrians.

They came closer and Nicole saw that the three men were young, shabbily dressed, and carrying rucksacks. "Out of work farmworkers," she guessed. They were probably carrying everything they owned on their backs. She felt sorry for them. How could she not? Times were indeed hard on the lower classes these days.

"Out'n out riffraff if you ask me," O'Henry snorted. "If'n a body wants t' work he can always foind somethin'. Don't ye be givin' them no handouts, Yer Grace."

But Nicole had no coins with her, although she would have gladly given the men a few pounds if she could have. Suddenly one of the men made eye contact with her. Nicole had been staring curiously, now she looked quickly away. The redhead's gaze was bold and rude—too interested in her appearance for comfort.

The trio had suddenly fallen silent. Nicole did not look at them again, suddenly stricken with uneasiness, but she knew they stared at her and the stablemaster. "Ride roight around 'em," O'Henry said in a low voice, moving his mount into a trot.

Nicole was about to do the same when the redhaired man grabbed her stallion's bridle. Her eyes went wide in shock.

"G' day, lass. Nice bit a' horse ye got there."

"Let go, please," Nicole said calmly, not wanting to make an incident out of what, hopefully, would be nothing more than a request for alms.

"Got a pound or two?" he queried with a gap-toothed grin.

"Let her go," O'Henry said. He had ridden past the group and now he turned his mount around and came back towards Nicole. He had to rein in abruptly when one man stepped in front of him to block his way.

"Please," Nicole said. "I have no coin. As you can see, I don't have my reticule with me."

"She ain't got her reticule, boyos," the redhead laughed.

"I'm agoin' to ride right over ye, lad," O'Henry warned the man barring his path. "Let Her Grace go!"

"Her Grace?" Nicole's assailant laughed. "If she's Her Grace than I'm the Duke! Well if she ain't got any coin, she sure does have a fine horse—and a fine set of legs of her own. Guess I got use for both."

Nicole gasped. O'Henry rode forward, about to make good his threat to run down the man in his path. At the same time, Nicole urged her stallion on. The redhaired man holding her horse did not let go, in fact, with his other hand he grabbed her leg. The stallion halted, confused and growing distraught.

The redhead did not get any farther. O'Henry rode up to him from behind, forcing the one man to jump out of his path, and sent his riding crop slashing down on the redhead's back. The man released Nicole and her horse with a yelp, turning on the stablemaster with a cry. At the same time, his two friends lunged for O'Henry, and in the next instant the stablemaster was being dragged from his horse.

Nicole screamed when she saw the three vagrants began to pummel him. She rode her stallion into the melee. Weilding her crop, she began slashing frantically at the men.

The gap-toothed redhead turned to her with vengeful intent gleaming in his eyes. Nicole tried to strike him across his ugly face, but he caught the crop and yanked it from her grasp, flinging it away. Her heart stopped. He grinned. In that split second she knew her fate was in his hands and that it would be worse than death could possibly be.

But her stallion, already frenzied, now smelling human blood, screamed and reared. His hooves flailed wildly, striking Nicole's attacker. The man screamed, going down under the animal's front legs. Nicole wrenched her stallion backwards to avoid trampling the man.

He scrambled to his knees. Nicole glimpsed blood on his face and his torn clothes. He lurched to his feet and suddenly he and his two friends were running away.

For an instant Nicole sat staring after them, trying to bring her stallion under control, panting wildly. Then she turned her gaze on O'Henry, who was sitting up and reeling. His face was bloody and he spat out a tooth.

With a cry, she jumped from her saddle and ran to him. "Oh dear God! Are you all right?"

He looked at her, his face sporting several bloody bruises. "I'm right as can be, Yer Grace. They didn't hurt ye, did they?"

And before Nicole could reply his smile faded, his eyes glazed, and he fell back to the earth, unconscious.

Isobel's stomach churned.

She paused beside Woodward as the butler rapped twice on the door to Hadrian's study. Her visit was not unexpected. Yesterday she had sent her son a note requesting an audience with him. The note had been uncharacteristically formal, and Isobel had tried to reword it twice, but had failed to achieve the casual intimacy that had once existed so naturally between her and her son. In the end, she had left it as it was.

She had not had a meaningful conversation with her son since she had revealed to him the truth about his birth, almost a month ago. In all the time that had elapsed since then she had barely seen him. In no small way, Isobel had been avoiding her own son.

She had volunteered to help the Countess of Dragmore with the wedding preparations. Jane had agreed with no small amount of relief. Isobel had known Lady Shelton for some years, but not intimately; now they became partners in deed—and in spirit. They got on fabulously. Isobel had always liked what she knew of Jane, and after these past weeks she liked her even more, and admired her, too. For, like Isobel, Jane was secretly a rebel at heart. She was intelligent, independent-minded, compassionate and wise. And like Isobel, she was a woman of experience—not a cloistered paragon of womanhood. Isobel was well aware that once upon a time the Countess had been the popular stage actress, Jane Barclay. She did not think it a demerit upon her character, to the contrary,

Isobel's admiration for her only grew.

Knowing the Countess now as she did, Isobel was more certain than ever that her daughter was the perfect mate for her son.

Planning such a grand, elaborate wedding had been a distraction for Isobel from the fear that had haunted her for nearly thirty years, and which continued to haunt her now. Daily she tried not to confront that fear. Daily it worsened. Now she no longer had wedding preparations to be consumed by. Now she no longer could avoid what was in her heart.

The last time she had really spoken with Hadrian, the encounter had ended in anger. He had been angry with her, and rightly so, she knew, for denying him his father all of these years. She had been afraid of his disdain for her behavior, just as she had been afraid that he would be angry with her for concealing the truth. Her worst fears had been realized. He had been furious with her. Was he still angry with her? She could not continue to tolerate the unknown. Facing each day had become a chore filled with anguish.

Hadrian rose from behind his desk as Isobel entered. She could not smile, although he did. "How are you, Mother? What a strange request. You ask me for an audience?"

Nothing seemed to have changed. Isobel dared to hope. Tears suddenly filled her eyes, blurring her vision. "I did not want to intrude."

"You are not intruding," he said, somewhat sharply. He came around his desk. "Something is the matter. What is it?"

She dabbed at her eyes with her handkerchief and gazed up at her son. "Hadrian," she asked softly. "From your demeanor, can I conclude that you are no longer angry with me?"

"Maybe you had better sit down," he said, guiding her to a chair.

"Are you still angry?"

He stared. "Mother, it was wrong of you not to tell me the truth about Francis and Hadrian Stone as soon as I was old enough to understand. But I have been trying to empathize with you. I can see how you would not want to admit to having an affair. Yet I would have understood. And admitting to a long ago, forgotten affair is insignificant in comparison to a man knowing his father's identity. How could you not see that?"

"I knew I was wrong," Isobel whispered.

"Then why?" Hadrian demanded. "Why did you not tell me sooner? I understand why you did not tell Hadrian Stone, after all, he was no longer a part of your life. But I am your son. I needed to know. It has been the greatest relief knowing that Francis is not my real father."

"I was afraid."

"Of what? The secret becoming public? That will never happen, Mother. I will guard your reputation zealously."

"I was not worried about my reputation," Isobel said, twisting her handkerchief relentlessly in her hands.

"Then what? My inheritance is secure even should the truth be found out. After all, grandfather Jonathan made you his heir after Francis. You are the rightful heiress of Clayborough, and me after you. I have many cousins who would love to dispute my ownership, but their claims would be jettisoned from court."

"I was afraid you would never forgive me for my actions and for not telling you."

Hadrian blinked. Then he smiled softly. "Mother, that is ridiculous."

"You do forgive me?" she asked incredulously.

"Mother, I was angry, but that is in the past. Nothing has changed. Although I am somewhat insulted that you would think me capable of condemning you for finding love with a man other than Francis. I am glad, terribly glad, that you had some small amount of happiness in your lifetime. God knows Francis did his best to make you miserable."

Isobel covered her face with her hands. Relief swamped her. She trembled and wanted to weep. She should have known that her son, her beautiful son, would never turn from her. Yet how could she have known? Hadrian was so straight-laced, sometimes even a prude. He was so honorable. He was the most honorable person she knew. And what she had done was nothing but dishonorable, even though it had been for love.

Hadrian patted her shoulder awkwardly. "Don't cry, Mother. The past is past. We have the future ahead of us now."

Isobel managed to smile.

"I have put investigators into the field. One should have arrived in Boston two weeks ago. If my father is there, if he is alive, he should have received my letter. I know it is too optimistic, but I cannot help but hope that even now a response is on its way back across the Atlantic."

Isobel stood very still. She also should have known that Hadrian would have instigated the search for his father immediately.

"When I hear something, I will let you know."

"No." Isobel shook her head vehemently. "No. I do not want to know. I do not want to know if he is alive or dead. Or married. No."

He stared at her.

Isobel's heart was pounding. After all these years, it was unthinkable that he might be alive, a bachelor, and still in love with her. Unthinkable. The pain of seeing him if he were happily married, or indifferent to her, would be unbearable. Just as it would be if he were dead.

"All right, Mother," Hadrian said softly. To change the subject, he asked her if she would like stay and have supper with him and his wife.

Isobel smiled tearily. She was about to decline. She knew very well that the newlyweds deserved more time alone to sort out their relationship, even though she was eager to know what was transpiring between her son and his bride. Before she could respond, the doors to the study burst open.

Both Isobel and Hadrian were startled as Nicole flew into the room, panting and wild-eyed. "Hadrian!"

At the sight of his wife, rather disheveled and clearly distressed, in muddy breeches and boots, Hadrian leapt forward. But Nicole skidded instantly to a stop, her frantic gaze darting to the Dowager Duchess, who watched her calmly enough. Nicole's pale countenance instantly turned a dull shade of red. "Oh, no!" she moaned.

Hadrian had already grabbed her, turning her abruptly to face him. "What's the matter? What has happened? Are you all right?"

Nicole tried to regain her breath so she could respond. She glanced desperately again at the Dowager Duchess, barely aware that her husband was shaking her. It was just her luck that her mother-in-law would have to glimpse her for the first time in her new role as a duchess dressed like a stableboy!

Hadrian continued to shake her. "Nicole! What has happened? Are you all right?" he repeated anxiously.

Her attention was jerked back to her husband. "Hadrian! You must come quickly! There has been a terrible accident! The stablemaster was set upon by ruffians and they beat him up! It took me forever to get him on my horse—he was unconscious—and get back to Clayborough! Woodward has sent someone for the doctor, but I am so afraid!" These last words turned sob-like.

He still gripped both her arms. "Were you hurt?"

She managed to shake her head no.

Hadrian abruptly released her and strode across the room. "Stay with her, Mother," he ordered, and then he was gone.

Nicole covered her mouth with her hands, which were trembling. O'Henry had still been unconscious when she had finally returned to Clayborough with him lying prone and face-down across her stallion, as Nicole led the horse on foot. She was afraid he was dead.

"Here, dear, take a sip of this. It will calm your nerves."

Nicole started, realizing again that the Dowager Duchess was a witness to her most unseemly manner and dress, which in itself constituted behavior too sordid to be acceptable. She wanted to burst into tears, instead she accepted the glass and took several jerky sips. The Dowager Duchess patted her back soothingly.

Nicole stared at her. The woman was being kind—not condemning.

"How badly was Mr. O'Henry hurt?" she asked.

"I don't know!" Nicole moaned. "And it was all my fault!"

"I'm sure you are exaggerating, just as I am sure everything will be all right."

"I am afraid he is dying—or dead!"

The Dowager Duchess patted her again. "Do you want to talk about it?"

Nicole knew she should not. The incident was beyond the pale for any lady, much less a duchess. Then Nicole looked at her. Isobel's eyes were warm and kind and concerned. Nicole's resistance crumbled, and before she could stop herself, she was babbling the whole story. "I insisted we ride alone. One of the men attacked me! I'm sure I could have ridden away, but Mr. O'Henry immediately began hitting him with his crop! There were two others and they dragged him from his saddle and jumped upon him. I was afraid they were going to kill him then and there! I beat them the best I could with my crop, and thank God, my stallion went berserk. He injured their leader, nearly trampling him, and they all ran away."

"Oh dear," the Dowager Duchess said.

Nicole gazed at her miserably. Her tone was so kind that it invited further intimacy. "I have made a terrible mess of things, haven't I? I am not a very good duchess, and I so wanted to be!"

Isobel rubbed her back. "Well," she sighed, "your husband will most likely be furious with you, but thank the Lord you were not hurt."

"I'm so sorry you must learn of this—and see me like this," Nicole whispered despondently.

Isobel did smile. "It doesn't change my opinion of you, if that is what is worrying you."

Nicole groaned. "I am sure it only confirms it!"

Isobel blinked. Then she led the distraught Nicole to the sofa and they both sat down. "My dear, do you think I am disposed unfavorably towards you?"

"You're not?"

"Not at all."

Nicole was shocked.

Isobel smiled. "To the contrary, I approve of this match. In fact, I am positive you are the best possible choice of a wife for my son."

Nicole would have choked if she had been sipping the sherry. "You do! But, why?"

"You are an independent woman, my dear, that's why. You are daring and unconventional. In some ways, you and my son have a lot in common. In others, nothing at all. And it is that precise balance that I am counting on."

Nicole was now truly dazed. "You are?"

Isobel patted her hand. "You both love the country and a simple life. Common interests are important. Yet Hadrian is much too prudish and self-contained for his own good. You are not. He needs to be set on his ear now and then. Yes, the two of you shall do just fine."

Nicole could not believe what she was hearing. "I am afraid I have more than set him on his ear today!"

"Well, it was a bit reckless to participate in the fistfight," Isobel said cheerfully. "But I will not tell a soul."

Hadrian did not think he had ever been angrier in his life. Will O'Henry was no longer unconscious, and he had related every detail of what had happened that afternoon. His strides deadly, the Duke returned to the library.

He paused before Isobel and Nicole, towering above them as they sat together on the sofa. "Mother, tonight would not be a good time for you to join us for supper."

Isobel got to her feet. "I understand. Be gentle with her, Hadrian. She has suffered a great deal today."

"That is nothing in comparison to what she is about to suffer."

Nicole stiffened.

"Be brave," Isobel said, leaning down to kiss Nicole's cheek. She again gave her son a warning glance before departing.

Silence filled the room. The grandfather clock standing on one wall ticked away the seconds loudly. "Can you explain yourself?" Hadrian finally asked.

"I am sorry," Nicole tried.

"You are sorry?!" Hadrian was incredulous. "Madam—you were about to be raped and you tell me you are sorry?"

Fearfully, she said, "We won't ride on the public roads again."

Hadrian exploded. "Damn if you will ride anywhere again!"

Nicole jumped to her feet. "Hadrian, be reasonable!"

"Be reasonable! Why should I be reasonable while you are nothing but unreasonable!"

"I did not seek this adventure out."

"Adventure!" he shouted, beyond control now. "Only you, Madam Wife, would refer to a near rape as an adventure!"

"That's not what I meant," she cried.

He wanted to tear at his hair. His fists clenched. "I have done everything that I could—from the very beginning—to protect you from mishap of your own making. Yet every time I turn my back, you are at mischief again. But this is beyond belief! Your welfare—your life—

could have been seriously jeopardized!"

"And I'm sorry!" Nicole shouted back. Tears streamed down her cheeks.

Hadrian was beyond stopping. "Look at you!" he raged. He shook her, ignoring her attempts to twist free. "You look like some stableboy—except clearly you are no boy! Good god! You might as well be naked! Did you ever think of how I might feel, having my wife run around in clothing so tight that every man can easily imagine her nude?"

Anger flared. "Now you are exaggerating."

"Oh I am? William told me everything, Madam. You attracted those men's worst intentions. Had you been dressed in a proper riding habit—had you had a proper escort—they would have never dared to attack you—the Duchess of Clayborough!" It was a roar. "Or need I remind you of whom you are?"

Nicole wrenched free of his grip. "No, you do not need to remind me of whom—and what—I now am! I know damned well that I am now your duchess! How could I forget?"

"Ahh, so we *do* have regrets!"

"Yes! I mean, no!"

"Clearly you have no idea what you mean," he shouted. "Just as you clearly have no idea of the kind of havoc your thoughtless behavior continually wreaks."

How his words hurt. "Now I suppose you are going to tell me that I must never ride astride, I must, at all costs, at the cost of my own pleasure, maintain appearances."

"Yes, damn it!"

Nicole was aghast. "Surely you jest!"

"Believe me, Madam, there is nothing to jest about right now."

"Then you lied!" Nicole cried hysterically. "You told me I could do as I chose. You told me many times. I chose to ride like this, I always ride at Dragmore like this."

"This is not Dragmore, and in case you have forgotten, as you so obviously have, you are my duchess now. Damn it, Madam, I am sure it's all over town that you have an inclination to dress like a boy. The gossips must be having a field day. Do you eternally want to be the focus of malicious gossip?"

"No," she admitted tearfully. "But . . ."

"There are no buts." Hadrian released her and wheeled away from her, breathing deeply. He was still shaken to the core by how close she had come to being raped, or even killed. He was still shaking and in the worst kind of fear, an overwhelming fear for his wife. If something had happened to Nicole he would have never forgiven O'Henry or himself, when it was Nicole herself to blame. He ran trembling hands through his hair, seeking control which he could barely summon up. He was afraid he might do something unthinkable—like turn her over his knee and beat her until she metamorphosed into a rational being and a lady of decorum.

It was a long time before he finally turned to face her again.

"Is—is Mr. O'Henry going to be all right?"

"He will undoubtedly be confined to his bed for a week or two, but he is not at death's door. Although he could have been." He ignored her increased pallor. He could not shake the image from his mind of Nicole riding directly into the fray and striking at O'Henry's three assailants with her crop. "Go upstairs. Get out of those clothes. Immediately."

Nicole hugged herself. "What are you going to do?"

He grimaced. "For one, I want those breeches burned." He ignored her protest. "Secondly, you, Madam, shall stay away from the stables indefinitely."

Nicole was outraged.

"Thirdly, I intend to apprehend those outlaws and have them thrown into Newgate."

"Hadrian," Nicole gritted, "you are not being fair."

He whirled. "Do not ever dare to accuse me of being unfair! I have your best interests at heart! Clearly someone has to when you do not! I suggest you leave me immediately!"

"When you calm down," she managed, "we can continue this discussion."

"Go upstairs, Madam. I mean *now*. I mean this instant. Before you make me behave in a manner I shall regret."

Nicole no longer hesitated, she fled.

It was a long time before Nicole managed to stop trembling.

It was a combination of all the circumstances that beset her so. She had been accosted with violent intent, and the kindly stablemaster had almost been killed defending her. Those circumstances alone would have been enough to keep her nerves quivering uncontrollably, but her husband's reaction to it all and their furious fight was the coup de grace. Nicole had run to him for comfort more than anything else. Instead she had received a scalding setdown.

And perhaps, what made it unbearable, was that Hadrian was right. She was wrong. She had acted more than recklessly, she had been foolish. Had she at least been on the public roads with a proper escort, the three vagrants would have never dared approach her. But not only had she not had an escort, she had not even been attired as the Duchess of Clayborough should be. In any case, Nicole could not deny that it was her fault. *Because of her nitwit behavior, a man had almost been killed.*

She sat on the sumptuous pink velvet bedspread in her dirty clothes and hugged herself. She had to sadly admit that she was botching up being a duchess in full form—as well as ruining her chances for a happy relationship with her husband.

She heard riders galloping away from the front of the house. Nicole ran to the window. She could make out her husband in the lead on his raw-boned black hunter. Her stomach clenched. He was going after her assailants.

There was a knock on her door. Nicole answered, and both Mrs. Veig and Annie stepped in. Annie was white-faced and anxious, and Nicole silently blessed her little maid for her loyalty. Mrs. Veig was somber. Nicole knew that her unusually impassive expression was an attempt to cover up her disapproval, the first instance of it that Nicole had yet to discern.

"Draw Her Grace a bath, Annie," Mrs. Veig said. Annie scurried to obey. Mrs. Veig set a tray of cakes and hot chocolate down besides the chaise. "I thought you might like a bit of something sweet to calm your nerves."

Nicole had no appetite, but she nodded.

The housekeeper busied herself in Nicole's closet, pulling out a warm wool robe and brocade slippers lined with fleece. Nicole shed her boots, breeches and shirt on the floor. Annie called to her that her bath was ready. Nicole was about to strip off her underwear when she saw Mrs. Veig pick up her scattered clothing. Mrs. Veig never attended to her dirty clothes, and an alarm sounded in Nicole's mind. "Mrs. Veig," she said, "what are you doing?"

"I'm sorry, Your Grace. But His Grace ordered me to take these clothes."

Nicole stood very still. "And burn them?"

"Yes."

Her entire body tensed.

"I'm sorry, Your Grace," the housekeeper said again. She left with the clothes, thankfully leaving Nicole's custom-made boots behind.

Nicole closed her eyes. She was truly sorry for her role in what had happened, but this was going too far. Yet instead of anger, there was only hurt. This past week had been paradise. Now where had it gone?

Nicole did not leave her rooms. She waited for her husband to return to Clayborough with no small amount of anxiety. She hoped that he would be calmer and more reasonable when he did return. She was determined to undo the damage she had done, she was determined to get their relationship back on the track that it had been on. She would meet him in the library before supper as always, and she would be a paragon of propriety. If he did not bend, if he chose not to forget or ignore what had happened that day, then she would be more aggressive in her plan of attack. She would steal into his bed and seduce him. A night of passion would surely distract him from his anger with her.

It was a simple plan. She prayed she would not have to use it, she prayed that when Hadrian returned he would be in a better, more forgiving mood.

It seemed that Nicole passed an eternity waiting for her husband to return, but a glance at the clock told her it was not even an hour. She waited uncertainly in her rooms, her heart lodged like a stone in her chest. Would he come to see her? Wouldn't he come to tell her if he had been successful in hunting down the ruffians who had attacked her and O'Henry? Then she would have a chance to judge his mood before she went to meet him in the library. She could not bear the uncertainty, the waiting.

But he did not come. She heard him enter his apartments, which adjoined hers. She waited. She listened acutely to the sounds coming from his rooms. She could not decide what he was doing, but it seemed as if he were changing his clothes. Her hopes lifted briefly as she thought that he was readying himself to meet her in the library, but then they abruptly sank. For she heard him leaving his suite and heading down the corridor—not towards her door, but away from it.

And a few moments later she heard a coach and horses coming around to the front of the house. Nicole ran to the window. Shocked, she watched her husband, dressed for travel in a many-tiered greatcoat, step into the Clayborough coach. A moment later it rolled away amidst its cavalcade of liveried outriders.

* * *

Three days later, Nicole began to be quite angry. Hadrian had left without bothering to inform her of where he was going. And he had yet to send a single word to her as to when he would return. Separated as they were, she could not gauge his mood, but she found it hard to believe that he might still be angry over an incident that was fast becoming ancient history.

Nicole had too much pride to ask Mrs. Veig where her husband had gone. But he had taken his valet and butler with him—not an encouraging sign. Again, Annie was put to the task of ferreting out information. She soon told Nicole that he had gone to Clayborough House in London, and that no one had any idea of when he would return.

Could it be possible that he was still angry with her?

Or was he merely indifferent—and completely inconsiderate?

By the third day, Nicole was becoming thoroughly angry. Was this his way of punishing her? Hadn't she apologized? She had even learned her lesson! In the future she would ride in public with an escort and in proper attire. No one would have any grounds to say one accusatory word about the Duchess of Clayborough. Her husband would be proud of her. Privately, however, she would continue to do as she chose. She thought this the fairest of compromises. She had yet to exercise this last step, though, wanting to resolve her relationship with her husband first. She could imagine only too well that if he happened upon her riding in breeches, even if it were on Clayborough land at the crack of dawn with a few grooms, he would jump to the wrong conclusions. She would put this disastrous argument behind them, not fan the flames of another fiery fight.

Nicole had just decided to go to London to join her husband when Mrs. Veig informed her that she had a caller. Nicole raised a brow, surprised, wondering whom it could possibly be. She had yet to receive anyone other than her family, and Nicole was glad that they had come when she was still living in a state of paradise, and not now, when she felt as if she were about to walk through the gates of hell.

Mrs. Veig told her it was Lady Stacy Worthington.

Nicole got a very bad feeling.

She resolved to be gracious. She would be a role model of propriety, the perfect duchess. Quickly she had Mrs. Veig help her change into a spectacularly expensive gown, one suited to an afternoon in the city, not at home in the country. With it she donned her diamonds—all of them.

A half an hour later she descended the stairs like a queen to greet Stacy in the rose salon. That particular room was the size of many a gentleman's ballroom. Of course, Stacy had undoubtedly been to Clayborough many times, but being a guest, she could not have done more than glimpse a quarter or less of the palatial residence. Even if she had been in this room before, it was still imposing.

Stacy rose to her feet from the sofa where she sat. "Good afternoon, Your Grace."

As Nicole came closer—and it took some time to cross the room—she saw the gleam in the other woman's eyes and her sense of suspicion grew. "Hello, Stacy. What a surprise. Mrs. Veig, please bring us more sandwiches. And some sweets." Nicole smiled at Stacy. She had addressed her without her deferential title purposefully. For Stacy would not really be Lady Stacy until she married a nobleman.

Stacy smiled back. It was feral.

Nicole sat in a bergere facing her visitor; Stacy sat back down on the sofa. The two women looked at each other. Silence reigned.

Normally, Nicole would have bluntly asked Stacy what she wanted. But she was resolved to be the epitome of a hostess. "The roads are becoming bad, are they not? I hope it did not make traveling too difficult for you."

"They're not too bad, not yet. So, when will Hadrian return?"

Nicole was dismayed at the possibility that Stacy might know that Hadrian was in London, and not here with her. "Excuse me?"

"From town." Stacy was still smiling.

"Why, as soon as he concludes his business."

"How urgent it must be. After all, you have not been wed more than a week or so."

Nicole held onto her temper. "It was of the utmost urgency."

"Hmmm. But he still had time to go to No. 12 Crawford Street."

Nicole blinked. Whatever Stacy was driving at, she had no notion what it might be. "Yes, well, I imagine he has business there as well."

Stacy hooted. "You don't know, do you! You don't know what No. 12 Crawford Street is!"

It was very hard to maintain her poise. "No, I don't." But she suddenly had an idea, a distasteful idea.

Stacy was gleeful. "Hadrian has apartments there. He has had apartments there since he was eighteen."

Nicole tried very hard not to understand. "I see."

"You still don't comprehend me, do you! He keeps those apartments for his mistress!"

The color drained from Nicole's face. When she spoke, it was numbly. "I don't believe you." She didn't—she did not believe her! She would not believe her!

"Surely you did not marry Hadrian with ignorance of his reputation for women! Why, his current mistress is considered to be the most beautiful woman in all of London. She is French, an actress they say. Her name is Holland Dubois."

No, Nicole thought, it is not true. He could not. He could not. He could not have gone to another woman, not after what they had shared. *But she had known he had a mistress. She had known of his reputation. Hadn't that been the reason she did not want to marry him in the first place? Hadn't she known that one day he would tire of her and go to other women?*

"If you do not believe me, then why don't you go and see for yourself?" Stacy was triumphant.

Although Nicole's numbness was rapidly turning into a searing pain, she spoke with the utmost calm. "Why should I do that? All men have mistresses, and yes, I certainly knew of my husband's reputation before we were wed. The news you bring me changes nothing. I am, after all, the Duchess of Clayborough. You think I care about his dalliance with an *actress?*"

Stacy was taken aback. Her glee was gone. "Well," she said in a huff. "I was only trying to help you."

"How kind you are."

Stacy rose. "I can see you don't want my friendship! I think I had better leave!"

"You can certainly do as you choose." Politely, Nicole also stood, summoning Mrs. Veig. "Please escort Lady Worthington to the door," she said.

She knew it was true.

She would not believe it, not until she saw Holland Dubois at No. 12 Crawford Street with her own two eyes.

She would not believe that Hadrian had left her after what they had shared—after the promise that had been inherent in the blossoming beginning of their relationship—to go to another woman.

She would not, she did not.

But of course it was true.

He was a womanizer. Everyone knew it. She had known it. She had learned of his reputation early in their relationship. Elizabeth had probably known, too. But she had probably not cared. Ladies were not supposed to care about their husband's lovers. If anything, they were supposed to be relieved that their husbands cavorted elsewhere.

Nicole was not relieved. Nicole was sick.

How could she have forgotten for a moment why she had not wanted to marry him in the first place? But in one short week she had forgotten, because of the carnal bliss they had shared. But it was only that, carnal bliss, yet she had foolishly, naively, thought it something more.

Nicole peered out of the carriage window. Her gloved fists were clenched tightly in her lap. As soon as Stacy had left, she had immediately departed Clayborough for London, taking only Annie with her and not even informing the distressed Mrs. Veig as to where she was going. Once in the city, she had ordered her driver to Covent Garden. (A place Hadrian would never go, and thus never chance upon his own carriage.) She had ordered her driver and Annie to await her there. She had climbed into a hansom, and now they were pulling up in front of No. 12 Crawford Street.

It occurred to her that Hadrian might be within that residence even now.

If he were there, she would die. No—if he were there, she would be strong. She would be impassive, cool, perfectly composed. *She would not let him know how he was hurting her.*

Nicole barely looked at the townhouse with its wrought iron fence and its painted brick facade. She climbed from the hansom, asking the driver to wait. She was numb, as if in a dream, or a daze. Slowly she walked through the gate and up the steps. She banged an old-fashioned brass knocker.

A butler immediately answered the door.

Nicole's mouth was so dry that she could not, for a moment, speak. "I would like a word with Miss Dubois."

The butler let her enter. "Whom should I say is calling?"

Nicole hesitated. He had not said that there was no Miss Dubois there. Briefly she closed her eyes, nausea overwhelming her. So far, Stacy had not lied. *Just as Nicole had known.*

When Nicole opened her eyes, she had regained control. "It does not matter. Tell your mistress I am here." Nicole was imperious. She had at least learned to be a duchess—when it was too late to matter.

She walked past the butler, head high, strides graceful and fluid, her fabulously expensive gown swirling about her silk shoes. She walked right into the parlor. She did not sit down, just as she had not taken off her gloves or coat. She gave the butler no choice but to do as she asked.

While she waited, Nicole took in all of the fine furnishings—the delicate furniture, the Persian rugs, the papered walls and landscape paintings. Miss Dubois lived well. She lived well beyond the means of an actress.

Several minutes later a woman said from the doorway, "You wish to see me?"

Nicole turned. She turned to see a small, petite woman in a stunning and expensive gown, one too low-cut to be appropriate for midmorning at home. The woman was as exquisitely beautiful as any woman could possibly be, she was as perfect as any china doll. Her blue gaze was puzzled, but as Nicole stared at her, the truth hitting her like a sledgehammer, the confusion left Holland Dubois' lovely cat eyes.

"Oh dear," Hadrian's mistress said. "It's you! Oh dear!"

For another long moment, Nicole did not move.

"Your Grace," Holland said breathlessly, "I am not sure what you want, but please, do sit down!"

Nicole had seen enough. Quickly, before the other woman might start to see the moisture forming in her eyes, she moved past her and into the hall.

"Wait!" Holland Dubois called. "Why did you come? Wait!"

But Nicole did not pause. Her long strides carried her through the hall and out the front door in a blurry haze.

Somehow she made it into the hansom. She made it into the hansom before her tears fell, and with it, all of her dreams, crumbling into the dust on the floor at her feet.

Hadrian shifted forward in his seat. He peered out of the window of his coach and glimpsed his home. Tension lanced through him.

He had left Clayborough four days ago. Four agonizingly long days ago. He had not left in a fit of anger, although he was still half-heartedly angry at Nicole for putting herself in the danger that she had by riding alone with O'Henry on the public roads. He had left in a moment of fright. He had, in fact, been running away.

But it had not worked.

He could no longer run from himself, his feelings, or his wife.

The episode with the ruffians—all of whom had been caught and dispatched forthright to the local gaoler within an hour of Nicole's return to Clayborough—had brought Hadrian into a violent confrontation with his deepest, most heartfelt feelings. Knowledge he had sought to avoid—probably from the very start of his relationship with Nicole—loomed up bluntly and inescapably in his mind. The instant that he knew, without doubt, that he loved his wife, was the most terrifying moment of his life.

He had spent a lifetime maintaining cool control of himself and his passions. He had spent a lifetime keeping his emotions rigorously in check. As a very young boy he had learned how to hide his feelings, even from himself. For to feel was to be vulnerable. To feel was to be hurt.

And now he was no longer invulnerable. To the contrary, he had never been more vulnerable in his life. He loved Nicole so passionately that it bordered on obsession. Those vagabonds had almost hurt her, perhaps they might have murdered her. The mere thought, even now, four days later, terrified him and consumed him.

After apprehending the three men, he had quit Clayborough immediately for London. As if to outrun his emotions. As if to outrun the knowledge he now faced. He had intended to regain control of himself—and his heart—no matter the cost. Even if it meant abandoning his wife indefinitely at his country home and seeking refuge in the arms of other women.

Neither escape route had succeeded. He had gone to Holland Dubois with the intention of bedding her so soundly that he would never think about Nicole again, yet he had found himself politely terminating their relationship instead. He had intended to remain in London, immersed in his business affairs, yet instead he was heading home eagerly.

The knowledge, so new, so powerful, was still there within him, and it was still frightening. There had been moments in the past few days when he had awakened in the middle of the night feeling the kind of panic and aloneness he had felt as a very young boy. As sleep had fled, so had the anxiety, but not before he had recognized it and his own vulnerability. His own humanity.

He had finally given up, and given in, to himself, to her. She was his wife and he was in love with her. She had rejected him many times in the past, yet he had survived—just as he had survived Francis' cruel rejections. Recently, though, she had no longer rejected him. Recently there had been a truce between them by day, one that, at night, vanished completely into the most compelling form of intimacy. There was hope. Their marriage could succeed. The first week of their marriage promised that. Yet Hadrian knew he would never be content with what they had shared so far. Now he wanted so much more. He wanted her love, and he wanted it to be as fullblown and passionate and obsessive as his.

As the coach rolled up the long graveled drive he began to perspire. The last time he had seen her, they had been in the midst of a furious confrontation. One that he had initiated, due to his own heart-rending fear for her safety. He had probably compounded matters by leaving without even a word about his plans. He was not sure what kind of reception he was about to get.

He carried with him a peace offering. A large box, gift-wrapped, lay on the seat opposite him. When she saw its contents she would recognize his sincerity in wishing to make amends for the extent of his rampaging anger and for his inconsiderate departure from Clayborough.

The coach came to a halt in front of Clayborough's oversized, engraved front doors. Hadrian alighted from the carriage, the box under one arm. Mrs. Veig greeted him on the steps. He inquired after his wife and was told that she was upstairs in her rooms.

Hadrian was as nervous as he had been as a schoolboy being called before his principal. He moved somewhat slowly up the two flights of stairs. In the corridor his stride lengthened. His heart jack-hammered anxiously now.

Her door was open. He stepped into her sitting room and heard sounds of movement coming from her bedchamber. He walked to that doorway, a sudden fierce joy filling him. He would always feel a rush of exhilaration upon seeing her, he realized. And then, when he was standing on the threshold, his exhilaration died.

Nicole's back was to him. One large trunk was on the floor, open and nearly filled with clothing, none of which was folded neatly. On her bed were piles and piles of gowns, petticoats, chemises, drawers, shoes, gloves, scarves and reticules. Annie hovered anxiously by one side of the bed. As Nicole picked up another heaping pile of garments, Annie saw him and froze. Nicole dumped the heap in the trunk and saw him as well.

He stood very still. "Madam," he said stiffly.

Her eyes snapped with fury, but her tone was more

than polite, it was formal and arctic cold. "Your Grace." Abruptly she turned her back on him and grabbed another pile of clothing.

The Duke set the box down very carefully against the wall and folded his arms across his chest. "May I ask what you are doing?" But he didn't have to ask, for it was obvious. The curtains of numbness started to part a little, and pain pierced through his chest.

"Can you not see?" she retorted, dumping the clothing in the trunk. "I am packing."

"That is obvious. Where are you going?"

She stared at him, her gray eyes as brilliant as diamonds, and equally hard. "I am leaving."

There was no numbness now. Yet because the Duke had spent a lifetime learning to keep his reactions masked, nothing showed on the exquisitely chiseled planes of his face. "Leaving?"

"I am leaving you."

"I see." His composure threatened to crack. Quickly, he walked into the room and to the window, staring unseeingly out of it, his back to her. He heard her resume her packing. Thrusting his hands in his pockets, he fought to get an iron grip on the panic swirling in him. He turned. "May I ask why?"

She whirled. "You dare to ask me why!" It was a scream. As the words erupted, she reached him in three agile strides and slammed her open palm across his face as hard as she could. He reeled back under the impact.

She did not move away. She waited, eyes glittering wildly, eager to do violent battle with him. But he would never hurt the woman he loved. "That is, I believe, the fourth time you have struck me."

"And the last."

No words could have given greater testimony to her irrevocable intentions. Her irrevocable resolve. To leave him. *The panic was there, lurking beneath the surface, a black mist threatening to choke him, to drag him down.*

When she saw that he would not rise to the challenge,

she nearly snickered, with great bitterness. With hate. She turned her back on him abruptly and slammed the lid down on the trunk. "Annie. Get two servants up here to bring this down."

Annie could not speak. She fled the room. The Duke had not even been aware of her presence during their exchange.

He reached deep within himself for more strength than he had ever required of himself for any endeavor, and miraculously, he found it. With apparent casualness, he moved towards his wife. She did not back away, and he dispassionately comprehended that she still wanted a confrontation with him. He was not about to give her one. Not now. Not when he was in complete control. He took her chin between his fingertips.

"A warning, Madam," he said dispassionately. "If you leave me now, you will not be welcome back. Not ever. Do I make myself clear?"

She laughed, the sound maniacal. "I am never coming back! Not ever!"

He still did not know why, but he no longer cared. *For the colors were all gone now, and the blackness had consumed him. But it was familiar, almost soothing.* "Very well," he released her. His smile was cold. "You have been forewarned. This time, Madam, your reckless nature will lead you where it will, and you will not be rescued by me."

"Good."

He turned on his heel. He quit the room. He was more than numb now, but it did not matter. He had left behind the splintered pieces of his heart, so he was incapable of feeling, and that suited the Duke of Clayborough as well as anything could.

Life quickly returned to normal. The Duke forgot that he had even had a wife, that his wife even existed. He slipped back into a routine he had adhered to for too many years to count. He rose with the sun and tended to the many operations that required his supervision on his vast estates. He spent his afternoons and evenings locked in his study with his papers or his managers. He slept heavily, dreamlessly.

Except he always awoke in the middle of the night. Always, he felt like a boy of six, not a man nearing thirty. In the dark midnight hours, panic engulfed him, and it was real. It was only then that he remembered her, and hated her. Again, hatred was his refuge, his strength.

One week later, the Duke rose from his desk to greet his mother. Her visit was unexpected. He was not pleased to see her; he was in the middle of a meeting with the manager of his timber farms who had spent an entire day traveling south for this appointment. The manager was told to wait, and the Duke closed the door behind his mother. "Mother, this is a surprise." His tone was polite but nothing more.

"Hadrian, what is going on? I have heard the most impossible rumor! That your wife has taken up residence with the Serles at Cobley House!"

"My wife?" He was cool. "Ah, the Duchess." He shrugged, distinctly disinterested in the topic of conversation. But a sudden throbbing began behind his temples.

"Have you two had a row? Or is she really just visiting the Serles? I pray the latter is the answer, but what bride of a few weeks runs off to visit a friend and leaves her husband?"

"Mother, this is a matter I do not wish to discuss. However, I shall answer your question this once—and then we shall drop it. We have chosen to live apart."

"To live apart!" Isobel was horrified.

Sudden anger swept him. It was so strong and consuming that it almost knocked the Duke off of his feet. "It is done all the time," he said coldly. "Indeed, I must thank you for reminding me. I must see that a proper residence is provided for her."

"A proper residence! Hadrian—what has happened?"

His brow lifted. "Nothing. Absolutely nothing." But a

part of his mind clicked, and a thought materialized, its vast meaning condensed into one word: *everything*. He quickly shut his eyes, not wanting to be conscious of what his subconscious mind already knew.

"This is ridiculous,?" Isobel cried. "Go and fetch her back. The two of you are meant for each other! If she has left you, forget your pride—put your foot down!"

Instead of answering, the Duke walked around his mother and opened the door for her. "I am in the middle of a meeting," he said bluntly. "I believe that this discussion is over."

Nicole dressed for dinner. She did so with vast concentration. She did every minor thing with vast concentration. Even the simplest tasks consumed her mentally, wholly, such as brushing her hair or drinking a cup of tea. She found that by focusing completely on whatever it was that she was doing, she could survive each and every day.

She had arrived at the Serles' country home a week ago unexpectedly. Martha had taken one look at her face—tear-stained, her eyes swollen—and hurried her upstairs into a guest bedroom. Nicole, having no facade to maintain, had wept copiously in her best friend's arms. In between the tears were bouts of near violence, where she had punched at the pillows with all the strength she had, wishing it were Hadrian she were pummeling into shreds instead. And she had told Martha everything.

She existed, but that was all. She took each day moment by moment, keeping her mind blessedly blank or thoroughly occupied with mundane chores. She dared not think of him, she dared not feel. The heartbreak lurked within her, threatening to erupt. She had dared to hope, she had dared to dream. For the briefest of times, it had seemed as if her dreams would come true. And that made his betrayal impossible to bear. The grief that lay buried deeply and solidly within her was so immense she knew she must not ever uncap it.

And he had not even tried to stop her. He had let her go without the slightest hesitation. She was so unimportant to him that he had not even fought for her.

Nicole dared not allow such knowledge to slip into her conscious thoughts.

At the end of the week Regina appeared. Nicole had known it would only be a matter of time before her family learned of her whereabouts. Nicole was glad to see her, but she was also afraid to see her.

"What have you done!" Regina cried, never one to beat around the bush. "Nicole, you had better think about what you are doing!"

Nicole had a flashing remembrance. She recalled how Regina had last seen her when she had come to visit her at Clayborough with Jane and Martha. Nicole recalled exactly how she was dressed, right down to the last detail of the tiny pearl studs she wore in her ears, just as she recalled exactly how she had been feeling. She had been on a sky-high cloud, in an impossible state of ecstasy, she had been in love.

She closed her eyes, hugging herself, fighting for control. She found it.

"Please, Regina, do not even bring the topic of my marriage up. It is over. I am never going back."

"You fool! You fool! What could he have possibly done to make you behave so stupidly! A few weeks ago you were ecstatically happy and madly in love!"

Nicole managed to smile at her sister. "Are you returning to London soon? Are you still seeing Lord Hortense?"

Regina blinked. "Don't change the subject!"

Nicole was instantly angry. "Don't badger me! It is my life! If he cared at all he would come after me—goddamn him to hell!"

Regina was shocked.

And Nicole had almost allowed herself to feel the immensity of the grief which she did not want to feel. She buried her face in her hands. Regina suddenly moved to her and embraced her.

"I am sorry," her sister whispered. "You are right, it is your life. It is only that I love you so and I want you to be happy." She released her.

Nicole wiped away a tear and managed to nod. "What would I do without you? And without Martha? Please, please, be my ally. Please don't take his side."

Regina bit her lip. Her expression very serious and very concerned, she finally nodded in agreement. "Do you want to tell me what has happened?"

"No." Nicole took a deep breath, then managed a smile. "There, I feel much better. And as soon as I put this marriage completely behind me, I will be a new person. I will return to Dragmore. My life will be exactly as it used to be—and I will be as happy as I used to be." Her smile was too bright.

Regina looked at her sadly. "And how are you ever going to put *him* behind you?"

Nicole did not dare answer the question honestly, much less consider it. "I imagine a man as powerful as he shall be able to obtain a divorce posthaste."

"A divorce!"

Nicole nodded. "This marriage was a mistake from the start. I have sent him a letter, asking him for a divorce."

He reread the letter. Not for the second time or the third or the fourth. He had read it so many times that he knew its contents by heart. Again, the words blurred. The tears were of both joy and sorrow. *Dear God, he had a son.*

Dear Sir,
I am the son of Isobel de Warenne Braxton-Lowell. I can only hope that, despite the passage of so many years, you do remember my mother and what once transpired between you. Recently she confided in me. I was as shocked as I am sure you shall be, for she not only revealed to me that she had known you so long ago, but that you are my natural father. I hope to find you alive and well and to make your acquaintance, at your convenience of course. Such a meeting can take place upon the soil of your homeland, or mine.

Until then, Sincerely,
Hadrian de Warenne Braxton-Lowell,
the ninth Duke of Clayborough

He folded the worn letter carefully for it was already beginning to tear, and tucked it in the inside breast pocket of his suit.

He had a son.

Although it was weeks now since Hadrian Stone had first received the miraculous news that he had a son, he could not recover from the discovery. He was still overwhelmed by the knowledge of his son's existence.

His son—who was hoping to meet him.

Hadrian Stone could barely wait for that day himself.

As always, his thoughts were preoccupied with that one topic, his son. Stone's speculation ran rampant. The letter's tone was so formal and so proper that he could not put a face to the words it contained, or emotions. Was his son being proper in addressing him as a stranger—which indeed he was—or was he being cautious? Was he enthused to meet him, or just curious, even dismayed? Perhaps he was even angry. His son was the ninth Duke of Clayborough. It was apparent that, until recently, he had thought the eighth duke to be his father. Would he not be angry? Perhaps he even felt threatened. Hadrian Stone only knew a few British lords, but he knew how they set a great store on their blue blood and titles, and it was quite obvious that his son's title could now be easily challenged by brothers, cousins, uncles or any sort of distant male kin.

But for whatever reason, his son had requested a meeting, either in America or in London. Stone had not even bothered with a reply. He had jumped aboard the first ship setting sail for England the very day he had received the missive at his home in Boston.

He stared at the jumbled London skyline as it came into view, the iron-clad ship moving with little grace up the Thames under steam. It was a chill gray day and it was drizzling, but Hadrian Stone was used to inclement weather and he was barely aware of the cold or the dampness. He tugged at his tie, feeling uncomfortably restricted by it and the suit he was wearing. He had probably not worn a suit more than a dozen times in all of his sixty years.

The joy almost choked him. It came over him in a hot tide, abruptly and completely, as it did so often. *He had a son. His son was the Duke of Clayborough.* It was a dream that had come true.

He had no children. He had never married. Only once in his life had he ever wanted to marry, had he ever loved a woman enough to want to marry. But that was long ago, far in the past. His regrets were few, for he was not an introspective man, being a man of action, but he had always regretted not having children, and recently the yearning had become more intense.

And now he had a son. A son who had, like himself, just learned of his existence. Again, Stone wondered what he would be like. Was he too proud or too proper to reveal any of his feelings in a letter to the stranger who was his real father? Hadrian Stone was a very proud man also, but he knew when to eat his pride and he always had. On the other hand, he wasn't the least bit interested in decorum. Stone did not have a formal bone in his body, but from the tone of the letter, he was starting to suspect that his son had more than one.

He could not inagine his son being proper, or worse, a straight-laced blue-blooded Brit. Yet there would be many more vast differences between them. Stone was a man who had built up a shipping empire from nothing but sheer determination, with nothing but an iron will and his own two strong calloused hands. Those who met him would never guess he was a successful business magnate. When he was at his offices he worked in his shirtsleeves like any common clerk, his manner open and familiar—although he was quick to temper should those working for him fail to do their best. Whenever he could, he abandoned his offices to captain one of his ships to a distant port. His love for the sea had begun when he was a small boy—at thirteen he had first shipped out. He had never been a man to be chained for very long to a desk. He had always been a man of the outdoors, of the sea. The sea was his life, his love.

Stone tried to prepare himself for the inevitable. His son was not just aristocracy, but a duke. Stone did not have to know anything about him to know that he had probably never lifted a finger in his life in labor or for himself. It was very hard for Stone to come to terms with this. Not only had he reached the top but he had done so by coming from the bottom, by not being afraid of any form of hard labor. He must honestly face the distinct probability that his son had never raised an honest sweat in his life. Stone was resolved not to judge him for it, even if his son openly disdained the work ethic.

But would his son judge *him?*

He prayed that it was only polite formality he had discerned in his son's letter—not cool indifference or haughty snobbery. But the question was there, one that had haunted him from the moment he had learned of his son's title. *Would his son be able to accept him, a simple hardworking man who saw himself as a sea captain?*

His stomach lurched at the thought. He had been afraid of very little in his life, but he was afraid of his son's rejection of him. He was afraid his son would look down his nose at him. He had met enough nobly born men, whether British or European, to know that they saw themselves as superior to the common man—that they were snobs.

As much as he anxiously awaited their meeting, he dreaded it, too.

And he was quick to blame the circumstances on Isobel. Had he known he had a son, he would have claimed him, and rightly so. The boy would not have grown up in the salons of the rich British upper classes, he would have grown up on the decks of seafaring ships. He would have learned the value of hard work, and to be proud of himself for himself, not because of some damned title.

But it wasn't to be. Because of Isobel, *who had denied him his son.* Isobel, who had deceived him for all of these years.

Rage engulfed him.

For all of these years, she had denied him his son. Isobel was the only woman he had ever loved. He had not understood her notion of duty and loyalty, he had not understood how she could really love him and leave him to go back to her husband, although, God knew, he had tried his best to comprehend her. Yet his love for her had never wavered. Not in nearly thirty years, despite the anguish, despite the heartbreak. Until now.

She had denied him his son. She was not the woman he had thought her to be for all these years. She was self-serving and dishonest. She had deceived him. Purposefully, she had kept the fact of his son's existence from him. *She had denied him his son.* It was the bottom line. He could not get past it. Rage burned in his heart where once there had been love. He would never forget, and he would never forgive.

The moment the Duke read his wife's short, blunt letter—the moment he comprehended her request for a divorce—all of his carefully exerted control vanished. With a roar he tore the note to shreds and shouted for his horse.

He was well aware of the fury consuming him, well aware that this was not how he should be reacting, but it was too late. All the control which he had exercised since she had left him was gone. Anger pumped through his veins until he felt nothing else, and he welcomed it.

He chose to ride Ruffian, the fastest mount in his stables. He rode with one burning ambition, and that was to reach Cobley House before the next dawn. Yet after the first crazed moments as he galloped away from Clayborough he slowed, regaining his sanity. Although adrenaline still coursed through his veins, he was astute enough to know that to kill his mount in a madcap ride would not only be an action he would later regret, it would not get him to Sussex any faster.

To hell with his pride, he thought savagely. She was his wife, and he would never, ever give her a divorce. Nor would he allow her to continue this nonsensical game. If he had to drag her back to Clayborough unwillingly, so be it. If she wanted to sulk and resort to feminine vapors, so be it. But she could sulk and pout at Clayborough—where she belonged.

Because he was not giving her up.

He had had enough.

When Hadrian arrived at Cobley House, it was several hours past first light. Both he and his stallion were covered in mud and soaked to the bone from sweat and rain. He was traveling alone, with no fanfare, and when the butler opened the Serles' front door he was not recognized. The man did not invite him in, but barred his path.

Hadrian wiped his face again with a muddy handkerchief. Ignoring the butler, he stepped around him and into the foyer, dripping mud and rain upon the gleaming parquet floor.

"See here, now," the butler protested. "You cannot be barging in—"

"Where is my wife?" Hadrian ground out.

The butler froze.

The sanity which had returned to him the day before in the course of the long, exhausting ride was gone. Cold, hard anger was in its place, and with it, glittering resolve. "My wife," Hadrian repeated. "The Duchess of Clayborough."

The butler paled. "Your Grace, forgive me! I did not know—I mean . . ." He grew even whiter under Hadrian's unrelenting, increasingly hostile stare. "She is in the guest room upstairs on the second floor. Her door is the first one on the right!"

Hadrian whirled, his greatcoat floating around him like a big black winged creature, and he bounded up the stairs. He did not pause before her door. Without missing a stride, he kicked it in off of its hinges and entered the room.

Nicole screamed. She was dressed only in a silvery blue nightgown and wrapper, and she had been sipping hot chocolate in bed. The chocolate spilled across the pristine white sheets, the cup tumbling to the floor. She sat up in sheer fright, then grew very white as comprehension of the very real presence of her husband filled her.

"I have come to take you home."

Nicole gripped the bedcovers. She was momentarily speechless.

Hadrian smiled, not nicely. He flung open a door to the armoire, revealing her neatly hung clothes. He tore a dress off of one hanger and threw it at her. It fell across her legs. "Get dressed."

Nicole came to her senses. "How dare you! Get out! Get out now!"

"I did not come here to argue with you, Madam Wife," he gritted. "You do not have to dress at all. The choice is yours."

Nicole kicked the dress to the floor, kicking aside the bedcovers in the process. "I am not going with you. Get out now. You cannot force me."

Hadrian laughed. "You underestimate me, Madam." An instant later he was reaching for her.

Nicole screamed again when he grabbed her. Her screams became even louder—enough to wake the dead—when she realized what he was doing. She writhed like a banshee as Hadrian slung her upside down over his shoulder with no more care than he would have given a sack of feed.

"Let me go! Let me down! This instant!" She howled furiously.

"I have had enough," he warned, and he smacked her hard across her thinly clad buttocks.

Nicole went silent in shock. Hadrian strode into the hall. He came face to face with his wife's hosts. Martha was white, her hand covering her mouth, her eyes wide. However, the Viscount was trying not to smile.

"Hello, Serle. Forgive me for disturbing you," the Duke said evenly.

"Think nothing of it, Your Grace," Robert Serle replied politely.

"I would greatly appreciate the use of one of your carriages."

"My pleasure" Serle said, turning and calling downstairs to his butler to order round the coach.

"Traitor!" Nicole cried, coming to her senses. "Help me, please! Martha—"

Hadrian smacked her across her buttocks again. Nicole was dumbfounded into silence. "And my stallion needs tending, if you please."

"Do not worry, he shall be fed and groomed immediately."

"Put me down."

"Why?" the Duke asked calmly. "You choose to misbehave like a child, so you shall be treated like a child. Errant wives get what they deserve." He began walking down the stairs.

"Oooh!" Nicole was momentarily incoherent with rage.

"Test my patience one more time," he said too conversationally as she began to twist frantically, "and I shall put you over my knee as if you were six."

She stopped struggling.

They paused in the foyer. The butler nonchalantly pretended not to see them. Martha came hurrying downstairs. Nicole tried to catch her eye desperately, but Martha was careful not to look at her. "You will need this," she said to Hadrian. She gave the butler two heavy blankets and a full-length fur coat.

"You too!" Nicole cried, almost sobbing now.

"The coach is here, Your Grace," the butler said. He could not quite keep the relief from his voice.

"Thank you, Lady Serle. Again, forgive the intrusion," the Duke said, following the butler outside and to the coach. Fortunately it had stopped drizzling. When the servant opened the door, Hadrian unceremoniously tossed Nicole onto one of the seats. He heaved himself in after her, reaching past her to lock the opposite door before she could even move to leap out that side of the carriage. He pocketed the key.

"Wait!" Martha cried, running from the house with a bottle in her hand. "You will need this too!" She shoved a bottle of brandy at him. The butler slammed that door shut.

Hadrian nodded his thanks and knocked on the ceiling sharply. The coach moved off. Then he stretched out his long legs and turned to look at his wife.

"I hate you!" she cried, heavy tears sparkling on her lashes.

"I am sure that you do," he said calmly. He threw the fur coat at her. "After all, if you loved me you would not have asked me for a divorce, would you?"

Nicole's nostrils flared. Tears slipped from her lashes, tracking down her cheeks. She stared at him as if incapable of responding.

"Just to set the record straight," the Duke said quite conversationally, "a divorce is out of the question."

"Why?"

"Because I do not wish it."

"And my wishes do not interest you in the least!"

"That is correct."

Nicole stiffened, then covered her face with her hands. She was not going to cry. She was not going to unleash all the grief and anguish which she had so carefully and deeply buried. She was not.

But she could feel it boiling up in her like a volcano about to spew forth its hot, molten contents.

She grappled with herself and finally, she won. She parted her hands to see the Duke regarding her impassively. "I will make your life unbearable."

"It already is," he said calmly.

Nicole blinked.

His smile was tight, cold. "I am damned if I do and damned if I don't," he informed her. "But I may as well get something out of this marriage, such as an heir."

She did not understand, and did not care to, not when he was stating his intentions so badly. "Is that what I am to you? A brood mare? Damn you! I will not bear you a son!"

He leaned towards her abruptly. There was no longer anything casual about his posture or his expression—hot rage glittered in his eyes. "You may make your position as my wife as elaborate—or as mundane—as you choose. And you *will* do your duty. You *will* bear me my son."

"No!" Nicole cried, frantic. She lunged past him for the door. It was locked, as she had known it was, but she shook it wildly anyway. Immediately he pulled her away, from behind. With a wild cry that was half a sob she twisted to claw at him viciously. He caught and restrained her hands instantly, forcing her body into an intimate embrace with his and pushing her backwards against the seat cushions. Nicole writhed and writhed hopelessly while he held her pinned there, panting and bucking, tears of rage and frustration and despair streaking her cheeks. Finally she had no strength left and she went limp against the seats in defeat.

He did not move. He made no attempt to free her, even though they both knew she was exhausted—and that she had lost. As Nicole's breathing slowed, as the mad rage which had blinded her diminished, she grew more aware of the feel of his chest against hers, his hip against hers. His arms were around her, his hands grasping her wrists, pinned behind her back. A day's growth of beard was rough against her cheek. His steady breathing was warm against her skin.

Panic flared.

It flared the instant all of her senses kicked into total awareness of his strength, his power, his heat, his maleness. And their intimacy.

"I will not try to escape," Nicole whispered, turning her head slightly. To her horror, her lips brushed his chin as she spoke. "Let me up." Her voice quavered.

He did not move, nor did he answer. The silence lengthened. Her heart was beating madly now. Although he still gripped her wrists, it was loosely now, and she became aware that she was actually in his arms. She was afraid to lift her gaze, afraid to look into his eyes.

She knew what she would see there.

She looked up. Their glances met. His was burning, but not with anger. "Please don't," she begged.

He shifted slightly and his heartbeat came into contact with hers. Her breasts were crushed fully by his chest. His coat was open, his shirt soaking wet. Nicole's nipples tightened instantly in response to the sensation of hot male skin covered only by the thinnest layer of silk; her own silk bodice was now equally wet and equally disturbing. Dismayed, she knew he could feel her body's exuberant response.

"Please," she begged again, her voice catching breathlessly.

He shifted. Nicole thought he was moving away from her, and she wanted to weep with relief. But he only moved to release her hands so he could slide his palms up to her breasts. "This is where we suit," he said roughly. "Rather, this is how we suit. You won't deny me now, Nicole, will you?"

She wanted to deny him, she did. But he crushed her breasts gently in his hands, his fingertips grazing her nipples, his gaze never leaving hers. And instead of protesting, Nicole gasped in pleasure.

He locked his arms beneath her back and lifted her abruptly in an arch to his mouth. He took one silk-clad nipple into his mouth, sucking hard. Nicole grasped his head, not to push him away, but to hold him to her.

He released her. He gripped her knees and pulled her down onto the seat. As he loomed up over her their gazes met again. Puffs of vapor formed with each rapid, hard breath he took. Nicole looked at his exquisitely handsome face, strained with a passion as dark and consuming as her own, and her heart lurched. His eyes were golden flames, burning intensely. Promising intensely. But promising her what? A moment's paradise? She wanted eternity.

She realized what he was doing. His hands fumbled with the clasp of his trousers. She watched him reveal his phallus, engorged and fully erect. Abruptly he flipped the silk skirts of her nightgown up over her waist and out of his way. Nicole closed her eyes, unmoving, waiting.

He came down over her and slid into her in one fast, fluid motion. Nicole instantly rose to embrace him. Her arms coiled around his shoulders, her legs around his hips. He filled her completely, instantly, hotly. For one moment he was still and she was still. Again their gazes locked. Again she glimpsed the promise she did not understand. Then he took her mouth with his, just as completely as he had taken her body with his.

He moved. He moved fast, deep. Nicole strained with him. There was no gentle introduction, no playful prologue, just hard, rough thrusting. Nicole slid back on the seats, thrusting up her own hips to meet him in a series of violent dead-on collisions. Harder. Faster. Their bodies met with fury, punishing one another. Nicole gripped him fiercely as a tidal wave of intense, mindshattering pleasure swept over her. She shouted her release.

He laughed. He laughed as he rode her in a final thrust that was deeper, more complete, harder. His powerful buttocks tensed as he drove her up against the opposite side of the carriage. Nicole held on tightly, her nails penetrating his skin as another wave of savage spasms attacked her as he swelled and swelled and finally burst inside her.

They lay limp, drained. The carriage rocked them back and forth. Nicole grew aware of his full weight crushing her, of his wet shirt and trousers abrading her bare breasts and bare legs. Her nightgown was tangled up hopelessly around her waist. Yet she wasn't cold. His body steamed with heat, warming her own flesh.

Realization of what they had just done and her own active, eager participation, brought despair swiftly into her heart. Nicole turned her face away from him, closing her eyes. The moment she did so she became aware of his regard upon her.

She would not meet it. She would not. For if she opened her eyes she would cry. He was already the victor, and he did not deserve another victory.

She still loved him. Despite all that had happened, she did. And she hadn't forgotten why she had run away, or how he had abducted her from Cobley House. And now, now she was reminded of just how hopeless her resistance to him was—in any way or any form.

"Nicole," he said.

She refused to answer.

"I know you are not sleeping."

She screwed her eyes tightly shut. She wished he would get up so that she need not be reminded of how warm and hard his body was, but he merely shifted to one side. The anguish was there again. She choked it down. He had forced her to return to him, she could not escape him, just as she could not escape her love for him. And his only interest in her was sexual—just as was his interest in Holland Dubois and God only knew how many other women. It was hopeless, so hopeless. To love such a man was hopeless. She was not going to cry, for if she did, she would never stop.

He touched her face. Nicole refused to respond. But his fingers were light and gentle, and despite her distress, his touch seemed tender, which she knew was an overwrought illusion on her part. His thumb stroked her mouth.

"Please don't."

"Then look at me."

She did, and tears welled up in her eyes. She didn't know what she had expected to see in his gaze, but it wasn't the softness that was there. It was her undoing, and she choked back a sob.

"Perhaps if you cry you will feel better."

"No."

"I doubt you will feel worse." He smiled slightly.

She could not smile back. Suddenly she wanted to be in his arms, when that was the last place she should ever think of looking for comfort. Quickly she closed her eyes and turned her face away again, praying in one breath that he would put some distance between them, and in the next, that he would reach for her and hold her.

"Is it truly that bad?"

His tone was gentle. He still loomed over her. He was too close. Nicole knew she must say something inflammatory, she must. Instead, she opened her eyes and again met his gaze.

The softness was still there. His expression seemed caring, but she knew he did not care, not for her, not really, not any more than he did for his mistress. Her hands found his chest and she tried to shove him away, panic choking her. "Please!"

He sat up and pulled her into his arms.

"God, no!" She cried, flailing at him blindly and missing by a wide margin.

He cradled her against his chest. "Cry."

"Please don't do this," she said, but she was already crying. He didn't answer, but he ran one large hand up and down her back repeatedly. "Damn you," Nicole wept. "Damn you," she sobbed. Her fists balled and struck his chest, the blows pitiful, overwhelmed as she was by her tears. "I hate you," she sobbed, flailing at him. "I hate you."

He tensed, but he did not let her go and he continued to stroke her. She continued to weep, giving vent to such a storm of tears that he was shocked at the depth of her grief. He could not understand why she cried, but he could identify with this kind of pent-up, bone-deep hurt. His arms tightened upon her. He rocked her as if she were a child. And holding her, he was sad.

He was sad for her—for whatever was causing her such anguish, and he guessed it was him. He was also sad for himself. Because now that he had recognized his love for her, and how much he needed her, he could no longer deny his feelings, and they were not about to go away. Apparently his love would remain unrequited. His heart seemed to bleed. And as she wept in his arms like a child, he suddenly felt like a small boy again, and he, too, felt like crying. Tears came to his eyes.

He tried to remind himself that he was not a small boy, that he was a grown man, but it did not work.

She vented her anguish for a long time, but eventually the sobs became hiccups, eventually the small blows she aimed at his chest lessened and disappeared. He did not let her go and he continued to rock her. Her fists uncurled, only to turn claw-like, and she was clinging to his shirt.

Although she no longer cried, a tremor swept her body. He swept his hand down her back, soothing her. He realized that she was falling asleep in his arms. "You will feel better tomorrow," Hadrian promised her. "Tomorrow it will not seem so bad."

She sighed. "I don't hate you," she whispered into his shirt. "Not really."

He almost smiled, and another tear sparkled on his lashes. "Sleep now. In a few hours we will be home."

Her grip on his shirt tightened. "I love you, Hadrian. I don't hate you, I love you."

He was shocked.

Her grip loosened and she sagged in his arms. Still stunned, he looked down at her and saw that she was in a deep, exhausted sleep. Very carefully, very gently, he laid her down on the seat. And he stared at her tear-ravaged face.

I don't hate you, Hadrian, I love you.

She had only been delirious. Hadn't she?

It was late that evening when the Duke and Duchess arrived at Clayborough. The Duke stepped down from the Serles' coach first, his own doormen gaping at him when they recognized him before quickly recovering. But Hadrian had more surprises in store for them other than his disheveled appearance in another gentleman's coach. He reached for his sleeping wife. She had not moved or made a sound in hours. Never had he seen a human being in such a deep sleep. Now he did not want to wake her, and very gently he lifted her into his arms.

Nicole stirred.

Hadrian carried his wife up the steps and into the foyer. Woodward, Mrs. Veig and his valet, Reynard, were hurrying into the room as he entered. No one so much as blinked at the sight of the Duke carrying his errant wife, barefoot and clad in a fur coat and asleep in his arms. Without pausing, he addressed Mrs. Veig. "When Her Grace awakes she will undoubtedly want a hot bath and a hot meal."

As he started up the stairs, Nicole sighed, gripping him with her hands. He watched her face as he strode into her bedroom. Her eyes fluttered open. Gently Hadrian laid her down on the bed. "We are home. Go back to sleep. It is late."

Nicole smiled at him. It was an artless, sleepy beautiful smile, and Hadrian's heart somersaulted. Her eyes instantly closed again. He could not help wishing that he could receive many more of those smiles, and that they would be purposefully directed at him.

He had removed her wet nightgown hours ago and she was naked beneath the fur coat. He took it off quickly, pulling the many heavy quilts and bedcoverings up over her. Then he went to the hearth and started a fire.

The last words she had spoken to him still rang in his ears. He had been able to think of little else during the remainder of the journey to Clayborough. *I don't hate you, Hadrian, I love you.* He knew she had not meant it. Had she?

He was afraid to hope. If she had meant what she had said, he would be the happiest man on this earth.

The fire beginning to blaze, Hadrian left the room, but not before giving his wife one last long glance. Hadrian strode into his own rooms, where Reynard was waiting for him. He handed him his greatcoat. "I too would like a bath and something to eat."

"I've already drawn your bath, Your Grace. And Woodward is bringing your meal."

Hadrian was suddenly restless. He patted the Borzoi, who had bounded forward to greet him, but he did so mindlessly, still thinking about Nicole. Woodward appeared at the door with a butler's table. He wheeled it into the room and laid out the Duke's napkin with an efficient flourish.

"Will you be taking your bath first, Your Grace?"

"Absolutely," Hadrian said. He doubted he had ever been filthier in his life.

"Before you do, Your Grace, may I tell you that you have a visitor?" Woodward asked.

Hadrian was unbuttoning his shirt. "What visitor?"

"He arrived most unexpectedly yesterday just after you left. He had no card, and I would have sent him to the Boarshead Inn, but being as he had come all the way from America, I thought the better of it and put him on the fourth floor in one of the guest rooms."

"Is it my courier returned from Boston?" He demanded

sharply, hope leaping in his chest.

"No, Your Grace. His name is Stone, but he would not say what he wants. Mister Stone is presently taking a brandy in the fourth-floor library. I can tell him to await you there until after you have dined, or I can tell him you will see him on the morrow."

Blood rushed from Hadrian's head, and for the first time in his life, he felt faint.

"Your Grace? Are you ill?"

He recovered. He recovered to turn and stride towards the stairs, taking the steps two at a time, leaving Woodward staring after him. *His father was here*. He could not believe it—he would not, not until he himself laid eyes upon the man.

Hadrian Stone restlessly inspected the collection of volumes in the library—which was just one of several in the Duke's residence. A terrific feeling of unease assailed him. He shouldn't have come. He knew that now.

The anxiety that had gradually intensified during the long days he had spent crossing the Atlantic as meeting his son became more imminent was nothing compared to the distress he now felt. He had known his son was a duke, but nothing could have prepared him for his son's estate, nothing could have prepared him for Clayborough.

He had expected luxury, yes. He had expected wealth. What he had not expected was a home fit for royalty as they lived a century ago, a home of palatial proportions and palatial pretense. All of his doubt came rushing to the fore. He was a simple man. His father had been cobbler, his mother a seamstress. He saw himself as a ship's captain, not as a shipping magnate. He was wearing expensively tailored clothes, but he felt like a fraud in them, and would have much preferred a seaman's wool sweater and rainslicker. Even this one small library overwhelmed him, for in truth there was nothing small about it.

What kind of man was he?

Hadrian Stone greatly feared that he was an arrogant one, and that he was about to be judged as unworthy by his own son.

A movement by the open door made him turn from his perusal of the stacks. A tall, powerfully built man stood in the doorway, half in shadows. Then he moved into the room.

Hadrian Stone knew the moment that the man stepped into the light that it was his son. His face was Isobel's. Barely able to breathe and unable to move, he stared at the man—the grown man—who was his son.

And the Duke of Clayborough stared back.

Stone saw that although his son had gained most of his stunning looks from his mother, his jaw was strong and square like his own, and it saved him from being too handsome. And his eyes, his eyes were the same golden amber as his own. But the resemblance did not end there. The Duke of Clayborough also possessed the same immense height, the same powerful build, as his father.

And then Stone noticed his clothes. He saw a damp silk shirt and tan, soiled breeches. The Duke's boots were glistening with rain and crusted with mud. Stone's gaze again swept to his son's face. There was nothing dandified about the man's clothes—there was nothing dandified about his face, either. His son was a man, in every sense of the word, and one who had, by the look of him, endured an incredibly long, difficult day.

Relief filled the father's veins.

The Duke was busy with his own inspection. Wide-eyed, Hadrian could not take his eyes off of the other man. His father was here. *His father*. Long moments passed. Hadrian shook himself out of the very real daze gripping him. "I had not expected such an immediate response to my inquiry."

Stone hesitated. The cultured tones coming from the other man were a surprise, reminding him again that not just a different country but a different class separated them, and his anxiety renewed itself. "How could I not come immediately?"

Hadrian shut the door and entered the room. "I must apologize for not being in residence when you arrived."

Stone waved at him. "Obviously I was not expected."

The two men fell into an awkward silence. Hadrian broke it by crossing the room. "Would you like another brandy?"

"Perhaps I'd better," Stone murmured.

Hadrian meticulously poured his father a drink. "Have you seen Isobel?" The question was casual, without intent, as he desperately sought a topic to break the ice between them.

"No."

Startled, Hadrian looked up, seeing the darkness passing over his father's face. He knew when to withdraw—he knew better than to continue with the topic of his mother, although his father's vehemence puzzled him. After so many years he would have expected indifference, not anger. He approached the other man for the first time, handing him his brandy. With no physical distance separating them, the two were silent and immobile, standing eye to eye and nose to nose, staring at each other.

"Damn," Hadrian finally breathed. "This is damnably awkward. How in hell does one greet one's long lost father anyway?"

Stone laughed suddenly. "Damn is right!" He exclaimed. "Thank God you can curse!"

Hadrian suddenly smiled, equally beset by nervous tension. "You wish me to curse?"

"It's not that I want you to curse," Stone said, his smile fading, "I was merely wondering if we would continue the conversation so formally."

"We Englishmen are sticklers for formality," Hadrian said.

"Yes, but you are half American."

Hadrian stopped smiling. Finally his mouth softened. "I was eager to meet you," he admitted. "Thank you for coming."

"What father could stay away in such a situation?" Stone asked frankly.

"Many, I should imagine."

Stone gained an inkling, then, into his son's soul. "I have always yearned for a son. I have no children. None. Rather—" and he smiled, "until now."

That smile told Hadrian everything. He had already learned from Isobel that this man was everything Francis was not. But he had been afraid, secretly afraid, that fatherhood would mean little to the stranger who had sired him. Yet it did not. His father was pleased to find out that he had a son. More than pleased, if the haste with which he had come to England was any indication. "And I always wanted a father like all the other boys had," Hadrian admitted.

Stone looked at him. "You had a father."

Hadrian's face turned to stone. "I did not have a father. Francis knew I was a bastard. I did not know the truth, however, so I could never understand why he hated me. Finding out the truth has been the greatest relief of my life."

Stone's face was grim. "She should have told you long before this—she should have told me."

Hadrian heard his tone—the condemnation—and stared. "She had her reasons."

Stone instantly recognized the loyalty his son had for his mother, and he backed off. If he were to accuse Isobel of treachery, he would alienate his own son, whom he was aching to befriend. "The past is the past. I am thankful that I am still alive to see this day—to see you, my own son, in the flesh."

Hadrian smiled. "I have looked forward to this day, too. Isobel only talked of you once but when she did, she made it clear that you were everything Francis was not."

"Was he so bad?" Stone asked softly, terribly concerned.

"He was a drunk and a sodomite who hated not just me, but his wife. He was a coward and a bully. He abused us both. Until I turned fourteen and knocked him down with my own two fists."

Stone was horrified. He suddenly had a clear image of Isobel as she had been thirty years ago, slender, proud and exquisitely beautiful, being struck by some featureless man who was her husband, a small boy holding onto her skirts. He shook off the sympathy he did not want to feel, not for her, and concentrated on his son instead. "Perhaps some day you will share your story with me."

"Perhaps." Hadrian turned away.

Stone knew that he had pushed too far, too quickly. He was an uncomplicated man; his son was terribly complicated. Yet despite what had to have been a horrific childhood, he was clearly a strong and honorable man. No one could talk with the Duke of Clayborough for long without recognizing his virtue and his power.

Hadrian turned again. "Do you want me to send for her?"

"No!"

Hadrian was again shocked by the vehemence in his father's tone. A hazy comprehension, still unformed, began to fill him. "You said you have no children. Did you ever marry?"

"No." Stone's expression was ferocious. "As I said, the past is the past." He softened his tone. "I have no wish to dredge it up, and I am sure your mother does not, either."

In that precise moment, Hadrian disagreed. He disagreed and sensed the power of emotions too private and complex for him to identify, nevertheless, shrewd instinct made him decide to ignore his father's wishes. "You are probably right," he said placatingly. "How long will you stay?"

Stone smiled. He realized he was no longer anxious

or afraid, not at all. To the contrary, his heart was ripe to bursting with love for his only child. His feelings were so consuming they left him breathless. He had never dreamed one could feel like this. "As long as I am welcome."

"You will always be welcome here."

Stone's heart soared. He looked at his son and saw the faint blush on his cheek and instinctively understood how hard it was for him to be so frank, so soon. "Thank you."

"There is no reason to thank me. You are my father. You will always be welcome here," Hadrian repeated firmly.

A new thought which Stone had not really considered made him grow somber. "Does not my relationship with you endanger your position?"

Hadrian looked amused, he lifted a brow. "Ahh, I see. My position as the Duke? No, it does not."

"But how is that possible?"

"Isobel was made a legitimate heir to Clayborough when she married Francis. Her father, the Earl of Northumberland, is a very shrewd man. I do have many cousins who would love to see me dethroned, so to speak, who would love to challenge Jonathan Braxton-Lowell's will. But it will not come to that. Not because I covet power or position—which I do not. Not because I love Clayborough and would be loathe to give it up—which I would be. But because, no matter how important it is to me that you are my father, it is more important to me that Mother's reputation remain intact. The truth about our relationship can never be revealed. For if it were to be revealed, I would deny it to protect her. And should I deny it, no one would dare to pursue the matter."

"I see." Stone was not disappointed, although a part of him would have dearly loved to claim Hadrian Braxton-Lowell as his son. Instead he was proud almost to the point of tears of his son's fierce, unwavering loyalty and sense of honor. Yet he thought that there had been a warning in Hadrian's tone. "I admire you, Hadrian," he said quietly. "And I am proud of the man you are. I did not come here to claim you publicly or to disrupt your life. You need not worry on that score."

"I know," Hadrian said, equally serious. "I know without your having to tell me. You are not vengeful, you are not a fortune hunter, you are not petty. I do not need to know you better to know all of that." And with rare humor, the Duke of Clayborough smiled. "You may be an American, but you are a man of honor."

And Hadrian Stone laughed.

Isobel wondered what could be so urgent. It had been several hours past suppertime the night before that she had received an urgent summons from her son, requesting her to meet with him the following morning at Clayborough. Isobel was worried; she assumed the summons had something to do with his wife. What else could it be? What else could possibly be so important?

Of course she would never ignore such a request. She had risen with the sun and set out for Clayborough an hour later. When she arrived at the ducal estate, it was still early morning. She nearly flew into the house.

"His Grace is still dining, Your Grace," Woodward informed her.

Isobel blinked. Hadrian never took such a late breakfast—it was half past nine—and she could not imagine why he was doing so now. Her worry increased. "Is the Duchess with him?" She was almost afraid to ask, but hoping beyond hope that she was.

"No, Your Grace, the Duchess is still abed."

Isobel almost swooned with relief. "So then she has returned!" she cried happily.

For a rare moment, Woodward also smiled. "Indeed she has. We are all most pleased, Your Grace. Although she did not exactly return."

Isobel had known Woodward for too long to be surprised that he would volunteer information she did not ask for; obviously he wished to tell her something. "What do you mean?"

"His Grace brought her back."

From Woodward's barely suggestive intonation, Isobel surmised the worst. Hadrian had undoubtedly fetched his wife back; she could imagine the fight they must have had. She sighed and hurried on down the hall to the dining room.

"He is not there, Your Grace," Woodward hurried after her. "He is dining in the music room—Her Grace prefers it so."

Isobel lifted a brow, knowing in that moment that all would be well. Nicole Shelton Braxton-Lowell was taming her son, inch by scanty inch. It was about time that someone softened him up. She let Woodward open the doors to the music room and entered with a cheery smile. A second later she froze.

It was Hadrian—*her Hadrian*—Hadrian Stone. He was sitting at the table with her son, the two of them engrossed in earnest conversation, taking breakfast as if they did this every single day of their lives—father and son together. Her world spun crazily. She was sure that she would faint.

"Mother!" Hadrian cried.

Isobel had a will of iron—she always had. She willed her heart to beat, she willed herself to stand still and strong and tall. But she could not will the blood to her face, which was deathly pale. Nor could she drag her gaze from Hadrian Stone.

He, too, stared.

Hadrian, their son, was standing. He looked from the one to the other, from his mother, frozen and ghostly white, to his father, sitting in shock at the table. It was Stone who recovered first. "Is this a joke?" he asked coldly.

"I have sudden, urgent business to attend to," Hadrian said, and then he was gone, slamming the doors behind him.

Stone stood. "Is this some kind of rotten joke?"

Isobel blinked. This was no dream. The man she had once loved with all of her heart and soul—the man she still loved—stood before her in the flesh. He was older, his hair was no longer a lustrous chestnut but threaded with gray, and there were many new wrinkles about his eyes and mouth, but he was still tall, still muscular in build, and he still enthralled her instantly with his male magnetism. He was still the most handsome man she had ever seen, and he always would be. Her entire body quivered in response to him, just as her heart pounded frantically and erratically.

He kicked back his chair. "I had no intention of ever laying eyes upon you again," he said in hard tones. "But apparently our son decided otherwise."

Isobel jerked. It was suddenly apparent—and it struck her like a cold, steel-edged slashing knife—that he hated her. His eyes burned with hatred. He stood there looking at her as if she were the lowest sort of vermin. Pain ripped through her, nearly knocking her from her feet. Dear God, how could such love have changed to such hate?

And how, oh how, how could she face him when he felt like this?

She found more strength than she knew she had. She straightened her shoulders, she lifted her chin. When she spoke, her voice barely trembled. "Apparently."

She glided towards the table. She did not look at him, although she could feel his burning eyes upon her. She had never been vain, but now she felt her fifty years, and she felt sick to know that, while she had taken one look at him and melted with hot, turbulent desire, he stared at her with nothing but hatred, seeing nothing but an old woman. She reached for the teapot, and began refilling his cup before filling her own.

He grabbed her wrist from across the table. She cried out as he hauled her forward so that their faces almost touched. "Good God!" he shouted. "After all you've done—*after all you've done*—you see me and you pour me tea?!"

Tears filled her eyes as she gazed back into his furiously angry gaze. "Unhand me."

He did so, instantly.

"It is not like you to behave like a brute." She was amazed at how calm her voice was, when inside she felt like she was dying.

"If I am behaving like a brute, it is because you have made me into one."

"Francis always blamed me for his weakness, too."

He froze. His face went white. Then, his jaw so tight that hollows formed beneath his cheeks, he said, "I am sorry."

He was nothing like Francis, he could never be like Francis, and Isobel knew it. "So am I," she said softly.

His head whipped up. His eyes blazed. "Being sorry now is a little bit late!"

Isobel stepped backwards.

He hurled himself around the table and she thought that he would grab her again. But he did not, he just stood there before her, shaking in rage. "Just what the hell are you sorry about, Isobel?"

The tears came then, filling up her eyes. "I am sorry for everything."

"For everything?" He was sarcastic. "For lying, for being deceitful, for being nothing more than a self-serving bitch?"

She reeled away from him. "Oh, God!"

He grabbed her. There was immense power in his hands, but he did not hurt her. He shook her once. "I loved a woman who did not exist! Who never existed! I loved a lie! I loved a lovely lie!"

She wept. "Why are you doing this? Why are you hurting me like this? Why do you hate me so?"

"You denied me my son and you dare to ask me why I hate you?"

She tried to focus on him through the flood of tears. "I did it because I was afraid. I was so afraid!"

"Afraid?" He became still. "Afraid of what? Of Francis?"

"No! I mean, of course I was afraid of Francis. He hated me for running the estates so well, and then he hated Hadrian for not being his son, and for reminding him of his impotency. He needed only the slightest excuse to hurt me. Hadrian was like you, though, even as a little boy. He was brave. He tried to protect me so many times!" She sobbed.

"I would have protected you!" Now he shook her hard. "God damn it, I would have protected you both! I would have taken you both away from here!"

"That is what I was afraid of," she wept. "I knew you would come if I told you of Hadrian. I knew you would come to claim your son. Just as I knew it was wrong to deny you the truth. But, Hadrian! Dear God, try and understand! Leaving you and returning to Clayborough was the hardest thing I have ever done. It was a miracle that I did so. A tenuous miracle. Somehow I survived each day without you. When I learned I was pregnant with your child, it gave me the will to live and to fight again. I didn't tell you the truth because if you came, you would destroy the existence I had just barely managed to attain. I knew if I ever laid eyes on you again I would willingly leave Clayborough and my husband, I would willingly violate my honor and my own integrity, to run away with my child and you. And if I did that, I would hate myself for the rest of my life."

He released her. He ran a shaking hand through his hair, staring at her wide-eyed. "Jesus. So much damn nobility. Self-sacrificing nobility!"

"If I had taken Hadrian and gone to you, I would have not just hated myself. In time, I would have hated you, too," she whispered.

He froze. Then he walked away from her. She watched him, the tears streaming freely down her face now, her shoulders shaking. But she did not make a sound.

When he turned to look at her, his own eyes were wet with unshed tears. But the anger was gone. "Life is never black or white, is it?" he asked sadly. "So many damned shades of grey. Why did you have to be the woman you are, Isobel? But then," his laugh was bitter, "it is that woman that I fell in love with."

"I chose to be apart from you, loving you, rather than be with you, hating you."

He absorbed that with great gravity. "I would not have been able to endure your hatred, either."

"Do you understand, then?" she cried.

"Yes, I understand self-respect," he said very heavily.

She collapsed on the nearest chair with overwhelming relief. "And," she whispered, daring to look at him, "and can you forgive me?"

"I don't know."

She was crushed.

"How bad was it for Hadrian?" He had to know. "Did you sacrifice him to your damned nobility, too?"

"No!" She cried. "Francis never loved him, but I more than made up for it. Francis hit him a few times, but I soon made him stop with blackmail—the same blackmail that made Francis accept him as his son. I threatened to reveal to the world the entire truth about Francis—his nature, his drunkenness, his preference for boys, and how he had to be rescued by his wife from his debts. It was that last that assured his silence about Hadrian not being his son—Francis could not bear for the world to know how inept he was. Hadrian did not have a father's love, but I tried to make up for that. You have met him, you have seen the fine man he has turned into. Look at how strong he is. You can be proud of him, Hadrian, you should be proud of him. He is like you in every way."

"But he grew up suffering."

Briefly, Isobel closed her eyes. "He suffered. He suffered a vast hurt that has haunted him to this day. The hurt of being unloved. The hurt of being despised by one parent. I protected him as best I could. Perhaps I was selfish. Perhaps you are right, I am self-serving. Perhaps I chose wrongly. I have wondered so many times if I did make the right choice. You would have given him love. But our relationship would not have survived if I had turned my back on my marriage and my life. Would that have made Hadrian a happier child?"

It was impossible to speculate upon the myriad possibilities, Hadrian realized. He watched Isobel cry silently into a handkerchief. It was a relief to no longer be angry. In its place, he felt curiously numb. He watched the outline of her small, shaking shoulders and her delicate hands as she held the linen to her face. A fabulously large sapphire glinted from her fourth finger. He noted that she no longer wore her wedding rings.

She raised her face, lifting her gaze to his.

His breath caught. There was no numbness now. Isobel was no longer a girl of twenty, but she had aged magnificently. Her face had not changed. Oh, there were deeper lines around her mouth, and a few crow's feet about her eyes, her hair was much paler now than it had been, almost platinum, but her features were as exquisite as ever. He was stunned to find himself staring at her, filled with the kind of raw desire he hadn't felt for any other woman in thirty years, that he had only felt when with her.

Her eyes widened.

He clenched his fists hard as the surge of lust swept him. Their gazes met cautiously. He saw that she knew. And he saw something else—the bright wild hope in her gaze.

"You are still beautiful, Isobel," he said carefully.

"I am old."

"You don't look old."

"Don't do this."

He approached her. "Don't do what?"

"Don't do this!" She tried to dodge his hands but they closed quickly on her arms and she was pulled up against him.

He shuddered violently at the contact. Every bit of her was slender and soft, feminine and familiar. She stared up at him, pinned in his embrace, her eyes as vivid and lovely as he remembered.

"Don't do this," she said again.

"Why not? This hasn't changed, has it? We still want each other. I want you."

Tears filled her eyes. "But I love you," she whispered.

He froze. Then he stopped thinking. His embrace tightened, his mouth came down on hers. Suddenly all the years that had passed vanished; yesterday and today became one. He was no longer sixty, but thirty, and the woman he held in his arms was a girl. They might have been embracing on the deck of his clipper ship, the Sea Dragon, or on the shores of Virginia. Time had ceased to exist. All that existed, for him, was Isobel, and the enormity of his love for her, which had never died.

His hands slid over her, remembering. His mouth moved slowly on hers. He stopped when he realized that he was tasting her salty tears. "Don't cry," he murmured, holding her tightly. "Don't cry, Isobel."

She wept harder. "I love you, Hadrian. I can't do this. Not with you hating me." But she clung so hard to the lapels of his fine suit jacket that the threads ripped.

"I don't hate you," he cried. "How could I ever hate you? I have spent my entire life loving you." And remembering his son's words, he said, "Even an American can be loyal."

She laughed, crying. "You mean it? You do not hate me? You can forgive me?"

"Isn't there a saying," he asked softly, holding her splendid face in his large hands, "that love heals all wounds?"

Now she really laughed, clasping his hands with hers as he held her face. "That is 'time heals all wounds,' I think."

"Then for us it is love," he said simply. His grip tightened as a new and frightening thought occurred to him—what if the past could repeat itself? What if she still felt some miserable sense of loyalty to Clayborough or the dead duke? "You are going to marry me this time, Isobel."

"Yes," she cried wildly. "Yes, yes, yes!"

"It wasn't a question," he said, sudden tears blinding him.

"I know!" And she flung her arms around him.

It took Nicole only a moment to realize where she was. She blinked, raising herself up on one arm and staring at the fat poster of the heavily draped, canopied bed. Remembrance rushed in upon her. Abruptly she fell back on the pillows.

Yesterday Hadrian had dragged her forcefully from Cobley House. Yesterday they had made love in his coach, with no inclination on her part to resist. Yesterday her anger had fled in the wake of her love, which just wouldn't die. And yesterday she had broken down in his arms, finally giving vent to her heartbreak.

Cautiously, Nicole sat up. She was naked, but she did not recall undressing or climbing into bed. Indeed, the last thing she remembered was sobbing wildly in Hadrian's arms in the Clayborough coach. His embrace had been so tender.

Her heart quickened.

She seemed to remember telling him that she loved him, too. She fervently hoped she had not, that it had only been a dream.

Dear Lord, what was she going to do now?

An image of the gorgeous Holland Dubois rose up in her mind.

Nicole rose from the bed and slipped on a robe. She washed her face and brushed her teeth, trying to concentrate on the task at hand. She could not. The memories continued to beckon her, larger than life. Nicole stood very still in the bathroom, gripping the marble-topped vanity. She was fully awake now, and it was impossible not be aware of what she had been avoiding all that past week. During her stay at Cobley House she had been like a zombie, unthinking and unfeeling. Now she could think and she could feel. She was afraid to analyze her emotions too closely. Yet they were there, unavoidable, a bit tender and a bit raw. It still hurt to think of Hadrian and Holland. Yet she did not seem to feel too bad. Her heart was miraculously intact.

What was she going to do about Holland? What could she do? Had Hadrian really been so kind and caring yesterday? Or had that, too, been a dream?

Nicole's grip on the vanity tightened. She wanted to see her husband. She felt compelled to see him. She must find out if she had imagined all that softness and compassion and caring she had seen in his eyes. Suddenly that was what was important, and she didn't give a fig about anything else.

She willed that it had not been a dream. She willed it so hard that it had to be the truth.

Nicole moved swiftly across the bedroom. She knew she should not go out of her suite in her current state of deshabille, but now she was propelled forward by a force she could not identify. She entered the sitting room. She was about to move into the hallway when she saw the gift-wrapped box.

She stopped. It was a large rectangular parcel, leaning up against the wall. It looked as if it had been carelessly placed there and forgotten. Nicole knew it was for her. Just as she knew it was from Hadrian. As if drawn to a magnet, she approached the package. And then once it was in her hands she tore it open like a demon possessed.

The first thing she saw beneath the green tissue paper was doeskin. She blinked, pulling out a pair of riding breeches. She pulled out another pair, and another. There were half a dozen in all, each a different color—cream and tan, gray and brown, and hunter green. She held the last pair up, the garment jet black. She did not have to try on a single pair to know that the breeches would fit her perfectly.

Nicole was moved to tears. She clutched the ebony pants to her face. What did this mean? Oh, what did this mean?

Abruptly she tossed the breeches aside, frantically rifling through the garments and tissue for a card. She found one. It only said: "To my dear wife." Hadrian had scrawled his name illegibly below.

She hugged the tiny card to her breast. *To my dear wife.* He had written "to my *dear* wife." He had not been merely polite, she was certain. Just as she was certain she had seen caring and compassion in his gaze yesterday.

He cared.

Nicole leapt to her feet. Nothing was going to stop her from finding him now.

She ran down the corridor, ignoring the busy maids she passed, who paused in their chores to blink at her attire before offering her their chipper good mornings. Nicole fled down the stairs, rapidly becoming out of breath. Her heart was thundering. Anticipation filled her. She must find Hadrian immediately!

One the ground floor she ignored the doormen, whom she really did not even see, and hurried towards his study. Voices coming from the music room drew her attention. Happy voices, a man and a woman's. Nicole skidded to a stop. The tone they shared was conspiratorial, intimate. The man's voice almost sounded like Hadrian's, and for a second, Nicole thought the worst even as she knew her suspicion could not be correct. She flung open the door.

For an instant she stared at the Dowager Duchess being intimately embraced by a man. Isobel and her lover both turned to look at her. Hot color flooded Nicole's face. "Excuse me!" she cried, backing away. "I am so sorry!"

She slammed the door shut and stood outside of it, panting. Whatever was going on? Did it matter? She must find her husband, she must!

He was not in his study. Now running, Nicole turned around and raced back up the stairs.

When Hadrian closed the music room doors on his parents, he was feeling more than a little bit guilty and very anxious. He was no longer sure that he had done the right thing. It was clear to him that they both still loved each other, but he was not a romantic, he knew better than that, yet he had been acting like one in trying to bring them together. In reality, so much water had passed under the bridge, it was doubtful that they would be able to recover what they had once had.

As he strode up the hall, he glanced at his pocket watch, not for the first time. It would soon be ten. His heart tightened. Nicole had been sleeping for almost twenty-four hours and he was growing very alarmed. Last night he had checked on her three times, each time becoming more anxious. She slept like one dead. That morning at six she had still been coma-like. At eight she had been stirring. Yet she was still not up.

Taking the back stairs because it was quicker, he decided to wake her up. And as he approached her suite, he began to tremble. He felt as if their next encounter would determine the course of their entire marriage, he felt it in every marrow of his being. He knew such a feeling was ridiculous. But he could not shake his certainty.

What if she really loved him? By now, he was wondering if his eager imagination had been playing tricks on him, if he had heard a declaration only because he wanted to.

Her rooms were empty. Vast disappointment claimed him. And then he heard a movement in the doorway behind him, and he turned to find her standing there.

"Hadrian," she whispered breathlessly.

His glance slid over her while the way she said his name, and the way her eyes brightened at the sight of him, made his heart yearn dangerously. He struggled for composure when he wanted to demand forthright if he had indeed heard what he thought he had heard yesterday in the coach. "Good morning, Madam. I was beginning to grow alarmed; you have slept an entire day away."

"I have?" she asked, still breathless. "And you were worried?"

"Yes."

Suddenly she smiled and held out her fist. He saw that she clutched a scrap of paper. Then she opened her hand and he saw that it was not a scrap of balled-up paper she held, but a small card—the card he had inserted in the gift he had intended to give her a week ago.

They stared at each other.

"Hadrian," she cried, "what does it mean? What does your present mean?"

He hesitated. "It means I behaved like a jackass and I am sorry."

Hope flared. Joy welled. "You are sorry about Holland?" she whispered.

He blinked. "Holland?" It just did not occur to him that she would know the name of his ex-mistress. "Holland who?"

Nicole stiffened. The joy started to dissipate. "Holland Dubois."

An inkling flooded him. He took her hand. "Nicole, what does Holland have to do with this? And how in God's name did you even learn of her?"

Nicole made no move to pull free. "I thought you were sorry you had gone to her. But I can see I was wrong. Wrong again, and foolish again."

"Wait!" He did not release her. "What in hell are you babbling about?"

"I cannot share you, Hadrian," she said simply. "I will not." Suddenly she straightened as a fierce determination filled her. "Oh, how stupid I have been! Why did I not think to fight for what is mine before?"

Hadrian could only stare at her. Then a smile tugged at his mouth as the beginnings of comprehension came to him. "And just what is it you are going to fight for? And whom are you going to do battle with now?"

"I am going to fight for you," she stated, her eyes blazing. "And I am going to fight Holland. And it is too late for you to change your mind, for I have made up mine. I no longer want a divorce."

"I see," he said, wondering if he looked as absurdly pleased as he felt. "And what about what I want?"

She eyed him. "I shall fling your own words back at you. What you want is no concern of mine."

"Indeed?" He laughed. "Why do I think you are lying?"

She blinked at him. "I do not understand your attitude, Hadrian, but perhaps I should make myself clear."

"Please do," he said, immensely happy. He had never been happier.

"I do not want a divorce. But I will not share you. I know I cannot physically restrain you from visiting that woman, but I can prevent *her* from entertaining *you*."

He chuckled. "Dear, you most certainly can restrain me physically, and you already have, but pray tell, what do you have in mind for poor Holland?"

"Forget any feelings you may have for her, Hadrian," Nicole said, scowling. "She will no longer see you, not once I call on her again."

He groaned. "Now I begin to understand! Let me guess! You saw her while I was in London!"

"I was not the only one," Nicole said sharply.

"You are jealous! Admit it!"

"Did you know that I have a drop of American Indian blood running in my veins?"

The Duke smiled and pulled her into his arms. "I cannot say I am very surprised."

"What are you doing?" Nicole cried as he caressed her back.

"I am holding my wife. My very dear wife."

That threw her. She froze, trembling. "Did you mean it? What you wrote on the card?"

"Yes, I did. Nicole, please do not take your crop to poor Holland's face as you did to mine. I hate to tell you this, dear, but you have been sadly misled."

She clutched his shirtfront. "I have?"

"You have. Holland Dubois is not my mistress."

"She isn't?"

"Not anymore. Our relationship was terminated when I was last in London."

"It was?"

"It was."

Nicole was flooded with relief, dazed with joy. She clung to her husband. "You mean, you did not even have a er—sweet parting?"

"I have all the sweetness I need here, dear."

She felt faint, but he held her up firmly. "Oh dear," she whispered. "And to think I was going to carve up her beautiful face with a kitchen knife."

Hadrian groaned.

"Oh, how could I have acted so precipitously and run away?!" Nicole moaned.

"I have no idea," the Duke said, cradling her face in his hands. "But something tells me it won't be the last precipitous thing you do." He silenced Nicole's protest with a long, lingering, intimate kiss. "But I shall be here to rescue you, darling, have no fear."

"Darling?" she whispered, dazed. "Why do you keep calling me dear? Why do you now call me darling?"

"Because your jealousy pleases me," the Duke said very tenderly.

His gaze was softer than it had been the day before in the carriage and Nicole melted. "Oh Hadrian," she sighed. "When you look at me that way . . ."

"Yes?" he prodded.

"I can barely think," she murmured. "In truth, I can barely stand."

"Can you think long enough to tell me what you told me yesterday?"

"What did I tell you yesterday?" she squeaked nervously.

"I don't want to play games anymore Nicole," he said very seriously. Then he added, "Darling."

She groaned. "It wasn't a dream, was it? Yesterday, the way you held me, as if you cared."

"I do care."

She clutched him tightly or she would have dropped right to the floor. "And I do love you, Hadrian. But you already knew that, didn't you? Because I told you yesterday."

"I began to suspect it was true only a few minutes ago," he said, deliriously happy. "When you began to threaten poor Holland."

"She is not so poor! She is the most gorgeous woman I have ever seen!"

"She is not the most gorgeous woman I have ever seen," the Duke said.

Nicole was nearly reeling in joy. "Can you forgive me for running away? For embarrassing you again? Oh, I shall never forgive myself for humiliating you once more! I promise I shall never do anything so rash again!"

"Please, do not promise, I know now to expect the unexpected from you. As long as you love me, Nicole, nothing else matters."

"Oh Hadrian," Nicole said, gripping his shoulders. "This is too good to be true. I am afraid if I pinch myself I shall find out I have been dreaming!"

He laughed again and pinched her cheek for her. "There. You see? You are awake, you are not dreaming. You are my duchess," his voice lowered, "and I love you."

Nicole fell into his arms eagerly. She had waited forever to hear those words. And he was right. Her husband, the Duke, was right. Nothing mattered, not anymore, not when they loved each other, and not when they had finally laid old misunderstandings to rest.

Sometimes, she realized happily, dreams really do come true.

New York Times *bestselling author*

Julia Quinn

On the Way to the Wedding

0-06-053125-8/$7.99 US/$10.99 Can

Gregory Bridgerton must thwart Lucy Abernathy's upcoming wedding and convince her to marry him instead.

It's In His Kiss

0-06-053124-X • $6.99 US • $9.99 Can

To Hyacinth Bridgerton, Gareth St. Clair's every word seems a dare.

e Was Wicked

• $6.99 US • $9.99 Can

For Michael Stirling, Lon ost infamous rake, his life's turning point came the first time he laid eyes on Francesca Bridgerton.

To Sir Phillip, With Love

0-380-82085-4 • $6.99 US • $9.99 Can

Although handsome and rugged, the moody, ill-mannered Sir Phillip Crane was totally unlike the other London gentlemen vying for Eloise Bridgerton's hand.

Romancing Mister Bridgerton

0-380-82084-6 • $6.99 US • $9.99 Can

Penelope Featherington has secretly adored Colin Bridgerton from afar and thinks she knows everything about him. Until she stumbles across his deepest secret . . .

Visit www.AuthorTracker.com for exclusive information on your favorite HarperCollins authors.

Available wherever books are sold or please call 1-800-331-3761 to order.

JQ 0406